La Donna Detroit

Also by Jon A. Jackson:

The Diehard
The Blind Pig
Grootka
Hit on the House
Deadman
Dead Folks
Man with an Axe

La Donna Detroit

A Detective Sergeant Mulheisen Mystery

Jon A. Jackson

GROVE PRESS
NEW YORK

Published simultaneously in Canada
Printed in the United States of America

FIRST PAPERBACK EDITION

Library of Congress Cataloging-in-Publication Data

Jackson, Jon A.
  La donna Detroit : a Detective Sergeant Mulheisen mystery / Jon A. Jackson.
    p. cm.
  ISBN 0-8021-3822-5 (pbk.)
    1. Mulheisen, Detective Sergeant (Fictitious character)—Fiction. 2.
  Police—Michigan—Detroit—Fiction. 3. Detroit (Mich.)—Fiction. I. Title.
  PS3560.A216 D66 2000
  813'.54—dc21   99-086204

DESIGN BY LAURA HAMMOND HOUGH

Grove Press
841 Broadway
New York, NY 10003

01 02 03 04   10 9 8 7 6 5 4 3 2 1

To the memory of Leonard Robinson, 1912–1999 . . .
the raconteur supreme, the wit humane . . . *da capo al fine*

Contents

Thanks to the detectives of the Missoula County Sheriff's Department for their suggestions and expert advice.
—Jon A. Jackson, Missoula, November 1999

1

A Bad Beginning

It was as classical as Goldilocks and the three bears, or Hansel and Gretel . . . innocents in the lonely, spooky forest, surprised by experience, and reacting with violence.

This was not the forest primeval, but a pathetic remnant of the great American forest. It was no more than a few dozen doomed elms intermixed with the odd ash or oak, the sparse woods left by a suburban developer who had run out of cash, stalled by a war. It was one of those awkward places, a kind of limbo, where unsettling things can happen. It wasn't really part of suburban development, at least not yet. Maybe it would never be. The developer had put on hold his plans for Crooks Woods—named for the farmer who had owned these acres.

Children had delighted in the abandoned excavations of unsold lots and had roofed over the trench footings and half basements with cast-off pieces of building materials, scrap lumber, and tar paper. The excavations made ideal "bunkers." The kids were crazy about "bunkers," childish imitations of trench warfare, or bomb shelters—the influence of the previous war's stories and the present war's movies. They invented games to employ these bowel-like structures, crawling into them fearfully, stocking them with salvaged and stolen plunder: lanterns, bits of candles, boards hammered into secret altars, stashes for forbidden comic books, condoms from the dressers of lately drafted older brothers, items of daringly pilfered lingerie—including, in this one, an enormous brassiere and an accordionlike corset that could wrap two or three boys.

The bunkers were not for girls. Undoubtedly a few were invited, but they knew better than to crawl into these dens. Goldilocks was a cautionary tale, after all. Still, a few bold girls must have penetrated these caverns, rarely.

Some bunkers were larger, more labyrinthine, but this one was fairly simple, a rectangle twenty-four feet by twenty. The trenches were deep enough that two eight-year-old boys, Carmie and Bertie, could actually walk upright in most places, although they tended to hunch over to avoid striking their heads—there were sometimes nasty nails poking through the rough boards that roofed the trenches.

The bunker was well isolated from the others, almost in the center of the uncleared woods. Carmie and Bertie had known about this bunker for some time but they had never dared approach it until today. They knew it belonged to an older boy named Porky White, who led a gang of teenaged boys who stole cantaloupes from suburban gardens, beer from their parents' refrigerators, candy from stores. All of this exciting loot was stashed in the bunker. The gang, known as the Clawson Commandos—there was an inescapable air of militarism these days—naturally despised little kids like Carmie and Bertie. And they, in turn, naturally writhed in envy of the Commandos, from the helmet liners on their heads to the combat boots on their feet, and wanted to be just like them.

Porky White was a particularly nasty, cruel bully. He ruled this bunker like a Chinese bandit, something they had learned about from movies and magazines. But he lacked the charismatic attraction of their true idol, a Sicilian outlaw recently glamorized in the pages of *Life* magazine, the bold and daring Giuliano. Perhaps the fact that they were themselves of Italian heritage (fairly recent, their parents emigrants) enhanced their idolization of Giuliano. They truly feared, respected, and envied Porky White, but did not idolize him.

They attended a Catholic school. Porky went to public school. On this day, due to the funeral of a priest, the Saint Anthony school was out and public school was not. So they had a perfect opportunity to creep into the citadel of Porky White and see what all was there.

It was a bleak, cool day at the end of winter but before the beginning of spring. The sky was a familiar gray, a featureless overcast, with a feeling that it could rain but probably wouldn't. In this half-begun suburb, if one could climb the water tower and look down, one would see a mildly rolling terrain with woods to the north and east and a city to the south and sprawling to the west. But at one's feet were laid out streets with only scattered houses on each block. Off to the east were farms and the shrunken remnants of farms. There was almost no automobile traffic, because of gas rationing, but there was an interurban trolley zipping along on a distant arterial rail line.

The boys had an old tin flashlight with weak batteries—it was hard to get batteries these days—and it barely lasted long enough for them to get into the sanctum sanctorum, the little eight-by-eight-foot cellar at the heart of the scrappily roofed bunker. This cellar had been meant to house the furnace and water heater of the home that would eventually be built if the war ever ended.

When the light failed the boys were scared. They almost panicked. Carmie, the slighter, more handsome of the two, began to cry, fearing that they were trapped and would never find their way out of this pitch-black labyrinth. He wept, freely lamenting that they had ever crawled in here, evidently giving way to the belief that they had gone down into the earth, that they might be buried in a cave-in and never found.

The chubby boy, Bertie, was scared, too. But he didn't cry. He was almost certain that the bunker was not deep, that they hadn't actually crawled down into the earth, although it had seemed to them on their way into that darkness that they were descending. But he retained a fairly strong impression of the surface of the site, with the scrap-and-tar-paper covering that was itself meagerly covered by raw, clayey dirt—the Commandos had too soon wearied of camouflaging their bunker. Still, as children, the boys did not recognize this excavation for what it was; they didn't see the pattern. To them, it was a subterranean maze, not a simple square footing. But Bertie, at least, clung to the notion that in an emergency they could possibly break out through the roof, as it were, if they couldn't simply crawl back through the passageway to the entrance. He tried to buck up his cousin Carmie. He denied that, for instance, there were snakes in the dark bunker.

And then they saw a light. They almost squealed with relief, but this quickly gave way to a greater terror. The huffing, bobbling figure that lurched toward the inner sanctum, out of the pitch blackness, for a fleeting moment resembled a bear. But a bear with a flashlight? And then Bertie had the weird impression that this was . . . was what? Something familiar, something he had experienced but only obliquely, never face-to-face: his guardian angel, perhaps, or his doppelgänger, another self born at the same time as himself, but already fully formed, or more advanced, anyway, and always lurking on the periphery of his experience.

But in the next instant they both realized with horror that the bear, or weird ogre, could only be Porky White, the awful brute who ruled in this subterranean domain, who must inevitably discover them, and that he would be outraged at their violation of his secret castle. They tried to get away, frantically bolting for escape by another tunnel, like baby rabbits fleeing a badger or a weasel. But it was useless. Porky quickly caught them.

The older boy dragged them back into the pit by their heels. He pummeled them with his fists and shone his powerful flashlight in their eyes. The blows hurt their arms and backs and their heads rung. They cowered in a corner, moaning and sobbing, rubbing their sore arms while Porky lit a candle and placed it on a tin can that sat on a wooden pop carton.

"So, it's you little dago rats," he snarled, looking them over. His big moon face loomed evilly in the flickering candlelight. The little boys blubbered.

"Shut your damn traps, you shitty punks!" he commanded. "So, you snuck into my bunker, hunh? Thought you'd steal my treasure, hunh? Well, now you gotta be punished." He sounded just like a troll from a fairy tale. The little boys quaked in despair.

"You know what I'm gonna do?" the bully said. "I'm gonna beat the hell out of you, that's what! Or maybe I'll burn your fingers. Yah! Teach you a lesson, you little wops!"

The boys wept. They knew there was no escape. They stared aghast at his huge white face with his wet red lips and glowing eyes. He was capable of killing them, they were convinced. He might even eat them.

Porky relished their terror. He tormented them with spectacularly imagined savageries. He would break their bones, poke out their eyes, or even throw them to the snakes. He said he had a snake pit, filled with rattlers and moccasins. The snakes would bite them and they would swell up from the poison, puke, and die. They would never see their families again. Nobody would ever find their wormy corpses. He knew they hadn't told anyone where they were going. No one would look for them down this hole. They were in Hell, that's where they were! They might as well consider themselves dead already. The Devil was coming to get them.

Carmie was convinced that he would be murdered. Bertie wasn't so sure. As the older boy raged on he began to feel less frightened. It was the bit about snakes: Bertie knew from Sister Mary Frances's adamant insistence—"There are no poisonous snakes in Michigan"—that Porky was lying. Porky was just trying to scare them; maybe he would let them go. But when? And after what kind of torment and physical violence? Bertie wasn't so hopeful about that. He didn't know how to deal with this older boy's malevolence. He didn't want to anger him further, stir him up to a fury in which he might do something that they would all regret. He tried to get Carmie to hush, to calm down. Maybe this stupid boy would content himself with just punching them, some painful but not too harmful punishment, and then let them go.

"We just wanted to be in the Commandos," Bertie whispered. "We want to join up, be like you. We'll do anything."

"Anything?" the boy asked. He sat for a while, watching them, his eyes glittering in the candlelight like a goblin's. Then he said, addressing Carmie, "Come over here. You stay there," he said to Bertie. "You don't move, or I'll kill both of you."

Carmie crawled to the other boy. Porky rummaged in a box that seemed to serve as a kind of altar, covered with an old flag and supporting a candelabra and a dented urn of some sort. He pulled out a Boy Scout camping hatchet. He brandished it in the light. Carmie's eyes were like Ping-Pong balls. "Take off your pants," Porky said.

He had to say it again, twice, before Carmie understood. But then the boy unbuckled his belt and unbuttoned his corduroy knickers and let them down. He stood hunched over in the light. He still wore his white underpants. Porky was crouched before him. He reached out and pulled down the boy's cotton briefs, somewhat damp and stained with urine from his fright. Carmie trembled in horror.

"What . . . what are you gonna do?" he asked.

"If you don't shut up and do what I say," Porky said, "I'm gonna chop yer pecker off."

The boy stood still while Porky took hold of his penis and pulled on it, not roughly, but almost tenderly. Porky was breathing heavily. He stroked the child's penis repeatedly, his lips wet and nearly drooling.

"You ever suck a fella?" he asked, suddenly.

Carmie shook his head. "What do you mean?" he stammered.

Porky stood up. He was much taller, and like Carmie, he hunched. He unbuttoned his own trousers and took out his own penis. It was much larger than Carmie's, and it was strangely stiff, sticking straight out.

"Here," he said, his voice rasping, "get down on yer knees and suck it."

Carmie's eyes were locked on the well-sharpened hatchet, but he shook his head. "No."

"Okay, then," Porky said. "I'm gonna whack yer dick off." He grabbed the boy's penis again and held it, stretching it, brandishing the brutal hatchet threateningly.

"Fatty, help me!" Carmie squealed, inadvertantly using a nickname he often applied to his pudgy cousin.

His tormentor seemed to think that the name was applied to him. "I ain't Fatty," he snarled. "Get down, before I chop this weenie off!"

Carmie sank to his knees, moaning. The older boy hunched over him, breathing excitedly. "Open yer mouth," he demanded, hoarsely.

Bertie picked up a bottle that had been used to hold candles, its neck encrusted with wax drippings. He held it by the neck and smashed it into the side of Porky White's head. The big oaf stumbled backward, tripped over his own trousers, then the box altar, and fell on his back.

"Get him!" Bertie cried. The boys leapt on the fallen bully. The candle was knocked away and lay on its side, flickering, but not out. It cast lurid shadows on the walls as the boys screamed and pummeled their tormentor, striking with the bottle until it broke, striking with anything that came to hand—bricks, stones, the fallen hatchet.

Finally, they stopped. Porky was still, crumpled in the corner. In the flickering light they stared at each other, at their grubby hands and faces, smeared with blood and dirt. And then they stared at Porky. He lay with his eyes open, as if in surprise, catching the candlelight, his face gashed and bleeding, his mouth gaping, his front teeth broken. He didn't move.

The boys stood up. Bertie retrieved Porky's flashlight. He picked up the hatchet. It was wet with blood, but whether it had been chopped into the body of Porky he didn't know. Perhaps it had only acquired blood from the wounds. Perhaps it hadn't been used. Bertie looked at Carmie, who was pulling up his pants. He gestured with the hatchet.

"Did you chop him?" he asked.

"No! No, I didn't," Carmie declared. He buckled his belt. "C'mon, let's get going!"

Bertie shone the light around the little dirt room, which now looked like nothing more than a littered garbage hole. The sprawled body inevitably added a suggestion of the grave.

"Maybe we should take some of his stuff," Bertie suggested. The light fell on the stack of precious comic books, a wooden box filled with pop and beer, a deck of cards, some military medals and insignia.

"No! Leave it!" Carmie was possessed with anxious haste now. "Let's go! Let's get out before someone else comes!"

"Maybe we should cover him up," Bertie said.

That idea seemed right. They began to scoop dirt and hurl magazines and scraps of blankets, junk, at the body. They got caught up in this frantic activity.

Finally, Carmie said, "That's enough. Let's go. Let's go, let's go."

So they crawled, or rather scurried in a hunched duckwalk, through the passageway until they burst into the precious but blinding daylight. It was still a dull, overcast day, but it seemed bright to them after the darkness of the tunnel and oh, so blessedly welcome.

They ran from the site almost to the edge of the thinned woodlot before Bertie stopped.

"What?" Carmie said, looking back at him anxiously. "Let's go! Let's run." He was frantic to be away.

"You know what we did?" Bertie said. "We killed him. We murdered him! He's dead." He looked around. It was early afternoon, he thought, almost like coming out of a movie matinee, but earlier.

The world seemed abandoned. There were few houses here. The men of this half-built community were all away, enlisted in the armed services or at work, and many of the wives were at work as well, in factories that made tanks and bombs and airplanes.

It seemed to Bertie that Porky White must have had some unusual reason not to be in school. He must have stayed home, ill perhaps, or, more likely, played hooky. There was no sign of his gang. So there was no great rush. Bertie was not exactly calm—how could he be?—but he was not panicked.

They were in trouble, though. He knew that. And something told him that the biggest part of his trouble was his cousin Carmie. The handsome lad was visibly shaken. They could not go home, not yet. There was no reason for them to go home. They weren't expected. They had been shooed out to play, and normally that meant they would be outside until near dark, when Carmie's mother would stand on the porch and call, over and over again, "Carmie! Bertie!" He talked to Carmie and got him to calm down.

They found a cold puddle of water, where Bertie was able to wash the blood and dirt off Carmie's and his hands and faces and bare legs. The blood on their clothes he rubbed with dirt. Then they went for a walk. It was only a few blocks over to the railroad viaduct; they often played over there, although warned against it. They hung around there until a train came by and flattened some pennies they had put on the tracks. Then they walked to the filling station on Crooks Road and got a couple of Cokes and shared an Oh Henry! candy bar.

Carmie was in pretty good spirits by now. It was as if he had forgotten what had happened in the bunker. But as they walked back toward the neighborhood, Bertie pointed out some important things. When Porky White's buddies got out of school they would go to the bunker and they would find their leader. The cops would be notified. They would question the gang boys, who would deny having killed Porky. Maybe the cops wouldn't believe Porky's friends, but they might also come around and question Carmie and Bertie, and any other kid who lived in the neighborhood. Maybe the cops had some way of knowing that Carmie and Bertie had been in the bunker. Maybe there were fingerprints or something. Bertie didn't know. They had heard about fingerprints and stuff on the radio, in *Gang Busters* and *The Shadow*. Maybe there was something they didn't even know about, that detectives could use to find out who had been in the tunnel. Maybe they would be caught.

Bertie wanted to alarm Carmie, because he was genuinely worried on just these lines, but he didn't want him to be too scared. Still, he had to be scared enough to keep his mouth shut. And so he made him swear that, no matter what, he would say exactly what Bertie said, even if the cops split them up and asked them separately.

And what they would say was that they had gone out playing, had gone to the viaduct, had put pennies on the tracks, and then went to get pop at the filling station. And that was that. They didn't know what time it was because they didn't have watches. One thing they hadn't done, they hadn't gone anywhere near the woods. They had always been told to stay away from old man Crooks's woods, so they never went near. That was their story. Bertie wished he had thought to take the hatchet, to throw it away, down a sewer or something.

It began to rain.

This much of the story Umberto recalled with ease, even after fifty years. Indeed, he *knew* this story, at least to this point. There were other details, he was aware, but he had forgotten them. If he worked at it, however, he could recall—he thought—that nothing ever came of Porky's murder, or death, or whatever you want to call it.

Did they ever find the body? He was not sure. He supposed they must have. Some time after this, it may have been within days or weeks or even months, they had moved away. He remembered his uncle Dom saying Crooks Woods wasn't a good place for them to live and all the other grown-ups laughing. His other uncle was there, he recalled, Uncle Gags. That was his special uncle. Uncle Gags was somehow closer to him than Uncle Dom, Carmie's dad, although he didn't actually live with them. He came around a lot. Bertie didn't know why, then.

The move may have had something to do with Porky. But he was sure that, at the time, he had not connected the events. Still, Uncle Gags had taken him aside at some point and asked some questions about Porky. He couldn't remember what the questions were. It wasn't anything like, Did you do this? Or even, What happened? Or, Were you there? Bertie's answers apparently satisfied Uncle Gags.

Anyway, they moved. Bertie remembered feeling tremendously relieved, happy to move to the city, to the east side. He still lived with Carmie and his family. They were his family. Aunt Sophie was like the mother he'd never had. And then he didn't remember much of anything until Uncle Gags's funeral.

Uncle Gags had been killed, shot by another man. Lots of men came to the funeral, dressed in black suits. Very important men, it seemed. There were a lot of flowers; the body lay in a casket in the front room, dressed in a suit with a flower in the lapel, the hands crossed on the chest. The men drank whiskey and beer and smoked cigars. The women talked. There wasn't much crying. The priest came and they all drove in big cars to the cemetery, where the casket was lowered into the ground. For some reason, Bertie was treated with some solicitude, which he didn't understand at the time. Older women hugged him and said they pitied him. Men shook his hand and patted him on the back and shoulder and said he should be strong.

2

Birds of Prey

Ezio Spinodi was in trouble but he didn't know it. He was like a sparrowhawk who sees a songbird sitting on a barbed-wire fence and makes a casual pass. The songbird turns out to be a shrike that chases him down in a thicket and beats his brains out. He saw Helen Sedlacek, a pretty, diminutive woman sitting in a Colorado ski bar in one of those pricey new concrete hotels in Winter Park. She wasn't dressed like a skier or a local, but he would have noticed her anyway, because he'd seen her earlier, on the Amtrak train from Salt Lake City to Denver, and he'd seen her get off in Granby, just a few miles northwest of here.

It wasn't some huge surprise; Ezio was looking for her. He'd been sent by Humphrey DiEbola, the Detroit mob boss, to find her and Joe Service. When they got to someplace useful, like Denver, he was supposed to call in for further orders.

Ezio, popularly known as Itchy, was a moderately cynical man—he was a Detroiter. *Further orders* would mean only one thing, Ezio felt. But it was significant that he hadn't been given the order from the start. So he was cool. He was not about to drop the hammer until he heard the command.

Only, they hadn't gotten to Denver. Joe Service had been taken off the train in Granby in an ambulance. It looked to Itchy like he'd had a stroke, or a heart attack—some kind of fit. Surprising—such a young man. Maybe it had been dope, cocaine or something. Joe had been accompanied by a cop from Detroit, Itchy knew him—Detective Sergeant Mulheisen. If Joe's fit had incidentally removed "Fang" Mulheisen from the scene, Itchy could not complain, even if it complicated things. But he believed he had obeyed his right instincts in not following Joe and Mulheisen, rather than the babe. He'd definitely gotten the feeling that Humphrey was more interested in the babe than in Joe Service. Not that Itchy believed for a nanosecond that Humphrey had a letch for this babe, no matter how young and good-looking. This babe must have her mitts on some loot. That was his theory. There is a prevailing cynicism among Detroiters. They have an image of themselves as unsentimental, can-do people. They say: Screw *pretty* . . . does it *work?* To hear them talk, the rest of the world is more or less Disneyland. Of course, genuine cynicism gets nothing done; a real cynic doesn't believe in anything, much less that something will "work." So maybe Detroiters are just pseudocynics. Severe skeptics. Beauty is a hard sell, but there are some takers. The point is, practicality is poured on one's morning pancakes.

Helen Sedlacek was no less a Detroit girl than Itchy a Detroit guy. Born and raised on the east side, she had gone to Dominican, a Catholic girls school, graduated from Michigan State University, started her first business in Birmingham (once a suburb, but now the epicenter of the Detroit municipal zone). She had definitely eaten Motor City molasses on her hotcakes. Which is not to say that she hadn't her soft, feminine side.

Helen was about thirty, small, slim, and dark. She had gallons of black hair, with a silver skunk stripe rising from her right temple. She had a boy's physique and she was strong and lean-muscled. Fearless and brave; sweet and demure. Everyone has at least two sides: how they see themselves, versus how others see them. At least two, more like dozens, especially as the years go by.

At one point, when she was about fourteen, Helen had acquired the nickname Sonya. Schoolkids aren't notably discriminatory when it comes to ethnic origins. Or rather, they are very discriminatory, but careless: they don't distinguish between a Yugoslavian and a Russian, especially if both countries are part of what was then called the Iron Curtain, or the Red Menace. No Serbs or Croats in those days, before the walls came tumbling down. She was known as Sonya Bitchacockoff.

She wore nothing but black, and her black hair was long and generally draped over her pale face. She tended toward capes and hoods. She read poetry, especially Anna Akhmatova, and even affected an accent—"Vot do you vant," she would mutter. Or, with a wave of the hand, "Leaf me alone." To her credit, she genuinely liked Akhmatova's verse, although she was more attracted by the legendary image, and she enjoyed correcting the pronunciation of the name by her teenaged friends—"Perhaps you muss be Slaf," she would say, pityingly.

But the "Bitchacockoff" tag was derived from a bizarre incident. It hardly needs to be said that teenagers experiment with sex; it's required. She had a couple of girlfriends with whom she discussed the varieties of sexual experience, a lot. Each pretended to a greater experience than they possessed. They were all virgins, but denied it. One of them, a rapidly developing girl of Italian extraction, even claimed that she had "gone down" on her boyfriend.

"It's not bad," she claimed, "just kind of salty and a little sweetish-sour at the same time. You have to be careful not to gag, when it goes down your throat."

"You mean you let him come?" the others asked.

"Oh, no! Ugh! I could never do that. I mean when it pokes the back of your mouth, you know?"

One night a bunch of them were parked in a van, down by Windmill Point. One of the boys had stolen a bottle of his parents' booze, a fifth of Southern Comfort. It was sweet and palatable to their youthful tastes and soon they were all more or less tipsy, if not drunk. The toughest of the boys, Cazzie, started talking about oral sex. There was a lot of snickering and giggling, boasting, and the conversation evolved to the point where he dared the girls—there were three of them, including Helen—to show their nerve by "going down."

The other girls seemed at least cautiously willing to try, but Helen balked. She wasn't against a lot of kissing and feeling, even a furtive hand job, but she wasn't going to actually allow some boy to penetrate any of her orifices—not in front of other people. The boys, however, were intensely excited by the idea, naturally. The Southern Comfort had emboldened them all, lowered their inhibitions or, at least, had provided them with an excuse if it actually occurred. But not Helen.

"I want to go," she insisted, straightening her clothing.

"Aw, c'mon, Sonya," Cazzie said. He pulled her to him. "A little blow job never hurt anybody." He had actually unzipped and produced a throbbing penis that was about ready to explode. The other kids were thrilled and joined in.

"Do it!" they cried.

Cazzie, encouraged and sexually maddened, grabbed Helen by the head and forced her face to his groin. He was strong and clearly intended to force her to do it, thrusting his rigid organ at her lips.

With a snarl, Helen opened her mouth and then clamped her little, sharp teeth onto the end of his penis, biting down as hard as she could. The boy screamed and cuffed her head away. He howled in agony, then rage. Helen spit blood into the boy's face. That was a brilliant gesture.

Cazzie was so concerned with wiping his face—he wasn't sure that the spittle wasn't semen, an unsettling thought—and tenderly cosseting his penis that he didn't strike her again, or kick her out. The others were scared and the driver quickly started the van and drove to Helen's home. "You bitch!" Cazzie roared when they pushed her out of the van in front of the house.

It was an instant legend. But for Helen, the significant thing was that she had acted spontaneously. She analyzed her behavior incessantly. It was so unlike her, she felt. What was she thinking? She saw herself as poetic, introspective, though daring and unconventional. She entertained the idea that she ought to have made at least a feint at performing the act, and *then* to have recoiled in disgust. That would be the way to do it. Later she might advertise her disgust, so everyone would know she'd had the nerve, but she'd loathed the act.

Or she ought to have become hysterical from the start, perhaps. To have made a scene that would startle the other kids and awaken them to the enormity of what was being proposed. That probably would have worked. Even as far gone as Cazzie was in Southern Comfort and sexual arousal, he should have remembered who her father was. Yes, she could have invoked her father, the gangster. She'd already had some experience with that: often enough, she'd had to endure a definite social coolness, a certain notoriety, from some of the more snobbish kids. What was the good of having a mobster for a father if he couldn't protect her, at least with his reputation?

Her friend Julie, also from a mob family, had shared this semi-ostracization with her. Julie, however, had been in the van. It occurred to Helen that if Julie hadn't been there, the mob threat might have worked. But it was less easy to invoke when Julie was present. Julie, after all, was the one who had confessed that she'd gone down on her boyfriend.

So, faced with the apparent approval of her peers, faced with the penis itself, she had chosen violence. And she had *chosen* it, she had to recognize that. It wasn't just an automatic reaction. She had opted for attack. That surprised her. To say nothing of Cazzie and the others.

Now she was a teenaged legend: Watch out for Sonya, she'll bite your cock off. Before she was thirty she had done a lot more than that. She had killed men and not by accident. Intentionally. Murdered the boss of Detroit's mob, no less. She had all but leaped into the back seat of his Cadillac to blast him with a shotgun. In Montana, where she had gone to lie low with her lover, Joe Service, she had been tracked down and attacked by a hired killer. She had shot him to death in a bloody hot springs. Bitchacockoff, indeed—how about your head?

On the flip side, Helen thought of herself as a good, loving, and dutiful daughter, an ordinary, ambitious, and modern young woman. She'd founded her own consulting firm, she'd been successful in the most mundane of ways. She never thought of herself as a killer. Sure, she had killed, but only once on purpose. The others she dismissed as accidental. She was not sorry for having blasted Carmine Busoni. He deserved killing. He had ordered the death of her father.

In her education she had been told by the nuns and the priest that "Thou shalt not kill" was absolute, it applied across the board. But there were exceptions, obviously. It wasn't ever applied to soldiers in battle. And you couldn't be blamed for killing in self-defense; in fact, not to resist was seen as a kind of betrayal of one's self, one's group. And in her family, the principle of revenge was respected.

She didn't recall ever having a conversation with her father in which he said, "Honey, when someone kills a relative it's your duty to kill him." But there had been many stories recounted by her father and her mother in which exactly that principle was illustrated and approved. The only thing was, these events had taken place in the Old Country and, romantic posturing aside, Helen wasn't enthusiastic about the Old Country. Her parents' tales of the Old Country bored her—why couldn't they stick to the present? They weren't in the Old Country anymore. So some Bogdanovich, say, angry at a seduction of his wife or daughter or sister, had waylaid and killed a Simonich. Three or four generations of Simoniches and Bogdanoviches have to kill each other? Not in America.

She had pondered this after her father's death. There seemed to be a vague but important reservation that the revenge code applied particularly in the Old Country, not here. She thought it had something to do with the prevalence of family and clan traditions over there, and possibly with the doubtful legitimacy of successive governments. There, governments—the State—were not seen as adequate, reliable, or even just. In America, presumably, it was different. For Helen, there were no family stories about revenge in America *where the initial act of treachery had occurred in America.* Except maybe for hillbillies in Appalachia.

She considered the frequent accounts of gangland slayings where revenge was invoked by the perpetrators. Big Sid and Mrs. Sid would usually shake their heads disapprovingly and say, "Those Sicilians." The Sicilians, then, were to be seen as crude, primitive people—Old World hillbillies, still addicted to a system in which clans and families had reserved the final act of justice to themselves. In the Old Country, sure: revenge was a duty. Here: no. Those Sicilians, they forget that they aren't in the Old Country anymore.

Nonetheless, when her father was slain by Carmine's orders, shot down by a nameless, faceless, hired assassin, Helen Sedlacek clearly saw that justice was left in her hands. The police were helpless, hopeless. She felt that the investigating officer, Detective Sergeant Mulheisen, was unconcerned, possibly incompetent. And when she encountered the private, independent investigator for the mob, Joe Service, she found a sympathetic and attractive man who would help her obtain justice. She prepared almost religiously for her act of retribution and was thrilled when she was able to carry it out effectively, with Joe's help.

Since then, events had taken unexpected turns. She had soon resigned herself to the fact that her old, straight life was now closed to her. By now, she was caught up in more complex situations, for which she didn't always feel prepared. Joe Service had warned her about this. The mob, he'd said, would feel that they had to respond to her act of simple justice—it was the old code. They would pursue her. And they had. But she had prevailed.

Helen did not have the common attitude toward the mob. It wasn't the stuff of movies and novels for her. It was familiar. She knew the people involved, some of them intimately. She wasn't awed by them, not very impressed, even. She knew many of these people to be stupid and ignorant, incompetent. They had names and faces for her: half-witted James who drooled, incredibly vain Guido who wouldn't dance at parties because he wasn't good at it, neurotic Ari who was sure he was too short, hopelessly fat and blundering Nick who wouldn't go swimming because he was ashamed to be seen in swim trunks. She knew these dorks.

But knowing that her father was a mobster didn't mean that she had any clear idea of what he actually did. He seemed mostly idle, but he was always talking about "business." What kind of business? She didn't know and she understood that it was not to be inquired about too closely. She knew almost nothing about how the organization actually functioned. She was genuinely dismayed when they continued to pursue her after Carmine's slaying. Why hadn't they, of all people, understood that she'd had to revenge her father? Okay, they had to make a show of revenging Carmine, but when she'd survived the attempts to kill her, she felt that should be the end of it.

She had survived, she hadn't tried to retaliate in turn. In a curious way, she believed that her success had crucially altered the equation. It was the *mandate of heaven*, a concept she remembered from a college class in Chinese history, perhaps a little unclearly. Sometimes, it seemed, a perfectly legitimate and long-established dynasty had been overthrown. The new regime justified its usurpation under the handy principle of the mandate of heaven, which turned out to be a form of realpolitik, at least as she understood it. The emperor is defeated, long live the (new) emperor. Of course, she wasn't the new emperor. She was just an agent of change. Humphrey DiEbola was the new don. In fact, in the eyes of the most knowledgeable, he'd been the "real" don for years. So maybe it wasn't a change of regimes. But she had not thought that far.

The first hit attempt had separated Helen from Joe, but they'd finally been reunited, in Salt Lake City. Then they had survived another botched attempt. She'd thought they were through the bad part. Unfortunately, just when she and Joe were on their way to freedom—the vindication of success!—Joe had suffered a serious medical relapse on the train bound for Denver, in the very throes of sexual celebration.

By then, Helen was getting more proficient at thinking on her feet. Mulheisen had actually been on the train, hot on their heels, literally in the next compartment. Under the circumstances, Helen had been compelled to abandon Joe to the detective's mercy, which permitted her to get away.

Not incidentally, she had also managed to throw a couple of duffel bags full of money off the train, intending to salvage them later. This money, amounting to nearly eight million dollars, was the remnant of a larger amount that her father had originally skimmed from an unauthorized mob activity in Detroit. She felt it was her money. Joe Service, who had actually acquired the money, felt it was his, but he was happy to share it with her. Humphrey

DiEbola felt it belonged to the mob, and he wasn't interested in sharing. This complication helped to confuse the issue of revenge: was the mob willing to forget vengeance for money? Humphrey had hinted as much. Vengeance wasn't the primary principle it was construed to be.

Itchy was familiar with an old adage: When a guy says it ain't the money, it's the principle—it's the money. Humphrey's interest wasn't revenge, it wasn't sex. It was money, just as any Detroit kid would know. Itchy was no genius. He was one of those mob figures whom the press like to inflate when they get caught, or take the fall, instead of the real villains. Not that Itchy wasn't a genuine villain, but he was only the visible villain. He was loyal and didn't think too much. Years ago, he had gone to prison for Carmine and the press had described him as a deadly ice-blooded hit man who had taken a softer fall. In the present case, his function was to "bring Helen home."

That's what he told Helen now. Or did he have other instructions? Bring home the money? Cancel her? That's what she wanted to know.

She and Itchy discussed this issue in the hotel bar, in Winter Park. Itchy was a man of fifty years, not much taller than Helen, despite his expensive elevator shoes. He was a careful dresser. He had a very black mustache and was concerned about his thinning hair, which had once been his pride. Now it was streaked with silver, or would have been, if he didn't use dye regularly. He advised Helen that she could get rid of the skunk stripe in her hair with his special preparation.

Itchy was a competent fellow, to a point, and unlike Helen, his ethical concerns stopped with loyalty to the boss. He was willing to use violence, if necessary, usually in the form of a discreet bullet. He didn't like breaking people's limbs, or scarring them. But he would, if so instructed.

He had actually met Helen a couple of times, when she was a child. He had liked her father. Everyone did. And he liked her, as much as you could like a child. Although, it was obvious she wasn't a child anymore. He didn't consider it a factor. To Itchy, Helen was just a songbird sitting on a wire. He called Humphrey as soon as he saw her, sitting at the bar, alone. Humphrey asked about the money. Specifically: "Has she got it with her?"

Itchy: "Not that I can see."

Humphrey: "Well, find out."

Itchy: "And then what? That's why I'm calling. It's cold. I'm standing outside."

Humphrey: "I want to talk to her."

Itchy: "Okay."

Humphrey: "Don't you do a thing. Hear me? I gotta talk to her, first."

Helen didn't want to talk to Humphrey, initially. She felt it was something that she and Ezio—she did not once use that despised nickname, which he'd always resented but had come to accept—could work out. She wanted his help in recovering the money, she said. She brought it right up, without any probing on his part. It was somewhere out in the country, lying near the railroad in two not very conspicuous blue duffel bags. It wasn't very safe there, but it would be safe for a while, she thought.

Helen could see that she was stuck with Itchy, for the time being. He hadn't tried anything heavy, except that he warned her he wouldn't hesitate to gun her down if she tried to run off. She smiled and replied that if he even thought of taking a gun out she would blow his ass to kingdom come with the Smith & Wesson .38 in her coat pocket. Itchy wasn't sure if she was kidding, but anyway, it didn't matter. They were stuck with each other.

"Whether you talk to him or not, I gotta call the man back," Itchy said. "Okay?"

Helen sighed. "Okay, but you don't say a word about the money. I'll take care of that."

Humphrey convinced Helen on the phone that he bore her no ill will. She didn't say anything about the money and he didn't mention it either. But she knew it was her hole card. Humphrey wouldn't do anything until he knew where the money was and how he could get it.

Humphrey was concerned about her, he said. He'd always been like an uncle—Unca Umby. He cared about her and her mother. That was a good touch, just mentioning her mother, in a friendly, non-threatening way. He reminded her again that he had tried to dissuade Carmine from hitting her old man, she must believe that. Here he had precedent on his side. She must know that on an earlier occasion, when Big Sid had dipped a little too deep, it had been Humphrey who convinced Carmine not to whack the likable mobster. It was true. Humphrey had long believed that loyalty was overrated. Crooks will be crooks. You had to convince the underlings that their success was related to your success. You couldn't prosper, no one could prosper, if everyone was going to be ripping off more than was reasonable. A little skim, sure. But nothing messy or pretty soon there's no icing on the cake. That time, Humphrey had gotten Big Sid off with a wrist slap and a season or two of laboring in the latrines of criminal activity—enforcing and discipline.

Once back in good graces, however, Big Sid had gone back to his old sticky-fingered ways. On an earlier occasion Humphrey had told Helen that when the second transgression was discovered, he had felt that a little more severe discipline might be in order, but not a hit. Big Sid was a friendly, likable guy. The business needed these guys, a lot. It made the business a lot easier. But Carmine was pissed, he wouldn't listen. There was no way of proving that this was the truth, but Helen believed it, which, after all, is what mattered.

What was the big problem that was bugging Humphrey? It didn't seem to be the money, or he would have said something. It was something bigger. He couldn't say on the phone. It was too big. He'd tell her all about it when she got home.

Helen, of course, wanted to go home. Especially with Joe in the hospital, soon to be in the penitentiary, she figured. He was no good to her now. Maybe he'd never be anything to her again. She felt drained of whatever little sentimental sweetness her soul had ever possessed. Or maybe only the Detroit molasses remained. Time to cut your losses.

Cutting losses did not mean forgetting about the money. But it was the dead of winter. If the money hadn't been discovered already—and if someone, say a railroad worker or a rancher, had found it lying in the boondocks, next to the railroad, the story would have hit the news with a loud splash—then it could probably lie there till spring. It would take a bit of finding, obviously. She'd simply tossed a couple of duffel bags full of money off the train, somewhere west of Granby. She had a pretty good idea of the location—she'd noticed some signs—but that was not the same as having a dead fix on the site. The idea of it just lying out there, available to any passing hunter or cross-country skier . . . it wasn't a comforting thought. And for all she knew, one or both of the duffels might have broken open on impact and even now the Colorado winds were broadcasting money hither and yon.

She had an image from the old Kubrick movie *The Killing*, where the desperate robber's suitcase of loot breaks open on the airport tarmac and prop wash sends the dollars flying. That vision haunted her.

What the heck. She was here. Might as well go look. Itchy was agreeable. He had a rented car. They took off up Route 40.

The problem was, she knew that the money had to be somewhere west of Granby, not too far, but it was hard to judge distance on the train. It's not like driving your car, where you constantly pass signs, annotated landmarks. On the train you're just riding through the countryside. She thought she had a good idea, though.

Driving westward—that is, in the direction the train had traveled from—she was at first discouraged, because she thought they had been closer to Granby than they had, in fact, been. But when they drove into Byers Canyon, she realized it must be beyond that spectacular red-rock gorge, along which the Colorado River surged. Soon they issued out onto the high plateau, and then she saw, to the south, the mountains she'd noticed when she tossed the bags. Also, she recalled that the tracks had been close to the highway, on the north side. But her hopes fell when they got to Kremmling and the tracks shifted to the south and they couldn't follow them.

She told Itchy to turn around. It had to be on the stretch between Kremmling and the canyon. They were only a few miles east of Kremmling on the return when she saw a railway maintenance shack with the painted inscription H.B.D. 98.9.

"I saw that when I first lugged the bags to the platform," she said. The platform was in the middle of the double-decker car, at the foot of the stairs, with openable upper doors on either side of the passageway. She'd opened the upper half of the northside door and tossed the bags out, on the side away from the highway.

Shortly, the tracks crossed the highway, and now she knew she was close. They slowed and she looked carefully at the mountains to the south. And then another remembered landmark appeared: a large, wooden archway at the gate to a ranch. It was not far. They parked and hiked across the road and began to walk the track.

They walked about a mile and Itchy wanted to quit. He wasn't outfitted for this. He had snow in his fancy shoes; they were ruined. He was cold, and he'd lost confidence in Helen. She wasn't daunted, however. "Just one more curve," she begged.

And then they saw the bags. They were about a hundred yards apart, and no more than a hundred feet from the road. She urged Itchy to go back and get the car. By the time he returned, she was standing by the road with both bags.

Now the big question: How to split?

They discussed it on the drive up over the pass to the highway to Denver. Itchy's initial claim was simple: no split, return the money to Humphrey. But Helen's argument was also attractive: Humphrey had no idea if they actually could recover the money, or how much it was. He hadn't even asked if she'd had it with her. So he didn't know. They could split it, she argued, and he was free to return his share to his boss, if that was what he wanted. Or, he could take his share and go live on a tropical island. She would never rat on him, she couldn't. She was going back to Detroit. She might have to return something to Humphrey, if it came to that, but she'd decide that if and when it came up.

It would come up, Itchy was certain. But he was receptive to her suggestion that even if he returned to Detroit with his share, she would have no reason to tell Humphrey that he had taken a cut.

The first order of the day was to count the money. They drove south of Denver and checked into a new, almost empty hotel off I-25, near Castle Rock. It was an ideal place, comfortable, inexpensive, and isolated by a newly landscaped site that hadn't been completely cleaned up and resodded yet. In the room, they counted up $7,375,223. Fifty-fifty would yield $3,687,611.50 apiece.

Itchy had no visions of palm trees and margaritas. He was going back to Detroit too. And he wasn't going with no three million and change, a hefty chunk of which would have to be turned over to Humphrey. He proposed a 33-33-34 split, with Helen keeping the extra point.

No, no, she argued. Remember that Humphrey doesn't know how big the pie is, or even that they had it. Why not a mil for

Humphrey, maybe a few extra bucks to make it look realistic, and they'd split the remaining six or so? They could figure out a plausible story and Humphrey would have to accept it.

Itchy didn't buy it. They went on in this way for a while, then went for a walk down to the town, for a little air, and Itchy found some cheap cigars in a convenience store. On the way back, nothing resolved, they loitered around yet another construction site, another new roadside motel, while Itchy smoked one of the cigars. He perched on a low concrete wall, recently poured but now cured and waiting for a hotel to be erected on it. He puffed his cigar and examined his ruined shoes.

"Two hunnerd and fifty bucks," he said, disgustedly.

"You can buy yourself a dozen new pairs," Helen observed. "Why do you smoke such bad cigars?"

"That's all they got," Itchy said, poking at his shoes mournfully.

She paced about, gazing at the hazy mountains to the west, beyond which the sun had just set. She heard a cry and wheeled around. Itchy had disappeared. One shoe lay on its side on the earth, next to the wall.

She raced to the wall and looked down into the huge excavated basement. No Itchy. But there was a large circular concrete projection from the earthen floor, perhaps a drain or something. It looked like a concrete tube on end, a vertical culvert. She found a place in the wall where she could clamber down onto the floor, which would soon be poured with concrete, level with the lip of the tube. She could see down into the tube. It was perhaps eighteen inches in diameter, maybe more. She could see Itchy's feet, about three feet down, one of them stockinged.

Somehow, he had tumbled backward and into the tube, no doubt striking his head in the process. He was neatly stuffed in the culvert. She called, but there was no response.

She stood up and took a deep breath. It was horrible, but there it was. The answer to her problems. There was no way Itchy could extricate himself, if he wasn't already dead. He was headfirst down a drain, unable to move his arms. He would soon suffocate, or maybe . . . well, she didn't know just how he would die, but he would by morning, that was obvious.

She could call for help, but that would mean the fire department, the police, and then . . . well, she couldn't call for help. She looked down the drain. There was a muffled groan. She sighed and reached down. By nearly diving into the hole herself, just barely keeping her feet on the ground, she could seize Itchy's ankles. She began to tug.

The next morning, on the way to the airport, she explained the cut to him: with his million he could keep a low profile, and when he eventually retired he'd be in excellent financial shape. She knew of some excellent investments. As for Humphrey, he'd have to be satisfied with the news that they had been unable to locate the money. Hell, he didn't even know it had been on the train.

3

Blackout

It is disarming to find powerful persons engaged in common pursuits—Winston Churchill diverting himself from imminent invasion by laying bricks on his estate, or the archbishop on the first tee at Pebble Beach. Of late, in the middle of the night, the boss of organized crime in Detroit and its surrounding territory was sitting quite bemused at his computer terminal, surfing the Web. Lately, he had established contact with a remote outpost in northern Ontario, an indigenous peoples site. He was wholly engrossed.

It was a bitter-cold night in January. Humphrey DiEbola was finally going to bed. He stubbed out his last cigar, signed off on his machine, and padded across the hall from his study to his bedroom. He disrobed and put on his pajamas, then sat on the edge of the bed and stared across the room at a beady red light glowing at the corner of the ceiling. He was a few years beyond middle age, a man with a large face and a strong nose. His silk pajamas were bottle-green with yellow piping, and the drape suggested not a robust or athletic physique but rather one a little bulky; not obese, but recently reduced, perhaps.

"Bernie?" he said, hardly more than whispering into the gloom.

A crisp, calm voice answered immediately from a speaker mounted in the elaborate headboard of the bed, among the reading lights, the bookshelves, the hidden electronic panel that controlled things like a radio, the stereo, the lighting. "Bernie's gone home, Mr. DiEbola," the crisp voice stated. "This is John."

DiEbola nodded, as if John were in the room. He was aware that John was observing him on a monitor. He glanced at the digital clock nearby: 1:17, in red numbers. "Are the dogs out?"

"No sir. It's a little cold."

"How cold, John?"

"Below zero, sir. It's, ahhh . . ." He sounded as though he were checking his console. "Minus five, sir. I thought it better to keep the dogs in. They don't perform well in low temperatures. And the wind is kicking up. Fifteen knots with gusts to twenty. Sir. But I can put them out, if you—"

"No, that's fine. I just wondered," DiEbola said. He still sat on the edge of his bed. He didn't appear sleepy or confused to John but, rather, pensive, alert. There was a long silence, more than a minute. DiEbola just sat there, his head cocked as if listening.

John was uneasy. He wondered what the boss had heard. The house was very tight, the rooms well insulated; it was impossible to hear any but the loudest noises. One felt more than heard the wind gusts buffeting the house.

It was never quite dark in this house. In the evening, when everyone had gone to bed, or should have been in bed, the captain of the watch, as he was called, would dim the lights in the halls by remote control. At his console in the anteroom off the entry, the watchman had an array of video screens on which he could, by pressing the appropriate buttons, view almost all of the rooms and living spaces on the main floor of this large house: the hallways, the exits, the living room, the dining room, the boss's study, the kitchen, and even the boss's bedroom. He could also view the grounds from several positions. All of these discreetly placed television cameras could be manipulated from the console to scan these areas, to focus very tightly on suspicious shadows. And lights could be intensified to dispel those shadows, if need be.

The watchman must be prudent, of course. The boss liked security, but he didn't like to feel spied upon. If, for instance, he got up in the night to use the toilet, as a man of his age will do, he would expect the watchman to scan the bathroom quickly and briefly, just to make sure that there were no lurkers, but the beady red light on the camera had better wink off by the time the boss unbuttoned his pajamas.

In the same spirit, there were no cameras in the guest rooms, nor upstairs, where the servants and his chef stayed. There were microphones, well hidden, but they were not to be abused. If the boss, entertaining guests in the living room or study, wished his conversation to be quite private, he had a discreet means of silencing the microphones or shutting off the cameras.

And if the boss were to step across the hall from his bedroom to the room occupied by his so-called niece, Helen, the watchman might observe him arise from his bed in his silk pajamas and exit his room, but as soon as his destination was determined, the cameras would go dead, as would the microphone in her room. Presumably.

Outside, day and night, in balmy summer or bitter winter, the twenty acres of the well-fenced and electronically observed estate on the shores of Lake Saint Clair were regularly patrolled by a squad of young, athletic men in constant communication with the captain of the watch and armed with automatic weapons. Dogs were also employed, rangy Doberman pinschers.

From one day to the next, nothing untoward ever happened. But the drill was never relaxed. The captain of the watch served his eight hours, maintained his log of communication, watched his panel to see where his patrollers were, and, if he suspected that any man was goofing off, dawdling, not paying attention, that man would be instantly contacted and warned to "stay on the ball."

Over the years, due to the lack of incident and the perfection of the electronic surveillance, the staff of patrollers had been cut from eight to five, and recently to just three. Reserves of two or three relief men stayed on standby in the little dayroom in the barracks, so-called, over the garage. The security staff were carefully chosen and trained and paid well. Performance was all but impeccable, and morale was high. It was a good job, a piece of cake. Nobody wanted to lose a cushy position like this one.

"The men are on eight-minute patrol," John said. "That's standard for this temperature. Eight minutes out, fifteen minutes in. I thought I'd have them take the dogs out on the hour."

DiEbola seemed to consider this. Finally, he said, "John, let the dogs sleep. And keep the men in the barracks."

Without meaning to be insolent or disrespectful, but in shocked surprise, John said, "All of them? What for?"

"It's cold out, John. Too cold for dogs. You said so. Send the patrol to the barracks. They can catch a nap, if they like."

"Okay, sir." No hint of objection or argument; John had recovered. "What about the gate, sir?"

"What about it?"

"The guy on the gate, maybe he could have a relief, since all the patrol will be in the barracks."

"The gatehouse is heated," DiEbola said. "He'll be all right. But I'll tell you what, John, since you're concerned, why don't you go up and relieve him?"

"But who'll run the console?"

"The console can run itself," DiEbola said. "Anyway, the alarms are all on. If anyone climbs a fence you'll know."

"Well, sure, but. . . . . How long, sir? I mean till the guys should go back on patrol, and . . ." He meant, how long did he have to stay away from his precious console? And there were other concerns that worried him, but he said nothing about them.

"The morning shift comes on at seven?" DiEbola asked.

"Eight," John said.

"Fine. Until eight, then."

"We could run an hourly walk-around," John suggested.

"Just call the men, John. Now. And then go to the gate and send those guys to the barracks. Everybody in the barracks. It's too cold out there. I don't want anybody freezing his butt on my time. Leave the console on and take a headset. I'll call you if I need you."

"Yes, sir. Thanks, sir," John said, dubiously. The fact was, he was scared. Not twenty minutes before, he had observed the chef, Pepe, come out of his room on the second floor, dressed as usual in jeans and a T-shirt with a Dos Equis beer logo, in stocking feet. He had strolled casually along, down the stairs and along the corridor, until he had merely brushed against the door of the room occupied by Helen, the boss's "niece." He had appeared at the door of the control room a few seconds later.

"Hey, Juan," the young man called, his voice lowered in deference to the hour. He was a very pleasant young man; everybody liked him. "I'm going to get a snack from the kitchen. You want anything? I got some good salmon. I could make you a sandwich. Maybe some poppers? Ees very good."

John had been sorely tempted, but he'd decided against a snack, even though Pepe's poppers—jalapeño peppers stuffed with jack cheese, dipped in batter, and deep-fried—were delicious. He was a man of great circumspection: a snack was too irregular. He'd thanked the chef but said no.

He'd watched the young man go on his way, into the kitchen, where he rummaged in the refrigerator, got out various items, and quickly, neatly prepared the poppers, made a sandwich or two, and then prepared a tray, complete with a couple of opened beers. The chef stopped on his way back and offered the tray. It was too good to pass up: John had taken a popper. It was very tasty.

"Ees Miss Helen still up?" Pepe had asked, innocently, glancing at the array of screens.

"I don't know," John had lied. He had, in fact, just monitored her room. She'd been listening to pop music, played quite softly on the radio, and it sounded like she was smoking. He'd heard a match, a puff, a little sigh.

"Maybe I'll check," Pepe had said. "She might want a little snack."

"I wouldn't do that, Pepe," John had advised him. "You know the boss doesn't like her disturbed. You want to be careful about that. The boss . . . it's more than your job is worth." He had decided against telling Pepe that the boss was still in his study, doubtless engrossed in surfing the Web.

"I'll be careful," Pepe had assured him. He'd placed a forefinger on his lips, smiled, and gone on his way. A moment later, the door to her room had opened and he'd disappeared inside. On the monitor John had heard some whispers, giggles, and some muffled sounds.

Jesus, he'd thought, the man is nuts! Screwing around with the boss's girlfriend.

Now, with the boss back in his bedroom, just across the hall from Helen, John was terrified. He was tempted to say something. But it wasn't his business. He wasn't supposed to be listening. He decided to leave it. Let the kid take his chances. The boss had lain down, he'd soon be asleep. He got up, donned his parka, and went outside into the bitter cold.

After a few minutes, DiEbola rose, put on his robe, and left his bedroom. He did not even hesitate at Helen's room but went directly and quietly to the front reception room. John was gone. The console was fully operative. He sat down in John's still warm chair. From here he could monitor the two main corridors in the large house: the one on which his room, Helen's, the study, and so on, were located, and the upstairs corridor, on which the guest rooms and the suite occupied by his personal chef, Pepe Ortega, were. There was nobody afoot.

All these screens, he thought, and nobody to watch them. There was something pathetic, he thought, about an unwatched video screen. On the gate monitor he could see that John had arrived there. John looked a little put out, but he settled into the gate man's chair with a cup of coffee from the automatic maker, and glanced up uneasily at the camera. Then, shaking his head, he fished out a cigarette and lit it. He picked up a magazine from the desk, flipped the pages.

DiEbola watched the screen that displayed an automatic scan of the dayroom of the barracks. The men were all accounted for. They were hanging up parkas, kicking off insulated boots, stacking their gear on tables. "Did you see those northern lights?" one of them said. "Even with the lights from the city, they're pretty bright."

Another answered, "I seen 'em. But that wind's too fucking cold to be standing out there gawking."

"I'll take the first watch," said another man, and the relieved men trooped off to the sleeping bay, where two others were already lying down.

DiEbola was pleased. He dimmed the lights further in the corridors and entry. He flipped a switch and heard Mexican pop music playing in Pepe's room. Another switch: Helen was listening to a late-night disc jockey spinning "easy listening" music. She was moving around. He tried to imagine what she was doing. A clink. Pouring a drink? Then a low vocal sound, "Mmmmm. Yeah." A laugh.

She was talking to somebody. "You're crazy," she whispered. "What if he comes in here?"

A man's low laugh. "I'm just the delivery boy," the voice said, "the pizza man." It was Pepe.

DiEbola sat listening, anger and titillation mingling as the two bantered and played. He heard or imagined he heard cloth sliding on naked skin, the sound of a zipper. "You like that?"—Pepe's voice. "I got something you like better."

"What took you so long?"—Helen. Then they were in bed, judging from the sound of coil springs, rather muffled. In quick order: many oohs and ahs, gasps, moans, grunts. DiEbola listened intently, breathing shallowly. He was mortified to find that he could not suppress his own sexual excitement. But ultimately, he felt a strange, almost despairing sadness.

He shut the sound off. He also shut off the house alarm system and killed the lights in the back of the house, the ones that illuminated the grounds on the lake side. He doused the lights in the corridor and went back to his room, feeling his way and carrying an extra parka, insulated overalls, and boots from the reception closet. He donned these quickly in his own room, then went to the rear stairs and up to Pepe's room.

The Mexican radio station played, some kind of salsa beat. He began to look quickly through the drawers of Pepe's dresser. The room was lived in, but neat. A maid came in every day to change the linen, vacuum the carpet, and dust. There were magazines lying about, the bed mussed. Pepe had sat around, killing time, waiting until it got late enough.

In the closet there were a couple of suitcases, one of them empty, the other containing some summer clothing that Pepe clearly did not need. There was also a nice leather satchel or overnight bag. It contained a couple of towels. Household towels, good big Turkish bath towels. DiEbola couldn't believe that Pepe would steal towels—

anyway, he wasn't going anywhere, as far as he knew. But there was something under the towels, wrapped in a lightweight jacket.

The most important item, at first sight, was a snub-nosed .38-caliber revolver, a Smith & Wesson, Model 58. Under another shirt, however, was a 5.56mm Bushmaster automatic pistol and three fully loaded banana clips—nothing less than a miniature submachine gun. Next to it, however, lay the truly significant find: a leather folder that contained a badge and a laminated plastic ID card, identifying the man in the photograph as Special Agent Pablo Ortega, of the United States Drug Enforcement Agency.

Hastily, DiEbola replaced these items and restored the bag to its proper place in the closet. He took a second or two to see if he had disturbed any telltale devices that would alert Pepe that the trove had been found. But there was no way, he knew, to spot such things; their very essence was to be invisible to the unsuspecting eye. It didn't matter, he decided.

He got out of the room as fast as he could, sweating slightly, just a sheen on his forehead. Perhaps it was the warmth of the parka. He was halfway down the stairs when he encountered Pepe, on his way up, carrying a tray over which a tea towel was spread. In his left hand he carried a bottle of Dos Equis, from which he had apparently been drinking.

"Whatcha got there, Pepe?" DiEbola asked.

Pepe stopped, his eyes narrowed in the dim light. Then he smiled broadly. "A snack, boss. You want some? I got some jalapeño poppers." He gestured at the tea cloth with the brown bottle.

"No thanks. I was looking for you."

"For me, boss? So late?" Pepe stepped back down a couple of steps until he stood at the bottom of the stairs and allowed DiEbola to come to him.

"Yeah. I was restless. I got up. There's northern lights. I thought you'd like to see them. I bet you never saw the northern lights."

"Northern lights, boss? What's that? The aurora? No, I never seen them." He stepped away, putting the tray down carefully on the floor, looking over his shoulder at DiEbola, talking, still holding the beer bottle.

"So you were restless, too," DiEbola said, nodding at the tray. "Those things'll keep you up all night."

"Not me, boss." Pepe glanced at the door that led to the back entry. "Northern lights. It looks cold out there." The light at the back entry shone on snow swirling past the steps. "Too cold for me. I got no boots"—he glanced down at DiEbola's feet, at his parka— "no coat."

"There's some stuff here," DiEbola said. "I'll get you something to throw on." There was a little anteroom where the household staff kept kindling, firewood for the fireplaces, and various household tools, shovels and the like. The staff kept a couple of jackets and slip-on boots handy for fetching firewood. This equipment was normally stored in one of the garages or sheds, but in winter they brought it in here for convenience.

DiEbola rooted around until he found the boots, which he tossed out to Pepe, then a wool coat. "C'mon," he urged, "you gotta see this. We'll just step out for a second. It ain't that cold. Go ahead."

He prodded the young man and followed him out through the entry onto the back porch. It was rather light out, reflections of the snow from the lights on the perimeter and at the front of the house. Deep shadows, but light enough to move about. The wind was huffing, snow hissing across the crusted surface. In the distance it was black. The lake.

Pepe stopped on the porch and shivered, despite the coat and the boots. "I don't see nothing, boss."

"Well, you ain't gonna see nothing from in here. Go on out there. I'm right behind you."

"Ees fucking cold, boss!"

"Just a few steps. Down the path here." DiEbola prodded him with his gloved hand.

"Jesus, boss! Okay, okay, but I'm freezing my ass. This Detroit, ees too fucking cold!"

The man hopped a few steps down the path and stopped, looking up, his arms clutching the coat closed, still carrying the beer bottle. "I don't see nothing, boss."

"You know what, it's too light. Let me turn out these porch lights." DiEbola stepped back onto the porch and flipped off the porch light. He also picked up an axe that the help had left there for splitting wood. He held it behind him and rejoined Pepe. The lights were visible, now, like curtains of pale fire that swept back and forth across the heavens. The rosy lights of the city seemed to tinge them with color.

"Wow!" Pepe said. "I never seen nothing like it."

DiEbola swung the axe. The blade chunked into the man's head. He fell face forward into the snow. DiEbola hurried back to the house and raced upstairs. He stripped a sheet off Pepe's bed and ran as quickly and quietly as he could back down the stairs and outside. With fierce concentration, panting and sweating, he rolled the body into the sheet. There wasn't much blood, less than he'd expected. He kicked snow over it.

A few minutes later he had fetched the toboggan that the maids used to haul firewood from the shed, loaded the body on it, and begun to trudge out toward the frozen lake, dragging the loaded toboggan behind him. Twenty minutes later he was back at the house. He stowed the toboggan and carried the grisly package of blood-soaked sheet into the house. He returned the outdoor gear, carefully wiped clean, back to the reception closet. He turned up the lights in the corridor to their ordinary dimness, then listened to Helen's room. She seemed to be sleeping.

He turned on the alarm system. It was nearly three. He scanned the console. Everything looked in order. John was still poring over the magazine in the gatehouse, the guy on watch in the barracks was talking to another one of the guys who apparently couldn't sleep.

DiEbola sat and stared at the console. He could hear Helen's steady breathing. He imagined her lithe young body, sated with sex, lying warm and moist, curled in her bed. He had a great aching desire to go in to her. He would slip off his silk pajamas and crawl into the warm nest of her bed. Would she reject him? He was not sure. He could practically feel her slim, almost childish arms about his neck, her teasing little hands. Oh, how he wanted to go to her. But he could not.

Now why was that, he wondered. Why exactly? Presumably, he could do anything he wanted in his own house. He had, in fact, just murdered a man. A man he actually liked and considered a kind of protégé. A man, in fact, whom he had until recently considered worthy of his trust to the point that he had been at least tentatively grooming him for succession. But he saw now, of course, that Pepe had not been qualified for that trust, that confidence. Still, from there to the chopping block was a huge step. But he had done it. Only now he couldn't go in and even "check on" Helen.

Why not? Because she would be annoyed. And he would have no credible excuse. He wasn't sure if he could even speak, or if his hands would tremble.

Well, he was a patient man. Also a bold man. This night's work could undo him. But he wasn't worried. He contented himself with the thought that no matter how agonizing his desire, he was strong enough to wait it out. The ability to postpone gratification was, he thought, the very essence of genuine being. It was self-mastery, wisdom, power . . . just about everything.

He forced himself to concentrate on details. He had disposed of everything—body in one hole in the ice, clothes in another, farther out. The rest of it, the sheet, the head, the hands, those were safely tucked away in a bag that, tomorrow, would find its way into the incinerator at the plant. By now, the ice would have closed the holes, the wind would have blown the snow over the tracks of himself and the toboggan.

He went back upstairs and packed Pepe's bags, including the guns and the wallet, all the personal items. That took him a good long while, but no one disturbed him. He wadded up the rest of the bedding and left it on the bed for the maids to take care of. Pepe would probably have done that, he thought. Then he carried the bags downstairs and set them in the anteroom. In the morning, Itchy could take them to the airport. Perhaps it would be a good idea if Itchy took a little vacation, Florida perhaps, or even the islands. He could work out those details on his way to the Krispee Chips factory tomorrow. It would be done, he was confident.

He decided to rely on the alarm system and toddled off to bed without recalling John to the console. They could resume their usual routine when the morning crew arrived.

4

Busy Life

Roman Yakovich had heard a saying in his youth in the Old Country: Even a simple life ends sadly, but a busy life is all pain. Roman had tried to live a simple life, but these were busy times. Still, he had tried. He had devoted himself to a smarter friend, Sid Sedlacek. He thought that if he just did what Big Sid said things would be less complicated. To an extent, it worked: Big Sid's clever maneuverings had brought them through the war and to the United States, to prosperity. In Detroit, however, people didn't seem to agree with the old saying. These were upbeat, can-do kind of people—they loved complications. Life hadn't turned out as simple as Roman had hoped, but it was easier than it might have been.

But now Big Sid was dead, slain by an assassin's bullet. In the nature of things, given that Big Sid was a gangster, this seemed all but inevitable. Still, Roman took it hard, although he didn't show it, of course. The fact was, he felt rather to blame for not protecting Sid, although it was not his fault at all. Roman had not been with Sid at the fatal moment.

And then, besides his normal bereavement, Roman felt a powerful sense of loss of occupation. Fortunately, Roman still had Big

Sid's aged widow, Soke—no older than himself, actually, just sixty-five, but seemingly an ancient woman—to look after. That helped. They lived a quiet life on a quiet street in a huge house, a life that was now as simple as anyone could wish. They went for walks. Not very far. The neighborhood had declined into a drastic poverty, except for this block, which made it dangerous. But Sid was well armed and, anyway, they walked in careless ignorance of danger. The walks were short because Mrs. Sid was a dumpy, gray woman. Her legs weren't good. They walked to the end of the long block on which they lived, near Grosse Pointe, stopping at Kercheval Avenue and walking back. Roman drove her to the Serbian Orthodox church on Eight Mile Road, to the special grocery store in Hamtramck, where she got imported foods. She still cooked for him, heavy Serbian meals of pierogi, *sarma*, dumplings stuffed with liver paste.

The dozens of people who used to come for the Sunday meals—all-day buffet, actually—came no more. And the little angel who had brightened their lives no longer appeared. Little Helen, the only child of Big Sid and Mrs. Sid, was in trouble. She had run away with a dashing young man named Joe Service, who was some kind of trouble-shooter for Big Sid's one-time associates. Little Helen and Joe Service had disappeared after the death of the mob boss, Carmine. Helen had visited at Christmas, but she had stayed at the home of the new boss, Humphrey DiEbola, the one they used to call the Fat Man, although he was no longer fat. This might have seemed a scandal, and it upset Soke, but Roman understood that Helen's stay with Mr. DiEbola was of a business nature, and he calmed her mother with that. And then Helen had gone back out West.

She wasn't gone long. She reappeared in time for the Eastern Orthodox Christmas. Mrs. Sid was very happy and Helen seemed glad to be home, but Roman could see she was in trouble. He didn't ask any questions. He just made sure her room was comfortable and he took both the ladies shopping for Christmas, buying presents and lots of food. And then he called Mr. DiEbola, just in case he wasn't aware of Helen's reappearance.

Mr. DiEbola was very grateful. "The poor kid, she's had a bad time, Roman," he'd said. "Listen, I want to help her. She needs help. Let her settle down, relax. But keep me informed. You did good. If she calls anybody, see if you can find out who she's talking to. Some of these people she's been screwing around with, they aren't good friends. They don't look out for her like we would. She's just a young woman, practically alone in the world, now that her papa's gone. But we can help her. In a few days I'll come by, see what I can do. If she looks like she's running away again, let me know, right away. She's a little confused right now, don't know who her real friends are."

And after a few days, as he'd promised, Mr. DiEbola came around. He was slimmer than Roman had remembered him. He'd lost a lot of weight. Probably, now that he was the big boss, he was worrying too much. It was a difficult thing, running a large and complicated enterprise like the business. But he looked healthy, younger even.

Little Helen didn't seem unhappy to see him, but Roman could see she was anxious. She and Mr. DiEbola went into her papa's study and when they came out, an hour later, she seemed more cheerful. She no longer looked to Roman for support. She even patted his arm and said that everything was all right. So that was good, Roman supposed. He would never allow anything to hurt the little angel.

That same afternoon, Helen moved back to DiEbola's house on the Lake Saint Clair shore. It wasn't far from home, just a few miles, but it was a significant move. She visited her mother at least once a week, and occasionally Roman would drive the old lady to visit at Mr. DiEbola's house, especially when the weather got better. Spring had come early. It was still chilly, except for occasional days when it was nice enough to walk down to the shore across the huge lawn and sit on folding chairs on the deck that had a roof of exposed beams. Helen would bring a cashmere blanket and a shawl for her mother. Servants would bring coffee and even a decanter of slivovitz for Roman. Mr. DiEbola was dashing in a colorful windbreaker. Roman wore, as always, a heavy black wool suit and a white shirt and tie. He also wore the handsome checked wool cap that Helen had given him for Christmas. It sat so well on his large, square head and made him feel good.

He was pleased to see that Helen was happier and that she got along so well with the man she used to call "Unca Umby." There was something about her flirtatious manner with DiEbola, however, and his too eager acceptance of it, that disquieted Roman. But he decided it was just her lighthearted, girlish way and he dismissed it.

Still, all was not gaiety. Earlier, when Helen had first moved to DiEbola's, Roman and Mrs. Sid had visited a couple of times and they had been introduced to an interesting young man from Mexico, a fellow who was apparently Mr. DiEbola's cook. This Pepe had become more than a cook, it seemed. He was doing something at Mr. DiEbola's potato chip factory, but Roman wasn't sure what it was. But he joined them for coffee and drinks, at that time. Now, however, when the winter was ending, Roman never saw him. He didn't ask about Pepe, because he sensed that it was not a topic that would be welcomed. In his idle moments in his room (Roman had moved into the house from his old room over the carriage house, to be handy for Mrs. Sid, in case she felt ill), when he was not watching a hockey game on television, Roman would wonder if there hadn't been some romantic trouble with Pepe. It had been clear that there was some sort of attraction between Pepe and Helen and that Mr. DiEbola wasn't too pleased about it, although nothing was ever said and no incident had occurred in Roman's presence. Now that he thought about it, however, Roman supposed that Mr. DiEbola had sent Pepe packing.

As for Joe Service, his name was never mentioned. Roman had met him only once. That was after the death of Big Sid. Roman had been told to cooperate with Service, who was investigating the death of Big Sid. He seemed like a good fellow to Roman and he had gotten along very well with Helen, to be sure. Too well. When they had disappeared after the assassination of Carmine, Roman felt bad about it. He thought maybe he should have warned Helen about these young guys who come waltzing into town, no attachments, acting like they own the world. But, he had reasoned at the time, she was not a little girl anymore. She had to learn about these heartbreaking Lotharios. And her heart had been broken, he was sure. But she had survived. She seemed very happy now. The thing that bothered him, though, was that she should be so . . . well, flirty with Mr. DiEbola. The man was almost as old as Roman! He was no Joe Service, who, despite the misery he had evidently caused the little angel, was a more appropriate match for her.

Roman wasn't sure how to deal with this development, but it was a complication. He hated complication. He decided to stay out of it. Keep your mouth shut. Drive the old lady around, do the shopping. Play cards when you're asked. Otherwise, watch television, root for the Red Wings, despite their awful dependence on those Russian players.

Roman wasn't worried about little Helen. She might be small, but she was dynamite. He laughed to himself in his room, thinking of the word *dynamite*. He wasn't any genius with words, but he liked the combination of *mite* with the notion of explosiveness. That described little Helen, all right. A dynamic mite. He could pick her up with one hand. When she was a child she would ask him to do just that, delighting to perch on his outstretched hand. She shot around like a little rocket, all over the place, screeching like a devil. She would hide in the shrubbery while he blundered about, searching for her, then suddenly streak away out of the corner of his eye, disappearing around the carriage house, her squeals of laughter hanging in the air.

Now she was a woman, all right, with heavy black hair that incongruously featured a silver streak rising from her pale forehead. She wasn't a lot bigger than a child, however. And Joe Service wasn't a lot bigger than her, so maybe their attachment was natural and reasonable, Roman thought. Two perfectly made small people, very handsome, very well matched. They were grown-ups who still possessed much of the innocence and delight of children. Roman was sorry now that it hadn't worked out.

Unlike Roman Yakovich, Detective Sergeant Mulheisen was very much a Detroiter. Problems were his bread and butter. But lately, however, like Roman he had a desire for a more peaceful existence. In Mulheisen's case, this took the form of burying himself in routine. He'd been running around all over the country, out to Montana, Colorado, and points in between, in pursuit of Joe Service and Helen Sedlacek. He'd finally run Service to ground in Colorado and seen him safely confined to a hospital there, awaiting recovery, questioning, and, he hoped, a trial. Now, he felt, he could turn his attention to precinct work, catch up. This wouldn't last long, he was sure, but while it did, he was happy to immerse himself in local issues.

One major problem was definitely local: according to Chapter 3, Section 48, of the police manual, he was required to reside in the city of Detroit, an issue that he and numerous white officers had dodged for years. His boss (formerly his assistant), Captain Jimmy Marshall, had just informed him that the rule could no longer be ignored.

Earlier, Mulheisen had kept an apartment in the city, but for some time now he had lived in his childhood home, in nearby Saint Clair Flats, with his widowed mother. It was a convenient arrangement for both of them. She was rarely at home, often away for extended bird-watching jaunts or lobbying for some environmental cause. In theory, it was comforting and convenient to have one's policeman son around to mow the lawn, move furniture, and keep the burglars out. For him, it meant free housekeeping and even the occasional meat loaf.

Now the department had cracked down. Once he became resigned to the move, Mulheisen didn't mind. To his surprise neither, apparently, did his mother. High school kids could be hired to mow lawns and shovel snow; machines could answer the phone. Mul had never mowed the lawn once, could not program an answering machine, and often forgot to turn off the coffeemaker. Perhaps burglars had avoided the house—assuming they knew it was a cop's house— but they were welcome to take what they wanted, if they were into monochrome TVs, furniture that was antique but not valuable, old tennis rackets, and boxes of unused housedress fabric.

Mulheisen had looked at an apartment near the Cultural Center. It was small, but it had considerable advantages. It was located in the heart of the city, in an area undergoing extensive renewal and some gentrification. It was the upstairs back in a four-flat brick mansion. All newly remodeled. He could walk to the new ballpark, Comerica Park, or whatever they were calling it, when it opened. It had a tiny bedroom with a closet about the size of a refrigerator, a combination living room–dining room–kitchen, a bath with a new shower and tub combo. Not a lot of room, but maybe he didn't need so much. The rent was reasonable, he thought, at twelve hundred dollars a month.

As for work, there was plenty of it in the Ninth Precinct. For instance, with the breakup of the ice on Lake Saint Clair, some kids throwing rocks at the spectacular ice jam on the Detroit River had discovered a body. Not an ordinary drowning, for sure. This body had no head and no hands. The corpse had been badly mangled by the ice. According to the medical examiner, Doc Brennan, the body had been deposited on the ice several weeks before the breakup.

It was a male, in good physical condition at demise, aged about twenty-five to possibly twenty-nine. Probably about six feet tall, probably weighing about 185 pounds. Mulheisen had absolutely no leads on an identification, but he was a patient man. Something would turn up.

Besides this case, the precinct had a curious one involving a woman who had been shot while ostensibly holding up a supermarket. And then there was the odd incidence of some troubling E-mail messages received by a young boy in the precinct and addressed to Mulheisen himself. Oh, there was plenty to keep him engaged, all right. And all the while he was keeping one ear cocked, as it were, for news about the recovery of Joe Service, out in Colorado. When Service came out of his coma there would be plenty to do.

In the meantime, he was busily packing his books for the move. Or rather, he should have been packing. At the moment, he was engrossed in a history book, one he had purchased months before and had glanced at cursorily, only to set it aside and never open it again. He was leaning against a bookcase reading Richard White's *The Middle Ground*, despite its daunting subtitle: *Indians, Empires, and Republics in the Great Lakes Region, 1650–1815*. He had been in the act of adding the book to a box of other history books marked READ, SOON! when he made the fatal mistake of opening it. He had been standing like this for fifteen minutes, but now he absentmindedly shifted some other books off an easy chair and sat down.

He had innocently looked up what White had to say about Pontiac, one of Mulheisen's abiding interests. White's analysis of that historical figure was somewhat at odds with Mulheisen's own, though by the end of White's comments it appeared that they weren't so far apart. Just out of curiosity, he'd turned to another figure from early Detroit history whose name had also been borrowed by General Motors: Antoine Laumet de La Mothe, Sieur de Cadillac, the founder of Detroit.

The passage that so engrossed him was an account of what appeared to be the first murder in Detroit history. The aboriginal people gathered about Detroit included several tribes. Most, like the Ottawas, were Algonquian people, but some were Iroquoian, such as the Huron-Petuns and the Miamis. In 1706, when this important trading and administrative post was five years old, the Ottawas were warned by a Pottawatomi that when the Ottawa warriors left for a proposed attack on the Sioux, in their absence the Huron-Petuns and Miamis would attack their village. The old Ottawa chief, whom the French called Le Pesant—the Fat One, although he was said to have slimmed down in recent years—counseled a pre-emptive strike on the Huron-Petuns and their allies.

> The Ottawas ambushed a party of Miami chiefs, killed five of them, and then attacked the Miami village, driving the inhabitants into the French fort. The French fired on the attacking Ottawas and killed a young Ottawa who had just been recognized as a war leader. Although the Ottawa leaders tried to prevent any attacks on the French, angry warriors killed a French Recollect priest outside the fort and a soldier who came to rescue him.

This, then, was the murder case.

Mulheisen was puzzled. Which of these killings were actually murders? It was more like war. You didn't prosecute soldiers for murder. But evidently, the French saw it differently. The priest was clearly an innocent party, although one wondered how the Ottawas were to see it that way—he had intervened in an action, had thrust himself into harm's way. Presumably, his death was a regrettable accident, or at least an incidental consequence of his own foolhardy behavior. Not murder, in the intentional sense.

The soldier, moreover, was one of those who had fired upon the attacking Ottawas; he was a combatant. Nonetheless, the French wanted retribution for both deaths, an eye for an eye, specifically, a trial and execution of the perpetrators.

The Ottawas, like any of the indigenous peoples, made a clear distinction between these deaths. The Huron-Petuns and Miamis, while nominally allies under a treaty worked out by La Mothe, were traditional enemies of the Ottawas and they had instigated this conflict, if they had not initiated it. Blood retribution was the normal expectation of conflicts between enemies. But between friends—i.e, with the French—killings must be dealt with by two means: "covering the dead" (compensation in goods, gifts) and "raising up the dead" (providing a substitute, a slave). The Ottawas were sorry for the death of the priest and the soldier, and they eagerly offered to cover or raise up the victims, but they saw no reason to surrender their warriors to be executed. What purpose could be served by that?

Mulheisen was intrigued. To be sure, in the present day distinctions were made in the nature of killings—first-degree homicide, premeditated murder, manslaughter, negligent homicide, and so on. And, of course, acts of war exempted combatants from even these distinctions. Seen that way, the indigenes' attitudes didn't seem quite so odd.

He reflected that the indigenes' willingness to allow the killing of innocent parties to be compensated by gifts, letting the perpetrator go free, suggested a deep conservatism: these people were living so close to the bone that a warrior's bloody deeds could be excused, as it were, with ephemeral gifts—perhaps because every warrior was so valuable to the group. Imagine allowing a hit man to buy his way out of a murder conviction! After all, he was not professedly an enemy of the slain victim. (Although, Mulheisen speculated, perhaps the hit man could be seen as an enemy of all private persons, inasmuch as his actions were not undertaken in the service of society—any society—but for mere pay.)

As it happened, negotiations covered the Ottawa dead to that party's satisfaction. But the French were not satisfied with either covering or resurrecting the priest and the soldier. The problem was compounded by political considerations. The French knew very well that they were not powerful enough to continue to operate in the countryside without satisfactory resolution. Governor Vaudreuil, the French authority in Quebec, with whom La Mothe was not on good terms, insisted on French justice—the execution of those responsible. There was also the consideration that these issues must be resolved and seen to be resolved among the various factions of Algonquians and Iroquoians, or there would be widespread war in the frontier, a disastrous consequence.

Le Pesant was the key figure. He took responsibility for the Ottawas' actions. Vaudreuil was actually presented with two slaves to "raise up the gray coat" but rejected them, saying that if Le Pesant was responsible, only his blood would suffice. He ordered La Mothe to arrest him, although he knew very well that any attempt to seize the Ottawa leader would endanger the alliance and that no Ottawa had the authority to deliver Le Pesant to La Mothe. Evidently, Vaudreuil did not expect Le Pesant to be surrendered, which would embarrass La Mothe, Vaudreuil's rival. But it would cut Le Pesant and his band off from the alliance, perhaps punishment enough.

It was clear that neither French nor Algonquian ethics, by themselves, could resolve the issue. A middle ground was required. La Mothe's solution was novel. He let it be known that Le Pesant's death was not his primary aim, but that he wished "that great bear, that malicious bear" to be surrendered to him, after which time he would decide further. The Ottawas agreed. Apparently, they sensed the unique and unprecedented nature of the situation. Le Pesant was delivered as, in effect, a slave—a condition that had never attached to someone of his position. It was a kind of fiction, a staged drama. But it served the needs of the alliance and of both sides.

The drama itself was highly edifying. Le Pesant appeared at the fort with his escort of Ottawas. The Huron-Petuns, Miamis, and French officials (including Vaudreuil) looked on from a distance while La Mothe addressed the trembling Le Pesant imperiously. The Ottawa escort begged for their chief's life, offered another young slave, and asked to be allowed to return to Detroit. But La Mothe was not conceding anything.

That night Le Pesant escaped from his prison, "leaving behind his shoes, his knife, and his shabby hat." La Mothe locked up his escort for a day, in punishment, then released them. He declared that Le Pesant, nearly seventy, nearly naked, and unarmed, would surely perish alone in the woods. Privately, he assured the Ottawas that he had intended to pardon Le Pesant anyway. The matter was closed. Vaudreuil could do nothing and even grudgingly admired his rival's creativity; the Huron-Petuns were evidently satisfied by the humiliation of Le Pesant and the Ottawas, and the alliance was restored. That Le Pesant soon reappeared at his old encampment in Michilimackinac was ignored.

Ah, the beauties of fiction, Mulheisen thought. How gratifying. Le Pesant had yielded to French authority; he was allowed to disappear; a fiction of his death was accepted. Case closed, everybody satisfied. Mulheisen wondered if he had ever done anything like that, himself—accepted a fiction in order to resolve a sticky issue. Perhaps he had, but he couldn't remember it.

Unfortunately, history showed, as White conceded, that the drama was not completely successful: the Miamis were enraged and soon got their own revenge, killing Ottawas and even Frenchmen, kicking off another round of negotiations.

Mulheisen put the book on the top of the READ box.

5

Cigar

Humphrey was regaling Helen with amusing tales of "the guys." They were walking along the Lake Saint Clair shore in front of the house. A blustery onshore wind buffeted them, making their eyes water, yet it wasn't too cold. Spring was in the air. Already, Helen's mother had visited. But today, the lake was dark blue-gray and choppy. The overcast was like an iron lid coming down on their heads, but it didn't oppress them.

Helen was dashing around, playing with a dog, one of the rangy Dobermans from the guard kennel. She called it Fritzy, although that was not its name. Humphrey was smoking a large, torpedo-shaped cigar.

"His real name is Angelo," Humphrey said, continuing a story, "but everybody calls him Mongelo, because he's a biter."

"A biter? Well, he's supposed to be, isn't he?" Helen laughed and capered along the shore like a girl, tussling with the dog, tossing a stick for it to fetch. She looked like a teenager in her woolen cap. "He won't bite me. He likes me."

"Not the dog," Humphrey said, amused. "The guy I'm telling you about. Angelo. Mongelo. You know"—he made eating gestures with his hands—"*mangia, mangia*, like he eats a lot. He's fat. Fatter than me."

"Oh, Unca Umby," she cooed, snuggling him momentarily, caressing his cheeks and attempting a kiss, which he dodged. "You're not fat. Not anymore."

"Well, like I was," Humphrey said. He enjoyed her fooling. He liked her attempted kiss, but felt that for the sake of dignity, decorum, he should pretend not to like it. "Actually, Mongelo's fatter than I ever was. The trouble is, he's a *biter*. He bit a guy's finger off."

"My god!" Helen stopped, appalled. "Why on earth would he do that? Is he crazy?"

"Sure he's crazy, whaddaya think?" Humphrey puffed appreciatively on his cigar. "They're all crazy. Well, not all of them, but some. Yeah." He nodded, thoughtfully, gazing out at the cold lake. "There's some crazy guys we got working for us. That's one of the things, you know, when you're in this business. Some of the guys who work for us aren't wrapped too tight."

"Mongelo works for you?" she asked. She had taken his arm. The dog trailed along as they paced, patiently waiting for the stick in her hand to be thrown again. "What does he do?"

"He bites people," Humphrey said. They both laughed. He shrugged and took his cigar out of his mouth, holding it to the other side of him, away from her. "Well, though, that's really the truth: he's an enforcer for the loans. Guys don't pay their loans, Mongelo bites 'em."

Helen was amused and interested. She wanted to know about the loans. They walked back. They were chilled now. Humphrey tossed his cigar into the chop of the waves. The dog looked puzzled but didn't offer to retrieve it. "Let's get back to the fire," Humphrey said. He made a signal and one of the security men, discreetly standing beyond a fir tree, raised a device to his lips. The silent whistle instantly drew the dog away.

Humphrey explained about the loan business over hot choco-late for Helen, coffee for himself. "There are always guys who need money, need it fast, no questions. Maybe they gambled, maybe they borrowed from where they work . . . and they don't exactly have good credit, but they have access to money. So, you try to figure out if they can handle it. The interest is big, but so is their need. Can they pay it back before it's too big a problem for them? That's the question. It's like all loan business, like a bank . . . with a difference—we collect. We don't write it off. If they pay it back quick, the interest isn't a problem. You're doing them a favor. They're grateful.

"Say an opportunity pops up," Humphrey went on. "The guy finds out he can get his hands on some merchandise that will make him a lot of money, but he doesn't have the large. You want to help a guy, if he's got a chance to do something for himself. And a lot of the time you can get a piece of the action. So you say, Okay, you can have the grand, the five, the ten, whatever he needs. Give him more than he needs, even—Don't leave yourself short, you tell him. And you warn him, the vig can get steep, so pay up. The vigorish, the interest," he explained.

"But he doesn't pay," she prompted. This was not really news to her, but she'd never heard the actual details.

"Yeah, sometimes the deal goes haywire, he screws it up, he lied about it, or he's just stupid. Maybe it wasn't really his deal. Or it was really a gambling debt. He didn't borrow enough. All kinds of reasons." He got out another of his cigars from the humidor cabinet, the big fat ones, torpedo shaped. He waved it. "You mind?"

"Oh no," she assured him, she didn't mind. She liked the smell of cigars, good cigars. Her father had always liked cigars. "Let me try one," she said. "Do you have any little ones?"

Humphrey rummaged in the cabinet and found a small, well-made cigar, a "petit lancero." He clipped it and lit it for her, then lit his own. He had discreetly turned on a device that whisked away the smoke, the aroma.

"The vig can be a problem for the loaner," he said, "for us. It gets to be too much, more than the guy can pay. Sometimes he gets scared, afraid of the collector, and he'll do stuff he shouldn't do, to get the money. It can cause problems. But you gotta enforce it. You send Mongelo around. You can't have these guys thinking they can get away with this irresponsibility."

"And he bites their fingers?" she said. She enjoyed the little cigar, but she was finding the story a little distasteful. She was glad she didn't have to deal with any Mongelo, in any respect.

"That's the problem," Humphrey said. "He didn't used to be so screwy. Used to be, he'd go around, put a little pressure on, twist his arm, maybe even slap the guy around a bit. But then he heard about Action Jackson."

Action Jackson was a legendary collector in Chicago, Humphrey explained. Like Mongelo, he was a big, fat man who bit people. Humphrey told the story, but he didn't think he could tell her about Jackson's worst actions, such as when he'd bit a woman's nipples off. The woman was the mistress of the borrower, not the borrower himself. Jackson had gone to see the man but he wasn't home. Jackson had sat around, waiting, but after a while his attention turned to the woman. He thought he'd rape her. That would send a message. He overpowered the woman, tied her up, stripped her, but then he didn't have the urge—or so it was said. He ended up biting her nipples off. The guy got the message. He paid up. And then he went looking for Jackson.

"Jackson went too far" was all Humphrey would say about it. But Helen wanted to know what had happened to him. She meant, Where is he these days? But Humphrey, still in the train of memory, said, "Oh, they reamed him. The guy he was collecting from, him and some others. You don't want to know. He died from it. The guy was nuts, like I said."

Jackson had died hanging from a barbed plug hammered up his rectum, attached to a wire cable suspended over a girder in a warehouse. Humphrey remembered when he first heard about it, wondering how they had hoisted the man up and how the plug could have held him long enough for him to die of suffocation, his mouth duct-taped. It was a grotesque image: a naked fat man hanging by a wire up his ass. Like a great pig in a slaughterhouse. According to the stories, they'd gone off and left him, and his corpse wasn't found for several days.

Humphrey suddenly didn't like the image and blanked it from his mind.

He wondered how he could get it across to Helen that it wasn't all like this, tawdry and violent and even a little disgusting. It was mainly just business. Business like ordinary business, not a lot different from your friendly bank, say, but with the principles carried a little bit further, carried as far as they could go. It didn't happen that often. Guys needed money but couldn't get it at a bank or any legitimate source. So they had to pay a big price. They almost always paid it back; they were grateful and they knew they could borrow again. That's how it mainly worked. Mongelo was unusual.

What concerned him now, Humphrey said, was that it looked like Mongelo had gone off the deep end. He might try to carry his imitation of Action Jackson to the same extremes, and that would cause problems. He had to do something about Mongelo before he went too far.

"What Mongelo needs," she suggested, "is to diet."

Humphrey laughed. Then he looked thoughtful. "Not a bad idea," he said. "Maybe a forced diet." He abruptly changed the topic. "So, you like the cigar?"

"I like it very much," she said. "Is it Cuban?"

"Naw. You wouldn't like Cuban."

"Papa always smoked Cubans," she said. "Big ones. He used to give me a puff, secretly."

Humphrey remembered. He'd liked Big Sid Sedlacek. A man's man. Full of jokes, smart, a guy who would go out on a limb for a buddy and back him up. He had a lot of stories about Big Sid, though he didn't think his daughter would like all of them. But she was tough. He looked at her, thoughtfully. She'd been through a lot and she'd showed her mettle. She had her wits about her. Maybe she wouldn't be as shocked as he thought.

"Cubans are too strong," he said. "I don't even like them, most of 'em. I like the milder ones." He puffed the torpedo.

"That looks strong."

"But it's not, not really. Here, have a puff." He held it out to her and she bravely took a little puff.

She smiled. "It's pretty mild!"

"I told you. Most people don't know sh—, crap about cigars, even guys who smoke all the time. They hear other guys talking about Cubans, so they all want a Cohiba. Hell, most of the Cohibas they get—if they can get one—aren't even Dominican, much less Cuban. They're Honduran, or Guatemalan, sometimes not even that. Mexican, or Florida. But they got the label."

"How do they get the label?"

"That's our business," he was delighted to tell her. "A label is a hell of a lot easier to make than a cigar. A real cigar, like a Cohiba or an H. Upmann, you got to grow the tobacco right, select it, dry it, age it. You got to have top-notch rollers and makers, and then you got to age them again. There's a lot to it. A good cigar is worth what you pay. But in this country, especially since Kennedy did us all a favor and slapped an embargo on the Cubans, cigar smokers here don't know from Shinola about real cigars."

"What is Shinola?" she asked, abruptly. She tapped her little cigar on the crystal ashtray. She let it lie.

"You don't know Shinola?" Humphrey laughed. "It's shoe polish. I think it's still around."

"Shoe polish! I thought it was a cigar. So what is the business, your business?"

"I'll show you. Come on, let's take a ride." This was perfect, he thought. He'd been thinking about having her meet some of the people he worked with and Strom Davidson had come to mind, as a man of some class, not just another hoodlum. Strom would be interesting to her, he thought, but not too interesting.

They drove into the city or, rather, they were driven into the city by a couple of the guys, nice-looking young men who sat silently in the front seat, the glass up between them and the passengers. The Cadillac had dark-tinted windows. It rolled through the rough neighborhoods where every block was missing at least two or three houses that had long ago burned and the lots had been graded and sodded. Many of these empty lots were still weedy, but the general effect seemed to be to let light and air into the old, rundown neighborhoods. That hadn't been the object, presumably, but it was the effect.

Eventually, somewhere west of Saint Aubin, a very old part of town, they entered a kind of warehouse district. The limo pulled up at a door served by a simple concrete stair of six steps. The young man on the passenger side hopped out and opened the car door for Helen. The driver opened the door for Humphrey.

"You want us to go up, boss?" the driver asked.

"No, that's all right," Humphrey said. "You guys wait here. We won't be long."

They went into a little office. A young woman with a fancy hairstyle, all pushed up in back and then artfully messed up to look like a waterfall over her well-cosmetized face, greeted them with obvious interest. She knew who Humphrey was, clearly.

"Mr. Davidson's upstairs, in the shop," she said. "Want me to get him?"

"No, we'll go up. I just wanted to show Miz Sid the operation," Humphrey said.

They pushed through a door and climbed a dimly lit stairs, then passed through another door into a kind of loft. Here there were several rows of waist-high benches, at which more than two dozen women were busily opening plastic-wrapped bundles of cigars and dumping their contents onto trays that traveled along a conveyor belt. At the end of the belt another woman operated a machine that rapidly applied a colorful cigar band to the cigars, which were then carried farther along to be packed into boxes bearing the same "Cuban" label as the newly affixed band. At other tables previously banded cigars were stripped of their bands and new ones were affixed.

All of the women were young, dressed in jeans and shirts, over which they wore a variety of aprons—some of them very kitcheny floral prints, others more standard work aprons supplied by a linen service. Many of the women appeared to be Chicanas. There were no black women.

A tall man in his fifties was pacing about, barking at the girls fiercely. He was berating one young woman in particular, a rather pretty, dark woman of Helen's age who worked swiftly and competently, seemingly ignoring her persecutor.

"You could have done all this hours ago," the man was raging. "I told you to get them out by noon, but no, you hadda take your fuckin' break!"

"We gotta eat," the woman said, calmly, not even looking up. She worked on swiftly. "The girls don't eat, they start screwin' up, they make mistakes, it takes longer. We'll get 'em all out, don't worry."

"Worry! Yeah, it's me 'at's gotta worry! You bitches don't care! Get a fuckin' move on!"

He spun on his heel and strode away. As he came toward
them, before he even saw Humphrey and Helen, she could see that
he was actually laughing. She was shocked. He'd seemed so furi-
ous, so enraged. And yet, she could see the women shrugging, looking at one another, shaking their heads, getting on with their work,
brushing back their hair with grimy hands, deftly stacking and sort-
ing, placing bundles out, picking them up from the machine, or
loading boxes on pallets.

"Hey!" Davidson cried out when he saw them. "It's the man,
himself." He pulled up in front of them, towering. He hoisted his
trouser belt unconsciously and looked at Helen. "What'd ya bring
me, Hump? More help? I can always use more help." He bellowed
the last to carry over the din of the shuffling noise of the women,
the clanking and humming of the machines. "I'll fire all a these
bimbos, get me some babes who can work!"

Humphrey smiled and introduced Helen. Davidson seemed
pleased to meet her. He'd known her father, a good man, he said.
Then, "C'mon, let's get outta this racket."

He ushered them through a passageway, toward another
room. "It's going good," he told Humphrey. "Great! This fuckin'
cigar business is going through the top. You wanta know my biggest problem?" He stopped in the passageway and looked at them.
"I can't get enough crappy cigars. No shit. If I could get my mitts
on another ten million crappy stogies they'd be outta here in two
days, lookin' like Havana Supremos."

Humphrey told him he was showing Helen the business.
Davidson was happy to conduct a tour. He had a printing operation in the next room, where elegant labels were being created.
He had a couple of artists who designed them, then more
who transferred the designs through the processes leading to a
beautifully printed label. Helen had never heard of any of these

brands, naturally, and neither had anyone else. But they looked good.

"Hell, I'll create one for you," Davidson said, grandly. He bent over a thin, harassed-looking young man at a drafting table, explaining what he wanted. The man quickly sketched a picture of what appeared to be a Greek goddess wearing an Indian headdress, carrying a basket from which flowers, fruit, and cigars tumbled.

Davidson was delighted. "That's it, Ramón," he cried. "And we'll call it . . . " He paused, thinking as he regarded Helen standing there. "I got it! Call it LaDonna Helena. And make her skinnier. She should be sitting on a donkey. You know, some flowers around, a palm tree, maybe some parrots or colorful birds, whaddaya call 'em, macaws. One on her shoulder."

He leaned over the man. "No, skinnier. Not so much tits. She should be more like . . . like her." He pointed to Helen.

The young man tossed his lank black hair back with a habitual gesture and peered at Helen through his glasses. He poked the heavy black frames firmly onto the bridge of his nose with his index finger and smiled shyly. In a moment he had made the changes. "Perfect!" declared Davidson.

They went downstairs then, to his office. He poured a little glass of brandy for Humphrey, one for himself. Helen had declined to join them. "They'll have them labels on a thousand boxes by tomorrow," he boasted. "Our new brand. It'll sell like ice cream in July. You'll see. So, whaddaya think?"

Helen was impressed, even amused. She found herself caught up in the man's enthusiasm. "But why do you have to yell at them?" she asked. "They look like they're going full blast."

"You gotta," Davidson said. "They expect it. If I don't yell they slow down. Pretty soon they're taking coffee breaks, smoking cigarettes . . . as it is, every damn one of 'em has to go to the fuckin' can every ten minutes. This morning three girls didn't show. It's the same old shit. They got their period, their old man's in jail, the kid's got a cold. They come back the next day, but then another three or four don't show. It's a pain in the ass."

He cocked his ear, suddenly, at the ceiling. "See? They're slowin' down. I gotta get back up there. Hey, glad you could stop by."

He started to rush out, but Humphrey caught hold of him, then asked Helen to wait. He went out into the corridor and the two of them talked, the big man hunched over, listening to Humphrey patiently. It wasn't a long conversation. The big man seemed agreeable, slapped Humphrey on the back, and then went bounding up the stairs. Before Humphrey and Helen departed they could hear him screaming, even before he'd reached the top of the stairs.

In the car, Helen asked, "What was all the conversation?"

"Oh, just a little business," Humphrey said. "He's doing me a favor."

Three days later, two boxes of LaDonna Helena Petit Coronas arrived at Humphrey's house. The wooden boxes sported a splendid design. The label assured that the contents were "*Hecho a mano*" and very official looking stamps sealed the box. The principal feature was a picture of a svelte, dark-haired beauty wearing a diadem, with a macaw on her shoulder, strewing flowers and cigars, perched on a white donkey. She looked a lot like Helen, except that instead of her silver skunk stripe, this goddess had two golden stripes rising from her temples. According to the gold medallions surrounding the picture, these cigars had won prizes in 1898, 1910, and 1925, in Havana, Cuba, and Paris, France. Humphrey advised against opening the box. "It's the only good thing about those cigars, the label," he said.

Later that morning, in his office at Krispee Chips, DiEbola received Angelo Badgerri. He was a fat man, about Humphrey's age. They even looked a bit alike, although the resemblance was not so marked as it had once been, when DiEbola was carrying much the same weight. Badgerri's people were reputed to be from the same region in Italy as DiEbola's, though why anyone said that wasn't clear, since Humphrey's heritage was so uncertain. But, until just a year or so earlier, it wasn't uncommon for acquaintances to remark that they looked like brothers, or cousins, at least. After the slaying of Carmine and the accession to power of Humphrey, no one said that.

For all Humphrey knew they could be half brothers. He wasn't sentimental about connections like that. He'd never really known his father, at least not *as* his father. Humphrey had known Angelo all his life and he'd never liked him. As a boy he'd been a nasty little jerk, stupid and venal, and he'd only gotten worse with age. But they got along. Angelo did his job, he was useful. Unfortunately, he was becoming a liability.

Like many of his contemporaries, Angelo seemed unaware that times had changed in the business. Of course, they hadn't changed completely, but the old days of mob arrogance were fading fast. The modern mobster needed a slimmer, less obnoxious profile. That was what Humphrey wanted to talk to Angelo about.

He explained it to him as delicately as possible. "Monge, you're a pig. You gotta get rid of that lard."

Angelo wasn't offended. He grinned. "Like you did, Hump?" Evidently Angelo believed that the length of their relationship entitled him to the "Hump." Humphrey was unperturbed.

"Exactly," he said. "It's gonna kill you. I'm worried about you."

The fat man's padded brow furrowed. Humphrey knew what he was thinking. He was thinking that he was going to get chewed out for biting the finger off the deadbeat. "Boss, I warned that shithead, I—"

Humphrey shook his head. "No, forget that, Monge," he said, in a comfortable manner. "We'll talk about that some other time.

I'm serious. I'm worried about your health. I think you should see a doctor. Get a checkup. Look at you, you're wheezin', your face is red, I bet you don't sleep worth a damn—"

"I sleep fine. I—"

Humphrey cut him off. "I already made an appointment. With my own personal physician. Here." He handed the man a slip of paper with the name and address of a physician in Grosse Pointe. "You go see Dr. Schwartz. Two o'clock. And don't gag down an extra-big lunch."

Angelo squinted at the piece of paper in his hands. "Whatta I gotta see this guy for?" he said. "I got my own doctor."

"Your doctor ain't doing such a good job of looking after you," Humphrey said. He got up and smiled broadly, coming around the desk. He looked almost slim in his elegant blue pinstripe suit, new from his tailor. He patted Angelo on the shoulder and guided him to the door. "You go see Dr. Schwartz. Do it for me, Monge, you fuckin' monkey. And for your family. Don't worry, it's not gonna cost you a fuckin' cent. It's on me. That's how concerned I am."

Angelo was almost out the door before he balked. "I ain't goin' on no fuckin' diet, Hump!"

"All right, all right, I hear you," Humphrey said. "But go see the doctor. A checkup isn't gonna kill you. It might save your life."

That afternoon Humphrey checked to make sure that Mongelo had visited the doctor, that they had done a full workup. "What do you think, Doc?" Humphrey asked.

"Well, I can't discuss a patient's case, Mr. DiEbola," Dr. Schwartz told him, "but since you are a good friend—"

"I've known him since we were both toddlers," Humphrey interjected. "I'm worried about the man, Doc. I don't want to know any secrets and I'm glad you maintain strict confidentiality. I just wondered, how's he look to you? Generally. That's not violating anyone's privacy. I mean, the guy's not dying of some disease we don't know about?"

Dr. Schwartz laughed. "Well, anyone looking at Mr. Badgerri can see what he's dying of. But really, I mean . . . are you sort of in the nature of his employer, Humphrey? Yes? Well, the man's in amazingly good health, when you consider. . . . But if you're really a friend, I'd encourage him to go on the diet I recommended."

"I'll do it. I'm a believer, Doc. You know what it did for me."

Dr. Schwartz did know, although he wasn't as sure of the medical virtues of chili peppers as DiEbola was. That diet was something that Humphrey and his chef had concocted. Still, there was no question that it had gotten splendid results. "Well, I gave Mr. Badgerri a regimen that I believe will work for him," the doctor said. "If you can encourage him, we'd all be grateful, especially Mr. Badgerri."

"I'll do it," Humphrey said. "Thanks, Doc. And, if you don't mind, keep me out of it. You never heard from me."

"You're not in it, Mr. DiEbola. This is not part of Mr. Badgerri's record. But that reminds me, who is his regular physician? It might be helpful to see his medical history."

"Didn't he tell you? No? To tell you the truth, I wouldn't be surprised if the guy never saw a real doctor in his life. These old-fashioned Italians, a lot of them see grandmas . . . you know, some old gal from the Old Country who knows how to cure warts or constipation. But I'll ask him."

"Folk medicine," Dr. Schwartz muttered. "Well, I shouldn't say anything against it. But ask him."

Two days later, Mongelo was picked up by the two men who had driven Helen to the cigar factory and delivered to the back door of that same building. At first, he hadn't wanted to go along. He'd been approached at an awkward moment, when he was going to the bathroom of a restaurant in Harper Woods, not far from his home.

He went there every morning for breakfast, a meal that typically featured veal scallopini, eggs, freshly baked rolls, even tripe soup, and wine. So far, he'd only had a few biscotti and torcetti with his coffee before he'd had to piss. But the boys convinced him that his presence was urgently needed. They'd bundled him out the back door and into the limo, where a couple of other friendly fellas accompanied them downtown.

They entered the building through a disused basement entrance, an old stairwell with concrete steps and a steel door. Humphrey was waiting in the basement of the cigar factory. He was sitting behind a desk, under a hanging light. It was otherwise dark and cool, and an earthy, cellar odor filled the air. On the table before Humphrey lay a brutal-looking object, seemingly of metal, about six inches long and shaped like a large bass plug, except that it wasn't alluringly painted with eyes and scales. At first glance it seemed to be a basically smooth object, but it had many small, flexible steel leaves or scales, rather like a pinecone, and it terminated on one end with a sturdy eye, through which one might, perhaps, thread a wire or a line, except that it was the wrong end: if the object were trolled, or drawn through some medium, the leaves would tend to catch.

Mongelo stared at the object. "What the fuck is this all about?" he said. "You wannida see me, we couldn't meet at the chip fact'ry?"

"This . . . " Humphrey said, poking at the object with his now long and slender finger, then wincing slightly as it almost nicked him, " . . . is the actual dingus that they cut out of Action Jackson's asshole." Humphrey looked up with a smile. When he'd nudged it the device had partially rolled, then resettled itself. It was obviously heavy. "Can you believe it? I got it from the cops in Chicago. It cost me."

Mongelo recoiled. He looked about him. The other men were in the shadows, but they were there. "What the fuck?"

"I can't have no more of this Action Jackson shit, Monge," Humphrey said, quietly.

Mongelo drew himself up, puffed out his cheeks, then sighed. "All right, all right. I get the poi—" He stopped himself.

"Good," the boss said. "But it ain't enough to get the point." He smiled and there were mild, distant titters from the shadows. "All right, that's enough of that," he called to the men. He addressed Angelo again: "You like to play at being Action Jackson, you can get the dingus, like he did. It ain't enough for you to just say *Okay boss*. I want you to go on that diet."

"That diet! What that fuckin' doc you sent me to gimme?"

Now there were guffaws from the back. Humphrey ignored them. "Schwartz gave you a diet and you didn't take it seriously," Humphrey said. "That's your problem, Monge. You don't take what you're told seriously. So now I'm going to see that you do. Come here."

Humphrey stood up and walked toward the back of the basement. Mongelo followed fearfully. Humphrey stopped and flipped a light switch, revealing an open door. Beyond it, lighted, was what appeared to be an apartment. "Come on, come on," Humphrey urged, his hand out. He clapped Mongelo on the shoulder and guided him gently into the room.

Aside from the obvious feature of the steel bars that converted the room into a jail cell, it looked like an ordinary one-room apartment, what was usually described in newspaper ads as a studio apartment. Cozy, they would say. It had an ordinary, department-store couch and easy chair, a couple of lamps on end tables, a small television set, and a tiny little kitchenette, complete with a small refrigerator, a coffeemaker, a radio, some metal cupboards.

"The couch makes into a bed," Humphrey said. "It'll be comfortable enough. And you got your TV, magazines. Back there is a pisser and shitter, a little shower." He thrust the open-mouthed man through the open steel-barred door.

Mongelo caught hold of the bars. They held firmly, Humphrey was glad to see. He'd only had them installed overnight. They were anchored in the joists above. They would be all right if Mongelo didn't make too violent a move on them. They could be beefed up later, if necessary. But there would be someone around to keep an eye on Mongelo. He wouldn't be left alone to work on the cage.

"I ain't going in there," Mongelo declared. He clung to the bars like death, bracing himself against entering.

"Oh yeah, you are," Humphrey said. "And you ain't coming out until . . ." He paused. "How much do you weigh? Three something? Okay. You stay until you lose a hundred."

"A hundred pounds? You're fucking nuts!"

A hand snaked out of the dark and slapped him on the side of the head with a weighted cosh. He reeled and stumbled into the cage. The door clanged shut. It locked by itself.

Mongelo quickly recovered and began to rage, shouting, screaming. But the sound didn't resonate much and Humphrey had turned away, talking to someone in the darkness. "You give him the meals I told you. He can have magazines, videos, get him whatever he wants. He can smoke. Give him some of them cigars, the LaDonnas. He'll like those."

Humphrey turned to go. Mongelo fell silent. "I hope you like peppers, Monge," he said. And then everyone withdrew into the darkness.

6

Dying to Get Out

Every night Joe opened a door and across the room was another door, also opened, and a man leaning into the room between them. The man's head was large, cartoon large. Joe recognized the absurdity of this but also knew that it didn't matter. The man brandished something, a device, a tool. Joe knew what it was though he could not explicitly acknowledge it at first. But the gesture went on and on until Joe granted that it was a gun that the man waved. The gun was aimed directly at Joe and the man almost immediately fired it. It either happened very quickly or agonizingly slowly. Sometimes it never really got to the point of the gun being fired, but sometimes it was as if all this had already happened when the dream started. Usually, however, the bulk of the dream was taken up with the flight of the bullet.

The bullet traveled with enormous, impossible slowness. It hung in space, revolving smoothly, but it moved directly toward Joe with inexorable deliberateness. He always thought, as the bullet was so slow, that he ought to be able simply to duck away from the path of it. But that proved impossible. When he tried to move he found that he could only move rather more slowly than the already impossibly ponderous bullet. He could think quickly, like lightning, it seemed. And he could endure this eternity of waiting, as if he were in a much faster state than the sluggish bullet. He could actually see the bullet rotate, a smooth, machinelike rotation that was fascinating, even beautiful. But horrible.

What agony! He ducked and it took him forever. He could not escape the bullet, even though he had an eternity to observe its passage. He could meticulously examine the interior of the room—which he was not actually in, just thrusting his head within, as the shooter was similarly not in it, the two of them standing outside the room on either side, looking at each other through the doors. Joe peered about, even out the great window, looking out onto grassy slopes, odd-looking funereal trees of a dark color that Joe knew was black-green although there was no actual color in the dream. He also observed the room's curious equipment: wheels, dials, knobs, compartments, benches, handles—all arrayed low on the wall below the great window.

The room was familiar to him and yet not familiar. It belonged to him, but it didn't. And sometimes it changed. Sometimes it was more cavernous, almost a great hall, and the assailant so far away that he was no more than a figure with a pale blob of a face and arms and legs. He never recognized the assailant, but just sort of knew who he was. The assailant, the shooter, was just an agent, one sent to do a job.

And finally, when the bullet was upon him, in his face, as it were, he turned his head, slightly, and took it. And then he woke up.

The dream was unbearable at first. Well, bearable, obviously, since he bore it, but so frightening that he feared he would not be able to bear it next time. Yet as time went on, he bore it more easily and the intensity eased without him noticing. It seems one can get used to being murdered, but it may have been that he was more absorbed with daily events.

The crucial daily event was to determine who would deliver him from captivity. Very early on, within a week or so, he had singled out his man. At first he hadn't even bothered with the various men who came and went in the ward. He had concentrated on the women, as usual. They were the most likely, he felt. Only these women were remarkably invulnerable. As nurses, they had no deficiency of concern and interest in him *as a patient*, but they were remarkable for no interest in him as a man. He wasn't used to this. He was ill, he'd had a serious brain injury. He wasn't sure how long he had been unconscious, but he didn't think it could have been too long. He didn't think he'd been in a coma, although he admitted to himself that it was possible. He could have been "out" for weeks, he supposed. Maybe he looked like hell. He couldn't tell.

When last seen in a mirror, Joe Service had been a slim, fit young man. He was not quite thirty years old, below average height but with a large head that made him seem bigger. He had the sleek, smooth-muscled build of a swimmer. He'd had a beard, but someone had shaved it.

The ladies weren't interested, so he quit thinking about them. The guy he settled on was a cop. Tall, not bad looking, about Joe's age or a little older. Joe didn't say anything for days, just listened. His guy was named Kirk. He was a county cop, a sheriff's deputy, assigned to this boring guard duty at the hospital because he was being disciplined for some mistake. Over a period of days, Joe pieced out from Kirk's intercourse with other officers, nurses, and aides that Kirk had wrecked or damaged some superior's car.

"They told me to take the car," Kirk complained. The others laughed. "They didn't tell you *that* car," they said, and, "They didn't say run a light." Kirk had screwed up before, obviously. He seemed on the verge of something.

Soon, Kirk noticed that Joe was listening. Joe would catch his eye and make a slight movement of his head. It was very subtle, not really a look of commiseration, but at least neutral, willing to listen. Kirk began to air his gripes. It wasn't the screwup, that wasn't the real trouble. It was the lack of promotion, the fiddling with benefits, the lack of camaraderie, and his wife. All that and more, going back to his parents, his teachers, bankers who had turned down loan applications, even grocery-store clerks who refused his checks until the assistant manager came to okay them.

Kirk was one of those people: he didn't trust others and they didn't trust him. He looked more intelligent than he was, and pleasant and amiable, at first. Then you noticed he wasn't so bright, wasn't accommodating or efficient or careful, wasn't genuinely friendly but guarded and suspicious. And he seemed to know something was wrong but riled easily if he wasn't shown respect. In Joe's eyes, Kirk was ideal.

Joe had met people like Kirk. They didn't get along very well. He soon knew with near certainty that Kirk was not going to be a cop for long, that this was probably the fourth or fifth minicareer he had blown, that his wife was leaving him. Joe was happy with him. A guy like this was a cheap guitar: he could be tuned, after a fashion, and a melody or two could be picked out, as long as it was a well-known air that anyone recognized in the first few notes so they mentally helped you out when a fret didn't bite or the tuning slipped.

The problem, Kirk said to Joe one day—by now he was given to spending most of his free time in Joe's corner, sipping coffee and staring blindly out the window with its bars, talking over his shoulder softly, occasionally glancing back to see Joe watching thoughtfully, understandingly—the problem was bosses. All bosses, any boss. A man was never getting anywhere as long as he had a boss. That was obvious.

Joe sometimes wondered if Kirk was putting him on. He didn't think so, but the guy seemed too good to be true, too dumb. Joe couldn't afford to, however. By now, Joe was occasionally replying, tersely. This itself had taken a leap of confidence, for if Kirk were to mention to anyone, a nurse, another guard, that Joe was talking, was alert, he'd be transferred to the security ward. It was very important to Joe that this not happen. As it was, he had his three guards a day who were supposed to sit by the door and check everyone who came in or out. Joe was presumed to be, if not comatose, then barely out of that state and certainly incapable of moving. Definitely not talking. But somehow, Joe had perceived that Kirk wanted to stay, wanted this private audience for his gripes. And maybe something further.

Joe whispered, weakly, "Everybody's got a boss, Kirk."

Kirk shrugged. Well, yeah, he allowed, in a way. Maybe. Somewhere up the line. Even the entrepreneur, he's got backers, shareholders, regulators of one kind or another—too damn many, in fact. But really what Kirk meant was a *boss* boss. Some bastard you had to answer to or he could fire your ass.

Joe managed to look sympathetic, conceding the point. "Marry a rich woman, Kirk," Joe whispered.

"Don't I wish," Kirk said, devoutly. "Me, I got the reverse: Phyl could break Trump. She went out the other day and bought a trash compactor. What the hell we need a trash compactor for? On credit. Now I got to pay for a trash compactor."

"How much is 'pactor?" Joe asked.

"I don't know. Too much. A hunderd'n fifty, or something. Where'm I gonna get that? I need tires on the pickup for Chrissake. She think of that?"

Money is nothing, Joe told him. Kirk didn't agree. Money was everything. With money you were free. Without money you were somebody's slave. And money was hard to come by.

"No," Joe assured him. "Money . . . no prob. Money's free. The prob is . . . be free. Not free . . . do nothing." Or words to that effect.

Kirk was wary. He knew Joe was trying to bribe him. Joe knew he knew. The problem now was to move the dialogue to a point where a bribe could be offered, and accepted, without it being felt to be a bribe. It was an interesting situation, Joe thought, one that could be explored endlessly, right up to the moment when a doctor would say that Joe was physically able to leave the hospital, to be taken to a jail, and tried. Joe didn't have much time, he knew. You could fool the doctors for a while, the nurses for less, but very soon their training and knowledge and their instruments would tell them that Joe was ready to be thrown to the prosecutors.

So every day, every hour, every waking minute, Joe worked Kirk. He had just about got him to the point where he could present the bait when the woman showed up.

Her name was Schwind, which she pronounced *shwin*, like the bicycle. Dinah Schwind, special agent. She strolled in one day, showed her credentials to Kirk, and asked him how the patient was doing. Kirk shrugged, said the patient was in dreamland.

"Still out?" she said. "I thought I heard voices."

Kirk smiled guiltily. "I talk to him. I don't know if he hears anything, but it helps pass the time."

Agent Schwind nodded as if that was a good idea. Then she asked if he could step outside. When he was gone she pulled a chair up next to the bed where Joe lay with his eyes closed, not moving.

"I know you can hear me, Joe," she said. "Don't bother to nod or blink. It's not important. You won't be here much longer, so we have to move fast."

She told him the agency she worked for, but Joe didn't believe her. She described it as a liaison between various other federal agencies, such as Drug Enforcement, Securities Exchange, Immigration, even Central Intelligence. She didn't exactly belong to those agencies, but she worked with them. She was—she smiled self-deprecatingly—a superagent.

Dinah Schwind might smile but she didn't really laugh, ever. She was five feet, six inches tall, weighed about one hundred and thirty pounds, had brown hair cut short enough to show her ears, in the lobes of which she wore little gold studs. She had a square face, a square jaw with a wide mouth. Not very thick lips but a strong, straight nose; didn't wear much makeup; brown eyes and thick, straight dark-brown eyebrows below a high, smooth forehead. She was not pretty, but not homely either. She could doubtless be attractive, if she wished, but clearly she didn't wish. No one would call her nice looking. She didn't look *nice*. She looked determined and serious. She also had a faint suggestion of a mustache. Another woman would easily have effaced that—it wasn't really very visible—but Dinah Schwind couldn't be concerned.

She had a compact build and wore her blue suit well, with low heels. She also packed a gun—the shoulder-harness strap was visible when she reached into her inner coat pocket for a pad and pen—though she wouldn't have brought it onto a security ward for prisoners.

She had been to see Sergeant Mulheisen, a Detroit police detective, who had told her about Joe. Mulheisen had arrested Joe, although the arrest had taken place here in Colorado, which is where Joe was lying in a hospital bed. Mulheisen had obtained a special warrant.

Agent Schwind told Joe she was not concerned about Mulheisen or his interest in him, whatever that was, she explained. She was interested in a man named Echeverria, who was lying in a Salt Lake City hospital, slowly recovering from severe burns. To be exact, she was interested in Echeverria's friends and associates, some of whom were in the international drug trade, others who were in organized crime in Detroit.

Joe didn't know Echeverria, although he soon surmised that Echeverria was one of the men who had tracked him down in Montana, after the initial hit attempt had failed, the one he still dreamed about. Echeverria would have been after the money Joe had lifted in Detroit, the take from a drug scam. Joe wasn't at home when Echeverria got to his country retreat. Joe had thoughtfully booby-trapped that house when he'd left. Echeverria had been one of those caught in the ensuing blast.

Joe didn't say anything about this, or anything else. He was still playing semicomatose. But he didn't want to disappoint the lady. He had a feeling that his long courtship of Deputy Kirk had been blown, so Special Agent Schwind was now his fallback position. It was time to speak.

"Etch," Joe whispered faintly. "Heard of him." Which was true. He'd read about Echeverria's plight in the papers in Salt Lake. A friend in Montana had told him more. He knew where Echeverria was coming from: Humphrey DiEbola. Joe knew plenty about Humphrey. He supposed that was who Agent Schwind was really after. But all he said was that he'd heard of Echeverria.

Special Agent Schwind was not a woman to play games. "They won't stop looking for you, Joe. You've been working for DiEbola for a long time," she said. "Him and several other racketeers, in New York, Miami, Las Vegas. You have a reputation. They haven't forgotten you, either. I don't have anything on you, Service. I can't hurt you, but I can help you."

Joe thought about that one. He thought so long that she stood up and said, "I'll see you later."

"Going?" he asked, surprised.

"You think about it. I'll be back." And she left.

Joe Service pondered. He was an independent investigator who specialized in service to the underworld. He had grown up with close connections to the mob, particularly in the East, and at one point it had seemed that he would make his way in that world. But very early on he had realized that he didn't like the way the mob operated. He had no moral scruples, or not many, about the nature of their business, but there were many things about the way they functioned that he disliked. The mob was very big on loyalty, yet it was based on deception, brutality, and corruption. Inevitably, the mobsters cheated one another, or made serious mistakes in their interface with the general public. Normally, they had no one they could trust who could address these problems. That was where Joe came in.

It was a perfect role for a man like Joe Service. He was *of* the underground culture, familiar with its ways, on good terms with its practitioners, but he wasn't *in* it. For some people this would have been uncomfortable, but for Joe it was ideal. He liked living fast, liked the excitement, and he liked the money. In order to function, however, he had to hold himself apart. He couldn't take sides. He had to assess the situation, see where the virtues lay, such as they were, and implement to a limited degree the sanctions. It wasn't easy, but generally he could stay out of the internecine struggle. He could investigate, report, and recommend. Once in a while, if the price was right, financially and in terms of avoiding compromise of his own status, he could carry out the sanctions.

What was crucial, of course, and this was what was giving him these long thoughts, was that he had to operate in as great confidentiality as was possible. So. How was it that Special Agent Schwind knew who he was and what he did?

If he had never reckoned it before, he now knew just how greatly he had compromised himself when he fell for Helen Sedlacek and agreed to help her assassinate Carmine Busoni, the Detroit don who had ordered the death of her father. Obviously, to the criminal community that he had once served so ably he was now seen as just another rogue mobster. He had sacrificed an extremely valuable thing.

But—he sighed—no doubt it was inevitable. Even his vaunted special status would not have kept him immune forever from their suspicions, their paranoia, their treachery, endless devious plotting, and basic villainy. He reflected that the whole situation had devolved from Carmine's petty cheating on Joe's fees.

That special status, he reckoned, could never be restored. But that didn't mean that some viable similar status couldn't be achieved. He'd have to work on it. Maybe this lady could help.

But what help could she offer? She'd said she couldn't hurt him but she could help. Presumably, that meant help with Mulheisen. Well, no. He felt certain that she couldn't help him with Mulheisen. But maybe she could shield him, at least temporarily, or, at least, spring him. On his own, out of Mulheisen's clutches, he thought he had a better chance.

She returned the next day. He'd hoped it would be sooner; the doctors were starting to look at him speculatively. When no one was around, say on a night shift when one of the other guards was off chatting up the nurses, he could get out of bed, walk around, do squats, even push-ups, but when anyone but Kirk was about he lay as still as a corpse, his breathing as shallow as he could make it, his pulse as erratic as he could try.

Dinah Schwind wore the same blue suit. It looked the same, anyway. Maybe she had a dozen of them. It was well tailored. She wasn't exactly slim, but athletic looking. Good color. He was sure that she didn't smoke. No stained fingers, no dental problems, evidently; clear-eyed as hell.

"Okay, Joe," she said briskly, drawing up her chair when Kirk had discreetly vanished, "drop the possum act. We don't have time for it."

Joe opened his eyes, raised his head, and glanced about. He smiled. "Shoot," he said.

"Imagine," she said, "that you knew a private airstrip in, say, Idaho. Say that you had learned that a private jet would be landing there at a specific time. Say that you had the means to destroy that plane."

Joe imagined. "Just destroy the plane? Not a hit?"

"Just destroy the plane."

"Get a cowboy from a saloon," he said. "Boise's full of cowboys."

She shrugged. "There are usually problems, you know."

"Yeah. But not big problems."

"And then there is the question of deniability," she observed. "A cowboy has to be told something. There has to be a plausible story. And if he's caught, or implicated . . ." She let it hang.

"Whereas," she went on, filling in the blanks unnecessarily for both of them, "Joe Service is on his own. He knows why he's there, more or less, and if caught, well, he's a mobster, anyway."

"Who deals with the people on the plane?"

"That was just a scenario," she said. "A paradigm, if you will. But consider a new scenario. Say you knew when a couple of fellows were going to deliver, oh, fifty grand to another couple of fellows. The money is payment for some heroin, or cocaine, that would be delivered at the same time, somewhere else."

"Say a hundred thou," Joe said, getting into the spirit of this game.

"Why not?" she agreed. "But that's not up to us. It could be more. But say we knew. The way it works, these guys meet in, say, a rest stop on an interstate highway. They have cell phones. Not very secure, but then they aren't communicating anything implicatory. They call a number—the cell phone on the other end could be at a different rest area, or in a warehouse, a thousand miles away—and ask, 'Okay?' The other end says 'Okay,' the money changes hands, the narcotics change hands, everybody goes their own way."

"But I take the money, or the dope. Another agent takes the dope, or the money, depending how it works," Joe said. "Any more scenarios? This is fun."

Dinah Schwind almost smiled. She looked at him with a kind of pleasantness, anyway. She had a couple more scenarios. Like the first two they involved interdicting criminal behavior in what could only be described as extralegal ways.

"Do your bosses know?" Joe asked. That was a very important point, he felt. First of all, because it implied a kind of intervention that he didn't believe could be authorized by any accountable government agency, and if it were, how many people in the agency would know about it, what would be the level of security?

Schwind agreed that he had identified a key factor in the operation, assuming that it could be implemented. So far, she told him, only three people knew about it: herself and two of her colleagues, both of whom she could vouch for. They believed that operations like this could be mounted. They were all for it. They thought that authorization could be restricted to one more individual, but he wouldn't want to know any details. They were planning to suggest it, but they wanted to know they had the right man in the active role. They had the intelligence for several such scenarios, and had every reason to believe that they would continue to obtain further intelligence. Some of the action they would carry out themselves, but most of the scenarios they envisioned required an unofficial agent, an extralegal operative. If he was interested they would move to the next step of authorization. If it turned out that authorization was not forthcoming, or if it required even another step, another level of official involvement, then they would drop the whole proposal as too unwieldy and that would be the end of it.

"Nothing risked," Joe said.

She nodded.

"What's my end?"

"You get out of here," she said. "I can't get Mulheisen off your back, but you'll be outside those bars. And once you got into the prisoner population, of course, you'd be vulnerable to DiEbola and Echeverria." She nodded toward the window.

"How?" he asked. "You got paper? Or do I 'escape'?" He'd meant it as a joke, but it seemed that her scheme wasn't so different.

"I think you've already got a plan," she said. "We'd just see that nothing interfered with it. If we can."

"You mean . . . ?"

"Deputy Kirk has financial problems," she said. "I wouldn't offer him too much. If he gets rich it might attract attention. But if he's able to pay off some bills, that's not unjust."

This wasn't what Joe had hoped. Now he would be a fugitive. He'd thought that maybe she would at least get bail.

"They'll never give you bail," she said, saving him the trouble of asking. "There are a lot of charges pending. You're the world's worst risk for bail. Lee Bailey couldn't get bail for you."

Especially not now, Joe thought. Maybe Schwind couldn't get him out, legally, but he had a feeling she could sure keep him in. But he said nothing. Or rather, he said: "I'll talk to Kirk."

"Can you walk?" she asked. "Drive a car?"

"What do you think?"

"Go ahead," she said. "I'll talk to my guys."

After she left, Joe had a great new idea. How about if he just died? They could fake his death and somewhere between the hospital and the morgue he could be switched with another body. He was delighted with this scheme. He'd be free, not have to worry about Mulheisen, about the mob, about Echeverria and his gang. And he'd soon shake Agent Schwind. It was perfect. He was dying to get out!

7

Ex-Capo

The secret plan, known only to Humphrey, was to get out. It was the one thing he couldn't talk about. So he talked about everything else. Mainly, he talked about himself.

Helen observed that he was an erudite man (she used the phrase "well read") and yet he pretended to be not too bright. "I don't mean it quite that way," she said. "You don't act stupid, but you have this kind of *dumb* manner, most of the time. But I know it's just a facade."

"Nobody likes a brain," Humphrey said. "People say 'pointy-headed,' or something like that. Crazy, ain't it? Everybody wants to be smart, they don't want to be dumb, theirselves, but they don't like it if you're *too* smart. Sure, I read books. I like to read, always did. But I never went to college, I never even graduated from high school. Nobody ever called me dumb, though. What it is, you gotta act like an ordinary guy, a little dumb, and I guess that reassures people—you ain't *too* smart. But at the same time you gotta make sure that the people who need you, who rely on you, understand that you're not really dumb, that maybe you're pretty sharp.

"Everybody does that, to a degree," he went on. "You're a woman, you know about that—women do it all the time. There's some things you aren't supposed to be a genius about. Guy things. You don't know nothing about football, say. But you probably know quite a bit."

"I don't know nothing about football," Helen said, affecting a dull tone.

"Okay," he said, smiling, "so maybe it's cars, or guns, or something else that you aren't supposed to be interested in—because you're a woman. Me, I'm in the business, as we say. I'm not supposed to know about books. That's for pointy-headed intellectuals. But . . . I read. Machiavelli, for instance."

"Machiavelli," she said, and sighed. "What is it with you and him?"

The Machiavelli thing, he explained at length, came about for two reasons. He had noticed that people frequently invoked Machiavelli's name, generally as a byword for deceit or cunning, but if one inquired more closely, they didn't seem to know much, if anything, about him. He was supposed to be bad, almost the Devil himself, or a close associate. But few even knew when he had lived.

"Oh, they heard of *The Prince*, maybe," Humphrey said, "but that's about it. When I was a kid I heard grown-ups talking about Machiavelli and I thought he was some Italian guy, somebody they knew. And later, I heard him used in that way so much, to me he was like the original Italian. And I had this thing for wanting to be Italian."

"You are Italian," she said.

"You're Italian if your mama is Italian," Humphrey said. "It's like being a Jew. Everybody knows Sammy Davis Jr. is a Jew, but they also know he ain't a real Jew. That's the way it is with me. Everybody knows I'm Italian, but they know it like they know Machiavelli is Italian. Me, I don't know. I never knew my old man . . . well, I knew him, but at the time I didn't know he was my old man. And now I'm not so sure, again.

"My mother, I never knew her or even anything about her. I was raised by my 'aunt' Sophie, Carmine's mother, except she wasn't my real aunt, I think. She tried to be good to me, but she already had a kid—Carmine. I always understood that I was like a charity, or something. And Aunt Sophie would never talk about my mother. Nobody would ever say anything about her when I was a kid. Maybe they thought they were being kind. For a long time I dreamed she was an angel, or a kind of princess, like in a fairy tale.

"When I got older, I was on the street. I was caught up in that. The Life. You know? It's exciting. You learn something new three times a day. By then I didn't want to hear anything about my folks. I didn't want to think about them.

"A little later, now I know a little bit, I'm a little calmer, but still so young. I'm your basic Detroit guy, you know? Tough guy, a cynic. If I thought about my mother at all, I thought she was probably a whore that my old man—by now, at least, I knew who he was, but he's dead—that he knocked up and for some rea- son he got stuck with the kid and he managed to shuffle me off on Carmine's old lady, Aunt Sophie, who was a sucker for this kind of stuff.

"So I get a little older, not quite so dumb. I even went to Italy by now. Actually, I'd been once before, after the war, with Aunt Sophie and Uncle Dom, but I didn't remember too much about it, I was just a kid. To me they were my real folks. When Uncle Dom died, as a favor to my stepmother, I took the body back to be bur- ied. I also took a little trip to Eboli, to look up some relatives. It's inland a little ways from Salerno, in Campania."

"Eboli?" Helen said. "What's in Eboli?"

"I was born a Gagliano but Aunt Sophie used to say my folks were from Eboli, so when I turned twenty-one I took the name

DiEbola. Anyway, I had some time to kill. I was in no hurry to get back to Detroit."

"You were cooling off?" Helen said. "A little trouble?"

"Well, I escorted Uncle Dom's body, but yeah," Humphrey said. "And I was looking up my roots, you know."

"I thought of going to the Old Country," Helen said, "but I wasn't sure where I would go."

"Well, *your* ma's right here," Humphrey said. "Didn't you ever ask her?"

"Mama likes to talk about *her* home," Helen said. "You've heard her. When she was here the other day, she talked about Belgrade. But whenever I ask her about Papa, she just shrugs."

"Roman would know," Humphrey said. "Ask him."

"Roman!" She laughed. "They don't call him the Yak for nothing. Talk about playing dumb. He's the original dummy."

"Yeah, Roman plays it close to the vest," Humphrey said. "One of these days I'll find out if he's really so dumb. Well, anyway, I went to Eboli after I got Uncle Dom buried, but I didn't find out anything. I don't know what I expected, but over there, you ain't Italian. To them, you're American. I had a few names, people to look up, but they treat you funny. They're suspicious, they don't tell you shit. You sit around in some hotel, you don't know the language, everything's so strange. Finally I went to a church and talked to a priest. He laughed when I said my name was DiEbola. He knew it was made up. So I give him the old man's name, Gagliano, thinking there maybe was a record of the marriage. He rolls his eyes, makes this little hand gesture to ward off the Devil. He said Gagliano was a village way over the mountains, in Lucania. A bad place, he said. 'Don't go there. They eat Christians,' he said. He was half serious. 'Bad people. They won't tell you anything.' Guys leave Gagliano, they take that name, sort of like I did with DiEbola. I gave up on it."

"So you never found your Italian connection," Helen said.

"No, and I never said nothing to Aunt Sophie. I think she meant well. It's like my folks were hillbillies, or something, so it was better to say they were from a nice town like Eboli than from some shithole in the sticks like Gagliano, which I guess is why she'd encouraged me to change my name.

"Anyway, I settled on Machiavelli. He was my Italian connection. Some people, they think Italian, if they don't immediately think of DiMaggio or Sinatra, they think of Dante, or maybe da Vinci, somebody like that. But I started reading Machiavelli, and you know what? He wasn't hard, at all. Right off the bat I understood what he was saying. And he didn't bullshit. It all made sense to me."

Helen supposed a person could make that kind of indentification, but it seemed artificial. Still, if it worked for Humphrey . . . well, she guessed it worked for him.

"Mac—I think of him as Mac, for short," Humphrey said. "Mac talks about things like success, power, glory. Those are the big things. Success is survival, getting power, getting glory. The truth is, I never worried about glory much. Maybe it meant more in Mac's time. To me it's fame and notoriety. Today, everybody and anybody gets famous, at least for a little while. I don't care about that. In the business, which I like to think is a little like Mac's princedom, but after all, ain't exactly like it . . . glory is not in the cards. You get known among the powerful, that's the glory. I think I can claim a little of that."

"So, you are interested in glory after all," Helen said slyly.

"A little. But only a little. Power, though . . . that's the number. I followed Mac as closely as I could in getting to power, but I never lost sight of the fact that I was operating in a different field than Borgia and them guys Mac talked about . . . although, there are plenty of comparisons.

"Mac says that it's better to be feared than loved," he observed, thoughtfully. "People are fickle. When you're good, when you treat everybody good, they love you. They'll do anything for you, praise you, offer their children to you. But you can't always be a sweetheart to everybody. Right? The minute you turn somebody down, you're a bastard. So it's better to be feared than loved, he says. You don't go out of your way to piss people off, you treat 'em right, but when the deal comes down, you can't think about how much they like you."

Helen wondered if it wasn't a bit like being dumb and smart at the same time. Humphrey conceded the point. But he came back with the notion that sometimes, after an act of brutality, even just not being a hard-ass looks like kindness. That was from Mac, he said.

"When I was just the Fat Man, it was no problem," he said. "Carmine was the boss, but he never took the rap for the hard stuff—he said it was *me*." He laughed. "He'd tell 'em, whoever was bitching, that he'd see what he could do, but it was the Fat Man who was grinding them. And when they came to me, I'd say, 'See the man.' And, of course, being a Fat Man . . . everybody likes a fat man, they think you aren't tough. Only now, not only am I not fat, I don't have no Fat Man to lay it off on." He sighed and shook his head.

"The main thing, though," he observed, "is that Mac taught me that a man is what he makes of himself. You got governments, society, religion . . . none of it means shit, if you only got the guts to be your own man. And, of course, if you got the power.

"Everything comes from power," he said, after a moment's thought. "Money, pleasure, and survival. Only, it looks like it's easier to get, maybe, than to keep. Especially when you start getting on. That's why I'm glad you're here. I can use some help. Somebody has to run this business when I'm gone."

"You're not getting on," Helen hastened to assure him. "And I'm no Fat Man. Anyway, I don't know anything about running the business, but if I can help . . . "

"Forget the Fat Man stuff," he said, smiling his amusement. "That was yesterday. Maybe you could be the Bitch. That would help. Then I could be the Fat Man, again. I'll be the kindly old grampa."

"The Bitch!"

"Hey, I'm joking," he said. "But it's a thought. You don't have to *be* a bitch . . . some days I was the Evil Fat Man and the next day the Jolly Fat Man. What have you got goin' for you? You're smart, you're young, educated, you look like a million bucks, and you got connections from your old man—"

"I'm not sure that's a help," she interjected.

"It's a help. It don't matter what he did, how he screwed up. He was in the business. He was well known, and people liked him. The funny thing about something like that is, they don't blame you for his screwups, they just notice that you were born into the business."

"But when it comes to power," Helen observed, "they aren't ever going to give a woman any real power in this business."

"That's the tradition," Humphrey agreed, "and it'll probably go on that way for a long time, but that don't mean there aren't exceptions. You can be an exception. I was reading a while back about this Egyptian queen, Hashaput."

"You've been reading again, you cryptoscholar," she teased. "Who is this? Hasha—?"

"Hashaput, or Hatchep— Oh, I don't know how they pronounce it. Maybe it's Hotchapuss." They both laughed.

"Listen!" he said. "It's you. I saw it right away. In something like three thousand years of pharaohs, there's only one Hotchapuss. But she pulled it off. As far as anyone can tell she was a pretty good pharaoh. It's a long shot, sure, but there oughtta be *one*. Your odds are better today, 'cause we're in America. A woman's got a much better shot today."

"Maybe it's Hatchetpuss," she joked. "She's the Bitch. Hotch-apuss is the Honey."

They bantered this way for a while, but eventually they turned to a serious analysis of the present situation. The way Humphrey saw it, the traditional mob business of the past was in serious decline. The mob had been successful in the U.S., maybe too successful. They had forgotten how they got here. But that was all right. Things inevitably change. The mob had gotten into legitimate business so thoroughly that legitimate business had taken on some of the characteristics of the mob. Maybe it was always so, he wasn't confident of his economic history, no one was, really. There were a lot of theorists out there, but who was right?

This discussion became rather complex and confused, but Helen finally asked: What were the major problems facing them (she was thinking in terms of "us" by now) today?

"A major problem," he said, promptly, "is Mulheisen."

"Sergeant Mulheisen?" she said. "A precinct detective? That's a major problem?"

"Mulheisen is poking around in the Hoffa business," Humphrey said.

Helen was interested. "You were involved with Hoffa? With his disappearance?"

"You don't want to know," Humphrey told her. "It's all history. I knew Hoffa. I know what happened."

"What happened?"

"It's too complicated," Humphrey told her. He'd liked Hoffa, thought he was a good man, but excitable. Not easy to work with. Humphrey was vague. There had been a misunderstanding. An accident. It was nothing, but it wouldn't do for a guy like Mulheisen to dig too deep. It could bring the whole thing down, especially right now, when the FBI had brought a huge case against several guys who used to be major players in the Detroit business. Humphrey didn't think that case could touch him, but the Hoffa case surely could.

"The man's trouble," Humphrey said.

"Hoffa?"

"Mulheisen. He doesn't let go. He's one of those guys," Humphrey said, "they don't seem to be a problem. Like you say, you didn't think he was much help with your old man's case, but then he found out just about everything there was to know. The thing is, he doesn't give up. You think you've put him off the scent, you don't hear anything from him for ages, and then, there he is. He's been picking up a little something here, something there. And then, one day, he's standing at your front door, that weird smile on his face. I hate to see him coming. That face. It's so . . . so flat."

Helen didn't understand what he meant.

"Not physically flat," Humphrey said, "it's that flat, open expression. He seems simple. You think he don't know anything, but maybe he knows almost everything. Believe me, it's a big mistake to underrate Mulheisen."

"So? What are you going to do?"

He outlined a plan. It seemed overly elaborate to Helen. A Rube Goldberg device to catch a mouse. But Humphrey was serious. He wanted to set up a foundation, a phony historical research project. They'd hire a young graduate student, something like that, who would keep tabs on Mulheisen's activities in the guise of doing historical research. Only the kid doing the research wouldn't know what the research was really about, what it would be used for. From time to time they could feed Mulheisen a little info, through the researcher and some other outlets; kind of steer him in the direction they wanted him to go, keep him busy, running down old trails.

Helen thought it sounded dangerous and expensive. Humphrey was excited about the plan, however. He wanted Helen to set it up and run it. She had some expertise in things like that. She agreed to do it. It was something to do. But she couldn't shake her misgivings.

The other thing Humphrey wanted was for her to get acquainted with the business, at least the legitimate side of it. She could do that. If she didn't want to get into the other stuff, well, that was up to her. They'd see about that down the road. But anything she could do with the legitimate stuff would be a big help. Humphrey said he was getting to the retirement stage. He wasn't interested in all the detail work anymore. He didn't have the mind for it, these days, everything was so much more complex, and he had lost the old drive.

At one point, he said, he'd considered bringing Pepe into the business, but then the young man had taken off. Gone back to Mexico, apparently. It was a disappointment. Pepe was a smart young fellow, a lot more to him than he'd looked. But what can you do? Young men, they have other ideas. Well, more power to him.

Helen was sorry he'd gone, too, but she didn't say anything. She kept waiting for Humphrey to say something about the money, about Joe, but he didn't bring it up. Instead, he talked about how she had to start finding herself some allies, people who weren't necessarily *his* guys. "Not just anybody, of course," he said. "I know you're tight with Itchy, he likes you. That's good. But I don't want you getting cozy with guys who might not be friendly toward me, or who'd be thinking they'd be stepping into my shoes—my shoes are going to be empty before you know it. No, don't give me any bullshit about how young and vital I am. I mean it. You gotta be thinking about yourself. About how you would run things. You'll need some strong-arms around you, but guys you can trust. That's my problem now. Thanks to age and the FBI, and Mulheisen, most of my old guys are gone. That's why I'm talking to you."

"The only strong arms I want about me are yours, big boy," she said, playfully. She leaped onto his lap, throwing her arms about him.

Humphrey was delighted. He loved the close feel of her. It aroused him. He made some tentative squeezes. She allowed it, a little. It was amazing, he thought, how she knew just how much intimacy to permit before she stopped him, subtly, with a kind of stiffening or drawing away. Just enough, not too much. In truth, he was grateful. It was the way he saw it. The thought of actually being intimate, really intimate, with her was scary to him. He wanted it, he knew he did, but he couldn't give in to it. He had other plans.

Helen, for her part, was simply doing what came naturally. She loved to tease him, even to the edge of sex. But she was thinking about Joe. She was certain that Humphrey was thinking of Joe, as well, but neither of them could mention his name. "And what are you going to be doing while I'm learning to be HatchetHellion or HotchaHelen?" she asked impertinently.

"Puss. Puss," he urged. "Me? I'll still be running things, don't worry. But I'm gonna step back, as much as I can. I want you out there in the forefront, where the others can see you running the show. I'm like the old spider in the web. I'm thinking what I need is a kind of hidey-hole, a nerve center, where I can keep tabs on what's stepping on the wires, who's rattling the cage."

"You've got that," she said, referring to his security devices.

"That's nothing," he said. "That's sort of what gave me the idea, though. I got thinking, my sensors just go out to the gate. I gotta have real communications that go out to the whole . . ." He paused, searching for the right word.

"The whole kingdom," she said.

He shrugged. "Something like that."

* * *

He started
building his web almost immediately. Sending her out to learn about
the business, he immersed himself in a building project.

Humphrey wanted to construct the command post right at
the house. Why, in this electronic age, was he driving all the way
into Detroit, practically downtown, to Krispee Chips? Of course,
he'd still go out and check his traps, he said, but in the future he'd
keep tabs on things from his new office. It was being built in the
basement. A nice little suite, practically an apartment, with the most
up-to-date, powerful computers, a place to lie down, take a nap when
he got tired. He was amazingly enthusiastic about it. The builders
were there for weeks, putting everything in.

Once or twice a week, Humphrey would drive into town to
take care of business. Helen usually went with him, but she didn't
often stick very closely. She was busy with her projects. Besides the
historical foundation she was learning about the potato chip business, reorganizing that office. Another project was the cigar business.

She had done a lot of research. Apparently, Detroit had once
been a big cigar-manufacturing center. That had faded after World
War Two. The phony cigar business was one thing, but she considered it paltry, more a lark than anything else. She didn't see any
reason why they couldn't manufacture real, legitimate cigars in
Detroit. They had the facilities. She was looking into that.

Sometimes she and Humphrey would go together to Strom
Davidson's operation. She would look at the books, talk to the
people, especially the girls working in the loft and the people making the labels. Humphrey would wander off with Strom, for which
Helen was grateful. She found him abrasive and difficult. In the new
operation, if she got it going, there wouldn't be any room for Strom
Davidson.

One of the women, the one Strom had been raging at when
Helen first visited the operation, was particularly interesting. Her

name was Berta and it was her brother, Ramón, who had designed the LaDonna label. He was not well, and she was concerned about him. He needed to be in a clinic, but they had no health insurance. A business like illegal relabeling did not provide workers with benefits.

Berta was a very capable woman. Besides caring for her brother, she had two children at home, being looked after by her younger sister and her aunt. Berta often worked sixteen-hour days—ten hours packing cigars, then another four to six hours as a waitress at a Mexican restaurant in Dearborn. She herself was Cuban and had left the island with her mother more than ten years ago. The Cuban government had let them emigrate when it was confirmed that Berta's father had died in Miami. He had been a Castro supporter, a revolutionary, but the postrevolutionary executions had soon turned him into a disillusioned expatriate. Berta's uncle Jorge had fled Cuba with her father, but eventually made his way to Detroit, where he landed a fine job on Ford's assembly line. He had brought Berta and her family here. But then he died. Her mother died. Berta's husband ran away.

It was a long sad tale, but Berta wasn't one of those who liked to spin it out in detail. "He died," she said. "She died." No explanation unless asked, and then only if she knew you well. The husband: "Ran away."

Berta didn't seem crushed. While she wasn't delighted with her situation, she was not overwhelmed, not yet. The other women looked up to her, she was their leader. She didn't mind Strom Davidson, she said to Helen. She was being circumspect, of course, but Helen could see she was not intimidated by the boss. She confided that some of the younger, prettier women were the sexual prey of Davidson and he sometimes made a pass at her, but—she made an obscure gesture with her fingers, a scissors movement—"He knows he will not get me."

None of this really shocked Helen, but it disgusted her. She determined to put an end to it. She was also curious how she could go about getting into legitimate cigar making. Her new friend Berta was skeptical. Berta knew something about the business. "In Cuba, it is a matter of pride, of passion!" she declared. "You must grow the tobacco. You must have people who know how to pick it, cure it, age it. And buyers to find the tobacco you don't grow—binder leaf, wrapper leaf. It doesn't all grow in the same place. There is much involved and you must not rush this process. The big tobacco companies came to Cuba before and after the revolution, you know. They would make everyone rich. Lots of employment, big factories. But the Cubans could not see it that way. We preferred the old ways."

It was all very interesting, but not to the point. The problem was that because of the embargo on Cuban goods, the only tobacco that Helen would be able to obtain, if she wanted to seriously go into manufacture, was non-Cuban—Dominican, Mexican, Honduran, whatever. And what could she offer if she were able to get good tobacco? Berta could easily find her some cigar rollers, women who had been expert at this trade in the Caribbean and elsewhere, living right here in Detroit, but so what? There were already too many makers of cigars. Another brand would just be lost in the welter, especially one made in Detroit. Who would buy it? You could not make cigars cheaply enough in Detroit to sell them at a competitive price.

On the other hand . . . Berta had a cousin who rolled for a Canadian maker, in Toronto. That guy put out some very respectable cigars. They were about as Cuban as a cigar could be if it wasn't made in Cuba. The tobacco came from Cuba, the rollers were Cuban expatriates. The Canadian maker, Harold Jespersen, was from a Danish family that had been in the tobacco business in Copenhagen for generations, before relocating to Canada. Berta wondered if it was possible to buy cigars wholesale from Jespersen. The U.S. Customs wouldn't consider those Cuban cigars, would they? They could then be relabeled in Detroit, perhaps sold to a limited clientele. It wasn't what Helen had in mind, she knew, but it might be a start.

Helen would find out. In the meantime, she would do something about Strom Davidson. She went to look for him one afternoon, after a conversation with Berta. She had thought that he was with Humphrey, but he was not. He was perched on the edge of his desk, with his back to the door, when she walked in.

He swiveled his head, and when he saw who it was, he swore. "For godssake, don't you ever fuckin' knock?" He straightened up, adjusted his clothing, and then the secretary stood up, looking rather disheveled. She was beet red as she went by Helen without a word and disappeared into the bathroom.

Helen didn't comment on the scene. "Where's Humphrey?" she asked.

"Don't ask me," Davidson said. "Down in the warehouse, somewhere. What can I do for ya, honey? Or maybe you could do something for me." He glanced down meaningfully at his crotch.

"You can do something for yourself," she said. "Leave these women alone."

Strom's eyebrows shot up. "Leave them alone? Oh, dear! Is some little bitch complaining? She's not getting enough?"

Helen drew a deep breath. She was very conscious of how small she was next to this tall, rangy man. He was old enough to be her father, but he was a bastard. She was not afraid of him. She spoke calmly. "Leave them alone, Strom. I mean it. You've got a nice little racket here. If you want to keep it, concentrate on doing the job right. No more yelling, no more threatening, no more abuse. I don't want to hear one word of complaint or it's gold-watch time."

Strom's face darkened and he leaned over her. "Who in the fuck do you think you are, you dried-up little twat? I've been in this business for fifty fuckin' years. You're gonna come in here and tell me how to run my shop?" He leaned his face down and expelled a cigarish "Hah!" into hers.

Helen could hardly avoid reacting. But she didn't show any anger. Instead, she smiled. "I'm running this show," she said calmly. "I hope you weren't expecting *fair*. *Fair* ain't in it, is it, you stupid prick? No, don't raise your hand, Strom. Think. Think for a minute. How do I come off talking to you like this? Think! I'm not just some little twat. I can talk to you like this." She fixed him with her deep-set eyes, suddenly gleaming like coal about ready to burst into flame.

She could see it was sinking in. He was thinking. This was a woman who had blasted Carmine to shreds with a shotgun. And got away with it. She might not be aiming a Model 70 at him, but she had muscle behind her. She's doing all the talking, but there's heavy muscle here. He wasn't buying it without checking the label, however. He knew better than that. He stalked out, looking for Humphrey. Helen decided not to make the secretary hang out in the john any longer. She went out to the car.

Two of the guys were lounging there, smoking cigarettes. They straightened up when she approached. "Hi, boss lady," they said, almost in unison. They had taken to calling her that lately. She knew Humphrey had put them up to it. They were nice-looking young men, handsome even, in their early twenties. They had the dark looks of Italian men, with beautiful white teeth and flirty manners.

She smiled at the one called Mike. He had a vague European accent, not much. "How's it going, guys?" she said. It was going well, they said, pleased with the attention. "Listen," she said, "if that big old fart comes roaring out here, you know the one I mean?"

"Mr. Davidson?" Mike said, looking concerned. His hand went immediately to his suit jacket, to the bulge. "He bothering you, Miz Helen?"

"Not as much as he thinks," she said, with a smile. "I told him you guys wouldn't stand for it."

"We wouldn't!" Mike declared. They looked eager, staring at the door of the factory. Mike unbuttoned his suit coat and stood with his feet apart, balanced, his arms slightly bent.

She put her hand on Mike's arm. He flexed his bicep underneath it, his teeth gleaming. "I knew I could count on you." She looked him in the eye.

"You can count on us," his friend Alessandro said. "Why don't you sit in the car? We'll be here." He opened the door.

"Thanks," she said, and got in to wait.

But Strom Davidson didn't come out. He was down in the basement. He waited impatiently while Humphrey finished up his conversation with Mongelo.

Mongelo had lost quite a bit of weight. He was wearing some old clothes of Humphrey's, that Humphrey had kept when he was losing the pounds. He had also lost a lot of his anger. The first few times Humphrey had come calling Mongelo had raged. Then Humphrey would haul out the butt plug. He kept it in a leather bag.

"You know what Action looked like when they found him?" he asked. "He was a fucking fat bag of pus. He'd been hanging for a week. His face and arms and legs were swollen up like balloons, filled with old blood and shit. There was a lot of him in a puddle on the floor below him."

Mongelo was frankly scared. He had calmed himself and learned to relax and enjoy his confinement. Humphrey got nicer— or less brutal, which was the same thing. Never a devotee of exercise, Mongelo got out daily for a little workout with a treadmill Humphrey had ordered in for him, while a woman cleaned the cell. He watched a lot of television, especially an enormous supply of erotic videos that the boys replenished regularly. He devoured the food they brought, and although he couldn't say that he loved the peppery cuisine, he was more than a little proud of the way he was looking.

But the main thing that soothed his fury was the way the boss was talking to him, lately. Once Mongelo had adjusted to things, Humphrey had even apologized for the rude way they had kidnapped him and for the confinement. At first, that had made him wary. He still wasn't sure he wasn't going to be whacked. Today, however, the approach was different. The boss was confiding. "Monge," Humphrey said, after he'd sent the boys back out to the car, "I gotta talk to you. We got a huge problem, and only you can help. You heard about the guys," he said, mentioning three or four names of their acquaintance who were undergoing trial for racketeering. "The FBI has got them by the balls," he said.

"Those pricks," Mongelo said.

"Monge, when did you ever know the FBI to get so close? Think about it, Monge. There's no way those dumb fuckers could nail those guys. Unless they had help."

Monge frowned. He caught the drift right away. "Somebody ratted 'em out?"

"Somebody's in deep, Monge."

"Who?"

"We don't know, Monge. But you're gonna find out."

"Me, boss? I don't know nothin'."

"I know you don't, Monge. You're the one guy I can trust. You and me go back a long way. If I can't trust you, I can't trust nobody."

Mongelo nodded, a serious look knotting his face.

"I had to put out the word that you left town, Monge," Humphrey told him. "I even told Ellie," he said, meaning Mongelo's wife of thirty years. Monge shrugged. "And Carla," he added after a moment, referring to Mongelo's frequently battered twenty-eight-year-old girlfriend. He didn't tell him that Carla had said

"Thank God!" "Now sometime soon you'll be moving, Monge," Humphrey said. He could see that made Monge anxious. He was feeling secure here in his comfortable prison apartment. A move might not be a good sign. It might be a long car ride, one way. Humphrey let him feel that anxiety for as long as he could before he reassured him.

"You'll be moving out with me, Monge," he said. "I need you by me. Things are getting a little tight and, like I said, I don't know who's on the team and who ain't. I gotta have someone I can trust. The thing is, you can't breathe a word of this. When I come for you, we gotta be careful. No fooling around. I know it's hard on you, but you gotta keep up the diet, you gotta stay quiet, and no chatting with nobody. I don't want no one to know that you're with me, by my side. If they knew, and I don't know who they are, they'd grab you for sure. Wouldja even make it to prison? I gotta doubt it. They're after me, bad. You're my secret weapon."

Mongelo liked this notion. They talked about it in hushed tones somewhat longer. When Humphrey got up to go, he pointed at a plastic sack by the door and said, "That your trash?"

"Yanh," Mongelo said. "The wetback lady put it there."

"I'll take it," Humphrey said, bending to pick up the bag. He locked the door, smiling apologetically. "It won't be long, Monge. You'll like the house. I fixed it up for you."

Mongelo was grateful.

As he left Humphrey was surprised to find Strom pacing up and down at the other end of the dark cellar. How much had he overheard, Humphrey wondered? From the man's expression, evidently nothing. The man was very hot about something. Helen.

Humphrey listened to his raging as they returned upstairs. But before they got to the office he stopped and said, "So what are you telling me, Strom? You don't like your job?"

Strom looked shocked. Then he recovered. "No, no. I just thought you should know. I mean . . . you know me, boss . . . if that's the way you want it . . . I mean . . . "

"Well, what?" Humphrey said.

"Okay. Nothing."

At the car, Humphrey hefted the plastic bag. Alessandro opened the trunk. Humphrey put the bag in the trunk and then got into the back seat with Helen.

"So, which was it," he asked, "Hatchet or Hotcha?"

"Both, actually."

8

Flight Service

"**D**ead man doesn't walk," Schwind told him, before he'd even finished his pitch. She said it was too complicated, even if they could figure out some way to make him *look* dead initially. Too many complications.

Joe was crushed. Later, thinking about it, he realized that it suited Agent Schwind for him to be a fugitive and not a New Age Lazarus. She'd argued that it was all but impossible to fake a death these days, what with DNA testing and so on. And someone, surely Sergeant Mulheisen, would want to be sure that the corpse in the Denver morgue was really Joe Service. No, no, they would go ahead with the plan as sketched. Poor Kirk would have to take the blame, but then he'd be handsomely compensated. He could find an occupation more to his liking. An airline pilot, perhaps, or marine biologist. He'd have to go to school, but it would be fun. He could afford it.

The way it worked was two days later Kirk was on the night shift. He had to go to the bathroom. When he came back, Joe Service was gone. Kirk looked in the closet and found the money. He counted it. Then he gave the alarm.

Joe found the car, sitting in the parking lot. He shucked off his doctor's smock and emergency room scrubs and pulled on the pants and sweatshirt and shoes that Agent Schwind had left for him.

Joe never noticed any difficulty at all, didn't even see any police cars rushing to the scene. He got downtown and found the main post office, where he dumped the car that Agent Schwind had provided. One thing he had learned from dealing with federal agents was, don't use any car that they've had contact with. It will almost certainly be bugged, with direction finders, transmitters, who knows what.

He traded for an innocuous car belonging to a postal worker who would not get off shift, probably, for another five hours. But if Schwind's provisional transport was bugged, the feds would move in on it within a short time. They would know what he was up to. So he drove to the airport, parked, and rode back into town on the regular bus. He figured that would keep Schwind busy for a while. Even if they figured out he'd stolen a postal worker's car and they tracked it to the airport, they'd be checking to see which flight he had taken.

Despite all the screwing around he had a couple of hours to kill before the banks opened. Agent Schwind had provided him with plenty of money—well, a thousand dollars—but he needed much more and he wanted independence. He had a bank account or two in Denver, he was pretty sure. By the time they opened he had drunk far too much coffee, was a little wiggy, but still functioning better than he had expected. In fact, he felt great. It was great to be out and he'd had a good rest, although he was more tired than he wanted to be.

He'd remembered at least one bank account, from the days when he was flitting about the country unfettered. This one had a deposit box, too. In the box was a brown paper package. He was pretty sure what was in it, but he thought he'd better open it. As he'd thought: a Smith & Wesson .38 automatic, fully loaded with a box of cartridges. Also about $40,000 cash in old bills. He wrapped the package back up and hit the streets, feeling more free.

A good day's sleep in a pleasant suburban motel made him feel even better. Now he could consider his future with confidence. In an earlier day he would have headed immediately for Detroit. He was fairly confident that Helen would be there. She must have the money. If she wasn't there, she was probably dead. At any rate, the Fat Man—Humphrey—would know. But he'd had plenty of time to think about things. No zipping off to Detroit. First, he had to get to the bottom of this business with Agent Schwind.

He kind of liked the idea of being a rogue agent. That might be a good career choice. Just give up this whole idea of working for the mob. The United States government was every bit as powerful a mob. It might be interesting work. But he had a feeling that Agent Schwind's purpose might be allied to his own. She might be after Humphrey. First, though, he had to find out more about her. He went to a pay phone with a pile of change and began to call around.

In his wide-ranging travels, Joe Service had made many invaluable connections. He called five of them now. The usual proceeding went something like, "Oh, hi Joe. What's up?" As if the person had seen him only last week. Nobody asked why he wanted the information or where he was calling from. They just took the request and said they could tell him more in an hour. An hour later, the answer was the same from all five. Dinah Schwind was not known to be an employee of the FBI, the CIA, the NSA, or the INS (Immigration). Joe had not wanted to give too long a list of agencies, so he'd stuck to the federal ones. There were others, of course, but Agent Schwind had mentioned at least two of those. Maybe she was so deeply covered that none of his contacts could find a shadow. Or she might be with a state or municipal law-enforcement agency, he supposed. Detroit? Denver? Colorado? Michigan? He had no doubt that she was some kind of cop. He would find out.

Feeling less secure than an hour earlier, he nonetheless thought that he should contact Schwind now. He called the number she had given him.

She didn't seem upset that he had ditched the car and severed their contact. She had expected him to do that, she said. "Are you ready to go to work?" she asked.

"Sure," Joe said, cheerfully. "What did you have in mind?"

"I'll tell you when I see you," she said. "You're still in the Denver area, I take it."

"Close enough," Joe said.

"We'll have to meet. I want you to meet my partners."

Joe told her to forget that. He had met her, that was enough. It was probably better if he didn't even know their names.

She consented to that. "But I need to see you," she said. "I have to see how you are."

Joe assured her he was feeling fine, not quite up to full speed, but a few days on the outside would cure that. He agreed to meet her, alone. She should drive west on Interstate 70, toward Salt Lake. She might have to drive for a while, he told her, but she would see him. Keep her eyes open.

He passed her in an old pickup truck he'd bought for five hundred dollars, as they were approaching the exit for Route 40. She followed him for several miles, halfway up the mountain road to Berthoud Pass, before he pulled over at a roadside cafe and gas station.

"Sorry to drag you so far," he said. He stood by the car, taking deep breaths and stretching. "Smell that. I love that smell of the firs."

Agent Schwind didn't mind, she said. It was sort of on their way. She was glad to see that he was in good enough shape to go to work. The first job, she said, was in Salt Lake City. Did he want to drive there? They could go back to Denver and fly, or they could take the train from Granby.

"Granby! Hey, that's where they took me off the train," Joe said. "I forgot this road goes through there. I just wanted to get up in the mountains. Smell the firs." Joe was through with trains for a while, he said, with a smile. If she didn't mind, he kind of liked driving. She offered to drive and he could ride, see some scenery. Why not, he said.

They drove right past the spot where Helen and Itchy Spinodi had stopped to look for the money, but, of course, they had no way of knowing that. She drove precisely the speed limit. After they got over the second pass, Rabbit Ears, and were driving through the Yampa River valley, they ran into a cattle drive. Schwind was delighted. She said it was like the real West. Driving cattle right down the highway! Joe pointed out that the cowboys were riding all-terrain vehicles and the cattle were some kind of boutique breed of red Angus, along with a few Charolais. He didn't think that the Goodnight trail was like this.

"Did you raise cattle," she asked, "up in Montana?"

"My neighbor did. They stink too much. Besides, that place is gone."

"Thanks to Victor Echeverria," Schwind said. "You could say he drove you from your home. Well, here's your chance to get back at him." It appeared that "Vetch," as he was known, was well enough to be moved and the Colombian government had issued a request for his repatriation. The United States government had reluctantly consented, although federal officials wanted to question him. But they had no pretext, so they were allowing his transfer.

"A plane will arrive in Salt Lake City in five days," Schwind said. "I'll have everything you'll need to take it out."

"Parked?" Joe said. She nodded. "No one in it?"

She shrugged. "It would be best if Mr. Echeverria was in it."

"But then," Joe said, "there would be an innocent pilot, a co-pilot, maybe some medical people . . ."

"Maybe, maybe not. I'll know more when it leaves Colombia. But we were thinking it might be Echeverria's plane, which is a Gulfstream V. The pilot—we know him—isn't exactly innocent. Medical personnel . . . well, I don't know. You have qualms?"

"Sure I have qualms," Joe said. "The question is, do you?"

"Not many. We want to take out Echeverria, but we'd also like to take out the plane. It would really be better to do this off American soil. We're not real keen on blowing up a plane in the Salt Lake City airport, but we may not have another choice. If we do . . ."

"I like to travel," Joe said. "Let's take a trip to Bermuda. What outfit did you say you worked for?"

"I'm kind of like you, Joe. I don't work for any one outfit, as you put it. But I have worked for just about all the federal enforcement agencies. Do you want to see my I.D.?"

She fished out her card from her coat pocket and handed it to him. Joe peered at it closely. It was her face, her name, her general description. It had a thumbprint. He asked to see her hand. She extended it. He looked at the thumb. He wasn't a fingerprint expert but it looked close enough. He dropped her hand and returned the card. There had been no telltale "void" marks, so it appeared to be a genuine card, issued by the Central Intelligence Agency, signed by the director, George Tenet. Joe didn't know Tenet's signature from Bill Clinton's, but it looked good.

"Could I see your gun?" he asked.

She glanced at him, briefly, eyebrows raised. Then, "Sure, why not?" she said. She unholstered the Browning automatic, deftly ejected the magazine, and checked the chamber to be sure it was empty before handing it over.

Joe handled it lovingly. It had a dull, dark finish. "Model M35," he noted. "A very nice piece. You like 9mm?"

"It works every time," she said. She reinserted the magazine when he returned it. "What are you packing?"

"S&W .38 auto," Joe said. "Want to see it?"

"You show me yours?" she said, one heavy eyebrow arched. "No thanks. You find the .38 more stable, I suppose."

"It's enough gun," Joe said. "What did you have in mind for taking out the plane?"

"Well, not a .38," she said. "Or a 9mm. I was thinking an RPG. I've got a six-pack of them in the trunk."

"Throwaways," Joe noted, nodding. "That'd work. What about an M203 launcher, on an AR-15?"

"I can get it, if you want," she said.

"Trouble is, with the M203 or the RPG, you'd have to be fairly close. Not more than two hundred yards, better closer. I wonder if an incendiary in an AR-15, or some similar target rifle, anything in .225, would touch off the tanks."

Schwind was skeptical. She thought it was too iffy.

"They're very accurate," Joe said. "I could get my hands on one that's as silent as an air gun. I could plink away for an hour till I made the right hit. Nobody would notice."

"They'd notice ricochets," she pointed out.

"Who's your RAC officer?" he asked.

She smiled. "For these purposes, I'm the resident."

When they stopped for coffee and sandwiches at a little restuarant in Craig, Joe said he had to make a phone call. Schwind rattled off the serial number from her handgun.

"You'll find it's registered to me," she said. She didn't smile.

Joe made the call anyway. Before they left he had the confirmation.

"Doesn't prove anything," he said as they got back into the car.

"No, just that I own a gun," she agreed. "Maybe you should have met with my associates."

"What would that prove? Who do they work for?"

She shrugged and they drove on. Later, she said, "Remember, Joe, *you're* the fugitive. I could get in trouble just being seen with you."

"Good thought," he said, and went to sleep. When he awoke she told him they were only an hour or so from Salt Lake.

"I've been thinking about it," she said, when he seemed alert. "You deserve to know what this is all about." She explained that she had been working in various agencies for some years and the most frustrating thing about the work was that oftentimes valuable, hard-won, and dangerously obtained intelligence was tragically wasted because of bureaucratic wrangling and confusion. "We find out a drug deal is going down, or somebody is leaving the country, or expected to slip in, and by the time we get authorization to act, the opportunity has passed. Or a bureau chief refuses to take responsibility, or he's mad at some guy up the line, or in a competing agency. It's a shocking waste. And yet . . . it seemed to a few of us that if we had simply acted, without bothering with authorization, there would have been little or no fallout. You follow me?"

Joe followed her, all right. But he expressed his immediate objection, which anyone would have, that you can't have governmental agencies just charging about, without authorization or accountability. It was too dangerous. Scary, in fact.

Schwind agreed. "But sometimes . . ." she said. "Sometimes . . . take Echeverria, for instance. The man is a known scoundrel, the scum of the earth. He deals drugs on an enormous scale. He practically funds minigovernments. People are killed, others are enslaved, their lives made miserable, because of this, this vermin. Yet he flies in here, no problem. He attempts to kill you—which some would have said would have been no great loss—and we save his life. Now he'll fly out of here, off to do more mischief. No sane and sensible administrator that I know of would authorize any kind of action against him, certainly not what we are thinking of. Yet if he were to be thwarted, harmed, or even killed, none of those same administrators would object or do anything more than cheer."

"Unless you got caught," Joe said.

"Unless we got caught," she agreed. "My friends and I realized that given the intelligence resources we have, we could do a lot. But we have to be very, very careful. And we have to especially be careful that we consider from the outset the value and . . . well, the moral weight of any proposed action."

Good Lord, Joe thought, these people are already out of control. He wasn't so sure he had made a wise choice, getting involved. Still, he'd *had* to get out of the hands of the law. He'd had no choice, really. When a man was hanging on to the edge of a cliff, any bush, no matter how many thorns, was worth grasping.

They talked about it some more and Joe concluded by saying, as cheerfully as he could muster, "I'm with you, Dinah. Sounds to me like you're doing the right thing."

Dinah Schwind shot him a glance that may have been gratitude. But she remarked, "You can call me Dinah, Joe, but don't ever let me hear you refer to me as 'Dinah-mite.'"

Joe smiled and promptly effaced that epithet from his vocabulary.

9

Hell Gate

Schwind was around somewhere, but Joe couldn't see her. Her management style was to let the dog hunt. As long as she didn't get in the way, or complain if he didn't come when she called, he was content.

He was ready. It was getting dark. The mountains to the east reared up huge, their snowcaps red-gold in the last of the sun. Another beautiful day in paradise, here in the Salt Lake valley. No clouds, just sun. But cool, even for March. And a breeze, as always. Joe wondered if airports caused breezes. It wasn't a sea breeze, not a salt breeze, although the lake was just over there to the west. All he could smell was jet fuel.

He watched the Gulfstream V from about three hundred yards. He sat in a used pickup truck, not quite as old and beat-up as the one he'd abandoned in Granby. This one was a GMC. It had a big engine and everything worked. It had cost him fifteen hundred dollars—or rather, it had cost Schwind. Paid in cash to a young fellow who had run an ad in the *Salt Lake Tribune*. This kid would probably be able to identify Joe if anyone asked, providing they showed a picture of a cowboy with a mustache. But it was just a description. It would be a stretch to connect the buyer with Joe Service, an escaped prisoner from Denver. And no reason, for that matter, to connect Joe Service with the kind of activity he was about to initiate in Salt Lake City. And if all those connections were made . . . so what? Just something else to attribute to Joe Service, if you ever saw him again.

When they had finished fueling and the truck had moved away, Joe began to get ready. He'd tried out the RPG in the desert and he felt he had a good chance to make a hit with the second or third shot. Hell, he might even get lucky and score on the first. But he didn't have a lot of time. He figured that from a range of less than two hundred yards, at the fence, he could fire three times for sure, and if nothing interfered, he could fire more if he had to. A week to practice would have been better, but he didn't have it.

What he wanted now was for the attendants and others to leave the scene. But it didn't look like that was going to happen. Regardless of what Schwind wanted, he had no intention of waiting for Echeverria and his friends. He would knock out the plane and that was that. The trouble was, as he'd feared, there was always somebody in the plane, or close by. Obviously, there was a guard—he saw a man in quasi-military fatigues who occasionally left the plane by its open exit ramp, took a little stroll around, and looked like he desperately wanted to smoke a cigarette. This man looked professional, perhaps a former soldier.

This guy appeared to be unarmed, but on one occasion when he had appeared at the door of the plane he'd carried a weapon in a casual way, in one hand, aimed upward. Joe got only a brief glimpse, but it looked like a Heckler & Koch MP5. He wore aviator sunglasses and a beret. It must have taken some kind of clout to be permitted an armed guard on the flight line, although the guy was pretty circumspect—maybe he had orders not to show the gun. It looked like there was only the one guard. Sorry Raul, Joe thought, gazing through the binoculars, you can pack heat, but no smoking on the flight line—that's the American Way.

There were also a couple of women in uniform-type outfits, rather like stewardesses, who came out now and then, presumably to get a little air. There were people who drove up to other nearby aircraft: just people, businessmen, pilots, secretaries, service workers. There were just a heck of a lot of people coming and going. And then there was occasional traffic on the service road, which was why he wasn't parked on the service road. He was parked back off the road, behind some old earthen mounds, grassy piles evidently left over from construction.

The aircraft was larger than he'd envisioned it, having pored over photographs of Gulfstream Vs in aviation magazines at the library. This was a beautiful piece of work, painted fancifully in azure blue with a broad, sweeping swash, a leafy jungle-vine motif in brown and green that started at the base of the low, short nose and ended high on the tail. The aircraft had two big Rolls-Royce jet engines mounted on either side of the rear of the fuselage. The wings were swept and low. He knew from the magazines that the Gulfstream was noted for speed, cruising altitude, and, especially, range. In one of these a drug lord could check on his poppies in Asia or the Mideast, zip to Paris to make a deal, buy the wife a frock, and then head home to Lima, or wherever, with hardly a glance at the fuel gauge.

Obviously, the drug business paid well, but Joe was impressed. The drug dealers he was familiar with drove around in Cadillac splendor, and maybe the odd Rolls. This was spending money on a scale that declared, We gotta get rid of it.

The plane was angled away from the fence, its lofty tail toward him. In this posture it presented just about the smallest target profile it could have. He'd go for a direct hit on the left engine for the first shot. He had just decided that, after watching the scene for forty minutes. It was much as he'd seen three days earlier. Just too many innocent bystanders. The tail assembly was the closest, biggest target available. It was also, he thought, the least likely site for a general explosion, although he wasn't at all sure about that. The magazines he'd looked at had provided very little technical information about the location of fuel tanks. He assumed the main tanks were in the low wings, but then the engines were in the back. If he were designing it, he'd have put as much of the fuel as he could back there, in case of accidents. But he knew there were aerodynamic reasons for spreading the weight around, and fuel was a big part of the plane's weight.

If he could hit the tail assembly, the explosion of the rocket would frighten the people away from the plane. The exit was right up front, just behind the flight deck, a combination ramp and door. The crew would have maximum access to the exit, and he'd allow them as much time to flee as he dared. But there would be unforeseen problems, he was sure.

The guard would not run away, or not far. He would locate the source of the attack. He would see Joe, for there was really no place to hide. Standing by the fence would not give him a clear view to the target; he would be a little below grade. Anyway, there wasn't much cover value to standing at a wire-weave cyclone fence. The service road was elevated, however. If he stopped on the road and he stood in the back of the pickup truck, using the cab roof as a rest, he would have a good view, could fire over the fence instead of having to cut a hole to fire through. Of course, the elevated position, in the pickup bed, would make him very visible to the guard.

Joe accepted the probability that he would have to take some fire, probably automatic fire, probably 9mm, if that was an H&K. And he'd have to wait until he was sure the women had fled the scene, as well as anybody else who might be idly present, before he launched two and three. And, of course, the explosion would bring the cops.

The cops would come from inside the fence, first, rushing to the site, but there would be others who would quickly block the access roads. He had no idea how long it would take them to do this. There was doubtless a way to find out, but he hadn't had the time to do it. Today was moving day; Echeverria was leaving tonight. It was a major hole in the plan, but Joe had weighed the options and decided to go, regardless. There were two alternate exit routes; if either of them had been the primary route he wouldn't have agreed to do it, but as the primary was simplicity itself, he quit fretting.

It was only common sense to make all the preparation you could, but sometimes it was better not to make too fine a plan. Things always went a little wrong. You could never imagine exactly how things would go, so it was better just to have a loose, rather flexible plan—within limits.

He loved the intricate plans he saw in caper movies, usually of bank robberies. He could see the artfulness of the director and the screenwriter: the otherwise uncommitted viewer was drawn into the plot by its seeming explicitness. Everything seemed to be carefully mapped out. One wanted it to succeed, just as one listened in anticipation for the resolving chord of a musical phrase. And then, of course, the enactment was drawn out, heightening the viewer's tension, until some ludicrous little incident cropped up, some dumb little thing that one couldn't have anticipated or predicted, like a kid wandering into the scene, or a car double-parked and blocking the getaway route, whole traffic-stopping parades that materialized out of nowhere. People panic and start screaming, noon whistles blow and startle a gunman, who begins to fire wildly . . . a fire alarm next door, a tiny barking dog that won't go away . . . always a bunch of things. And, of course, it screwed everything up.

Well, it would, wouldn't it? This released tension into action, into another more rapid train of events. Usually it ended in a hail of bullets, sometimes quite satisfyingly in an exhilarated gangster looking back and laughing as he somehow managed to elude pursuit.

And now, Joe realized, at the last moment, something seemed to be happening on the flight line. It was time. It was getting late. Visibility was already reduced. The guard came out and so did the women, not casually but purposefully. They descended the ramp and walked together the few steps to the nose of the plane. Terrific! He couldn't have asked for better. Even the pilots had come out. And the guard didn't seem to be armed.

By god, he saw what it was! A group of vehicles was driving from the air terminal toward the aircraft parking area: a sedan, an ambulance, another car. The reception party was standing by the nose, on parade.

Joe tossed the binoculars onto the seat, started the engine, and drove out to the point he'd selected on the road. He hopped out of the cab and vaulted into the back. With no haste, he hefted an RPG, armed it, and took up his position. He looked up and down the road. No one in sight, which was a great relief. He had a fine view of the target.

He aimed and fired. The rocket whooshed, he tossed the launcher aside and stooped to get another ready. He tried to keep his eye on the rocket while he got the next one ready. It wasn't easy. The rocket took only a few seconds to reach its target. It had a better parabola than he'd anticipated. He'd aimed a little high and to the left, accommodating the breeze. The rocket swerved and smacked into the fuselage, about forty feet aft of the open door. It struck just in front of the left engine pod and exploded. These rockets were supposed to be armor penetrating, but this one exploded externally.

Joe figured the basic weight of the aircraft to be some twenty-four-plus tons. He hadn't expected it to move much, but the explosion kicked the tail of the aircraft sideways, bringing the entire plane now nearly broadside to him. He hadn't reckoned on that, and he was grateful that it worked in his favor. The target was much larger, and everybody was on the other side of it. He could hardly have asked for a better deal.

There was a gaping hole in the side of the plane, and smoke was pouring out of it. People were running, doubtless screaming, but he was not aware of that. Where was the guard? He at least ought not to be running away. He must realize what direction the rocket had come from. Joe couldn't wait to look. He aimed at the spot where the wing joined the fuselage and fired. Whoosh! Toss the launcher. Get another.

Now he heard shots. The guard must have gotten his weapon somehow and unleashed an entire clip. It was 9mm, all right, but Joe couldn't see him, didn't see any bullets kicking up dirt. No impacts on the truck. The second rocket struck the fuselage too high, blew a big chunk off the top of the plane. The approaching cars had turned away, Joe could see them driving away from the plane. But whoever was driving the ambulance was either confused or determined to make delivery. The ambulance swung clear around the nose of the plane and skidded to a halt, nearly crashing into the wing that was extended toward Joe.

The doors of the ambulance flew open, personnel in white uniforms ran wildly, running toward nearby parked planes, frantically seeking cover. Also two men in suits. There would be one person in that ambulance who couldn't run, Joe realized. A man who had intended to kill him. This was an unlooked-for opportunity. If he weighed the ethical factors at all, they didn't compute, didn't even register consciously. This was just too good to pass up. He aimed directly at the ambulance. But then . . . he let the sight drift away, toward the fuselage. The target was the plane, wasn't it? He fired, then tossed the launcher and bailed out of the truck, scrambling into the cab and driving as rapidly as he could down the road toward the terminal parking lot.

He never saw the rocket veer and strike the wing, just above the ambulance. The explosion, the fire on the wing, then another, much larger explosion. But he heard the blast, saw the flashes. It took him less than a minute to reach the spot where he had decided to leave the truck. The service road did not communicate with the passenger parking lot. From where he left the truck it was exactly a minute and forty seconds of walking purposefully, no panic, to reach the lot. That was twenty seconds faster than he had estimated. Must be adrenaline, he thought as he slipped through the hole he had cut in the cyclone fence. He slowed to the halting pace of the man who is pretty sure where he left the car, but not dead sure. He peered about, stopped, and then walked directly to the car he had rented two days ago. It was a white car, like so many rental cars, but also like a huge percentage of cars in the Salt Lake area; for some reason they liked white cars here, he'd noticed. He got in and drove to the exit, where a striped wooden barricade stopped him next to a windowed hut. The attendant had come out and was looking back toward the terminal.

"What's going on?" Joe called, extending his parking ticket.

"I don't know," the man said, coming around. He took Joe's ticket, glanced at it, said, "Be right with you. Some kind of explosion over there. Jeez, I hope it wasn't a crash!"

"My god," Joe said, "I hope not. It didn't sound that loud, did it?"

"No, I guess not," the man said. "It was a couple of bangs. You hear it? That wouldn't be a crash." He took the ticket back into the booth, ran it through a time-stamp device, and said, "That's thirty dollars and seventy-five cents, sir."

Joe paid, got his receipt, and when the barrier went up, drove cautiously out onto the terminal exit road. There was a lot of activity, sirens, flashing lights, that kind of thing, but he just drove onto the freeway and it was soon behind him.

In Salt Lake City he found a parking lot two blocks from where he had earlier left another car that he'd bought with his own money, a very nice four-year-old Ford Taurus, not white but green. He checked the rental car for any evidence that could connect it to Joe Service. There was none, of course. He locked the car and took five blocks to travel two blocks, checking his tail, crossing a hotel lobby, doubling back, entering a large department store, exiting by the parking structure. He was clean. He drove his new car out of yet another lot and back to the freeway. Traffic in the Salt Lake area was nuts. There was still a lot of construction going on because of the bid for the upcoming Olympic Games, but Joe didn't mind. The more confusion, the better. He patiently followed the temporary signs and got onto Interstate 80, then onto I-84, and finally, well north of the valley, onto I-15, headed toward Idaho and Montana.

This was more like it. Even though it was night, he could sense the wide-open spaces. Especially after he got over the ridge, out of the basin. He'd never cared for the basin. The Snake River reminded him of the last time he'd driven up this way. He'd turned around, just north of here, and gone back to Salt Lake City. He wasn't sorry he'd gone back, but thinking about it he was reminded of an odd guy he'd encountered there, a Colonel Tucker. He was pretty sure Tucker had been a federal agent, probably narcotics, but maybe Immigration or Treasury. The guy had staked out Helen's house in Salt Lake City, obviously intent on recovering the money that Helen had boosted from Joe's cabin. Not that Helen would see it that way, Joe thought. It was peculiar, though, that he had not given a thought to this guy before now. He wondered if Schwind knew this guy.

From here it was little more than two hours up over the Monida Pass to the turnoff that led up the road to his now ruined house, near the town of Tinstar. This really was a foolish idea. He'd thought about it as he drove. Almost no traffic at all on that freeway, from north of Idaho Falls, over the Monida Pass, until he turned off at Dillon. A couple of trucks. Then hardly any traffic to here. And all that time he'd known it was not just foolish but stupid.

If anyone was ever going to look any particular place for the fugitive Joe Service, it would be right here. He'd asked himself if this was just a blind, gut thing—a coyote running for his den. But he didn't feel like he was running from anything. He'd soon recovered from whatever adrenaline rush the attack on the plane had given him. Was this some primal thing? He didn't believe it. He decided it was just curiosity, and maybe a little bravado.

Then he laughed out loud. He was not a man to kid himself. There was at least one cardboard liquor box still stashed up there, full of money. Possibly two. As best as he could figure, there was between $500,000 and a cool million up there . . . assuming that the cops or somebody else hadn't found it.

He wanted to see the place, but it was the middle of the night. The house, of course, was just a charred hole in the ground. Too bad—he'd loved that house more than any other place he'd ever lived, but he was a remarkably unsentimental man. He parked and walked up the hill to a secret cache, an old mine shaft that he'd discovered only after he'd been on the property for some months.

Something had happened, he could tell right away. The door to the old mine shaft was pushed closed but not locked. He had no way of knowing the various events that had transpired here, after he had left. It didn't matter. What did matter was that, somehow, there were at least four boxes. And, he was gratified to see, their ghastly guardian, an unknown corpse, now rather mummified.

Joe recognized this corpse, although he hadn't the slightest notion of who this guy might have been. He'd first seen him on the highway, outside of Butte. Hitchhiking with a hired killer, or maybe it was the other way around. He'd stumbled on him months later, when he was trying to provide himself with a little cushion in his flight from Montana. Somebody had transported this corpse some forty miles from the highway and stashed him in Joe's private cache. Who? He assumed it had been Helen, but why? He'd never asked her when they had reunited in Salt Lake City. They'd been too busy with other things. But Joe was glad to see the guy. They were getting to be old pals. The guy didn't look much different, maybe a littler drier and thinner, his beard a little fuller, perhaps—it must be the excellent drainage, the dry air. The guy looked like he could hold out for years, till he resembled the husk of an insect, like a stonefly on a river rock.

More to the point: whoever had been here since Joe left, it hadn't been anyone official. This guy wouldn't still be on watch.

Joe had little curiosity about who the mysterious hitchhiker might be. He wasn't squeamish, but he had no desire to shift the body about. Still, it might be helpful to learn whatever might be readily available, so he took a moment to check the external coat pockets. All he found was a well-thumbed and grimy little spiral notebook and a stub of a pencil. By the light of the flashlight he read some lines of poetry, no name on the book. The last page written on contained a single, apparently uncompleted line: "The hour of transition is".

That was all. An epitaph, perhaps. He stuffed the book in his hip pocket and went directly to the remaining cardboard boxes. On his previous visit he'd been in too much of a hurry. He'd taken a box filled with old bills and records. Obviously, Helen had been more thorough. She had carted off the lion's share of the loot he had lifted in Detroit a lifetime ago, as it seemed. But to his relief, at least one of the boxes was filled with money.

He was tempted to whistle as he carried the box down the hill, but the hoot of an owl startled him and he kept his mouth shut. Also in the old mine were a few of his guns and plenty of ammo for them. He toted off a small arsenal, a couple of favorite pistols, a shotgun, and a special rifle he'd had made for him by a gunsmith over in the Bitterroot Valley. This was the gun he'd mentioned to Schwind, a .225 with a barrel that stifled sound like a vacuum. There was a companion piece, a similarly silenced .225 pistol. He took that as well.

Before he left he carefully closed the door and made sure it was locked. With any luck, the corpse would have eternal peace. Joe was looking for a little peace himself. He was dog tired, he realized, but he couldn't stay here. A freaky thought popped into his head: he knew a nurse in Butte. Nah. That would be too stupid. But where can you go when dawn is in the east? It's too late for a motel, especially in this remote territory. He didn't believe he could drive far. It would be the height of idiocy to pull over on the roadside: roads are empty out here, but eventually the sheriff or the highway patrol comes along. No tremendous danger, maybe, but not one to invite. Maybe the nurse, Cateyo, was not such a bad idea? She was in love with him, he knew, but they might have been watching her since he'd escaped.

He ended up taking a soothing bath and a catnap in the hot springs, just over the hill from the burnt-out house. It was still quite early when he dragged himself out and got on the road. To his surprise, he felt refreshed enough to drive as far as Billings before weariness forced him to stop. He checked into the largest hotel downtown, the Northern, and crashed into sleep.

When he awoke he was starving. It was morning, though. He had slept right through, some fourteen hours. Over breakfast he ransacked the papers, but there was no mention of any bombing or rocket attack at the Salt Lake City airport the day before. Maybe it was just that the *Gazette* was provincial, but he doubted it. Out here, Salt Lake might be a long way off in miles, but there weren't a lot of other large towns providing news. People thought nothing of driving to Cheyenne to shop. He thought it was some very good news management by Agent Schwind. Perhaps she'd convinced everybody that it was just an accident. That didn't make news unless a lot of people were killed. Joe didn't think anyone had been killed. It was possible, he thought, that yesterday's papers had carried a capsule news item, and when nothing further had developed, the story had died.

What next? He knew he should check in with Schwind, but he wasn't ready to yet. When he called her he wanted to be someplace where he couldn't be easily cornered. He hadn't made up his mind what he was going to do now, but he wanted to be free to decide for himself. He needed to be in a larger city. Montana had only a couple of roads out and only a few commercial flights. He needed to be in Denver, maybe. No. Not Denver. He wasn't ready to go back to Denver yet. And not Cheyenne. Nothing for it: he had to drive to Minneapolis. It took him two days and he enjoyed the drive immensely.

It was great to be out here, just driving, alone. He felt free, finally. Driving around America, checking out the scenery. Thinking the long, road thoughts. He thought about Schwind, about Helen, and Humphrey. He thought about his new career, whatever it might turn out to be. He didn't think much about who might have been in the ambulance. If it was Echeverria, so be it. He didn't know the guy, but he knew he'd been targeted by him.

He went to a mall in Minneapolis and bought a tiny tape recorder. Then he drove downtown. He parked and walked. He found a terrific used-clothing store, where he bought an amazing pair of python-skin cowboy boots that fit perfectly and a western-style sport coat that could have been tailored for him. A fellow he'd met in Tucson, many years ago, had shown him the joys of browsing in these kinds of stores. You could buy great clothes for next to nothing. He even found a cowboy hat, a genuine Stetson in dark gray, a modest rancher's hat. The whole shebang cost only fifty dollars.

He found the guy he wanted, on the street. A bearded young man with a backpack and a dog. One of those homeless but not helpless young guys who wandered around the country. This guy was happy to have lunch with Joe at a diner while the dog guarded the pack outside, where they could keep an eye on him. The man ate two big cheeseburgers, his fries and Joe's, and then gladly spoke into the tape recorder. Just a couple of cryptic messages. Joe gave him twenty bucks and left him smiling.

At a phone booth, he called the number Schwind had given him. When he got her voice mail, he played one of the messages. The homeless man's voice merely said, "Call this number," and carefully enunciated a number in Orange County, California. Joe figured Schwind would understand. What he didn't want was his own voice on her tape machine.

It was a beautiful day in Minneapolis, warm and sunny. He found a park near the river and strolled around. When he called the number in Orange County there were no messages. Too bad. Schwind hadn't figured it out yet. He called her number again. This time, she answered. He played the second message on the tape recorder. This one gave a number in Arkansas and asked her to leave a number in Chicago.

"Joe?" Schwind said. "Is that you? Listen, we've got to ta—" He hung up.

By now, he thought, she would know where he was and where he was headed. He could call her in Chicago, make further arrangements, and maybe even meet. That would calm her. Sure enough, when he called his Arkansas answering service, Schwind's voice was more relaxed. And she didn't use his name.

"Hi," she said. "You did a great job. Everybody's pleased. But we need to meet. Call me in Chicago, tomorrow, between noon and four P.M. Have fun."

Joe called the number in Chicago immediately. After four rings a recorded woman's voice, not Schwind's, asked the caller to leave a message, without providing any information. He hung up. That was all right, he thought. Maybe. He wondered where she had been when all the shooting started in Salt Lake. He called one of his old connections and asked for a location on the number Schwind had provided. The guy on the other end didn't take more than a minute. It was a residential number, at an address on the north side. The phone was registered to a D. Schwind.

There was no way he could get to Chicago before her, he knew. Not if he wanted to go armed, and he did. Maybe it was time to trust her. He'd think about it while he drove.

10

Kiddle-Dee-Divey

Helen wondered if Humphrey had ever been in love. They were down by the lake, by the pavilion, which stood next to the little dock. Humphrey's boat, a long low cabin cruiser elegantly crafted in rich, dark woods, had been brought out of storage in the boathouse for the first time this year and moored alongside the wooden catwalk. It was such a nice day, an incredible seventy-five degrees—Detroit got these days in March, sometimes—that they were actually talking about taking the boat out.

Humphrey was not fully convinced that it was a good idea. He kept asking the young fellows whose job it was to take care of and handle the boat if they didn't think it was a little early. Wouldn't there still be ice out there on the lake? No? But what about debris, all that flotsam left over from when the ice went out, some of it pieces of docks from as far away as Lake Huron? No problem, he was assured, they would keep a good lookout, wouldn't be running fast enough to damage anything even if they should encounter a log, to say nothing of a stray shingle or a net float. Heck, they said, it was worse in the summer, all the beer bottles. Clearly, they were eager.

Even Soke, Mrs. Sid, looked anticipatory. She had accepted one of her daughter's windbreakers, a shiny red one with a slick finish and a lightweight lining. Helen found her a pair of white canvas boat shoes and a bright Red Wings baseball cap. She said that she thought the Red Wings played hockey, not baseball, and they all laughed. But when Helen tucked her frizzy mass of iron-gray hair up into the hat, Soke looked ten years younger. Helen was very eager for her to go out on the water in this great boat. Roman was not eager. He was stolid, his dark suit bulging over his shoulder holster. But he said nothing, just watched.

At last, Humphrey agreed. Just for a little run. If it got too cold, if the water was too choppy (it was blessedly still, nothing more than an occasional warm flutter), they could come right back. But there were a few things to be done. Always some fussing by the boatmen, tinkering with the engine, testing the radio, the depth finder, something. And then there was the food and drink to be prepared and brought down. The boating party stood about on the dock, or the lawn, talking and watching.

Helen asked where the name of the boat had come from, *Kiddle-Dee-Divey*. Boat names were often silly, Humphrey told her. But had he named her? Yes, he had. He'd bought the boat a long time ago. He used to keep it down at Bayview, but when he bought this house with its boathouse, he'd moved it up here. He was quite proud of the boat. He said it was the only one of its kind. It had been built by a legendary boatwright from up near Traverse City. This master builder was famous for his many beautiful and fast sailboats, but sometime after the war he'd tried his hand at what he called a motor cruiser. He'd wanted to recapture the classical lines of powerboats from the twenties and thirties, and this was the lovely result. As far as Humphrey knew, he'd never built another. The builder had given the boat to his wife for an anniversary present. When she divorced him, she put it up for sale. Humphrey had bought it from her.

"But how did you come up with that name?" Helen demanded.

He reluctantly confessed that it was a lyric from a goofy song that was popular when he was a child: "Mairzy Doats." As a boy, he had thought at first that it was "Mairzy Boats." He had stubbornly insisted that everybody was mispronouncing the title. The grown-ups were so amused they often asked him to sing it. So when he bought a boat. . . . Helen thought that was funny and she begged him to sing the song. He refused. But he did finally recite some of the lyrics: "Mairzy doats and dozey doats, and little lambsy divey . . . a kiddle-dee-divey too, wouldn't you?" He added, "I still think it should be 'boats,' but that wouldn't work."

"Why not?"

"The words are just a goofy way of saying 'Mares eat oats,' and so on," he explained.

Helen cocked her head, smiling as she digested this example of an earlier generation's idea of comic wordplay. And then, for no reason that she could supply, she asked him if he'd ever been in love.

Humphrey was startled. "Well, I guess so," he said. "Everybody's been in love, once." But when she pressed for details, he would only say, "A long time ago."

"But you never married, or anything, did you?"

No, he'd never been close to marrying.

"It must have been that first love," Helen said. "What was her name?"

"I don't even remember," he said.

At last, the boat was ready. They all went aboard and found places to sit while the young man, Jamie, took the boat slowly out. The boat was surprisingly roomy inside, for all its sleek, low profile. There was a large open area on the back, or aft, with cushioned bench-type seats. But then you stepped down to an enclosed bridge, where the helmsman stood. Another door opened into an amazing saloon, so to speak, complete with a tiny galley, tables, booth seats, and beyond that sleeping compartments. Everything was marvelously worked out in deep, rich hardwoods. There were tiny windows that looked out onto a narrow catwalk on either side of the cabin roof. The builder had obviously not departed much from the design of a sailboat.

At first they all sat in the sunny rear cockpit. But Humphrey went to stand right next to the helmsman, in the cabin, directing him out to the northeast.

It was such a great day that soon they were all sipping drinks and eating grilled sausages, fancy cheeses, and a variety of crackers and tiny sandwiches; there was even a fancy genoise layer cake with caramel-hazelnut icing. Humphrey, true to his peppers despite the loss of Pepe, favored the jalapeño poppers, stuffed with pepper jack cheese.

Soon enough, Helen found an opportunity to bring up Humphrey's lost love. They were sitting side by side on the fantail, as it were. The others had drifted inside. Roman was playing a card game with Soke in the saloon.

Humphrey confided, finally, that the "lost love" had actually been his "first love"—maybe *only* love would have been more accurate. He had last seen her when he was fourteen and she was thirteen.

"My gosh," Helen said, "it's sort of like, what's his name, Dante and Beatrice. Or am I thinking of someone else?"

"It wasn't like that," Humphrey said. "We were just kids. But she was very nice to me."

"Ooh, that sounds a little risqué," Helen kidded.

"It wasn't like that," he insisted. "She was just nice. We didn't do anything. We traded books—I forget what. King Arthur, or something. Maybe it was Robert Louis Stevenson. Something like that. Poetry, maybe."

Helen was intrigued. She could see that it had meant a lot to him. It was sweet, she thought. A childhood romance, and then . . . "Well, what happened?" she asked.

He shrugged. "We moved away," he said. "Carmine's folks moved into the city. We grew up on the east side. Things got a little crazy. You know? Growing up, gangs, I had a little trouble. That kind of thing."

"Whatever happened to her? Didn't you ever call, or write?"

"I don't know why I never called," he said. "Maybe it was . . . well, I just don't know. She was too far away. She was history. I was into other stuff, like I said. She wouldn't have liked what I was doing."

"But you never forgot her," Helen said. It was sad, but cute. Still, he had never gotten married. She asked him why not.

"You know," he said, in a hopeless tone, gesturing at his torso. "I was a fatso. I had a few times with the bimbos, but it wasn't my thing. I wasn't into it."

Helen didn't understand. She knew Humphrey had been terribly obese; that was how she remembered him from her own youth—nice, fat, jolly Unca Umby. It was hard to believe, in fact, that this rather handsome, distinguished-looking man had once been a sweating, panting mess. But lots of heavy men, she thought, managed to get married, have children. Why not Humphrey?

He explained. Lots of men just gave up on sex and love, all of that. They channeled their energies in other directions. In his case, he got interested in the business. Carmine was enough of a playboy for all of them, him and her father. He apologized if it sounded disrespectful, but her dad was a lover. Humphrey wasn't. He realized in his early twenties that he had a lot of catching up to do, having dropped out of high school. He studied, he watched and listened and learned. He saw that he was going to have to be the brains behind Carmine, who was being groomed to take over. He had accepted this. He thought that his chance might come someday, and it had.

"But maybe too late," he added. "The business is all changed."

But Helen wasn't having another business pep talk. They were on an outing. She wanted to know how a man just "gives up" romance.

"You mean sex," he said. He was uneasy, but also excited. He had expected to have this conversation with her, as they had gotten closer these last few weeks. He hadn't dared to hope that anything could actually come of it, but it was hard for a man not to dream. He hadn't imagined that the conversation would come up just like this, on the back of a boat with her mother and Roman and the crew not far off. But they were effectively alone. Maybe it was the right time.

He gave it some thought, then said, "It's hard, at first. A man has natural feelings, of course, and you see these babes hanging around . . . I mean, they're there for the taking. Good-looking, too, a lot of them. I had a couple . . . well, I was coming up in the world, I had power, already. They *had* to go to bed with me. That's the way it was. I'm not gonna 'pologize. They were looking out for themselves, too. But it was no good. I could see why they were doing it. Eh? I couldn't do that, after a while. Besides, it was getting in my way.

"So . . . I just made up my mind: to hell with it. Forget about it. And it went away. I don't know just how it came about, but pretty soon I could see it was an accepted thing: the Fat Man ain't into broads. Something like that. And then, it's funny, the babes started coming around."

Helen didn't get it. "Coming around? You fell in love?"

"No, no," he said, with a snort of laughter. "Get over this falling in love thing. No, they saw . . . I guess . . . that I was safe. It was okay to horse around and be a little flirty, because it wouldn't come to anything. I was the Fat Man, right? I didn't like babes, not that way. I liked to kid around, but nothing funny. Right?"

She saw it, all right. It sounded awful, but she didn't say anything.

"And it was all right," he went on. "It didn't bother me. I forgot about it. But now . . ." He looked at her in a strange way.

Oh dear, she thought. This is it. She'd been afraid of this. But if he'd gotten over sex, a long time ago. . . . Maybe he was thinking of something else.

He was. Nonetheless, he took a breath and launched into a little speech. He had deep feelings for her, he said. Yes, very deep feelings. It went beyond their former relationship. He wanted her to forget about that. This was different. He wasn't her Unca Umby, see? But before she got any ideas. . . . He raised his hand, to stop her from replying. Just let him finish. He wasn't some dirty old man.

He actually used those words. "I'm not some dirty old man," he said. "I'm not interested in that kind of stuff. Oh, maybe a little kiss, a little squeeze." He laughed uncomfortably.

She sat there, gazing at him, wondering. Was she supposed to jump up and kiss him, hug him? She liked him. She thought he was smart, a strong, deep, mysterious man. She thought that, if it came to that, she would go to bed with him. She had long ago decided that sex didn't commit you to anything. But what did he want?

What he wanted, it seemed, was an intimacy. He felt they were practically there already. He wanted, he said, someone he could level with.

Well. That wasn't much, she thought, at first. But then she began to see what he meant. He hadn't had anybody for some time with whom he could talk unguardedly, someone he could trust and believe in. He was willing to eschew certain physical liberties to have this. He wouldn't be pawing her, wouldn't expect. . . . He left it unsaid.

Maybe he'd never had this intimacy, she thought. He'd had some kind of rapport with Carmine, his lifelong pal, almost a brother. That wasn't the same, at all, couldn't have been. He needed this intimacy with a woman, but a special kind of woman. Someone like her. Perhaps there wasn't any other such woman on the planet, she thought. She felt strangely proud to be that one person, that woman. Her heart filled with empathy toward him.

He had stopped talking. The boat rumbled along, its powerful engine nearly silent, but felt. The water was blue and the waves were light. The sun danced on occasional sprays. It was warm on their backs. They had turned and were angling toward the distant shore, toward home. He must have given some kind of signal to the helmsman. She hadn't caught it.

"So, whaddaya think?" he said, comically. He smiled sadly at her. He had brown eyes, she noticed. Well, she'd always known they were brown, but now she saw that they were. So this man wants me, she thought, gazing at him. She felt fond. He wants a—what was the word? morganatic? no—wife who can be intimate in a wifely way, but with a difference. An intimate. But not ultimately intimate. An arms-length romance.

"I could do that," she said.

They both laughed. He gave her hand a squeeze and she kissed his cheek. "You're sweet," she said. And suddenly, she was filled with affection for him. She wanted to say, "You know what? I love you, you big lug," or something coolly, movieish. But she didn't.

"You're great," he said.

"I think we can be great together," she replied. "But one thing. What about this what's-her-name? Are you still pining for her? You know, I can't have that."

"Oh, no way," he assured her, solemnly, shaking his head. "I've never even seen her again, I swear."

"Well, you don't have to swear," Helen told him. "Anyway, for all we know she might be dead."

He didn't like that thought, she saw instantly. That had been a mistake. But then he seemed to brush the thought aside.

"What about Joe?" he said abruptly. "You still carrying a torch for him?"

She almost gulped. She'd forgotten about Joe. Just thinking of him now made her feel like a fool. What had she been thinking of? Romancing Humphrey, imagining some kind of weird affair, and all the time. . . . What about Joe? Her foolish heart was wrenched.

"Joe?" she said, faintly. "Ah, well, Joe . . . I haven't seen Joe. I don't even know where he is, what he's doing." Firmly, she declared, "I haven't given a thought to Joe in weeks. That's over. That's past."

Humphrey looked at her closely, then nodded. He seemed satisfied. "Okay," he said. "Good. I like Joe. I always liked Joe. Me and him, we got along. The best I ever saw at what he does. So it wouldn't bother you to see him?"

"You've seen him!" She throttled back her sudden enthusiasm, tried to sound indifferent: "You heard from him?"

Humphrey elected to ignore her sudden excitement, she was relieved to see. "No," he said, offhandedly, "but I got a feeling."

"What kind of feeling?"

"A feeling like we haven't seen the last of Joe Service," he said. He wouldn't say any more. He had a feeling.

They soon docked. It had been a fine day. Her mother stayed for supper. Roman stayed too, of course, but he acted kind of funny around Helen. He looked at her almost reproachfully, she thought, but he didn't say anything. The new chef had prepared grilled salmon with two sauces, one of them a peppery one for Humphrey. Soke talked recipes. She sampled the peppery one. She used to cook with peppers, she said, Hungarian and Italian ones, but not this hot. This was too hot, she said. It was too much for the salmon. Humphrey disagreed, but politely. He had a theory that peppers never really masked other flavors but actually brought them out. Now, heavy cream sauces, he said, that could mask flavor.

After that day, things changed. There was a new intimacy. Not only did Humphrey begin to tell her inside things about the business, sometimes shocking her, but he began to act more possessive, in public. They would be talking to other men, his underlings, men with position, and he would insist that Helen be included in the talk. He'd ask her opinion, or voice "their" opinion—"*We* think . . ." or "In *our* opinion. . . ." And he'd sometimes rest his hand on her shoulder, or her waist.

She liked it. She was beginning to know her way around. She would talk about business practices, informatively, authoritatively, and Humphrey would beam at her, agreeing with her. Telling the other men, "You see? She's a bright one. That's the ticket. That's what we gotta do."

The one area where they didn't agree was the cigar business. He couldn't see her scheme. He listened to her spiel, discussed it with her and Berta. Unfortunately, Berta wasn't her best ally. She claimed that the problems were too intractable. Sure, Humphrey still knew people in Cuba, he could get tobacco, it could be smuggled in. But what was the point? They couldn't make as good a product as the Cubans, or even the Dominicans. And where was the market? Guys weren't going to pay the kind of prices they'd have to ask to make it worthwhile, not while they could get Dominicans and, even, smuggled Cubans. At best, over a period of time, they might build up a small, loyal customer base, but they could never be big while they couldn't go public.

The problem was, their major market consisted of guys who liked Cuban cigars, and even liked the added sense of adventure and danger that went with smuggling them in from trips to Canada or overseas. They couldn't compete with that. And these guys tended to know their cigars. They wouldn't accept a homemade version, even if somehow you could convince them that this cigar was what it was: a cigar hand-rolled by rollers from Cuba, using Cuban tobacco. It was not going to be a top-of-the-line Cuban cigar, not for a long time, anyway. But with the cost of production, her cigar—he called it "LaDonna Detroit"—would have to be priced up there with the real goods. It couldn't compete. And once the embargo was lifted, as it had to be, someday, the whole game was up. Who could compete then?

He finally conceded that maybe, what the hell, if she really wanted it, they could make a cigar and sell it at a loss. He figured the quality of the tobacco would guarantee at least a five-dollar price, maybe a little more. The cigar business was booming, after all, crazier things were happening. They'd lose money on every cigar they sold, but he could afford it. If that's what she wanted.

No, she didn't want that. She was too good a businesswoman. She believed that with Berta's help she could get her girls to turn out a quality cigar. They could go two ways: her girls would slap labels on them, any label she wanted, and they could be peddled as "illegal" Cuban "seconds"; and they'd also work on a public, over-the-counter cigar, the LaDonna series. Five bucks. Basically the same cigar, quality tobacco from the Dominican

Republic, Honduras, and so on; they'd be good cigars; they might lose money for a while, but they would slowly build a clientele. You could consider it a form of advertising, buying a market. Then, who knows, a year or two down the road . . . they could maybe jack up the price, get in the black.

She was satisfied, for now.

And then, Joe called.

11

Joe's Nature

Dinah Schwind watched Joe from her apartment. He had been by the building at least twice, but she had a feeling that he had been by more than that. She stood at the fourth-floor window, gazing through the muslin curtains. She had to smile. He looked goofy as hell, she thought. Where did he get that outfit? He was in jeans, very fancy cowboy boots, and even a hat. His mustache was full, already, she saw, and it had a western look, too—kind of droopy at the corners. Goofy but also, she had to admit, attractive. She couldn't imagine many men capable of carrying off this absurd drugstore cowboy look.

She had not liked very many men in her thirty-four years. She liked her dad. He was not what some would call a successful man—a finish carpenter. He didn't make a lot of money. He took too long. He was not a union carpenter. He worked in upstate New York. A nice guy. A family man. Her mother was nice, but she seemed to favor Dinah's older sister, who was pretty. Her sister had married a doctor, had babies, and that was her mother's interest: Jennifer and the kids, and Dr. Swanson. Her mother almost never called Jennifer's husband Glen, but Dr. Swanson. She was appalled that Dinah had become a federal agent. They sent her to law school for this? She'd done so well at the state university in Rochester. She had offers from many fine law firms but went into enforcement. What a waste.

Joe had disappeared. She moved the curtain aside, looked up and down the street. It was not a busy street, one of those north side Chicago streets with a store on the corner, a tavern, cars parked. Where had he gone? She let the curtain drop. Damn! Well, he'd no doubt come knocking when he was ready. But he must be pretty strung out, nervous as a cat. Although he hadn't looked nervous down there.

Some people, she thought, seemed to have a kind of unself-consciousness. Certain athletes, for instance. They moved about with remarkable grace but didn't seem aware of it. Joe had that. He'd looked natural as hell down there, a cowboy in a ridiculous outfit, perfectly at home on a residential street in Chicago. But he must be running scared.

She hoped he wouldn't be long. She was cooking something that she hoped he would like, braised lamb shanks. It had to be something of that sort, something that could be kept warm, because she hadn't been sure when he would show. It was a very tasty recipe; she'd picked it up in the Mideast.

She wasn't sure why she'd bothered. Maybe she felt that she owed him something. She had tossed him into a losing situation, as she saw it, and he had come out smelling like a rose and making her look like a genius. From Joe's point of view, of course, it was an opportunity. It had gotten him out of the hospital, headed off an indictment, almost certainly a long stretch in prison. But he'd hardly blinked. And now that she thought about it, she wasn't so sure that she had actually saved him from anything. His budding deal with the deputy sheriff had looked lame, grasping at straws, but now she thought he might have made that work. He might have been better off.

The problem was the colonel. He had absolutely insisted on Joe. You'd have thought he would be pissed, the way Joe had snookered him. Joe had, in fact, left the colonel handcuffed to a pipe in a house the colonel himself had staked out. The hunter wasn't supposed to be caught in his own trap. But the colonel was like that: extremely practical. No, the colonel just shrugged it off.

"Sometimes it's not the horse," the colonel said, "it's the jockey. That doesn't mean you want to trade horses, of course."

She looked at the lamb shanks. They were getting pretty tender, but the onions and raisins and cinnamon . . .

"Smells good," Joe said.

She somehow prevented herself from whirling about. She looked over her shoulder and raised an eyebrow. "It's an old recipe," she said. "Want some?"

"I'm starving," he said. He smiled.

White teeth. Some people were born with even, white teeth. That would be Joe. She was willing to bet that he'd never been to a dentist in his life, that he did not floss regularly.

He was leaning against the doorjamb, facing into the kitchen, his hands in his jeans pockets. He seemed totally at ease. For a man who had spent weeks in the hospital, he looked as fit as a gymnast. Good color. He appeared taller than five-whatever. Maybe it was the high heels of the cowboy boots. But he had such an elegant shape; even in the floppy ER greens he'd escaped in, he'd looked taller. He had a swimmer's build: wide shoulders, slim hips.

Dinah Schwind was suddenly shocked. For the first time in her life she had looked at a man and wondered what his belly was like, what his thighs were like, his penis. She had never had such a reaction in her life.

"Something wrong?" Joe said.

"I have to put on the rice," she said.

"I should have called to set a time," Joe said. "Put it on! I'm starving. Do you need some help?"

"No, no, I'll get it. I already made the salad, and I bought some flat bread. I saw you hanging around on the corner." She turned to her tasks, eager to be busy.

"Not too cool, eh?" Joe said. "Well, I came by earlier, but I guess you weren't here."

"Came by?" She looked at him. She was stirring the rice in the oil, before adding the stock. "You mean, you came in?"

"I didn't think you'd mind," he said. "We're partners, eh? I thought it was better than getting a place."

"You're not thinking of staying here?" She poured the hot stock over the rice and set it on a low burner.

"Whatever you say," Joe said indifferently. He pulled out a kitchen chair and sat on it, casually. "We going to eat in here? Or do you want me to set the dining table?" He nodded toward the nearby dining room.

"Open the wine," she said. "Will this Oregon pinot do? It's kind of full-bodied, but it has a dryness that should go with the lamb and the sauce."

He thought it sounded fine and he opened the bottle and poured for both of them. They tasted it. She was right. It was good, a solid wine, but a little young.

She didn't ask him how he'd gotten in. She might later. It was worth knowing. In the event, he volunteered the information: he'd told the super that he was her brother. Just back from Paris. Very friendly guy, the super. Thought Joe and Dinah were very much alike, not in looks, so much, although the nose. . . . She laughed. Later, she considered that he obviously had conned the super, but there were still a couple of details, field craft . . . that hadn't been the whole story.

The lamb was very good and they ate it all, and all of the rice and the salad. They drank two bottles of the wine. She couldn't wait to tell him how pleased they were with his work.

"It was surgical," she declared. She said it several times, with an enthusiastic emphasis on the first syllable, *surgical*.

"Just luck," Joe said. "Five minutes before the bell, I was ready to bolt. But then . . . everything worked out."

"You're kidding," she said. "You seemed cool."

"Where were you?" he asked.

"Inside the fence," she said.

Joe doubted that, but he didn't say anything. There was nothing she could do inside the fence. Unless . . . "You were set to pop Echeverria when I didn't?" he said.

She shrugged. "We considered it. If the operation didn't go well."

But then, he thought, you would be inside the fence. Maybe that would be all right, but he was skeptical. "Well, luckily, everything went well." He raised his brows. "How is Mr. E?"

She shook her head. "He didn't make it," she said. "You didn't know?"

"You did a good job of press management," Joe said. "Anyway, I did what I could. If I didn't succeed, well, that's life. Have to wait for another chance."

She was amazed. She thought she'd seen just about all there was on offer, killers, robbers, con men, revolutionaries, high-rolling mobsters, hardened janissaries . . . but she had never seen anyone so cool. "Do you enjoy this . . . work?" she asked.

Joe looked puzzled. "It's fun," he said. "It's exciting. Besides . . . well, what are we talking about this for? You know what I can do." He leaned forward, suddenly. They were sitting not across from each other but across a corner. "You know what I'd like to do?"

She shook her head, flustered. "What?"

"I'd like to go to bed with you."

That's what she heard—at first. But then she realized he'd said, "Do you have a bed I can use?"

She had a bed, in a guest room, for when her parents visited. But Joe told her he preferred her bed. "Don't get excited," he said, "I don't have any amatory plans. I just think I'd like you close by. Anyway, the last time I got amorous I ended up in the hospital. I think I'm going to have to ease into that."

When they were lying chastely, side by side but not touching, he said, "What happened with Echeverria?"

She explained that the fire had quickly engulfed the ambulance. Echeverria hadn't had a chance. It was a fluke. The driver of the ambulance had thought he was protecting the patient by driving around the plane. He'd thought the danger was from the guard shooting. But then, seeing the plane on fire, he'd panicked and fled. Nobody blamed him. Perhaps the attendants could have dragged Echeverria out, but. . . . Nobody was blamed.

"How about me?" Joe said. "Do they connect me with it?"

"Not so far," she said. "The cops might have, if they'd gotten hold of the truck you abandoned. But one of our guys spotted it and just hopped in and drove it away. Good thing you left the keys."

Joe didn't comment. He was asleep, but with his arm flung over her body. Presumably, he just wanted to make sure she didn't get up without him knowing, but she couldn't help hoping there was more to it. She lay there for a long time, willing him to wake up. They could talk, maybe make love. Then she drifted off.

In the morning, she woke to the sound of the shower. Joe came out shortly. He was naked, toweling himself dry. She looked up at him and tossed the covers back, frankly invitational. She was naked, too. Joe looked down at her and smiled. She looked a lot better naked. He admired that kind of lean, hard fitness. He sat down on the bed and laid his hand on her hip. She was very warm. She shifted lazily, her thighs opening. She laid her hand on his penis. It grew.

Joe was tempted. He had the desire, he was sure it would be satisfying, maybe even thrilling, and he didn't want to disappoint her . . . but he wasn't ready to trust her. He didn't want her to see that, however, so he opted for lameness. He leaned over the bed and kissed her cheek.

"Not today," he said.

"Scared?" she teased.

"You bet." He stood up and took his stiff cock in his left hand. "When this gets like this"—he shook his cock, while tapping his head with the forefinger of his right hand—"it's like the circuits get overloaded. Sometimes, fuses blow."

"It looks like it's functioning all right," she said. "Maybe a little exercise would be good for it."

"Maybe," he said. "Maybe later."

He dressed and went to make coffee for them. "Now tell me again," he said, as they sat at the kitchen table, "how you're going to pay me."

"Pay you?" She shook her head. "You got paid, for this one. We got you out. Maybe another time, another scenario, there'll be some money. You can keep what you find."

"You mean the scenario where I knock off some dope dealers?"

"Something like that," she said.

"Well, how about that," Joe said, disgustedly. "I bust my buns for you, I'm on the run, and you guys say 'Thanks, your country is grateful, but . . .' You are grateful, aren't you?"

"I said we were grateful, last night. And we've got more plans. Don't get so uptight. Of course, we can provide you with some money, a little, if you need it. But it's not like you're making a big score, you know. I explained all this from the start."

"You painted a rosier picture in the hospital," Joe said. He considered the situation briefly, then decided. "All right, this one's gratis. I'd have gotten out anyway, but you helped, you made it easier. So what's next? Do we fry another dope dealer?"

"First, the others have to meet you. It's absolutely essential," she said.

"What if I don't want to meet them?"

"Joe." She sighed. "Don't be this way. Don't force me to use pressure."

"You mean blow my cover?" He laughed. "And then I'd blow your operation. But you figure that A, I wouldn't do that, and B, who would believe me?"

"Something like that," she said. "But it's more, 'Why should you do that?' Your old role with the mob is blown, pretty much. You need something to do. This is a good job for you."

"You mean lots of kicks, fighting the war against drugs, Our Nation's enemies, that sort of thing?" he said. He paused and eyed her thoughtfully. "You said, 'pretty much.' What does that mean?"

"You caught that, did you? It means that we don't think you're *completely* blown with the mob. You've still got friends there."

Joe nodded slowly. He saw it. They figured he still had a connection. With Helen. So she must have been taken back under Humphrey's wing. And maybe they thought that Joe could still approach Humphrey himself. He wasn't so sure. But if it were so, what would be the point? Then he got it.

"You want me to hit Humphrey," he said.

"Gosh, what an idea! It's so crazy, it just might work!"

Joe was surprised. It wasn't like Schwind to joke. His amazement sobered her.

"Sorry," she said. "I didn't mean to make light of it. Actually, we weren't thinking of that, particularly."

"Any more than you were thinking Echeverria should get toasted," he said.

"No, really. It's just. . . . Here's the situation." She explained that recently they had become aware of a change in activity in Detroit. Humphrey seemed to be pulling back, or at least realigning his enterprises, changing his focus. People were being shuffled around, Humphrey wasn't making his normal appearances, money was being shifted. These phenomena were more felt than strictly observed. But the overall picture was getting distorted, hard to see.

"Something is happening," Joe prompted, with a musical lilt in his voice, "but you don't know what it is."

"Yes," she said. "We had an agent in there, a very good man. But he disappeared. A little while back, his body floated up, without a head. We think Humphrey tumbled to him and had him killed. We want to know what happened, and what's happening now. We think you could find out."

"And what's my end?"

"Your end?" She sighed. "You know, over the years I've had my hands on . . . oh, I'd guess about ten or twenty million bucks. Contraband, confiscated loot. I never took a penny, although in many cases there was not another person who could have said that I had, or even noticed, really. I was never even tempted, Joe. It wasn't my money. I couldn't have said, in most cases, whose money it was. Maybe it was no one's. But it wasn't mine. If you want money, Joe, I'm sure we can supply you with money, from those sources. It wouldn't bother me. Just because I don't take it, that doesn't mean that you can't . . . assuming, of course, that it isn't otherwise accounted for."

"That's nice to hear," Joe said, "but it's kind of iffy. I don't work on those terms. I like to know what I'm putting my ass on the line for. And," he continued, carefully emphasizing each word, "*I want to collect.* You see, that's what started all this: Carmine hired me to do a job, but then he didn't want to pay off."

"Okay, we'll pay you," she said.

"Pay me what? You keep saying that, but you don't mention figures. I'm just a simple guy, Dinah. I don't go in for philosophy. What's the payoff?"

"What do you want?"

"I want immunity. Freedom. Money. A new car. Time to myself. Better movies. Let's see . . ."

"I see," she said. "Immunity is the problem. You're in the system now, Joe. You have a number of charges pending against you. In order to get any of them dropped, to obtain official protection, we'd have to employ you. We'd have to be able to say what you were going to do for us. And we can't do that. But . . ." She pondered for a minute. "There may be something. I'll have to confer with the others. Possibly . . . I'm just thinking out loud, now . . . we could get you some kind of protection, get your name removed from the wanted computers, give you some kind of cover. But I think you'd still be vulnerable to arrest and detention, and prosecution, if some obstinate cop or prosecutor or judge insisted. I'll try, if you're content with that."

"It'll do for now," Joe said. "It just means being careful. But then, I'm always careful. The guy I have to watch out for is Mulheisen."

"The Detroit cop?" Schwind was surprised.

"I guess you don't know Mulheisen," Joe said.

"I've met him. He wasn't impressive. Seemed a little dense, even, a time server. I mean, the guy is a little long in the tooth to still be a sergeant of detectives, isn't he?"

"What is that, a joke? Look, I don't care what his rank is. The guy is a force of nature, or something. Water flows downhill, at thirty-two degrees it turns to ice, at two twelve it turns to steam. Mulheisen keeps looking. He probably doesn't even know why he does it. You've heard the story of the fox and the goose?"

"The fox wants a ride across the river?" Schwind said. "Is it like the scorpion and the frog?"

"I think so," Joe said. "The fox pleads mutual self-interest, but then he bites the goose's neck in midstream—"

"They're both going down and the goose cries out, 'Why?'"

"And the fox says, 'It's my nature.' Well, enough of fables, go ahead, find out from your pals." Joe gestured at the telephone. She seemed reluctant. He said, "I'll leave."

The next time she heard from him he was in Detroit and he wanted a boat.

12

Kiss and Make Up

Humphrey seemed a little uneasy. Helen hardly noticed, she was so excited about seeing Joe again. But she did notice, finally, when they were motoring out of the slip onto the lake, aboard *Kiddle-Dee-Divey*. Humphrey was running the boat, only the two of them aboard. Joe was supposed to meet them at Peach Island, in the Detroit River. Once again, it was pleasant weather, though not as sunny as on their last boating jaunt. It was the familiar high, thin overcast, quite bright out—they both wore sunglasses—but a little breezy. The lake was gray and choppy.

"What are you worried about?" Helen asked.

Humphrey shrugged. He looked very fit and nautical today, wearing a navy blue cashmere turtleneck under a windbreaker but, as always, no hat. If Humphrey had any vanity, it was about his hair, which was still dark and thick. He didn't like hats. He ran the boat with confidence, no fussing.

"I'm not sure about Joe," Humphrey confessed. Helen looked surprised, and he went on: "Joe can be difficult. Hell, he usually is difficult. But usually it's a put-on. Lotta swagger, the perennial wise guy. Most a the time, he had a legitimate beef—about Carmine. You know," he said, thoughtfully, "I ain't seen the guy in—what?

A year? Not since before he split for Montana with you. I talked to him, a couple times, but we didn't meet. I'm not sure of him, and I know he ain't sure of me. I'm countin' on you to make it good between us."

"Well, of course," she said, as if it were all agreed. "Can't we go a little faster?"

Humphrey looked at his watch. "We got plenty of time. I don't wanta get there before Joe. I don't want him thinkin' we're settin' something up."

A downbound freighter was looming in the eastern approach to the Fleming Channel. There was little other traffic out today, a few sailboats, a handful of motorcraft. Humphrey took the sleek cabin cruiser across the channel well ahead of the freighter and throttled back as they approached the upbound channel along the Canadian shore. They were still well east of Peach Island.

"Setting something up?" Helen said. "Why should he think that? He called us. I thought this was all for his security. I mean, he's the fugitive. He must feel pretty secure or he wouldn't have agreed to this boat business."

"Oh, I don't think Joe's too worried about being spotted by anyone," Humphrey said. "It's just . . . well, there's something a little funny here. You remember that plane that got blown up in Salt Lake City last week?"

Helen didn't. She hadn't noticed.

"You remember that guy, Echeverria?"

Helen remembered him all right. She had almost taken a plane ride with him, up in Montana.

"That was his plane," Humphrey said. "And Joe walked out of that hospital in Denver just a few days before. There was something about that, made me think of Joe. Vetch got torched in that plane hit. Now, I know it ain't like Joe to go around torchin' guys just 'cause they caused him a little trouble, but . . . I don't know, there was something about it. And now, a few days later, Joe calls. So, I set this up. This way, Joe can see it's just me and you, and we can see it's just Joe."

"So what do we do? Pull alongside? There could be people below. Or do we stand off, like in *Moby-Dick*, and shout at each other through megaphones?"

"We both pull up and anchor off the island. Actually, it's very shallow there, a couple feet. We can run right in and wade ashore, maybe even jump ashore. These boats don't have much draft. We'll probably get a little wet, but it ain't that cold."

They ran down toward the island. Helen pursued the question of Joe's activities. "You think he's working for someone?" she asked. "Like Mitch? The eastern organization?"

"I doubt he's workin' for Mitch," Humphrey said. "Those guys are still pissed he's out walkin' around. No, I don't know what the deal is. Joe don't like to work with other people, much, but he likes money. It took a little help to get out of that hospital, but maybe he just charmed his way out. Maybe he just misses us—you, anyways. Then again, maybe he's wacko. Maybe he's flipped out. I don't know. Do you?"

Helen had to admit that she'd had some thoughts along those lines herself. A man who has been shot in the head, seemingly recovered, but then had some kind of relapse. . . . Who could say?

"Could be he's on some psycho vendetta," Humphrey said. "But he's always been a kind of bold guy who did things different, so maybe this is just normal—for Joe." He tapped his forehead with a finger. "Could be, he's got some new clients. Well, we'll see. There he is."

They had swung around the head of the island, on the Canadian side, and there was the little sixteen-foot powerboat with an open cockpit, with Joe Service sitting jauntily on the gunwale. He was not in cowboy gear, but more like an outdoor-catalog version of what the sporty yachtsman wears: colorful windbreaker, light sweater, rainproof pants, bare feet in deck shoes. No hat, of course. But wraparound shades. Helen thought he looked terrific, but she didn't care for the closely clipped beard and mustache. She felt it hid his finely chiseled chin and emphasized his sensual lips too much. But she soon forgot that.

There was no uneasiness now. They pulled alongside and she leaped onto the deck, embracing Joe. They laughed and hugged, even kissed. Humphrey beamed and stepped across, a little more carefully than Helen, but still quite agilely. He too embraced Joe. Helen stood back for a moment, grinning at them. They were all clearly delighted to be reunited, though Helen noticed that Humphrey, for all his jovial exuberance, made sure to hug Joe thoroughly and practically pat him down.

Joe noticed it too, but he joked: "Hey, Slim, take it easy! I'm not wired. I'm not packing." It was clear, though, that he had made sure of Humphrey's lack of weaponry in their embrace. But now that formality was over. They were just glad.

"My god," Joe said, stepping back to look Humphrey over, "they said you were slimmed down, but this is amazing. You look like a fashion model." He laughed, and Humphrey laughed too.

"Actually, I gained back a few pounds, lately," Humphrey said. "Gee, it's good to see ya, Joe."

They all agreed, it was great to see each other. They quickly moved to the more comfortable boat, the *Kiddle-Dee-Divey*. They were standing in the well of the open rear cockpit, still delightedly patting each other's backs, when Humphrey looked over at Joe's speedboat and said, "Helluva nice little rig, Joe. How'd you get hold of her?"

"Ah, the Feds got it for me," Joe tossed off.

Humphrey and Helen both turned to stare at him, not quite with open mouths but clearly waiting for the punch line. "The Feds?" Helen said, after a while.

"Yeah, I'm working for the government these days," Joe answered innocently. "Hey, don't look at me! A guy's gotta make his car payments."

"You're working for the Feds?" Humphrey sounded disbelieving.

"Sorta," Joe said. "I get the feeling I'm still kind of on probation. But they like my work, so far."

"So far," Humphrey said. "You mean the Salt Lake City job."

Joe nodded. "They helped me walk, in Denver. I felt I had to return the favor. I got a new assignment, now." He waited. They waited. Finally, he said, looking at Humphrey: "You."

There was a silence in which the gentle slapping of wavelets against the boat's hull could be heard. It seemed longer than it was. Then Humphrey smiled. "How can I help?" he said.

They all laughed.

The ensuing discussion lasted for at least a couple hours. Fortunately, Humphrey had arranged for a lunch to be put aboard, of cold roast beef, fresh sourdough bread, three excellent cheeses, and a hot chili stew. He explained that this wasn't chili, per se, but a pork stew with root vegetables and chilis. They ate it all.

They ate and laughed and kidded each other, and Helen was pleased to see that Humphrey didn't seem at all disturbed by her obvious physical closeness to Joe. The two of them sat side by side on the banquette in the cabin and she stroked his hands, or his cheek, even kissed him a couple of times. Humphrey seemed easy with this. He smiled and nodded, almost like a real uncle.

Joe told them about Agent Schwind and her friends. He hadn't met the friends yet, but he was pretty sure he knew who was the chief, a guy who went by the name of Colonel Vernon Tucker, presumably a retired Air Force officer, now a federal agent of some kind. Helen was mildly amazed. She remembered the colonel from the incident at her rented house in Salt Lake City. She was curious about the colonel's attitude toward her, naturally. He had actually witnessed the attack by the hit woman Heather, in which Helen had managed to blast the killer.

Joe explained that it was her smurfing of money that had initially caught the attention of the Colonel and his team. They had staked the house out, hoping to rope in a few more confederates in what they saw as a scheme to launder dope proceeds. The intervention of Heather was inexplicable to everyone there, although Joe had encountered her earlier, up in Montana.

It was Humphrey's turn to explain. He swore he'd had nothing to do with Heather. He had explained it all to Helen, much earlier. It had been a faction of the mob that was working against him. This problem had been resolved, more or less, although there were some aspects of it he wanted to discuss further with both of them. The main item for discussion, though, was Joe's relationship with the Colonel and Schwind.

"Basically," Joe said, "they want me to take you out. But they don't put it that way. Not yet. They're a careful bunch. They want me to re-establish myself within your organization. I'm supposed to be some kind of spy. Now, I can tell you I'm not a spy and you can believe me or not, it's up to you. I come to you as a friend. You were always straight with me, F—, er . . . " Joe hesitated.

"You can call me Fat, Joe," Humphrey said amiably. "But only you."

"I'll call you Slim," Joe said. "That's what popped out before, without thinking. Anyway, you and I never had any problems. It was always Carmine. I understood that. But Schwind and the colonel don't know that. They think I've got a real beef with you, but it's something we can work out. Plus they think they have a hold on me, because I'm a fugitive, or maybe they think they can hang the Salt Lake City thing on me. Who knows, if we're talking about convincing a jury, they probably could. They'll have fingerprints on rocket launchers, cars, that sort of thing. They could make a case that I was seeking revenge against Echeverria. The point is: they think they've got leverage here, that I'm their man. They seem to be able to delude themselves, about that and a lot of things. They think they're lonely crusaders against crime, something like that. Me, I don't have any illusions. I'm just Joe Service, at yo' service."

He paused, looking from one to the other of them. When they didn't say anything, he went on: "See, their theory is that beef or no beef, I can get back in with you. I figure they're not so far out in that."

Helen and Humphrey both signaled their acceptance of this assessment.

Joe went on: "Once I'm inside, I'm supposed to feed them info and maybe, ultimately, I take you down." He pointed to Humphrey. "They didn't say anything about you, honey," he told Helen, with a smile. "They're very vague about this. But that's their style. On the one hand they're running this rogue-agent show, but then they're like any bureaucratic operation—it's in their genes, or something. Sometimes, I wonder if they even know what they want. It looks to me like they're trying to be the cowboys *and* the Indians. But here I am. So, what's the situation? How do we get out of this one?"

"It's amazing," Humphrey said, shaking his head. "I couldn't have asked for better."

"Really?" Joe said.

"These people are a gift from the gods," Humphrey said. "Let me explain. I already told Helen a lot a this, but not all of it." He told them he had concluded that the day of the old mob was over. He found it ironic, that he had worked to achieve something, to become someone, only to find upon attaining his goal that the game had irrevocably changed. It was a natural progression of events, he had decided. Times had changed. New people come in, new opportunities arise. New problems arise. If the old organization doesn't address these problems, these opportunities, it gets pushed aside.

"I got nobody to blame but myself," he said. "Well, maybe Carmine, too." He had not been shrewd enough, and Carmine had refused to change. Nowadays, most of the organization's income was derived from essentially legitimate enterprises—with a little of the old scamming and chiseling and muscle applied as part of the new business technique. Nowadays, he claimed, the regular business world had absorbed the mob's techniques, their hard policies. Whatever, he'd had enough of it.

"I'm too old to start over," he said. "But I ain't exactly old. I'm glad I'm still able to enjoy life. What I want is to step out, to pursue my own private interests. I'm outta here, as the kids say. But you guys, you're young, full of drive. You can take this show in any direction you want. Now, I've made some plans, and you can help . . . if you wanta."

Joe didn't seem very comfortable with this. He'd never envisioned himself as a mobster. He wasn't interested in running rackets. Helen wasn't either, not in that sense. She was interested in business, however. They wanted to hear more.

Humphrey looked at them, as if sizing them up, then plunged right in: "First, some old business. I ain't interested in that money Big Sid took. I don't wanta hear no more about it. I got plenty of my own. I made my arrangements. That's all I can say about that, for now. I could use your help, both a you, on a couple details. But you can tell your new friends, Joe, that you seen me and I said we could let bygones be bygones. Maybe that'll satisfy them for now. I think I got it set up, pretty much, so that Helen can step in and run things. It won't be much trouble, for a little while, and then you can figure out whether you wanta go on with it."

Their noncommittal stance didn't seem to bother him. He shrugged and continued. "The thing is, when I say I'm outta here, I mean outta here. There ain't no quiet retirements in this game. I been working out a way so it looks like I copped it. This business with the feds could be a big help. You guys could make it work, if you're willing."

Joe smiled. "Like you say, Slim: 'How can I help?'"

The three men arrived at Humphrey's compound separately, a few minutes apart. The first man was Kenny Malateste. He was thirty years old, a nice-looking fellow with a heavy beard that reappeared within an hour of shaving. He was smiling and flirtatious with Helen, familiar even, although they had met only a couple of times. Already he was holding her arm, talking her ear off. She got him a shot of Humphrey's favorite single malt, from a bottle that had a brown paper label that was hand-lettered—only a few hundred gallons of this whiskey were made in a year, and then put to age for twenty years or more. Helen couldn't pronounce the name. She told Kenny not to tell anyone: Humphrey would kill her if he knew it wasn't Glenfiddich in that glass.

The second man was older, a stocky middle-aged man who looked like a pile of rocks in a blue suit. The broad collar of his yellow sport shirt was spread on his suit-coat lapels, and he wore dully brushed brogans. He had a belligerent face and the manner to match. His name was Leonardo, but he was called Nardo. He stood by himself, rubbing his hands, not nervously but in a habitual manner, flexing his hand, forearm, and upper-arm muscles. He watched everybody, his eyes glittering. He refused whiskey, but asked for a Stroh's. "Bottle," he stipulated.

The third man was also middle-aged, but looked more youthful. He was a smooth, friendly man, well-dressed in a quiet way—a good suit, well cut, and deeply burnished cordovan shoes that could have been made for him. He was called Aldo Soteri. He happily settled for a Scotch and soda.

They stood around chatting for fifteen minutes with Helen and Humphrey and one another, although Nardo barely nodded to the other two guests. The talk was about the Red Wings, the Tigers, the weather, the traffic. Soteri and Helen talked about golf. But soon enough a young male servant, a Filipino, came to the living room and announced that dinner was served.

Dinner was prime rib, a crown roast. The guests looked relieved. They had fearfully anticipated another of Humphrey's peppery preferences. Nothing to fear with prime rib. It was delicious. The Yorkshire pudding was superb, the roast potatoes beautifully caramelized, the carrots done to the very edge of softness, but not quite. The wines were robust, not pretentious, very drinkable. For dessert, there was a delicious puff pastry filled with custard and drenched in chocolate syrup, but Helen and Humphrey did not eat theirs, so neither did the three guests. They all drank the good black coffee, however.

Afterward, back in the living room, they tasted Humphrey's excellent cognac and they seemed delighted with the LaDonna cigars that Helen offered around. She explained that they were, in fact, Cuban in everything but place of manufacture. Nardo, in fact, asked for and promptly received a box to take home. He liked a good Cuban cigar, he said. He was almost amiable.

Business. Humphrey said it was a shame, after a fine evening with friends, but, without business, what did you have? The news was generally good, except for this trouble with the sanitation contracts. Nardo was the garbage man, he should know who was behind these lost contracts. No? Well, Humphrey knew. It was an Armenian bandit named Pelodian, moving in from Cleveland, of all places. This could not stand: Pelodian had to go. If Nardo saw it Humphrey's way, he would take care of it. Nardo saw it just that way. He would take care of it.

"Good man," Humphrey said. "I gotta tell you, it was Helen who figured out who was behind this. The guy's been underbidding our contracts under a dozen names. Here's where you can find him." Humphrey gave Nardo a piece of paper with a couple of addresses on it, one of them circled. Helen said that if those didn't find Pelodian, give her a call, she had a couple of other leads, maybe she could even pinpoint when he would be at one of them.

"Don't worry, lady," Nardo rasped, "I can find the bastard." But then he remembered his manners and said, "Thanks anyway."

On to what Humphrey called "auto reclamation." That after-hours enterprise was booming, they should all emulate Aldo. His new acid technique was amazing. It took a number off the block like Ajax, and the new number was on in a matter of minutes. No muss, no fuss. A little hand for Aldo. They knew it was in fun, so only Humphrey, Helen, and Aldo applauded. Humphrey wanted a word with Aldo, later, so stick around, he said—and to Helen, "Remind me, in case I forget."

Kenny's security service was very productive. Humphrey and Helen wanted to take this opportunity to thank him for increasing his numbers. Just a super piece of work. Only, they'd heard vague reports of problems in the Eight Mile area. What about that? Kenny said, offhandedly, that they'd run into a thing with some Arabs, can you believe it?

Humphrey noted that the world was changing. These Arabs— he'd heard they were Palestinians—they don't got enough trouble in their own country, they gotta come over here and raise hell. Did Kenny know the outfit? Kenny didn't, but he was working on it, don't worry, it'll be taken care of.

So, that was that. Business was good. Humphrey and Helen thanked the guys for coming. The guys thanked them for dinner. Helen reminded Humphrey that he needed to talk to Aldo. The other two left and Aldo joined them in the study. Over a glass of the unpronounceable single malt (could it really be "Choigaloigach"?), Humphrey confided to Aldo that he was not as happy about Kenny's work as he'd let on.

"These Arabs are tougher than he thinks," Humphrey said.

"And they've got a lot of money behind them," Helen added. "This could just be the spearhead of a new invasion. The guy to watch is Hassan. He lives in Dearborn."

"Does Kenny know that?" Aldo asked.

She shrugged. "You know Kenny, if he knew he'd have said so. But he's not like Nardo—you don't hand him a piece of paper. He'll figure it out."

Aldo was clearly pleased to be let in on this inner-circle discussion. But he had little to contribute. He didn't know much about Kenny's field of expertise. It sounded serious. Did Kenny have any input on Humphrey's—and Helen's, he added, with a graceful gesture—personal security?

No, Humphrey assured him. Kenny wasn't really into "security," as such. His work was protection, which you could say was "security"—you had to protect the guys you collected from, but in the way of things, the problem almost never arose. Mainly, Kenny protected his clients from Kenny.

Anyway, that wasn't what they wanted to talk to Aldo about. Did he know there was a chop shop down on—Humphrey turned to Helen—"Where is it? Shoemaker?"

Yes, she confirmed. She gave an address on Shoemaker. Aldo was surprised. He hadn't known. But he'd check on it. Did they know who was running it?

They didn't. They were sure he'd take care of it. Just another encroachment. They were getting a lot of encroachment, these days. They hadn't mentioned it in front of the other guys, because they hadn't been able to check it out, and anyway, they didn't want to interfere. They knew Aldo would want to handle this his way. Maybe it was nothing.

Aldo appreciated their confidentiality. He hated being shown up in front of the guys. A guy like Nardo, his skin was so thick, nothing bothered him. While a Kenny, you couldn't tell him anything.

"Well, just between us," Humphrey confided, "I'm not so sure Nardo isn't slipping. This Armenian, he never coulda made any inroads in the old days. He's smart, too, which you can't exactly say about Nardo. Nardo's a tough cookie, but so is the Armenian. They eat rocks, you know. An Armenian told me that. They can live on rocks! I hope Nardo don't have no trouble."

Aldo was sure he wouldn't. And he'd be on this outlaw chop shop like . . . well, like frosting on a cake.

When he left, Humphrey shrugged. "Well, we warned them. I hope all that wasn't too much of a bringdown, baby," he said to Helen. "I know you're not into all this racket stuff."

No, she'd rather enjoyed it. It was amusing, all the posturing and grandstanding. She found Soteri a pain in the butt, but she thought Kenny was a kick, for all his strutting. She sat on the arm of Humphrey's chair and stroked his hair. She told him he was masterful, very suave. But she wondered if it was wise to take Soteri into their confidence?

"Oh, he might let it get around that we aren't so happy with Kenny and Nardo," Humphrey said, "but that's the point—he'll pass on the information. They need to know, and they ain't exactly the kind of guys you can tell to their face. They get all puffed up and belligerent. Plus, the rest of the guys need to know that we ain't sittin' on our hands, we're a little annoyed. This will put them on edge. Maybe they'll sharpen up."

Helen didn't comment, but she wasn't so sure of the strategy. "Where's Joe?" she asked. She'd held off asking all night.

"I can't have Joe coming here," Humphrey reminded her. "It don't look good. When I'm outta the picture, you can bring in Joe. That's your business. But that's how it's gotta be. I thought you understood that. Say, they liked your cigars."

Helen was pleased. "They're good cigars," she said. "You'll see, this thing will work out."

"Maybe you're right," he conceded. "The operation going all right?"

"Except for Strom," she said. "We should do something about him."

"Okay," Humphrey said. "We'll find something for Strom." He got up. "I'm headin' down to the bunker, play around on the Net."

"The bunker? Where did you get that?" Helen asked.

"I don't know," Humphrey said, thinking. "Well, you know what it is, that's what we called those underground hideouts we had when we were kids: bunkers. Sometimes, we called 'em forts. Pleasant dreams."

Humphrey's bunker was not as modern as one might expect, given the electronic gear installed there. It really was much like a bunker. The house had a perfectly modern full basement, providing more than enough room for the so-called command post. Presently, it housed a small gym, complete with a weight room, a sauna, and another exercise room, where Helen often worked out. There were the usual furnace, laundry, and storage rooms, but they were discreetly partitioned off, along with a temperature- and humidity-controlled wine cellar. Space was given over to a pool table, a Ping-Pong table, and a recreation room for servants, with a large television. And still there would have been room.

For reasons of his own, Humphrey had decided that additional excavation was needed. At the far end of the basement, toward the lake, he'd had a tunnel dug, slanting deeper into the earth. The tunnel was secured by a heavy steel door, practically a vault door,

with a locking system to match. The tunnel itself was not the standard eight feet in height but, rather, a mere six feet, which induced
at least a slight stooping by most persons who used it. Few did use
it. It was also merely thirty inches across, not really wide enough
for two people abreast, and it wasn't well lit.

The walls of the tunnel were roughly finished reinforced
concrete. The room at the end of this ten-foot-long tunnel, beyond
yet another steel door with a heavy lock, was again no more than
six feet high, a twenty-by-twenty chamber, a concrete box complete
with air-conditioning and venting and fully plumbed with a neatly
partitioned shower and bathroom. The walls were concrete sheathed
with painted Sheetrock on studs. The floor was covered with an
industrial-type indoor/outdoor carpet. The computer equipment was
housed in steel racks. There was a queen-sized bed in a partitioned
alcove, a refrigerator, a microwave oven, a table and a couple of
chairs, a number of television monitors, plus a large TV for recre-
ational viewing. It gave an impression of functionality. The lighting was more than adequate, but was usually kept fairly dim. The
whole effect was definitely that of a bunker.

Yet another steel door provided an emergency exit, served
by a roughly finished tunnel, less cramped than the house entry—
this was how the various appliances and equipment were brought
in—leading to a set of steps and another locked steel door that
opened on the lawn, discreetly shielded by shrubbery. From this exit
to the dock was only a hundred feet.

Humphrey punched in the combination to the lock and let
himself in. He went immediately to the long metal desk-counter
and dialed a telephone. "That you?" he said. "It's me, yeah. All right,
I told him. He'll be coming your way. It's up to you. Okay, I can do
the job, but if I do it, you don't get the franchise. We talked about
this. You want me to do it, I got no trouble with that. All right,
then. What are you bitching about? You do it."

He hung up and made two more calls, with much the same results. "Okay," he said to himself, when he was finished, "that's that." He grabbed a jacket out of an old wooden wardrobe he'd dragged in, and went out. He took a dark Ford out of the garage and drove out the gate. Fifteen minutes later, he picked up Joe Service. Humphrey went over the plan again, while he drove to the medical offices.

"Leave the computers to me. Like most of these guys, he's got two sets of files, some of it on the computers and some of it still in the usual paper-folder files. You take care of the folders."

"Couldn't you just crack into the computers? What do they call it, 'hack' in?" Joe said. "Why do you have to be along at all?"

"I awreddy did," Humphrey said, "but they got some crypto code, which I didn't know about. The key will be in the office. Anyway, I thought you'd like company."

Joe Service smiled. He felt quite easy, if not exactly relaxed, but he could see that Humphrey was tense and excited. "Been a long time, eh Slim?" he teased.

Humphrey scowled, but then he laughed. "Yah, like the old days. If bein' the boss was more like this, I wouldn't be quittin'. Instead, it's all meetin's, that kinda crap. Guy needs to get out once in a while, get his hands dirty."

Joe wanted to warn him that it wasn't just a lark. That kind of thinking almost always led to trouble. It would be stupid to get caught doing a simple break-in: the consequences could be out of all proportion to the act. Nixon's guys had learned that the hard way. But what could he say?

Dr. Schwartz's offices were typical, in a low brick building with its own parking lot. Humphrey did not park there, but in the much larger lot at Bon Secours hospital, a block away. They casually strolled across the way to Schwartz's offices. The entry was lit, in a kind of sheltered walkway. There was no guard, but there would be an alarm system. There was no money on the premises, not much to attract burglars, and there were frequent patrols.

Humphrey had taken sensible precautions: he knew how the system worked. Doctors often worked late, or had to return to meet a patient, look something up. And Humphrey had a key. He didn't say how he'd gotten it and Joe didn't ask. They simply strolled up, unlocked, and entered. Humphrey punched the requisite numbers into the alarm system, and they went to work.

It was time-consuming, but they did not hurry. Joe found Angelo's records and then Humphrey's. He went to the secretary's desk, located the appropriate forms, where possible, and retyped them. They made little sense to him, mostly numbers, so he made sure that he got them exactly right. The various signatures—there were only a couple—were a little tricky, but he thought that because they were largely hasty scribbles, his duplications would stand up. Where the forms were not available, as with lab reports, he made do with carefully replacing the name tags with labels that were in the secretary's desk and typing in the new name.

While Joe did this, Humphrey attacked the computer files. He soon located the access codes and he knew the technique, but it was more time-consuming than he had reckoned. They were both deeply engaged in the process when the phone rang.

Joe looked across at Humphrey. "The alarm company?" he asked. The phone rang again.

Humphrey considered. "It must be," he said. "Answer it."

"You," Joe said.

The phone rang a third time.

"No, you," Humphrey said.

Joe picked up the phone. "Hi," he said. "Who? Yes, this is Dr. Schwartz. No, I'm not on call. I'm just doing a little work. What is it? Who? Are you a patient? The who? No, you'll have to call Dr. . . . Well, who's on call? Me? You're sure? Well, wait a minute. Give me your number. Where are you? I'll call you right back."

He hung up and looked at Humphrey, a look somewhere between disbelief and bafflement. "Can you believe it? Schwartz is on call. He's got a patient on his way to Bon Secours with a heart attack. They tried his home, but no answer." He glanced at the wall clock: it was after midnight.

"Find his pager number," Humphrey snapped.

"Right."

They both hunted around frantically, looking at rosters, Rolodexes, until Joe found it on a list taped to the side of the secretary's phone. He dialed the number. It was not a pager, but a cellular phone. "Dr. Schwartz!" he said. "You've got an emergency. Heart attack—Mr. Cowan. He's on his way to Bon Secours." He slammed down the phone.

"Let's git," Joe said. "I'm done. If he sees the lights when he drives by . . ."

"I'm almost done," Humphrey said. He stared at the screen before him, pecking out numbers while Joe restored the files to the cabinets. "That'll do it, I just gotta log off."

A minute later they were outside. An ambulance whizzed by as they strolled to the car.

"You know what I forgot?" Joe asked as they got in. "I didn't call that number back, to tell them I was on my way."

"It won't matter," Humphrey said. He started the car. "It's an emergency. He'll be there. Somebody called, he came. Nobody'll even remember."

"The alarm company will have an entry on their log," Joe said. "The alarm was logged off and back on, such and such a date."

"Nobody'll notice. Why should they?"

"I hope you're right," Joe said. He relaxed, then added, almost to himself, "There's always some little thing. Well, what's next, the dentist?"

Humphrey pulled an envelope out of the glove compartment. He tossed it on Joe's lap. "X-rays," he said. "Full set. Just pop 'em in my file and take the others. I already took care of Angelo's."

13

Lucani

Dinah Schwind was wishing that while they had Joe Service in the hospital, they had thought to implant a locator beacon in his ass. She hadn't seen him in days, nor heard from him. She was kicking around in Detroit, visiting various federal agencies, police, just killing time and trying to convince the Colonel, who was in Washington and calling every day, that everything was fine. She had no such confidence. Beyond that, she missed Joe.

Two events tightened her tension. The first was a slaying in Pontiac, a city north of Detroit that doesn't like to think of itself as a suburb, because it had a fairly long separate history. The deceased was a well-known Detroit hood named Kenneth Malateste. He'd been shot in the head in a municipal parking garage. The woman who ran the booth at the entrance told the police that there had been two other men in the car with Malateste, but she hadn't paid much attention to them.

The car had been left, with Malateste lying on the front seat, slumped over. It had been there for several hours before someone noticed that there was blood on the windshield. Obviously, he'd been shot by someone in the back seat. No robbery; his identification and money were left on him. The doors were locked. Of no particular interest to Schwind, when she read the report, was that Malateste had a couple of cigars in his suit-coat pocket, in a plastic bag of the pressure-fastener sort. She was interested, however, in the fact that the victim was considered to be a key enforcer for Humphrey DiEbola, in recent times the administrator of the mob's protection racket.

Two days later, another body was found, another known associate of DiEbola's. This was Wallace Leonardo, a tough waste-removal contractor, popularly called Nardo. He'd been found by some kids playing around a flooded quarry in Lapeer County, north of Detroit. He had been pretty badly battered. The coroner thought his fatal wounds had been inflicted either in falling or by the skull being crushed with rocks. In addition, his abdominal cavity had been cut open and filled with rocks, presumably an attempt to keep the body submerged, but that hadn't sufficed. He had not been robbed. His personal effects were still in his pockets, including a couple of cigars.

Schwind could no longer ignore Joe's failure to report. Colonel Tucker flew into Detroit to confer, along with two other agents from other federal agencies. Counting Schwind and one other man, they constituted the ad hoc group that Schwind had described to Joe. Besides the Colonel and Schwind, the members were Bernie Acker, Dexter Collins, and Edna Swarthout. They had all worked with the colonel in one group or another. They were united in their impatience with bureaucratic bungling and corruption, coupled with a bold willingness to take direct action. Edna Swarthout, who had been with the colonel in his encounter with Joe and Helen in Salt Lake City, had not been able to make the meeting.

They were staying at a hotel in Southfield, in the northwest Detroit metropolitan zone. They conferred in the colonel's room. "Do you think this is Joe's work?" the colonel asked.

Dinah did not think so. She was emphatic. "If you're suggesting that Joe is initiating a campaign, no way," she said. "I never mentioned these men to him, and he's not an enthusiastic killer. I've talked to the police investigators in both cases. These appear to be unrelated killings, by different assailants. The techniques are different. What links them is the relationship to DiEbola and the closeness of events in time. This is either more evidence of the diffusion of criminal hegemony in the Detroit area—a natural consequence of the decline of mob power—or it may be a kind of weeding-out process instigated by DiEbola himself. Neither of these men were considered very staunch allies of DiEbola's, but neither were particular enemies, as far as anyone knows."

"What does Joe say about it?" the colonel wanted to know. Schwind was unable to say. She hadn't heard from Joe. "Well, we better find him," the colonel said.

"Any ideas?" she asked.

"I'd keep an eye on the woman," the colonel said. "He came looking for her in Salt Lake. He must be in communication with her here."

Schwind saw his point. She had been observing local events, but that had not extended to physical surveillance; she was contacting police and other investigative organizations, trying to get a clearer picture of general activity.

They were only a small group, and their activities had to be carried out while ostensibly on other missions. Schwind's presence in Detroit, for instance, was being attributed to a larger investigation of organized crime.

The colonel saw the problem even as he spoke of it. "I'll get you some help," he said. "I'm supposed to be liaising with the INS here. I'll clear it with the director."

Two days later, after tailing Helen to the cigar factory, Schwind was sitting in a surveillance van with a couple of INS agents, parked down the block, when she saw Joe Service enter the building. She wondered what Joe saw in this skinny little woman with too much hair, with that ridiculous silver streak. Some men might find Helen attractive, she supposed, but in her eyes the woman was superficial, affected, pretty but insignificant.

Joe and Helen came out together and took her car to the Renaissance Center hotel. They went up the elevator together. Presumably, one of them had booked a room. They stayed there for more than an hour, then returned to the cigar factory, where Joe got into his car. They followed him in the van to Saint Clair Shores—at first Schwind thought he was going to DiEbola's, but he didn't stop in Grosse Pointe—where he pulled into a parking lot at a marina and entered a restaurant. Schwind went inside.

Joe was waiting for her. He had reserved a table. They sat, looking out over the boats at the lake. He was pleasant and friendly, apologetic for not calling her. "I kinda figured you'd be around," he offered. He had noticed the van when they were coming out Jefferson Avenue. Schwind found it difficult to be annoyed.

When she asked him about the killings he readily volunteered the information they sought. "Humphrey's up to something," he said. "Malateste and Nardo were hit by rivals. I think Humphrey tipped the killers. I don't know what he had against the two. Maybe incompetence, but now he's got a couple of new allies, only they aren't traditional mob guys. Maybe that's his plan, to broaden his base. The thing is, you'd think that it would weaken his support among the traditional guys, but the feeling seems to be that it was another guy, Soteri, who screwed up. Soteri talks a lot. He was telling everybody in town that Kenny and Nardo were screwups, that they couldn't run their own show. I don't know where he got his poop. Maybe Humphrey put him up to it."

Schwind knew who Soteri was, a dealer in stolen cars. She wondered what advantage DiEbola could get from this.

"Malateste was a protégé of Rossamani's, who was one of Carmine's boys," Joe said. "Rossamani was involved in some kind of action behind Humphrey's back, with your buddy Echeverria. He got his when my cabin blew up. Maybe Malateste was thinking of making a move on Humphrey, I don't know. Nardo? He was an all right guy, maybe a little old-fashioned. I heard that his operation was under pressure from outsiders. Maybe they bumped him. Maybe Humphrey sold the franchise. Who knows? Humphrey is very deep."

Schwind digested this. She was very pleased with Joe. He was giving them great stuff, she felt. "What's next?" she asked.

Joe had a theory. "I think Soteri's in trouble. The mob guys don't like him. Things are changing around here. A lot of incompetent people are getting weeded out. It looks like Humphrey is building a leaner, more effective mob."

"Who else?"

Joe told her about Mongelo's disappearance. "Word is, he was run off," Joe said, "several weeks ago. He hasn't been seen. But they say that he was an old friend of Humphrey's, they were kids together. The word is, he got paid off and told to retire. Rumor says he went to the Bahamas, or maybe even farther."

"Another step toward the New Look?" Schwind offered.

"Trimming the fat," Joe said. "I guess Humphrey is remaking his organization in his own image. You might want to keep an eye on Soteri. They say he's making a move on some rivals." He gave her an address on Shoemaker.

Schwind, grateful as she was, still naturally wanted to know his sources. Joe said he'd gotten some of it from just talking to Humphrey; other pieces had come from conversations with a variety of old Detroit hands. None of it was ironclad, just speculation, but it sounded plausible. When you saw Arab gangs operating Malateste's business without retaliation by DiEbola, or the Armenian prospering in the suburbs, you had to conclude that the rumors were valid. But who knows? Maybe Humphrey was biding his time. Maybe he'd crack down.

"How are you getting along with Helen?" Schwind asked.

"All right," Joe said. She couldn't tell if he had been aware that he'd been followed to the Renaissance. "Helen's okay."

"What's her role in all this?"

"She's Humphrey's new pal," he said. "Well, he's known her since she was a kid. He relies on her to take care of the legitimate side. She's pretty capable, you know."

"Just the legitimate side?" Schwind said.

"Yeah," Joe said. "What are you doing for dinner?"

"What did you have in mind?"

"Do you like Arab food?" he asked. "I heard about a place in Dearborn."

"I'd be delighted. I'm sure the colonel would like to join us, and a couple of other guys. It'd be a good opportunity for you to meet the Lucani."

Joe raised an eyebrow.

"That's what we call ourselves," Schwind explained. "It's from Lucania, a province in Italy. DiEbola is supposedly from there."

"It's a date," Joe said.

Dinner was great, if you like tabbouleh and that sort of thing. The colonel was very affable, as were Acker and Collins. The colonel was congratulatory about Joe's progress. He made no direct reference to their encounter in Salt Lake City, when Joe had thwarted an operation aimed at breaking up Helen's attempts to smurf the cash that she and Joe had taken, but he asked after "the lovely Miss Sedlacek."

Joe took this opportunity to say that he would have no part in any operation that targeted Helen. The colonel was quick to allay his fears. "We have no interest in Helen Sedlacek," he said. "You have my word on that."

Joe noticed that Schwind looked steadfastly at her plate.

They were eating some kind of spicy goat stew when the colonel got a call on his cell phone. There had been a shoot-out on Shoemaker. Aldo Soteri was dead. There were some federal agents on the scene. The colonel suggested they all take a run across town. Joe didn't think that was such a good idea. It wouldn't be good for him to be seen in their company. The Lucani conceded the point.

Sometime earlier, at about the moment the Lucani were sampling the tabbouleh, Humphrey was at the cigar factory. He'd asked Strom to meet him there.

They met at the loading dock. Strom was alone, as was Humphrey.

"Where's your boys?" Strom asked.

"They had work to do," Humphrey said. It was dark, just a few minimal lights. The parking lot and loading area were empty. "Don't you have a watchman?" Humphrey asked.

"Don't need one," Strom said. "This ain't a great neighborhood to be out in at night, and the guys who make it not such a great neighborhood know who runs this biz. They don't fuck with us. Besides, you got your boy downstairs, watching Mongelo. If anybody tries to break in, he can tend to it."

"That's not why he's here," Humphrey pointed out, "but never mind. Let's go see Monge. You got a piece?"

"Sure," Strom said. He patted his breast.

They went down to the basement. The guard was a young fellow from the potato chip factory. He didn't speak English. He was sitting outside the cage, watching a porno movie through the bars, with Mongelo. He jumped up when they approached. Humphrey's Italian was poor, but he managed to convey to the young man that he was relieved, he could go.

After he left, Humphrey told Strom to leave him and Mongelo alone, but not to go too far. He was unarmed, he said, and while he didn't expect Mongelo to make any trouble, it wouldn't do to give him too much slack.

"Why'dja let the kid go?" Strom said.

"None a your business," Humphrey said. "I gotta talk to Monge. Just back off, but stay handy. Capisce?"

When they were alone, Humphrey unlocked the cage and went in. He could see Mongelo was edgy. "Relax," he said. "Listen, this is it. You're gettin' outta here." That didn't seem to relax Mongelo. Obviously, he was thinking that "gettin' outta here" might mean something final. Humphrey tried to calm him.

"You're lookin' good, Monge. I'm proud a ya." It was true. Mongelo looked ten years younger. He had lost over a hundred pounds. He looked better than he'd looked in . . . well, ever.

But he was a chronic complainer. Tonight, it was the fillings that Humphrey's dentist had put in. They had gone to the dentist a few days earlier. The dentist hadn't been a very fancy one. Mongelo had been surprised that Humphrey would go to such a sleazebag dentist, but Humphrey had assured him that he'd been going to this guy forever. And the guy had found some cavities that Mongelo didn't know were there. His teeth were fine, he'd thought, but the dentist said no. All those X-rays, before and after! Who takes X-rays after? But that was what made this guy so good, he was told: he X-rayed after to be sure the fillings were right and all the decay removed. Mongelo was still sore, though.

"Monge, forget the dentist," Humphrey said. "I told you I was having trouble, remember? Well, now I need you with me. I want you to come to my place. I got a 'partment all fixed up for you. Together, we'll fix these bastards that are ratting us out."

"Who is it? D'you find out?"

"I got a line on them. Malateste was one. I took care a him," Humphrey said. "But there's others. We'll discuss it. So, you ready to go?"

Mongelo was ready.

"Can I count on you?" Humphrey asked, fixing him with a sharp look. Mongelo said he was ready. He was Humphrey's man.

Humphrey called out to Strom. When he loomed up in the light, Humphrey beckoned him in. "Give me your piece," he said. Strom looked surprised, but readily pulled out his gun. It was an automatic, a nice, flat, compact .38. He handed it to Humphrey, who held it on the flat palm of his gloved hand. Then he turned to Mongelo.

Mongelo's eyes grew round. His mouth fell open. But then Humphrey handed the gun to him. He nodded toward Strom. "Do him," Humphrey said.

Strom whirled and started away, but Mongelo did not hesitate. He blasted Strom down with three quick shots. Strom's body sprawled on the concrete, in the semidarkness. The shots had reverberated in the chamber, but there was no response in the silence that followed. No one had heard a thing.

Mongelo stood outside the cage, staring down at the body. Humphrey took the gun from his hand and dropped it into a plastic bag. "We'll get rid of this," he said. "C'mon, let's get outta here. Leave him."

In the parking lot, Humphrey explained that Mongelo would have to ride in the trunk. "Boss, I don't wanta," Mongelo said.

Humphrey produced a revolver from his pocket. "Get in the trunk, Monge," he said. "Trust me. I ain't gonna hurt you. It's only, you can't be seen."

Mongelo got in the trunk. Humphrey drove home. When they passed through the gate, Humphrey stopped to tell the gate man that he was home for the night. He drove around to the other side of the house, toward the boat slip, and parked. He went into the house. The watch commander was at the console. "Go relieve the gate," Humphrey said. "Tell him to go to the relief room. I might have a visitor tonight and I don't want nobody around. I'll give you a call."

When the man left—it wasn't John, tonight—Humphrey switched off the monitors. He went down to the bunker, let himself in, then went out through the emergency exit. He got Mongelo out of the trunk. "See?" he told him. "It's all right. I told you."

When they were in the bunker, Humphrey showed him around and explained a few things. He had to understand that he was there in secret. It was crucial. The rats in the organization couldn't know he was on watch. Nobody would know. Together they'd root those bastards out. Mongelo seemed ready. The bunker was not luxurious, but it was better than the cage. There was plenty of movies, plenty of food.

14

Mouse Hole

Much to his surprise, Humphrey found Mongelo to be an amiable companion. They had known each other all their lives and had more in common than Humphrey cared to admit. Considering the bums they'd hung out with, the fiascoes they'd endured in common, this wasn't necessarily a happy congruence. But they had an enormous fund of mutual experience. Down in the bunker, they worked out together on the fancy machines that Humphrey had installed: StairMaster, treadmill, weight machines. It was good that the ventilation system was so effective, but it was certainly being fully tested. Even the copious numbers of LaDonna cigars that they smoked could not daunt this system.

Humphrey appreciated a situation in which he was free of just about any social constraints. They swore, farted, belched, made scurrilous comments about everybody, speculated on who was on his last legs and who was still getting it up. They bragged about monstrous acts and indulged each other's exaggerations and bullshit. It was all quite harmless and foolish, and after a while it palled on them both, although both continued to make tired gestures at it, to keep up the pretense of youthful exuberance.

But soon enough, Humphrey remembered why he had always disliked Mongelo: the man had an appallingly narrow focus. You could start him on a track and he was like the bunny in the television ad: he just kept banging away until he was redirected.

In the evening, after Mongelo had finally sunk into a snoring sleep, Humphrey would take care of his electronic business. He did some of it during the day, but it wasn't easy, with Mongelo hanging around, yapping and watching amazingly sordid pornography all day on the VCR. Humphrey had not bargained for this. He was glad it wasn't going to last long.

One thing he needed was for Mongelo to wear his clothes, all of them, and to take showers, to leave his hair and sloughed skin everywhere. Humphrey had some of it cleaned up and bagged, as he'd been doing from the start, when Mongelo was in the cage at the cigar factory. He washed this crud down his own drains upstairs, sprinkled hair on his old hairbrushes, and kept the sheets Mongelo slept on. It was all part of the big plan.

He was happy to see Helen and Joe getting along so well and taking more interest in the operations, although Joe kept pretty clear of that end. Joe had a profound distaste for the prosaic drudgery of business. He could work pretty hard at something that directly concerned his own well-being, but he wasn't much for financial intricacies. They did get into a conversation once about the possibility of setting up what Joe called "hospices" for AIDS victims, ones in the terminal phase. But here again, Joe seemed to think there were great possibilities in it, for himself. Humphrey couldn't see it: it was too much trouble for the prospective value of having a ready supply of dead folks who could inherit and leave money—an overelaborate money-washing scam.

Humphrey was busily collecting money and transferring it to offshore accounts, much of it from new franchisees for old mob operations—Russians, Arabs, various South Americans. He was also putting the finishing touches to his grand exit strategy. One of these touches, perhaps the most crucial, was selecting Mongelo's executioner. For this, in a step that he found wonderfully appropriate, he drew in Mongelo himself.

Mongelo was eager to help, idle as he was, and unaware as he necessarily was of the true end of the process. Together they pored over information that Humphrey had carefully compiled on personnel in the organization. The ostensible purpose was to determine who were the traitors, the rats, and who were their allies and fellow conspirators. Mongelo was very useful here, doggedly sifting through lists, relating anecdotes, remembering who had done what. He knew everybody, knew their backgrounds, and by now was thoroughly into a paranoiac frame of mind.

Mongelo agreed that Nardo was a traitor. "I was allus 'spicious of da bastid," he said. "He was such a fuckin' hard-ass. He never had much to say f'hisself, an' nothin' good about nobody else." He approved of the way that Humphrey had set it up, having him beaten to death with rocks and thrown into a stone quarry. That would point the finger at the Armenian, all right.

As for Kenny Malateste, he'd never liked the punk. "What a fuckin' wiseass," he said, "thought he could screw any bimbo walkin'. You ast me, these guys, some a them, all they think about is gittin' their ashes hauled, they don't take care a bidniss. Well, he's gettin' his ashes hauled now." Mongelo was a little curious if Kenny had actually been popped by the Arabs; Humphrey just winked, and Mongelo nodded with a little smile.

Soteri? What a bum! Always talkin' down the next guy. Mongelo was surprised the jerk had lived as long as he had. As for the late Strom Davidson, well, Mongelo could see it had to be done and he was glad to have been of assistance.

Mongelo spotted, without much prompting, what all these guys had in common. They were all allies of the late "Rossie"

Rossamani, one of Carmine's old buddies. Who else was in that circle? Mongelo named a dozen guys. They went over them, one by one. By and large, they were okay fellas, capable enough, seemingly loyal to Humphrey, not too upset with Carmine's demise, and none of them in a position to do any harm. Who could the rat be? Who to pin the tail on?

At last they came to two figures, John Nicolette and Matty Cassidy. Nicolette was particularly interesting because he was married to Rossamani's widow's sister. Humphrey hadn't known that. In fact, the only reason he was on the list (although he hadn't told Mongelo this) was because he was the crew chief of the security group that had been working the night Pepe had disappeared. He now became the number one candidate.

Humphrey shook his head, marveling. "Imagine that," he said, "the devious bastards! The guy who is actually supposed to be watching my back turns out to be one of the traitors. It's a wonder he didn't cut my throat while I was sleepin'."

They had to do something about Nicolette, that was for sure. And Matty Cassidy. Matty was the guy who had brought the killer Heather to Rossamani, who'd suggested her to Humphrey as someone who could take care of Joe Service. She had come close to succeeding, and she'd almost taken down Helen, as well. Humphrey didn't mention any of this to Mongelo. But it was clear that Matty was another old Rossie buddy and he'd have to go.

"How do you want to handle it, boss?" Mongelo asked.

Humphrey had a plan, but he pretended to think. Finally, he said, "We'll have 'em down here. I don't want to take them out unless I'm sure they're guilty. They oughta have a chance to tell us their side, anyway. With these other guys, Nardo and them, I had them in before you came in on this, and I kinda felt them out. And you know from your own experience, I like to give a guy a chance to do what's right."

Mongelo thought that was pretty white of Humphrey. "You just ask 'em right out, eh? An' then, if they 'fess up, you . . . ah, what do you do then?"

Humphrey had to laugh. "It don't work that way, Monge. You ask 'em about somethin' else, some kinda innocent questions, then, when they're kinda relaxed, you lay it on 'em. See how they react. That's where it all comes down. A guy can kinda show his hand, sometimes. Sometimes, you don't learn nothin'. But, you at least gave 'im a chance. So then you gotta fall back on what you learned. You make your decision. That's about it."

Mongelo was impressed. This was a valuable management tip. He was pleased to have a suggestion when Humphrey asked what he thought would be a good excuse to ask the guys in. "A card game," he said.

"A card game?" Humphrey suppressed a smile. But then he saw that Mongelo wasn't so stupid. Matty was a gambler. He'd had to cough it up for Mongelo at least once, for getting in too deep. They'd invite Matty and then, just to fill out the table, they'd get Nicolette down from his post. It was ideal. An evening of poker, a lot of talk, plenty of beer, maybe even a little pizza—he could see Mongelo salivating. Small talk that turns a little serious, maybe revealing.

"An' we could prob'ly win a coupla bucks, too," Mongelo suggested. Humphrey laughed.

Things were getting close. Humphrey had a world of details to take care of. He was sending men out left and right, all hours of the day and night. On one occasion, just to get away from the fug in the bunker and Mongelo's monomaniacal drivel, he and Helen took a moonlight jaunt out on the lake to meet Joe.

This time they met in midlake and tied up together out of the shipping lanes. It was a great place to meet, a beautiful warm night. Humphrey told them over coffee that he was getting a little frazzled, but things were going well. The thing that worried him, though, was that Mulheisen seemed to be getting somewhere on the Hoffa case. If he could just hold him off for a day or two.

Joe didn't see much of a problem. "Just put him off, give him a little something, send him on a wild-goose chase. What do you care what he finds out? You'll be gone."

"I sure hope so," he said.

Helen watched him. Suddenly, she said, "This whole thing is about Hoffa, isn't it?"

Humphrey equivocated. "Not exactly. Well, maybe. I always knew it would blow up one day. It was a mistake, a big mistake. You can't . . . well, let me put it this way: you can maybe cover something like this up, but there's gotta be a payback, somewhere down the line. So, yeah, it's Hoffa, but it's all the other crap I been telling you about. So, I'm doing what Mac kinda showed me, when he was talking about Borgia and them. You gotta know when to fold your tent. I'm folding. But I'll be damned if I'm gonna leave the business in the hands of these pricks we got around us nowadays. I'm gonna clean up some a this trash."

More than that Humphrey would not say. He firmed up his plans with them, to the extent that he wanted them to know them, anyway. On the big night, Joe would wait for Humphrey pretty much where they were right now. Helen did not like this plan, Humphrey knew, but she kept her peace. She would not be involved. That was crucial. She would stay to deal with the aftermath, and when that was accomplished . . . well, it was up to her and Joe.

"I give you kids my blessing," Humphrey said. "Whatever you decide, I'm sure it'll be for the best."

The next day, in an amusing little performance at the Krispee Chips offices, Humphrey and Helen met with Mulheisen and gave him the very strong impression that they were lovers. It was a bittersweet act for Humphrey, one of the few occasions when he'd actually had his hand up Helen's skirt. He'd miss that, he thought, an intriguing possibility there. But he knew he didn't stand a chance as long as Joe Service was around.

Still, Mulheisen had jarred him. The detective was much closer than he'd realized. Humphrey had left things dangerously tight. It was time to set it all in motion.

The day before, he had invited Matty Cassidy for poker, tonight. When the gambler appeared, Humphrey talked to him in his study, prior to joining Mongelo downstairs. They were alone. He needed Matty's help, he explained. He had Mongelo downstairs, he said. The guy had been ill, he was a little crazy. Well, everyone knew Mongelo was nuts. He'd taken the guy in, nursed him. Now, whaddaya think? He had discovered that Mongelo was out to whack him.

"Jeeziss," Matty said, "and you got him right here, in the house?" He looked around nervously.

"I'm not worried," Humphrey said, "just careful. I got my eye on him. Only, I can't have no guns in the room. You understand."

Matty understood, but he said, "What if Mongelo's got a gun hidden somewheres? Wouldn't it be better if I could back you up?"

Humphrey nodded. "Good thinking. I tell you what, give me your piece. I'm not really worried about Monge, you know, but if he gets a little squirrelly, like if you're winning too much—which you prob'ly will be, if I know you . . ." He smiled at Matty.

"Monge never could play cards worth a shit," Matty said, chuckling.

"Yeah," Humphrey agreed. "But if he gets actin' crazy, I'll slip the iron to you. Maybe we could pull that old gag, stashin' it in the john. We'll see. If I get up and go to the john, you go in next. The gun'll be in the drawer of the washstand. Anyways, I'll have Johnny Nicolette down to play. He's the night man here. You know him?" Matty had met him, but they weren't well acquainted. "John won't be armed either, but between the three of us, we won't have any problems. The guy is actually a lamb, I really don't expect no trouble, Matty. But I figured, better safe than sorry. If he gets excited . . . you just don't know with psychos." Humphrey patted Cassidy on the shoulder.

"The guy is sick," Humphrey explained. "He's a little pissed at me because I did what hadda be done, I locked him up, kept him under wraps. It was for his own good, but he can't see that. The guy was a walkin' time bomb. But he needs a little break. I want the guy to have a little fun, he's been cooped up so long with this . . ." He whirled his finger around his ear. "Just keep your eyes open and we'll have a good time."

Matty handed over his gun, a 9mm Glock. Humphrey stuffed it into his belt and pulled his bulky cable-knit sweater over it. "Make yourself a drink," he told Matty. "I gotta talk to John, he's working the console. We'll go down in a few minutes."

Humphrey went directly to the control room, carrying a box of cigars. "John, we're gettin' up a poker game, downstairs. We need another hand." He glanced at the monitors. "Things are quiet, why don't you come on down?"

Nicolette looked pained. "Gee, Mr. DiEbola, I'd love to, but I'm kinda light just now."

"No problem," Humphrey assured him. "I didn't expect you to spend your own money. Here." He got out his wallet and thumbed off five hundred dollars in fifties. "Play with this. If you lose it, forget it. If you win, you can pay me back and keep the winnings. If you need more, just give me the nod. No, no. You're doing me a favor."

"Great! But what about the—" He gestured at the monitors.

"I'll tell you what," Humphrey said. "You go around, check everything out, and . . . oh yeah, be sure the dogs are in. It could get kinda stuffy down there, if we're all puffing away on cigars, and I wanta leave the passageway open to the yard, get a little fresh air.

I'll open up the yard door and you can come down that way. And don't say nothing to the other guys, eh? I don't want anybody thinking I'm favoring one guy over another, you see what I mean? The patrol guys can hang in the relief room, maybe they'll get up their own game. Who knows? The gate man can handle things. Anyways, you can keep an eye on the monitors down there. Oh, and one more thing—I told these guys no guns down there, so don't bring your piece."

"Won't that look kind of odd?" Nicolette said. "I mean, I'd have to leave it in the safe, in the relief room."

Humphrey thought for a moment, as if stumped, then said, "Tell you what. I'm glad you're careful. I'm careful, too. Maybe it would be better if your gun was handy. Let me have it. I'll stash it in this cigar box." He opened the box and scooped out the cigars, tossing them onto the desk. "I'll carry this box down there. You'll see it on the counter. Anything crazy happens, you can grab it. Okay?"

"What if someone wants a cigar, opens the box?"

"There's a couple boxes down there already. I'll make sure they're open. They'll be handy. Nobody'll bother this one. They won't even notice. It'll be where you can see it."

So that was settled. The gun fit nicely into the box. John said he'd start his rounds right away and he should be able to join them in fifteen minutes or so, when he got the dogs and the patrols settled in the security quarters. Humphrey told him to take his time. He went to collect Matty and they went downstairs in the conventional way. Matty was very impressed with the security arrangements.

Mongelo greeted Matty like a long-lost friend. He was clearly pleased to see a fresh face. He gave him an embrace that clearly included a weapons check.

Matty smiled, confidently. "I can't believe how skinny you are, Monge," he said. Then, remembering that the man had been ill, he said, "You feelin' all right?"

Mongelo frowned. "I feel great. How 'bout you?"

They popped open a couple of Stroh's and sat talking while Humphrey went to the desk to call for refreshments. "Guys," he called over his shoulder, "I gotta go up to get the pizza. The help has already gone home. Help yourselves to more beer, or whatever. I'll be back in a minute."

He went upstairs quickly. John was out. He could see him on the various monitors, making his rounds, getting the dogs in. He went to Helen's room. "You all set?" he asked her.

"I'm staying," she said.

Humphrey shook his head.

"I can do it," she said. "You know I can do it."

Humphrey looked at her. "Got your Hatchet Puss on," he said. But it was too late. He hadn't told her all his plans; they didn't include her. Still, he owed her something. "I know you jumped in the car and blasted Carmine," he said. "You can do it. But you don't want to. You don't want this racket."

"Maybe I changed my mind," she said.

"Too late, babe. Get outta here."

She saw how it was. "I'll be at Mama's, if anything goes wrong."

He nodded. "Go to Soke. You gotta be away from here. You gotta establish that. Make sure somebody else is there, as a witness."

She kissed him. "You're something else, Unca Umby."

"Yeah, yeah." He was embarrassed now. "I'll miss you baby. But . . . what the hell. This is the way to go. You take care of yourself."

"Say hi to Joe," she said.

"You say hi yourself," he replied. "You'll see him soon enough. Listen, I gotta go. I'm choking up, here." He kissed her again and they went out together.

The last she saw of him, before she went out the door, he was picking up a huge tray filled with pizzas. He had tucked a box of LaDonnas under his arm, saying, "The guys'll like these."

* * *

Roman Yakovich had made up his mind. Mrs. Sid had told him that Helen was coming over. She had invited some of her lady friends. They were going to have a good, old-fashioned hen party. She had cooked innumerable little goodies, *flancate*, walnut *povitica*, *priganica*. She prepared a selection on a plate for Roman and told him to get lost. "Go watch your hockey game," she said.

From his upstairs window, Roman watched Helen and the women arrive. When they were starting to laugh and gabble downstairs, he crept out the back way and drove to DiEbola's house. What he had seen in recent weeks had troubled him greatly. DiEbola was making a fool of himself over Helen. Roman had seen this sort of thing before. A rich and powerful older man can have his way with many a young woman, but not with the Little Angel. He would be polite; he would be respectful; but Mr. DiEbola must know that Little Helen was not one of these silly girls that he could tamper with.

At the gate the guard would not let Roman in. He recognized him, all right, and he knew that Roman was an old friend of Mr. DiEbola's, but the boss was entertaining guests. No, he would not call the house. Mr. DiEbola had personally given him strict orders: no one was to be let in. No one. Sorry.

The guard stood within the ornamented steel gates, wisely out of arm's reach. Roman stalled, a hulking bundle of a man with long arms stuffed into the sleeves of his suit coat like sausages. He stared around the area, looking toward the distant house, which was not visible from here. He seemed lost. Finally, the older man said, "He got women in there?"

The young guard sneered. "Sure, he's got women. Miz Helen went out for the night, so he ordered in a buncha whores. He's having a fuckin' orgy. Now get lost, old-timer." He stood and watched until Roman got back in his car and drove away. Then he went back into the guard booth, to his girlie magazine.

Roman drove several blocks away, then stopped when he came to a small stone bridge over a canal. He parked the car and walked back to the canal, then followed a path alongside it toward the lake. Several large estates had boathouses on the canal, he saw. These estates, like DiEbola's, were well fenced, and the boathouses effectively blocked anyone from walking farther. But a lovely little skiff was tied up to the piling of one of the houses. He would have to wade in the dark water to get to it, and he had no idea how deep it was, but he was determined.

The water was well over his waist. And it was cold. But Roman was not daunted. He waded to the boat and nearly swamped it crawling in, his gun in his hand, to keep it dry. It was a huge cannon, a .44 magnum revolver. He set it on the thwart before him and began to row out toward the lake.

It took him the better part of an hour to find the slip at DiEbola's. He had noticed that the dogs were not out, so he didn't worry about them, and he had no notion of patrols anyway, so that didn't concern him. Nonetheless, he was quiet about rowing up to DiEbola's sleek, low-slung cruiser and tying up. He clambered onto the dock and then walked across the lawn.

What luck! Some kind of cellar door was open, light spilling out and illuminating a faint haze that rose from the opening. It was cigar smoke; Roman smelled it. The opening was not attached to the big house, but from the voices—among them DiEbola's—he realized that he had found his man.

Humphrey glanced at the clock on the desk. It was a glowing red digital-readout device. It was 9:48, time to start the ball rolling. In fact, the ball had been rolling for some time. He had initiated a series of sly digs at Matty, mentioning the late Rossamani, and as he had expected, Mongelo had taken it up. Unlike Humphrey, Mongelo was wont to be less than subtle.

"That fuckin' Rossie, what a prick," Mongelo said, "and he was fuckin' queer, too. Gimme two fuckin' cards, you little chiseler."

Matty was dealing. He looked at Humphrey nervously. Humphrey smiled and nodded. Matty dealt. "Rossie wasn't queer," Matty muttered.

Mongelo looked at his cards and threw them down with disgust. "Jeeziss, what a shit hand. You deal like you fuck, you little prick. Sure, Rossie was queer. Maybe you are too. You deal like a fuckin' pansy." He sat back and stared, daring Matty to respond.

Before Matty could say anything, Humphrey showed three jacks, whereupon John triumphantly slapped down a full house, aces and eights. It was a big pot and John crowed, "Come to me you sweet things" as he raked it in.

"Whatta you so happy about?" Mongelo demanded of him.

John shrugged, unfazed, and nodded toward his full house. "If you can't beat it, you gotta eat it," he said with a laugh.

"Now you're callin' me a fuckin' pansy," Mongelo challenged him.

Humphrey put a hand on his shoulder, rising. "Take it easy, Monge. It's just cards. I gotta piss. You keep an eye on these crooks, make sure they don't steal anything." Behind Mongelo's back, when John was stacking his chips, he made a curt gesture with his head toward the bathroom, to Matty. When he returned a moment later, he nodded again and was pleased to see Matty got the message.

"My turn," Matty said, getting up to go to the bathroom. He would find the Glock there. Humphrey was all but certain that he would not check the magazine; that would make too much noise.

"Don't be playing with your dick in there," Mongelo bellowed after him. "You'll get the cards all sticky."

"Up yours," Matty retorted and shut the door.

John laughed and picked up the cards to shuffle. Humphrey nudged Mongelo's leg under the table. That was the first sign. Mongelo let his hand drop to his knee and then advanced it slightly under the hanging edge of the green felt table cover. He would be able to grasp the grip of the .38 taped there.

There were two bullets in this gun. Humphrey had given this number a good deal of thought. Would two be enough? Or too many? He figured that Mongelo would shoot Matty first. Then he'd try to shoot Nicolette, assuming that he actually hit Matty with his first shot. If he didn't hit him, he would surely fire again. Then he'd try to shoot Nicolette.

Or, Humphrey thought, he'll try to shoot me. Not likely. Mongelo trusted him, he was into the game.

What would happen next, however, couldn't really be predicted. Humphrey had read somewhere, maybe in Machiavelli, that after the first shot all battle plans change. But they wouldn't change much, of that he was confident. Nicolette had only one bullet.

Matty came out of the bathroom. He looked more assured. He had found the Glock. Humphrey didn't need to look at his face: he could see the bulge in his pocket. The idiot had put the gun in his pocket! Of course; he had removed his suit jacket. He had no other good place to put it, except in his waistband, under his shirt, and then he wouldn't be able to get at it easily. So he had his hand in his pocket, as if to mask the presence of the gun.

Nicolette didn't notice. He was shuffling cards. But Mongelo noticed. His eyes flickered toward Humphrey, who smiled. So this was it. The curtain was going up. Humphrey rose immediately and went around Mongelo toward the desk-counter, where the clock and the monitors were, the cigar box—and the Bushmaster he'd stashed last night. He didn't even look at the monitor, which would have shown him Roman Yakovich, stealthily descending the steps from the lawn.

"You son of a bitch!" Mongelo roared. He jumped up, knocking the table away, holding the .38.

Matty yanked the Glock out of his pocket, but he never got a chance to fire. Mongelo's bullet hit him in the chest, knocking him backward. The din of the shot was shocking to the ears, but Humphrey didn't notice. He scrambled for the Bushmaster, ready to hand in a desk drawer. In the same moment he slid the cigar box down the counter, toward Nicolette, who was reaching for it when Mongelo's second shot struck him in the back.

Nicolette fell to the floor but managed to carry the cigar box down with him. He fished out the pistol. He almost pulled the trigger on Mongelo, but he heard the click of Mongelo's empty gun just in time. Mongelo stared down at the gun in disbelief, then at Nicolette.

Nicolette said, "Drop it."

Humphrey said, "Shoot!" He pointed at Mongelo.

Both men turned to look at Humphrey. Then Roman's arm came through the door and he shot Mongelo. The .44 made a much bigger racket than the .38 had. Mongelo was flung backward, crashing into the treadmill.

Nicolette fired at Roman, but he had a very poor angle and Roman was all but hidden in the door opening. The bullet ricocheted off the concrete wall and zinged around the room like an atomic wasp. Roman pumped two shots into the security man. The blasts tossed the body back under the counter.

The smoke lay in dense reefs—cigars and gunfire. Roman was only dimly visible to Humphrey, who considered blowing him away with the Bushmaster. Instead, he suddenly realized he'd been hit himself. He didn't feel any pain, not exactly, but a shock. It must have been the ricochet. The bullet would have been badly deformed, doubtless fragmented. It had hit him in the right side, in the ribs, about three inches below his right breast. He wasn't sure if it had penetrated deeply, but there was blood.

"Jesus!" he cried, "I'm fuckin' hit!"

Roman lumbered forward hesitantly, still holding the .44 before him.

"Watch whatcher doin' with that thing," Humphrey barked. "Here, help me. I feel a little woozy." He had his right arm clamped against his side. He slid down to the floor, sitting in a puddle of spilled beer. "This ain't workin'," he said.

Roman peered through the smoke, waving the gun as if to clear the haze.

Humphrey was having trouble staying conscious. "What the fuck are you doing here?" he said.

Roman spoke, almost casually: "I come to talk to you."

"What about?"

"Liddle Helen. You gotta leave her alone." Roman was stern, reproving.

"I am leaving her alone," Humphrey said. "I'm leaving everybody alone. What do you think all this is about?" He gestured weakly with his left hand, at the bodies. "I'm leaving town. But I need a little help."

Roman couldn't take it in. Who could? "Leaving?" he said. "For good?"

"For good or bad," Humphrey said. "Give me a hand, here."

Roman jammed the .44 into his holster and stooped to hoist Humphrey to his feet. He helped him to the door, practically carrying him. But Humphrey stopped at the passageway.

"No," he said, "we gotta make it look right." He leaned against the doorjamb and directed Roman to drag Nicolette's body up the passageway and outside. Humphrey followed. He felt better in the fresh air. He looked around. Nothing. No sounds. No lights. No sign that anyone had heard a thing. He had been certain that they wouldn't.

"Can you get him to the boat?" Humphrey asked. Roman nodded and hoisted the body onto his shoulder. Humphrey waited. He tried to examine the wound, but it was too awkward, too dark. Nonetheless, he felt reassured. He could breathe all right. He was afraid of shock, but he wasn't bleeding too badly. He told himself he'd be all right.

When Roman returned they went back downstairs. Humphrey ignored the sprawled bodies, for the moment. He scanned the monitors. There was no activity. The man on the gate was reading a magazine. Nothing was stirring.

Not even a mouse, he thought, or a rat.

He had a few tasks for Roman, such as smashing quart canning jars filled with gasoline on the floor, especially around Mongelo. He had a nice little bomb, packed into a cigar box. He managed to kneel and clasp Mongelo's hands around it.

What next? He glanced around, picked up Nicolette's service revolver, and stuck it in his pocket. He wiped the Bushmaster and put it into Matty's right hand and closed the fingers, then tugged his left hand over to grasp the receiver, then let the gun fall away.

A few other touches . . . time to go. Roman helped him up the passageway, up the steps to the lawn, and let him sit. Then at Humphrey's direction he went back down the passageway with a Molotov cocktail. A moment later, there was a muffled *whump!*

A moment after that, smoke roared out of the passageway, followed by a coughing Roman. The bomb had gone off quicker than he'd expected. Roman was almost clear of the passageway, but the blast actually knocked him down. He got up and scrambled out onto the lawn. Together they hobbled to the slip.

Humphrey struggled aboard while Roman cast off the lines to the cruiser, then jumped down into the cockpit, treading on the body of Nicolette. Humphrey had started the engine and they pulled away. Flames billowed out of the hole in the ground, lighting up the night. Humphrey heard a splintering and a crushing noise.

"What the fuck is that?" he yelled.

"The liddle boat," Roman said.

They left the wreckage sinking at the end of its painter at the slip and roared out into the lake. Fifteen minutes later, they idled up next to Joe's boat.

"What happened?" Joe called out. He jumped into their boat to help. He and Roman got Humphrey into the other boat.

"I fucked up," Humphrey said. "Get my bag. Here." He handed Joe another jar of gasoline. "Break that in the boat."

Joe did as instructed and, at the last moment, noticed another box of LaDonnas. He tossed it to Humphrey. "Souvenir," he called. Then he came aboard. From ten feet away, he tossed another bomb into the cockpit of the *Kiddle-Dee-Divey*. This bomb took longer to react to the heat. The burning boat was visible for half a mile, then came the explosion, and shortly the flame snuffed out.

Humphrey thanked Roman for his help. "I couldn't have done it without you," he said. "I don't know what I was thinking about. I should've known something would go haywire. That goddamn ricochet! But you came along and saved my ass."

Joe examined the wound. "Well, it's in you," he said. "I can't tell how deep, or how much bullet is left. But that's a nasty situation. You have to have a doctor."

They argued about this. Humphrey was sure he'd be all right, and finally he said, "That's where we're going, anyway. Let's just go with the plan."

"It's a long ride, Slim," Joe said. "But if you've got someone at the other end. . . . Let Roman go with you, to help. I don't want to just drop you off."

Humphrey consented to that. Roman helped him down into the bunks and Joe set their course. After a while, Roman came back to the wheel with a cup of coffee. He sat in the seat across the companionway and watched through the night, occasionally going below to check on Humphrey. When Joe would ask how Humphrey was doing, he would just shrug. But he seemed content.

15

Moving Day

Mulheisen was moving. Or rather, he wasn't moving but he should have been. Instead, he sat in an old easy chair in his bedroom, gazing out at the shipping in the channel, across the field behind his mother's house. It was very quiet, very peaceful. He wondered if he was making a mistake. He glanced at the clock radio next to his bed. It was nearly three in the afternoon on a Sunday. He was all packed. Becky would be here soon with the truck. He looked around him, relishing the quiet familiarity of this room, his boyhood bedroom. When would he sit in this room again?

Becky was a small, fast-mouthed woman in her late thirties. Mulheisen wasn't sure of her last name. She'd lived with a man named Marvin Berg for years, until he died. Had she taken Berg's name? Had they ever married? He was shocked at his lapse, as a detective, in not knowing this. She had helped Mulheisen on a case not long before, and given him some nice, vintage H. Upmann cigars left over from the days when Marvin had owned a great little cigar store down on Fort Street. Becky's help had consisted in providing Mulheisen with some notebooks, left in Marvin's care by the late and not much lamented detective Grootka, that had proved useful in the never-solved disappearance of Jimmy Hoffa. It had been nice to see her again. Mulheisen thought she was . . . attractive. Not beautiful or cute, but nice looking. And she had been only halfheartedly insulting.

The house she had inherited from Berg was much too large for Becky. Mulheisen had mentioned that he was looking for an apartment and they had kidded about him moving in, but he had told her that it was pointless. The house was in Pleasant Ridge, one of the numerous little suburbs that ringed the city. It wouldn't qualify as a Detroit residence.

Then, soon after he'd found the apartment downtown, Becky had called. She had discovered something interesting: the village of Pleasant Ridge had only a single police patrol, so they had contracted with the city for additional services. Could it not be construed that Pleasant Ridge was, in effect, part of the Detroit Police Department responsibility and, hence, its employees could legally reside there? It was worth an inquiry. He had pitched it to his boss, Captain Jimmy Marshall, and he'd approved.

Still, Mulheisen hadn't been sure. What would sharing a house with Becky entail? He had decided to take a run out there and investigate.

Becky looked better than on the previous visit. She was not so pale; maybe it was makeup. Also, she was dressed better: instead of dungarees and garden boots, she wore shorts and a tank top. She was lean and muscled; evidently she worked out. Her body might be hard, but her new life since Marvin had died seemed to have softened her. She wasn't so caustic as before, though given to occasional sarcasms.

She said he ought to pitch his beloved H. Upmann cigars— not the vintage ones she'd given him, but the new ones. They were overrated, she said, living on their past glory. Before Mulheisen could voice misgivings, however, she was quick to add, "Don't look like that. I didn't mean you should quit. I like a good cigar as much as the next guy. You know me, Mul. I'm just saying, as an old cigar seller, Upmanns are what we'd call a parlor pitch. You can price 'em like a virgin, but they're more like an old slag. Here, try some of these."

She gave him a box of LaDonna Detroit figurados. They came in a fancy wooden humidor-style box with a clasp, and the picture inside was a splendid painting of a woman on a milk-white mare, strewing flowers and cigars on the world. They claimed to be hand-made in the U.S.A., in Detroit, of "highest Cubano-quality to-bacco." That was a nice touch, he thought. It didn't actually say Cuban. He raised an eyebrow at Becky.

"Try 'em," she said. "You'll see. It's as good a cigar as you can get, and only five dollars per. No, no charge for this box. I got 'em as a promotion."

"I didn't know you were still in the business," he said.

"I do a little wholesale," she said. "Why waste experience and connections? It keeps the money tap open. Try one."

He took one out and sniffed. It wasn't cellophaned, which he liked. They seemed handmade, all right, and well made. Tight, no large stems obtruding. The shape was terrific, a true torpedo with a double taper, thicker on the smoking end. He clipped and lit it. She was right. It drew very well, though a little tight at first. It was mild in the mouth, but had a full body. There was no disagreeable aftertaste. Kind of earthy. He liked it.

"Five bucks," he said. "How do they do it?"

"Somebody's underwriting it," Becky said. "You can't sell that for five bucks, not made in the U.S. Or anywhere else, probably. Maybe they figure on building a clientele, then raising it to ten. But you oughta take advantage of the introductory offer, as they say. I get 'em at wholesale, of course. That'd be one of the advantages of living here."

"What are the others?" He looked at her through the smoke.

"Low rent," she said. "No upkeep. Of the house and grounds, I mean. I'm not washing your clothes or sheets. Maybe you can run them out to your ma's." She laughed then, evidently envisioning him lugging an armful of sheets out to his car, stepping on the trailing edges. "Maybe I could do the sheets," she said, grudgingly. "Throw 'em in with mine. And you could help me put up the screens and take 'em down. But no leaf raking, lawn mowing, painting, or. . . I don't suppose you know anything about plumbing? Good. I do. I hate a man screwing up the plumbing with his ignorance. Rent's five bills. That'll pay my utilities and help with the taxes."

He decided to look at the room. It turned out to be most of the second floor. He'd have a large bedroom that overlooked the parklike street. A private bath that she had totally remodeled, much more splendid than the one in the flat he'd looked at: this had an enormous walk-in shower with a built-in bench, plus a huge, jetted tub. Heated towel racks, infrared heat lamps in the ceiling, full-length mirrors.

He could also have a large, shelf-lined study that adjoined the bedroom. She had repaneled it herself with old cherrywood she'd found up north and had remilled. Everything was rewired, new lighting that could be adjusted with a rheostat. There was room for his stereo equipment, and she said that she'd insulated when she'd repaneled the rooms. With the insulation he could play music fairly loudly without disturbing her, in her downstairs domain.

She showed him her fabulous kitchen. All new appliances, beautiful maple countertops with inlaid marble and lovely Mexican tiles where one would need that kind of surface. Professional- quality ovens and cooking surfaces, and hearty exhaust venting. A couple of huge refrigerators. "You could have a designated reefer," she said, "if you think you'd need it. Otherwise, help yourself from these. I don't eat much, but I like to cook. Kind of hard to cook for one, though."

The whole tour took quite a while. It was a huge house. They could stay out of each other's way. He'd noticed that it was a nice place when he'd visited before, but he hadn't seen much, just the basement, where the cigars were kept and she'd put in a lot of exercise equipment. He was glad to see that she was not a neatness freak, but liked things pretty much picked up and stowed in the obvious places. And she didn't mind cigar smoke.

"Be pretty weird if I did," she said. "I kinda got this joint jerked back into shape after the slob kicked. Oh, Marv was a good man. I miss him. Once or twice a month. But he was hell to pick up after. You don't look like a slob."

Mulheisen said he didn't think he was. An early stint in the armed forces had left its impact. He made his bed tight every morning. Clothes up off the floor, that kind of thing. His desk might get a little messy.

"How come you didn't sell those vintage Upmanns?" he asked her. She had twenty boxes, stored in a walk-in humidor that was bigger than the apartment downtown—another enticing feature (or was that two?). She had offered them to him at the time and he'd had the impression that she wanted to get rid of them. Now it seemed she was still in the cigar business.

"Marvin said he kept 'em for you," she said. "Don't you want 'em?"

"For me? Well, sure. How much?"

"I figured it was a bequest. From Marvin."

Mulheisen was not sure how to take this. Could it be true? Marvin had retired at least a few years before he'd died. He'd never called, never mentioned any such thing. But who could object? As far as he knew, the cigars—vintage Cuban—were perfectly legal pre-embargo goods. Perhaps Marvin had forgotten, or was just too ill to pursue it, had put it off until the right moment—which never came. Mulheisen certainly didn't care to debate the issue, in case the offer was withdrawn.

"One big thing," she said, when they were back in the down-stairs living room. She stood there with her hands on her slim hips, engaging his eyes frankly. She looked younger than her mid-thirties. Maybe it was the sandals or the short hair. "Fucking."

Mulheisen laughed quietly and glanced about, embarrassed. "Hey, I'm only renting a room. Rooms. Thinking about it," he amended.

She nodded briskly. "I know. But a man and woman live in a house and fucking inevitably pops up, causes a lot of tension. I'm not agin it."

There was a silence of perhaps ten seconds, although it seemed much longer. Mulheisen looked at her.

"I hate tension," she said. She smiled. She had wicked little teeth. Like a baby panther. "How do you feel about it?"

Mulheisen didn't know what to say. "It's . . . ah . . ." He watched her for a clue, thought he had one, and finished, "It's bad. Oh, you mean the other? I thought you meant tension. The other is good. I like it. I wasn't thinking about it, just now."

"You got a girlfriend?" she asked. "I didn't think so. Me nei-ther. I'm not a lez, I mean. No boyfriend, either, although I don't mind going out once in a while, maybe getting laid. Used to, any-way. That's over. AIDS and stuff. Bad times for fucking. It was fun while it lasted, though. I had the tests. I'm clean. You?"

"Oh, yeah. Well, we have to get regular checkups."

"So that's all right," she said.

"Ah, well," Mulheisen said, hoping this discussion was con-cluded, "that's good." He nodded and glanced around the room.

He was about to make a comment about the nice fireplace when she sighed.

"Shit," she said. "I guess I could have put it better. Let's see." She furrowed her brow in thought. She looked up. "I'm not saying we should . . . no, that's not it. How about this? If you wanta fuck, we could try it. We might like it. Maybe we'd hate it. But I hate the tension, waiting for it to happen. You dig?"

"You mean . . . now?"

She shrugged. "If you wanta. *I* don't, particularly, right at the moment. But it's there if you wanta give it a whirl. I just don't want it hanging in the air, screwing everything up. So to speak." She laughed, a throaty chuckle.

"Okay," he said, relieved. "That's good to know. Thank you. Uh, I wouldn't, you know, dream of bringing a woman in if that's . . ."

"Well, I don't think I'd care for that," she said, "but it'd be none of my business, I guess. Those things happen, sometimes. I'm not likely to be partying down here, either. The thing is, two people live in a house, they want to keep their own lives, you know? Their own space, as the kids say. That's important."

He agreed. "But the thing is," he said, "I've found an apartment, downtown."

"Oh." She lifted her eyebrows. "Nice place?"

"Yeah. It's all new. Not as big as this, but . . . I already made a deposit, first month's rent, that kind of stuff."

"How much?" she asked. When he told her twelve hundred dollars, her face registered shock, then relief. "Well, hell," she said, "I can get your deposit back for you. No big deal."

So that was settled. They proceeded on to other things, like when he wanted to move, whether there was room in the garage for his Checker. He wondered what his mother would make of her. Fortunately, Cora Mulheisen was in Galápagos, or was it Ulan Bator?

Someplace where they had cranes. She knew he was moving, of course, but she'd have to be told about Becky, some time.

Becky arrived with her pickup truck, right on time. Mulheisen's gear would take at least two trips. When they had taken one load across town and returned for another, she came up to his room and suggested he might like to take his chair. She was pretty strong for as slim as she was; she hauled as many boxes as he did and didn't get winded, either. And she didn't even comment when he did.

Mulheisen was exhausted. He offered to take her to dinner, but Becky insisted on cooking a tremendous grilled flank steak with a special barbecue rub. Becky had some good wines. A rather boisterous cabernet seemed appropriate. It revived and yet relaxed them.

After that, they went to bed. It was . . . energetic. Becky was as lively as a trout and as hard to hold. Sometime during the night she eluded his embrace.

In the morning, he found her in the kitchen, where he'd gone in pursuit of a delicious aroma of freshly ground and brewed coffee. Becky thanked him for his efforts of the previous night in a friendly, matter-of-fact way and accepted his compliments.

"You were better than I'd hoped," she said. "That doesn't mean you get breakfast. I mean, you were excellent. Really. It's just, I've got stuff to do. We'll have to do it again. I'm glad we got that out of the way, though. No tension, see?" And she disappeared into the basement to work out.

Mulheisen went to work. It was a long drive to the Ninth Precinct, but he had a LaDonna figurado and thought about that slim body as he waited for lights. He felt great. He wondered what she had hoped. But she was right. No tension.

* * *

"You look like the shark that ate a whale," Jimmy Marshall said. "You get laid, or something?"

"What do you mean? What makes you say that?" Mulheisen came back at him. But Jimmy wasn't listening.

"We've got a guy here, wants to talk to you, about the Fat Man," Jimmy said.

"Why me?" Mulheisen said. "That's a Grosse Pointe case. Or the FBI. Why didn't you send him to them?"

"He's been to them," Jimmy said. "They brushed him off. He asked to see you. Said he'd heard about you. I'll send him in."

A stocky, muscular man about fifty appeared in the door. He was blond, with thick blond eyebrows and pale eyelashes, an old-fashioned G.I. haircut. A tough guy, it seemed. He was Jimmy Go, he said. "Golsen, but they call me Jimmy Go." He seemed to think that Mulheisen would know him, or know of him, but Mulheisen didn't. Mulheisen got him to sit down. They were in the cluttered cubicle that Mulheisen called an office. He wondered, as he cleared some files off a chair for Jimmy Go, what Becky would think of the mess.

"What was the name again? Golson, with an *o*, like the tenor man?" he asked, scribbling in a notebook.

"*E*," the man said. "I thought Golysczywzki was bad. I had to change it. Nobody could pronounce it, or spell it. 'Specially at the motor vehicle department. Now I gotta spell Golsen. I'm a trucker. Gravel, stuff like that. Got a fleet of trucks. Yeah, it's about the Fat Man. Diablo, or whatever they call him."

He sat foursquare, hands on his powerful thighs, looking directly at Mulheisen. The detective waited.

"He ain't dead," Jimmy Go said.

"FBI says he is," Mulheisen said. "They did an autopsy, forensics identified him. They seem satisfied, from what I've heard."

"That's what they say," Jimmy conceded. "But it ain't him. It's somebody else. It's bullshit."

"What do you know, Jimmy?"

"The Fat Man ain't gonna get whacked by some security guard, a guy he hired, like the papers said. It's a put-up job. I know the guy. I had dealings with him, for years, the prick."

"What kind of dealings?"

Jimmy explained that for years the mob had tried to muscle in on his business, had harassed him, harassed his drivers, had tried to push him off jobs, sabotaged his trucks, and so on. It was a familiar story. Jimmy had fought back. He was tough. And finally, he made a deal with Wally Leonardo. Nardo was running that end of things in those days, when Carmine was boss.

It turned out that Nardo and Jimmy Go's sister had been acquainted. His sister had been a whore. He said it as if she had been a waitress. She had been Nardo's mistress for a while. And later, when his sister had fallen ill, Nardo had paid for an operation, even though they were no longer lovers. Jimmy Go's sister had died anyway, despite the operation. But Jimmy Go had found that Nardo played pretty straight with him.

Jimmy Go had been protected, for a not unreasonable price. It was the cost of doing business, he said. And Nardo had kept up his end. They got along. They were cut from the same stone, Nardo had told him. And now DiEbola had whacked Nardo. They had tried to lay it off on Pelodian, but Jimmy Go wasn't fooled. He'd talked to Nardo the night before he died. Nardo had told Jimmy Go he'd been to dinner at DiEbola's. Nardo knew it was coming. He knew what that dinner was all about. He'd said that the other two guys who were there, Malateste and Soteri, were gonna get it too. And they had.

Mulheisen didn't think that was much. What else was there?

Jimmy Go said Nardo had shown him a piece of paper. He'd given it to him. It was an address, where he could find Pelodian. It was way the hell out in the country, not far from the stone quarry where Nardo's body had been found. It was written in DiEbola's hand. Jimmy Go didn't know DiEbola's writing, but Nardo did. He knew it was a setup.

"Why did he go, then?" Mulheisen asked.

"I think he figured he could handle it, and if he couldn't, then it was his time," Jimmy Go said. "He wasn't scared. He said he'd gotten away with a lot of shit in his time, but maybe this was the payback. He never expected an angel chorus. But, what the hell, he might win! Only he couldn't. They must have jumped him."

"Maybe it happened that way," Mulheisen said, "but so what? DiEbola's dead. Well, maybe we could get the guys who did the deed. Did you show the paper to the FBI?"

Jimmy Go had. They didn't think it was much. They had taken the paper. They said they'd get back to him if something came of it. But they hadn't. Jimmy Go didn't think they were going to do anything. Trouble was, DiEbola wasn't dead. He was sure of it. Nardo had told him that he believed something funny was going down. The Fat Man was getting ready to cut. He was settling old scores, clearing the decks. He'd been knifing guys right and left, selling his operations to the highest bidders. That's what Nardo said and it looked like it was true. And if the Fat Man sold the biz out, could he stay on? No. He had to bolt.

"What do you care?" Mulheisen said. "He killed an old buddy of yours. Leonardo told you . . . what was it Nardo said?"

"He said he never expected to die in bed, flights of angels singing him home." Jimmy Go almost smiled, but he was a pretty mirthless sort of guy—his thin lips writhed for a second. "He was a pretty good guy, for a crook. He wasn't no Holy Joe, but he treated me good. Most of 'em out there"—he waved a thick, callused hand at the dirty window with its protective bars—"you reach out for a hand up and they'd as soon shit in your palm. Nardo was all right.

I gotta do something for him. He did something for Nita. He didn't haveta do nothing, but he did."

Mulheisen sat and stared at this knotty-looking man. He was impressed. The guy rambled on about his sister, Nita. She was never a nun, he said. They'd been orphans, stuck in a succession of foster homes, where they'd been kicked around. His sister had been raped when she was ten by one of the foster fathers. Jimmy had been younger by a couple years. He had tried to protect her, but it was she who had protected him from the beatings, she who had insisted that they couldn't be separated and had pitched such a bitch that the social workers had capitulated and found them homes together.

"She always thought she was so smart, but she wasn't that smart," he said. "She was good to me, though. I tried to look out for her when I got big. But you couldn't help Nita. She was into drugs, that kinda shit. But I ain't gonna let DiEbola get away with this."

He was raging inside, Mulheisen could see. But he kept it well muffled, choked off.

"I'll find the bastard, somehow," Jimmy Go said, getting up. "I'll find him and pound his fucking head in like he did old Nardo."

He was through talking to Mulheisen. He could see that Mulheisen couldn't help him.

"Well, wait a minute," Mulheisen said. "Where would I start?"

"Hell, I don't know," Jimmy Go said. "You're the fucking detective. There must be something that would tell you, some way to figure it out."

"I'll look into it," Mulheisen said. But Jimmy Go was gone, out the door.

An hour later, Mulheisen was talking to Brennan, the medical examiner. He had done the autopsy. Was there any way that the body was not DiEbola? No, Brennan said. It was DiEbola. The body was pretty destroyed, but they had plenty of identification, blood, tissue, teeth. They had ransacked the house upstairs, which hadn't been damaged. They were able to match hair and sloughed skin from the bedsheets. Good matches.

Good matches? Not perfect matches? Mulheisen asked. Well, there were some anomalies, sure, Brennan conceded, but there always were, and they were heavily outweighed. The medical files were the clincher. Nothing ever matched up one hundred percent. But the evidence was there. That was DiEbola.

What anomalies?

Well, there was some blood they couldn't account for, some fingerprints, some hair, some tissue. The investigators thought there may have been another man there, possibly he had perished in the boat that blew up and sank in the lake. Probably one of the assailants. They hadn't been able to make a match on him. No body. Probably never find it.

Mulheisen drove to the Federal Building offices, to visit the FBI. He was surprised to find a federal agent he had met before there, Dinah Schwind. She was kind of cute, he thought. He looked at her differently today, perhaps because of his experience with Becky. Women looked more attractive today.

The last time he'd seen her she'd been looking for a missing agent, evidently investigating Humphrey DiEbola. She was like a lot of federal agents in Mulheisen's experience: they asked the questions, but they didn't provide many answers to your questions. She had pumped him for details of his investigations of DiEbola and was particularly interested in his comments about Joe Service and Helen Sedlacek. As for the missing agent, she hadn't been able to provide him with much information; in fact, she'd said that he was more on the order of an informer, or a source, than an actual agent. He'd been working at Krispee Chips. His name was Pablo Ortega.

At the time, the name meant nothing to Mulheisen, but not long after he'd received a visit from Ortega's brother, from Mexico.

The family had heard from Ortega, months earlier, in a letter that suggested he was doing very well at Krispee Chips. But when Mulheisen and the brother had gone there to inquire about the missing man, they were told that Ortega had left the company and there was no information on his whereabouts.

Mulheisen mentioned this to Dinah Schwind now. "I'd have passed this on before now," he told her, "but you never said what office you worked out of. You're not FBI?"

"Oh, no," she said. "Right now I'm in and out of the country so much, I don't even know who I work for. My mother can't even get hold of me. But you did find Ortega?"

"No," Mulheisen said, "just his brother. But, you know, I've been thinking about it . . . you must have blood tests, that sort of thing, on your agents, eh? I've been talking to the medical examiner about the bodies they found at the DiEbola crime scene and they're still up in the air on some of the identifications. Maybe you should see if your guy wasn't one of the sources of some of the tissue and blood they found there."

Schwind was skeptical. The guy wasn't really an "agent," after all, but she was grateful for the suggestion. She'd get back to him on it. And before he knew it, she had run off. Oh well, it wasn't as if he didn't have other work to occupy him.

The FBI had a big file on DiEbola, but it didn't tell him much. They were totally convinced that DiEbola was a closed case. They weren't looking any further. They had listened to Mr. Golsen, but his information wasn't helpful about the actual perpetrators of the Leonardo murder. One of the other agents had the note. They could send him a copy if he needed it. They left Mulheisen to examine the file. He took some notes.

According to the records, Humphrey DiEbola had been born in Detroit, in 1935, and christened Umberto Gagliano. His mother had died soon after, his father in 1947. Custody of the youth had been awarded to Dominic and Sophia Busoni, of suburban Royal Oak, maternal relatives. He first attracted police attention in 1944, an Oakland County juvenile matter, no record. Later, the family moved into Detroit, and Umberto began to rack up a long series of police attentions, but no arrests and no fingerprints. At age twenty-one he had legally changed his name to Humphrey DiEbola, a simple matter of requesting the change through probate court.

Over the years, DiEbola was often suspected of violent crimes, often questioned, but never formally arrested. And again, no finger-prints. It was an amazing feat for a man so active in crime.

Mulheisen was strangely at peace as he left the federal offices. He stood on the sidewalk, among the tall buildings. It was a cool day in late spring, a milky sky. A good day for something. He felt good. Maybe it was Becky, he thought. But it had a old, familiar feel to it. He'd felt this way before, though not lately. He felt like doing some-thing, but he wasn't in any hurry. He was in a zone, as the kids said.

He went to juvenile court and was denied access to ancient records. He didn't blink. He called an old Royal Oak detective, a man named Hearn. They had met years ago. Hearn was in his eighties now, but he remembered Mulheisen. Did he remember any significant juvenile cases in 1944, involving a kid named Umberto Gagliano? No. But he remembered the Busonis.

"They were real gangsters," Hearn said. "They had a half dozen kids. The wife was something, a real beauty. She was Sophia before Sophia Loren. Nice gal, too. Busoni was always into some-thing. We were glad when he split to Detroit."

"Why did he leave?"

"I don't know. Moving up in the world, I guess."

Mulheisen called a friend at the *Detroit News* archives. She said she would put together a little file of DiEbola stories. They flirted a little. She hadn't seen him in a long time, she said. They should get together for a drink, or something. Mulheisen said he'd like to, but he was seeing somebody. It probably wasn't wise. His friend picked up on that. "Sounds serious," she said.

Hearn called back. He'd thought of something. "Busoni got run out of Royal Oak," he said. "It was funny, because it wasn't his fault."

"What do you mean, 'run out'?"

"The neighbors got after him. Him and his gang. They wanted him out. They even had a scene, what we'd later call a demonstration, in front of his house. We had to go out and break it up, protect him." Hearn laughed. "I mean, the guy was into a lot a stuff, but we had to protect him for something that didn't have anything to do with him."

"He had a gang? In Royal Oak? This was during the war?"

"Well, not a real gang, as such. But he always had guys, foreigners, coming around. Yeah, it was the war. People were wary of foreigners, you know. We had another deal out there, same neighborhood, where a baby-sitter saw a copy of *Mein Kampf*, Hitler's book. She told her folks, they told somebody else, next thing you know, a mob is shouting 'Nazi' outside the guy's door."

"I heard about that," Mulheisen said. "That was in Royal Oak? I thought it was Harper Woods. What happened?"

"Aw, nothing," the old policeman said. "The guy came out and said it was a free country, he could read any damn thing he wanted to, told 'em he wasn't a Nazi, just wanted to know what this Hitler guy was up to. That's all. We broke it up."

"Was the Busoni thing like that?"

"No, no, I don't even know if Busoni could read. Not English, anyway. It was . . . let's see . . . yeah, a kid had disappeared in the neighborhood. Didn't have anything to do with Busoni, though. He'd been out of town at the time. But maybe they were used to getting up mobs by then. Anyway, after that, Busoni and his family moved to the city."

"What about the kid?"

"The one who disappeared? They never found him. Oh, I take that back. They dug up his body, excavating. It was quite a while later, maybe ten years. Just bones. The guy on the cat, he didn't see it, at first. Bones were scattered all over, all crushed up. They figured the kid had crawled into an old abandoned excavation, got caved on. There were a lot of those old excavations, housing project that got started but then the war came along and there were no building supplies, no customers. After the war, though, they started to build like mad. By the late forties, they were . . ."

Hearn went on for a good long while about the postwar building boom. Mulheisen made some notes, hung up, and began to look at some of the other available records on DiEbola's career. Late in the day, his friend Sheila from the *Detroit News* called. She had a nice collection of stuff, if he wanted to come out and look at it. It was all in Sterling Township, at the *News* offices. Mulheisen felt a little odd about going there. He supported the *News* staff that had gone on strike some time back and hadn't been recalled. In the end, he figured that the archives belonged to an earlier, prestrike era. His union sympathies didn't apply. He said he'd come out.

He called Becky to say he wouldn't be home until late. "For godssake," she said, "let's don't start this crap. You're a big boy. Just because we had a little fun doesn't mean you have to call every time you're gonna be out. What, did you expect supper or something?"

She didn't sound cross, so he was relieved. "Oh, okay," he said. "I wasn't sure."

"So now you know. Jeez, no tension, remember?"

"Okay, okay," he said, "no tension." He almost made a crack about not feeling any tension all day, but decided against it.

When you look at old files a certain weariness sets in quickly. Especially if you don't know what you're looking for. Soon enough, he was grateful for the bad coffee that Sheila brought to the viewer.

Here was a depressing and seemingly endless parade of articles, many with pictures, of a younger, fatter Humphrey being questioned about and denying murder, theft, arson, you name it. In no case was he arrested or charged. It was an amazing performance. And at about age thirty, the pictures ceased. He was no longer even brought in, or if he was, it was handled more discreetly. That meant powerful lawyers.

Mulheisen knew, of course, who the lawyers were, but there was no point in approaching them. He wondered, however, if there weren't some documents that must now be made public, given the official demise of DiEbola. He would have to check.

He sat back and sipped the coffee. A thought struck him. He explained to Sheila about the disappearance of the schoolboy, in Royal Oak. About 1944. She soon found it. The boy was named Arthur Cameron White Jr. He had been fifteen. A large, heavy boy, certain to have been called "Tubby," though probably not to his face, not by his classmates. He was only in the eighth grade, so he'd been held back at least one year.

The original article described him as missing. The article hinted that he might have run away. He had run away before, it said. He had left the school that day for disciplinary reasons—sent home. But there was no one at home. Things were a little looser in those days, it seems. It appeared that for the first few days the police looked for him in bus stations, hobo jungles, highway stops, that sort of thing.

Mulheisen was entertained by the "hobo jungles." He remembered scouting them, in his uniform days. He supposed they still existed, in some form. Nowadays, they would look among the haunts of the homeless.

After a few days a more general search was made of the neighborhood. But it was too late. Evidently there had been "torrential" rains. He supposed that meant several days of pretty heavy, more or less constant rainfall. Not much chance. He'd participated in a search like that, once, as a young cop. There was nothing drearier than walking through parks and neighborhoods, looking but not knowing what to look for. Sort of like what he was doing right now. You soon fell prey to the conviction that nothing would be found. Nothing was found. It was rare to find anything that way. Just a bunch of men, stumbling around, wishing they were somewhere else, watching the leaders for the first sign that it was time to call it a day.

He didn't feel that way now, though. He felt interested. The story had moved to page 2, dropped to page 5, and then disappeared. It was revived by the mob that had besieged a neighbor's house. The reports didn't identify the neighbor. It was an unfounded rumor. Where the rumor had originated was unknown and not pursued. The story disappeared.

In 1950, Crooks Woods was finally sold and chopped down and the abandoned sites were bulldozed for a new subdivision. That's when the body was discovered—six years later, not ten. Much too late. The White family had moved away, to Ontario. They were from Ontario originally. An ambitious young reporter had evidently talked her editor into letting her do a lengthy Sunday feature piece on the sad tale. It wasn't much of a story. The family had believed that "Porky" (Aha! Mulheisen thought) had run away. They had never believed that anything bad had happened to him.

Porky was a bad boy, Mulheisen concluded from the article. They were secretly relieved at his disappearance. Anyway, he was the kind of kid who hurts others. Not a victim. The principal had expelled him that day for twisting a smaller kid's arm so violently that the child had to be taken to the hospital by the school nurse. (They had a school nurse!)

The main interviewee in the feature article was a teenage girl, Ivy, the younger sister, one of three girls. The youngest girl had died of diphtheria not long before Porky vanished. The parents were despondent and went back to a small town near Midland, Ontario. But the teenaged girl remembered that Porky "had a kind of hide-out somewhere, he never would say where." She thought he must have gone there, but they had no way to find it, no clue.

Oh, this is a waste of time, Mulheisen thought. He gathered up his stuff and thanked Sheila. She asked him what his new girl-friend was like. He said she wasn't his girlfriend, just a woman he was living with. "That's cute," Sheila said. He didn't feel like explaining. He promised to take her to lunch, soon, and drove home. He was tired. Becky had gone to bed. He didn't know whether to be pleased or disappointed. He just tiptoed upstairs and got in bed himself.

The sheets were clean. They smelled nice. He thought she must have washed them. This might work out, he thought. He fell asleep wondering if she was his girlfriend.

16

Netherworld

Helen was gracious. She looked tired, though. Mulheisen thought she must be finding the life of a don hectic. A donna? She did not look like a crime boss, none he'd ever seen, anyway.

"I thought you'd be around long before this," she said. "Mr. DiEbola has been dead for weeks."

"It wasn't my case."

She just looked at him, disbelieving. "What do you want, then?"

"I'm trying to close out another case," he said. "When did you last see Pablo Ortega, also known as Pepe Ortega?" He was pleased to see a flicker of alarm cross her face. Before she could answer, he hastily rattled off the standard Miranda warning.

"What's that all about?" she asked, carefully.

"We've identified Ortega's body. He was murdered. Do you want an attorney?"

"Am I a suspect?"

"Not the primary suspect," Mulheisen said. "But you could be an accessory." They were sitting in the living room of her mother's home. Helen had left DiEbola's estate, although she was the heir in his will.

"What happened to Pepe?" she asked.

"For one thing, someone chopped off his head."

"My god!" Her emotion was genuine.

"He was dead before that happened, according to the medical examiner," Mulheisen said. "His hands were chopped off as well. It was an attempt to conceal the identity. Effective, as long as we had no clue to his identity, but ultimately the DNA matchup was definitive." He had delivered this information in a calm, almost casual way. It allowed her time to recover her poise.

"I'm very sorry," she said. "Pepe was a nice man, very talented. Do you have any idea why he was"—she hesitated—"killed?"

"Yes. He was an undercover agent for a federal agency. Presumably, DiEbola discovered this and either ordered him murdered or did it himself. But you haven't answered my question: When did you last see him?"

She thought for a minute, then gave up. "Sometime in January," she said, "I'm not sure of the date."

"Think about it," Mulheisen prompted her. "It could be helpful." When, after a moment, she shook her head, he went on: "What was your relationship with Ortega?"

"What do you mean?"

"Were you friends? Lovers? Did you have any extended conversations?"

"We were friends," she said. "He was Humphrey's chef. So we talked, occasionally. Not anything extensive. He was funny, fun to be around."

"Not lovers?" When she shook her head, he saw that she was lying. "I'm going to tell you something," he said. "The M.E. thinks he made love just before his death. The FBI is pulling his room apart, right now. They may find evidence that will link him to a lover. A hair, fluids, maybe a note. I'll be surprised if they don't want to talk to you."

She denied again any intimacy, more firmly this time.

"DiEbola's the main suspect, of course," he said. "And he's dead. Did he say anything odd about Ortega's disappearance to you, or in your presence?"

She said that Humphrey had shrugged off Pepe's absence, he didn't seem to regard it as anything significant. She wasn't sure, but she thought that he may have said that Pepe had simply decided to leave. Her impression was that Humphrey and Pepe had discussed this, prior to his leaving. She wasn't sure, now, but that was always the impression she'd had.

Mulheisen asked if DiEbola had seemed excited, or disturbed, acting unusually during this period. She said he'd talked a lot about his life, his youth, but that she hadn't paid much attention.

"About his childhood? That's interesting," Mulheisen said. "Did he by any chance ever mention a boy, Porky White? From his youth?"

"I can't think of any names at the moment," she said, "but he talked a lot about some childhood experiences." When Mulheisen pressed her on this, she went on: "He told me about a boy who had been killed, a neighbor."

"Killed? When did this happen?" Mulheisen asked.

"When he—Humphrey—was about, oh, eight or nine. Maybe older. I didn't try to calculate it."

"What did he know about this killing? Was he involved?"

"I didn't think he was involved, but the incident seemed to have had a strong impact on him," she said. At Mulheisen's urging she described DiEbola's account of the incident: a neighbor child had wandered off into the woods, where he encountered some kind of pervert who murdered him and buried his body in a cave. The murderer was never caught.

Mulheisen was jarred. He didn't know what he'd expected, but it wasn't this. There were serious problems with this story, even if one hadn't any awareness of the events. He enumerated them for Helen: Arthur White had disappeared in 1944, his body found in 1950. Nobody knew how he had died. So: How did DiEbola know what had happened to the child? If the killer was never caught, how did he know he was a pervert?

"I thought it was a dream," Helen said. "The way he talked about it, and . . . come to think of it, he said he'd had trouble sleeping, nightmares. And then he told this story. I guess I just thought it was his dream, or something like that had actually happened, but this was his dream version. I got the impression that he'd been troubled by this dream before, a lot, since childhood. He must have talked about it a half dozen times."

"Tell me about it," Mulheisen said. "Was there any particular time, say the first time, that he told you more?"

Helen considered this. The first time was fairly early, not long after she had moved in, say early January. Humphrey had complained of a sleepless night, of nightmares. He didn't tell her about the dream right away, but later that afternoon, in the study. It was awful weather, they hadn't gone out. He'd been reading, then more or less spontaneously he had told her this story, which, at first, she'd thought was a variation on a fairy tale. But then, from something he said, which she couldn't remember now, she realized this was the nightmare. She really couldn't say if he'd told her all the details at that time, or if she was just conflating various versions that he mentioned, piecemeal, over the ensuing weeks.

"He started out talking about being buried alive," she said. "I think that was it. Or maybe he asked if I'd ever had that nightmare. That's pretty common, isn't it?"

Mulheisen supposed it was, but he was curious about the further details. What was that about a fairy tale?

"At first it sounded like Hansel and Gretel, or even Goldilocks," she said, "you know, babes in the woods. Lost children, ogres, giants. I didn't take it seriously, of course."

"But later?" he prompted.

Later, the dream and the fairy-tale element seemed to have faded away, somehow, she said. She was trying to reconstruct the sequence, but not having much luck. She really hadn't given it much attention at the time, although she could see that it was bothering him. At some point, she said, he began to talk about it as a real incident, something that had actually happened.

"I know what it was," she said. "There was another child involved. Humphrey had heard about it from him. It had always bothered him, it seems, because he had felt protective toward this second child, a cousin or something. This child had barely escaped, but was scared witless and had made him promise never to tell anyone, and he hadn't, not until he told me. Well, that's what he said, anyway."

The full story went like this, as best as she could remember: the neighbor child and his cousin—he had never named him—had wandered off one day, playing. They had gone to a woods, forbidden to them. There they had found a cave, which they crawled into, knowing it was wrong. In the cave they had found stuff.

"Stuff?" Mulheisen said.

"Grown-up things, maybe dirty pictures or something," Helen said. "He didn't describe what they found, but from his tone or manner I got the impression it was something like that. The whole story was very dark, very scary. Anyway, they found the stuff. Then, just when they decided they better get out, the Boogey Man came home. That's what he called him!" she said, pleased to have recovered this tidbit. "Or, another time, he referred to him as the Ogre. The Boogey Man punished them for messing with his stuff. That's how he put it. Then he tried to force them to do bad things.

It sounded sexual to me. The Boogey Man grabbed the neighbor boy, who was the smallest, and while he was fooling around with him, the cousin escaped. The neighbor boy never came out of the cave, and the Boogey Man, or Ogre, must have gotten away. The cousin was afraid to say anything, because he knew the Boogey Man was still out there, would get him. So they never told anybody anything. Let's see." She stopped to think, then went on after a minute. "I think that's all the details, all I remember, anyway."

"He never mentioned the name Porky? Porky White? Or Arthur?"

She was sure he hadn't. He'd also told her several stories about scrapes he'd gotten into with other kids, later, and she did remember some of those names: Carmine, Angelo, Howard, Denny. She couldn't remember all the names. But no Porky, or Arthur.

They went on to talk of Humphrey's surprising interest in books, particularly Machiavelli, his theories about power, influence, and so on. Mulheisen was intrigued. He asked about other people in DiEbola's life. She told him what she knew, but guardedly. It wasn't of much interest. He asked if she thought DiEbola was homosexual. She said she didn't think so. He seemed interested in women, although he didn't have any attachments. She told him about Humphrey's idealized love for the little girl. If he was gay, he was well closeted. The culture in which he operated was male, exclusively, but she knew of no associates of his who were even rumored to be gay. And no, she stated firmly, before he could ask, she had not been his lover. But she knew men. Humphrey had been a man. They'd been close, and, if he wanted to know, she'd considered it. The notion had been entertained, in a civilized way, by both of them. They had decided against it.

Mulheisen listened to all of this attentively, and not just because it reminded him of Becky's voiced dread of tension. Never once did Helen betray even a hint that she thought Humphrey DiEbola was still alive. That was convincing, to Mulheisen. He began to think that he'd been unduly influenced by Jimmy Go's stolid certainty. After all, he considered, Jimmy Go had strong feelings about the man and probably just wanted him to still be alive so that he could wreak personal vengeance.

Just to satisfy himself, he asked her, point-blank, if she thought there was any chance that the body found in the ruins of the basement was not DiEbola. To his surprise, although she claimed she had no doubts, he detected a measure of uncertainty. What was this? He pursued the question.

"He was talking about retiring," she said, finally, yielding to his pressure.

"But how could he retire?" Mulheisen asked. "Did he have somebody in mind to succeed him? Was he ill?"

She didn't know. She denied any knowledge of his plans, but she was unconvincing. At long last, she conceded that she'd had some doubts about the explosion and the fire. He had insisted that she not be present in the house that night. She had come home, to her mother's.

"Then, maybe it wasn't his body," Mulheisen said. "Maybe he ran away, like the Boogey Man."

"If he ran away," she said, "he ran away on the boat, the *Kiddle-Dee-Divey*. And that blew up. So he's dead, anyway."

"They didn't find a body," Mulheisen pointed out.

"You mean, he could have destroyed the *Kiddle-Dee-Divey*, to make it look like he was dead, just in case someone doubted the basement scene? Humphrey was a plotter," she conceded, "but that's too elaborate. If he'd gone to all the trouble to fake his death in the basement, he wouldn't want to do something like the boat. That would make the basement deal look fishy. No, no way. He was crazy about that boat."

"If he escaped on the boat," Mulheisen pointed out, "it would have been a dead giveaway."

"So maybe he wasn't on the boat," she said. "I don't know. But he wouldn't have purposely destroyed it."

"Why not?" he persisted. "He apparently abandoned everything else personal—assuming he escaped. Didn't he? Surely he had some other objects, books or pictures or whatever, that were dear to him. Is anything important to him missing?"

"Nothing that I know of," she admitted. "But he would never have destroyed the boat."

She was convinced, and Mulheisen could see she was convinced. "That's a funny name for a boat," he said. "It sounds like the old song 'Mairzy Doats.'"

"That's what it was," Helen said. "You know the song! He told me that was what he named the boat after."

Mulheisen reverted to DiEbola's health. Helen saw through that one. Humphrey had been in better physical shape than he'd been in in years, perhaps since his youth. Of course, losing a lot of weight could bring its own problems, she conceded, but he seemed fine. Still, you could never tell. It was possible that he'd had a terminal illness and had decided to go out in a grand blast, but the idea was too iffy. She suggested he consult DiEbola's regular physician, Dr. Schwartz. She thought he'd been to see him not too long before his death.

Mulheisen got up to go. He told her again that she could expect to see the FBI, about Ortega. Then he asked about Roman Yakovich. He wanted to talk to him. Here was another surprise: she seemed uncomfortable, said she hadn't seen Roman lately.

"When was the last time you saw him?" Mulheisen asked. She was evasive. She didn't know. Maybe a week. He kept to himself, she said. Mulheisen asked to see her mother. Her mother was ill, she said, under a doctor's care. She couldn't see anyone. Mulheisen insisted.

Mrs. Sedlacek didn't seem ill, but she was withdrawn and uncommunicative. She acted as if she couldn't understand English, or speak it. She spoke Serbian to her daughter, who translated.

"She hasn't seen Roman lately," Helen said. "She thinks he went on vacation, maybe he went to Florida."

Mulheisen hadn't heard anything in the conversation that sounded like "Florida." He persisted: How long had he been gone? Maybe a week, he was told. Had he ever gone away like this before? Oh, sometimes. He was a grown man, he didn't have to tell them where he went. That was the story. Mulheisen gave up.

"So what are you doing these days?" he asked Helen, as he was leaving.

"What's that supposed to mean?"

He didn't want to say, How do you support yourself now that your sugar daddy is gone? But that's what he meant, and she knew it. He tried to cover up the gaffe with a jest, but as usual he went too far. Mindful of the joke around the precinct that Helen Sid was now the don, he quipped, "Just as long as you don't start thinking you're La Donna."

"But I am," she said. She said it with pride.

"You're what?"

"That's me," she said, picking up a box of cigars and thrusting them at him. "La Donna Detroit. Take them. On the house. Or do you consider this a bribe?"

"These are you?" he said stupidly.

"All legit," she said. "I own the company. Hell, I invented the cigar. I know you'll like them."

"I do," he confessed. "They're very good. Thanks."

"I'll tell you a little secret," she said, leaning close. He was reminded of Becky. It was the feral mouth, perhaps, or the catlike litheness. "They really are Cuban."

"How can that be?"

"Trade secret."

He smoked one on his way to Dr. Schwartz's offices. Schwartz was not happy to see him. He'd been through all this with the Grosse Pointe police, the FBI, several times. He had verified the findings of the Wayne County medical examiner from his records of Humphrey DiEbola. He was frankly hostile, wanting to know why the Detroit police were involved. Mulheisen managed to present a vague justification that Schwartz could have refuted if he'd cared to take the time. But gradually, after Mulheisen allowed him to pontificate about medical expertise and the infallibility of his record keeping for a while, he grew more friendly.

"I know DiEbola was supposed to be this monster," Schwartz said, "but really, Sergeant, I can't say I found him to be so. The man was a pussycat, as they say. It's odd, isn't it? You read these newspaper articles, you'd think he was a cold-blooded killer, but he wasn't."

"No? Well, he was never indicted, anyway," Mulheisen said, "or even charged. An amazing record."

"Maybe he never did what they say," Schwartz suggested. "If you ask me, he was a businessman. A little shady, maybe, but basically just hard-nosed and pretty astute. He talked like a truck driver, but he knew how to run a business. And he could be generous, too."

"How is that?"

"Well, he sometimes sent friends or employees to me for medical care, and then he took care of the bills, out of his own pocket. That's pretty decent."

Mulheisen agreed. He recalled that Leonardo had acted similarly. He wondered if Humphrey had paid for medical care for a mistress. That would be worth finding out. He'd dearly love to locate a mistress of Humphrey DiEbola's, it could be a valuable link. But Schwartz said he'd seen no female referrals. All males. He didn't care to speculate, at Mulheisen's quick follow-up suggestion, on the possibility that DiEbola was homosexual. He doubted it. He'd seen no such signs.

"Who did he send, for instance?" Mulheisen asked.

Schwartz said he didn't mind discussing with the police a client who was deceased and under investigation, but he didn't think he should discuss or even identify other patients, even if they had been referred to him by the deceased. Of course, if Mulheisen could obtain a warrant, or a court-ordered deposition, that was another matter.

Mulheisen nodded agreeably. He could see the point. But had DiEbola sent him many clients? It turned out that he'd sent in only one, in the last year. That was about three months ago. The man was in poor physical shape, grossly overweight, but as far as he knew—he hadn't seen the patient recently—he had benefited from DiEbola's interest. He'd lost weight, gotten into shape. Schwartz supposed that it had interested DiEbola because he'd turned his health problems around in a similar way.

Mulheisen thought about this on his way back to the office. He hadn't pursued it with Schwartz, although normally the doctor's stiffness would have provoked him, but the idea nagged at him. He called Andy Deane at Rackets and Conspiracy and asked who in the mob was a fatso, someone DiEbola might have thought he could reform. Andy laughed. They were all pretty tubby, these days, he said. He named half a dozen notorious thugs who were seriously obese. Angelo Badgerri was probably the worst. A vicious swine, a collector. But he'd disappeared a few months ago. He was said to have retired, to have left the country.

"Who says?" Mulheisen wanted to know.

It was mostly rumor. Deane said that people were so relieved not to have Mongelo around that they soon put him out of their minds. He was an old buddy of Humphrey's, though, from the early days. They called him Mongelo, he said, because he bit people. But a lot of mobsters were disappearing, he said. He described it as a shake-up, the changing times. Besides the killings of Soteri, Malateste, and Leonardo, there was the murder or disappearance of minor hoods like Strom Davidson and Matty Cassidy. Davidson had been found in an alley, apparently the victim of neighborhood muggers. Cassidy, of course, had been identified as one of the victims in the explosion and fire.

Mulheisen remembered Davidson, a real loudmouthed creep. He realized now that Helen must have taken over Davidson's tobacco business. Deane said that was so, but that the word was that Davidson had been forced out, or sold out well beforehand. As far as he knew, LaDonna Detroit was legit.

Mulheisen asked about Roman Yakovich. Any rumors? No. But then, Roman had more or less retired when his boss was hit. No one ever saw him anymore. Andy would ask around, though.

In a mischievous mood, Mulheisen called Schwartz's office and identified himself as Badgerri, asking for an appointment. The receptionist didn't hesitate. She made the appointment, asking only if it was for any particular problem or just a checkup.

"Just a checkup," Mulheisen told her. "I thought I should. How long has it been?"

She checked and said it had been two months. He was due. The doctor would want to know how his blood pressure medication was doing. In fact, they probably ought to do another blood panel, so he shouldn't eat or drink anything but water after midnight before his appointment.

Mulheisen said in that case not to schedule the appointment just yet, he'd have to see when a good time would be, then thanked her and hung up. He sat for a long while, contemplating the circumstance of two men, closely related in age and background, one of them until fairly recently so notoriously obese that he was generally called the Fat Man, while the other was just as fat and was said to be on a weight-losing regime. And both of them lately being attended by the same doctor. Is that coincidence? He considered the possibility that a man who has successfully dealt with a personal health problem like obesity might be eager to help out an old friend with the same problem. Like a reformed alcoholic sponsoring an old fellow drunk at A.A., maybe. Except that this old pal—one of the worst assholes in Christendom, a man whom nobody, not even a notorious Samaritan like DiEbola, would dream of assisting out of an open latrine he might have tumbled into—had disappeared from public view . . . at about the time he had been treated to medical care by Brother DiEbola. Too much coincidence for Mulheisen. These guys were disappearing into the woods like . . . like Indians, like Le Pesant. Another "bad bear," or was it "malicious bear"?

He called Brennan at the medical examiner's office and asked what would be the difficulty of switching medical records, where both patients were treated by the same doctor.

"You mean physically switching them? Gee, what a primitive concept! You'd have to break into the offices, transfer records, fake some, probably. And then there's the records on the computers. You'd have to be computer literate, Mul. It'd be a laborious, time-consuming bit of business. But, oh sure, it could be done." There was a silence, then he mused, "It could work. The thing about doctors, they're very jealous of their record keeping. If something is in a file, the doctor would be insistent that it was no mistake. In such a case, the physician would prove to be a terrific ally if you were trying to say one guy is who you want him to be. And the thing is, you don't have to be absolutely ironclad about this, as long as the big important details are covered. I assume you're still scratching at the DiEbola evidence."

Mulheisen said he was. He speculated for Brennan that if, as he said, the "big important details" pointed toward one identification, then a smattering of noncorroborative evidence would be waved aside.

"Providing," Brennan expanded, "that A, there's no serious doubt or suspicion of faked evidence, and B, no single item surfaces that conclusively rules out the desired identification. If you've got that, Mul, you're on base."

Mulheisen felt it was worth pursuing. He called the legal guys and explained why he'd need a warrant. They said it sounded vague, but doable. They'd get right on it.

He put that out of his mind and went back to studying his notes. He focused especially on the Porky White story. DiEbola's version was fascinating. It was an obvious fabrication, even if it wasn't clear whether it was intended to deceive or an unconscious dream fiction: displacing the dead Arthur White with a nameless child, a defenseless victim, and distancing himself from the event while being able to describe the frightening, nightmarish scene, via a secondhand account. It could be a work of imagination, certainly. A child who had known Porky White, who might in fact have been frightened of him, could have devised this nightmare. Mulheisen was familiar with some psychology, and he thought he recognized some timeworn themes, such as guilt, the sexual associations. He supposed that a child who had been afraid of Porky White might have felt guilt as a price of relief at his disappearance. Or it might be a veiled fear that he might not really be dead, or . . .

He gave that kind of speculation up. For one thing, the body hadn't been found at the time. As far as children of the period knew, Porky had simply run away. The expected reaction would be guilt-less relief. Psychological speculation, especially when you had little hard evidence and couldn't interview the parties involved, was a great waste of time. It was bound to be wrong. He didn't doubt that kids might have had bad dreams about Porky White's disappearance, but so what?

He found himself humming the tune "Mairzy Doats." As he recalled, the nonsense verse was repeated in plain language, revealing the code. "Mairzy doats and dozey doats, and little lambsy divey" became "Mares eat oats and does eat oats, and little lambs eat ivy." "A kiddle-dee-divey too" finished out as "A kid will eat ivy, too, / Wouldn't you?" Amusing—once. When repeated endlessly, it quickly became tiresome.

A goofy thing to name a boat, though. He knew about boats, having grown up on the river. People gave them dumb names, sometimes. It was like vanity license plates, he supposed, without the restriction of space. People named them to reflect some jokey notion, like the expense—*Me'n the Bank*. Or a favored identification: *Serb-a-Rite* had been Big Sid's boat, he recalled, presumably a play on *sybarite*. Or they named them after their wife or girlfriend. He wondered if Humphrey had ever had a girlfriend, one named Ivy.

Suddenly, he recalled that Helen had mentioned that Humphrey had nourished a crush on a little girl. Perhaps.

He called Helen. She was skeptical, to say the least. To the best of her knowledge Humphrey had never mentioned anyone named Ivy.

"While I've got you on the line," he said, thinking about Brennan's notion of the difficulty of switching medical records, "was Humphrey what you would call computer literate?"

"Humphrey was a computer bore," she said. "He got into it late, but in a big way. I think he even took a private course from some guy, some whiz. No, I don't remember the guy's name. It was before I spent much time with him. He'd sometimes be up half the night fooling around on-line. He was a real nut for it. Maybe it was the bad dreams, afraid to go to sleep. He seemed apologetic about it, or do I mean regretful? He said it was eating into his reading. That's what that bunker of his was all about, I suspect. He had all kinds of computer equipment down there."

Unfortunately, of course, Mulheisen realized, all those computers had been destroyed in the explosion and fire. It would have been interesting to see what was on them. He wondered if the hard drives had been at all salvageable. He didn't know much about that kind of thing, but he thought he could find out. Of course, if Humphrey had staged the whole thing, he'd certainly have erased anything useful. But it was worth checking.

The other thing worth checking, he thought, was school records. Just out of curiosity. He supposed somewhere there would be a record of Humphrey's classmates. Perhaps there was a little girl named Ivy. The name seemed familiar to him, but he guessed it was from recalling the song lyrics.

It was too late for that today. He'd found out a lot. Too much, really. He had to digest it.

Happily, he also had Becky's special osso buco to digest. After dinner he set about shelving his books in his new library. He'd never had a library before, so much shelf space! Inevitably, he dug out White's *The Middle Ground*. He reread the account of Le Pesant with profound interest. He was struck anew by the treatment of the problem of murder. This notion of the differentiation between the killing of an enemy—i.e, an enemy of the group to which one belonged—versus the killing of a "friend," someone not an enemy of the group . . . it was difficult to comprehend.

How could any society treat the latter so lightly? Any society he'd ever heard of considered that kind of killing particularly heinous, a betrayal of friendship, trust, striking at the very heart of the social contract.

No, he saw that he misunderstood it. It wasn't that the Algonquians took it lightly. They killed their enemies without compunction or sentiment and expected to be slain by them, if caught in a weaker position. That wasn't particularly different from the traditional notion of the criminal inculpability of soldiers in battle. What was different was they absolutely rejected the concept of capital punishment for civil crimes, for murder. One man is slain; why should another valuable life be taken? What compensation was that? And yet, he had no doubt that there had been psychotics, murderers, among them. How did they deal with that?

A man like DiEbola, now, what was his ethic? He apparently killed at will, dispatching whomever he judged to be inconvenient for him. As far as Mulheisen could tell, DiEbola was quite conscienceless about it. Although . . . he was troubled by dreams. Possibly he was mad. Possibly his crimes were catching up to him. If what Helen had told him was true, DiEbola had become fascinated of late with his earliest experiences. Mulheisen couldn't help feeling there was something to this, that there was a significance to the Porky White episode. If he had been involved in that death, what a boon it would be to him if he could cover that body, or resurrect it, as the Algonquians saw it. What a concept!

Mulheisen had perceived no inclination on Becky's part toward further exploring their cohabitation. He went to bed thoughtfully, without tension.

17

Ontario

It was raining hard when Mulheisen got up, and it was still raining when he got to the precinct and called the Roman Catholic archdiocese educational offices. A very helpful woman supplied him with the information that Umberto Gagliano had attended their schools in Oakland County and, later, in Wayne County, from 1940 through 1950, after which he seemed to have dropped out. She was even able to locate class lists from the grade school, but there had been no little girl named Ivy in any of those rather small classes. She looked, as well, at classes a year or two on either side of Umberto's: no luck.

This was disappointing, but Mulheisen reasoned that Umberto's little girlfriend could just as well have attended public school. Through the Oakland County school district, with the help of yet another amiable official, he settled on Starr Primary School as the most likely place. If that didn't work, he was prepared to try private schools. It wasn't necessary. In 1944 and 1945, a girl named Ivy White had attended fourth and fifth grades.

Of course, he thought. Porky White's sister. He should have recognized it yesterday. Still, what did it mean? Just another connection to the White family, but they were neighbors, after all. Perhaps there was no more to it.

In the fall of 1945, her records had been transferred to a public school system in Peterborough, Ontario. This was way the hell the other side of Toronto—a little far to pursue a nebulous link, he thought.

The legal office called. They had his warrant. With the company of Detective Maki, Mulheisen visited Dr. Schwartz's offices. Within minutes they found enough questionable entries and irregularities in the files of Humphrey DiEbola and Angelo Badgerri to arouse the suspicions of even Dr. Schwartz. Mulheisen impounded the files and took them downtown to Brennan at the Wayne County medical examiner's office. Even a cursory glance convinced Brennan that the files had been tampered with. He would reopen the file on the corpse they'd identified as DiEbola, this time armed with data on Badgerri.

Mulheisen left him to make a definite determination, but he was now convinced, himself. He returned to the precinct and called Jimmy Go. The trucker was not in, but his secretary said she'd try to get hold of him on his cell phone. He called within minutes. From the sound of it, he was in a dump truck in high gear. He was clearly pleased at Mulheisen's news, but he was content to say "I told you so!"

Mulheisen warned him that the next step would be the hardest. Just because the evidence had been confused didn't mean that DiEbola was alive. People had died in that basement. One of them could have been Humphrey, regardless of the attempt to veil his identity. More to the point: if DiEbola was alive, where was he?

Jimmy Go was eager to know what Mulheisen's next moves would be. He seemed oblivious to Mulheisen's statement that the case was still in the hands of the FBI. Mulheisen assured him that he himself would pursue DiEbola as the no-longer-believed-to-be-deceased suspect in the murder of Pablo Ortega, whose body had washed up in Mulheisen's precinct.

"Atta boy!" Jimmy Go yelled over the roar of traffic. "Keep me posted, Mul! I'll make it worthwhile to you!"

Mulheisen didn't bother to respond to this artless bribery offer. He said Jimmy Go could read about it in the papers, if he was successful. For now, he had to do a lot more research into DiEbola's past.

"All I meant was, if you need any help," Jimmy Go said, "you can count on me."

Mulheisen thanked him and went back to work. One of the things that had interested him was the boat. What role had it played in DiEbola's plan? Like any Detroit policeman, Mulheisen had not only followed the case in the media but had supplemented that information by talking to other, official sources. By now he had seen the FBI report. The accepted scenario of the investigation had seen DiEbola as the victim of an assassination. Obviously, it had not gone well. At least one of the putative assassins, the security guard John Nicolette, had disappeared and was assumed to have died in the explosion of the *Kiddle-Dee-Divey*, although no bodies had been recovered. It was assumed that his original role would have been to let the killers into the grounds. That part of the assassins' plan had gone awry, it seemed, when Nicolette was invited to play cards with DiEbola. Questioning of the other guards had established that: Nicolette had informed the gate man of where he was going.

Mulheisen had thought that was a shaky assumption on the part of the investigators, but he hadn't considered it very deeply, as long as the original scenario seemed to hold up. Now Nicolette's role and the problem of access looked more interesting. It was thought that the assassins had gained access to the DiEbola estate via the lake, after they'd discovered the change in security plans. (Conceivably, they were notified hurriedly by Nicolette.) Why hadn't the conspirators just canceled and hoped for a better occasion?

The FBI had speculated that the change had been offset by the advantage of having a co-conspirator, Nicolette, on the spot.

A stolen rowboat had been found, smashed at its mooring at the dock. Obviously, that was how they got in, or so the grand theory went. No abandoned vehicle had been found, but the assassins must have been dropped off, made their way along the canal path, where they stole the rowboat and simply rowed out to the lake and on to DiEbola's. No one had seen the boat being rowed, but it was fairly late at night. Presumably, they had always planned to escape via the *Kiddle-Dee-Divey*, which was conveniently moored and ready to use—perhaps another benefit of Nicolette's collusion.

Now, with the indication that DiEbola had attempted to confuse identification of the bodies, a new scenario was required. Two bodies had been found in the basement, neither of them intact. One of them was presumed to be Humphrey DiEbola, the other a small-time mobster named Matty Cassidy. It was thought that Cassidy was the key, somehow. He'd been allied to one of DiEbola's less-than-supportive henchmen. The missing figure was Nicolette. He had some tenuous marital connections, but there was no reason to see him as a conspirator, Mulheisen thought. He was still missing. Who else had been down there? There was ballistic evidence from at least three guns. If one of the bodies was Badgerri, that meant a cozy four-handed poker game. The FBI had established fingerprints on two weapons found at the scene, and they matched with prints they had earlier established as DiEbola's: prints derived not from files, since there were none, but from household sources, like drinking glasses, cups, doorknobs. But what if DiEbola had planted those? The FBI presumably had Badgerri's prints—he had a long record—but they'd never had any reason to try to match them with the prints found at the scene.

Mulheisen presumed that DiEbola must have intended to use the *Kiddle-Dee-Divey* himself. Why? The obvious answer: to escape to Canada. The international border here was notoriously porous. He might have laid plans to fly out of Canada to some other destination. Or he might still be in Canada. A standard check of the airlines showed nothing, but Mulheisen had expected little from that.

And now, of course, another possibility raised its head. Say that DiEbola had escaped an assassination attempt, or even that he had staged the attempt himself, to make it appear he was dead. It was possible that he had died when the boat blew up. As yet, no sign of bodies had been found, and given the passage of a couple of weeks, it looked like none would be found. Was this just another subterfuge, to conceal the true nature of the plan? Had the assassins or, more likely, DiEbola destroyed the boat to close another channel of investigation? Had they, or he, then gone on in yet another boat? This seemed possible, even likely.

Mulheisen stared out through rain-blurred windows, pondering. It all seemed so speculative. Why bother with the boat at all? It just led the investigators on, provided them with another track. Very likely, it was a false trail. DiEbola was an intelligent man, a truly devious man. He had almost miraculously avoided arrest for decades. He probably could have simply packed his bags and taken a plane to anywhere in the world. Such a course would inevitably have been discovered, and pursuit would continue. Mulheisen, for instance, had been prepared to make an arrest on the basis of evidence he had discovered in the Hoffa investigation. Possibly, the FBI and other agencies were similarly poised to act.

DiEbola must have known that his long performance was about to end. He'd seen his fellow mobsters falling left and right, lately, to FBI investigations. Mulheisen couldn't help feeling that DiEbola had known that he, Mulheisen, was very close. No flight was likely to take him beyond the reach of the investigators, Mulheisen included.

It made sense to stage the death scene, if that is what had happened. Mulheisen now believed it. If that performance played as planned it could well have convinced everyone that DiEbola was dead. He couldn't help thinking about the farce that Cadillac had staged for Le Pesant. End of case. And here it had almost succeeded. But why the boat? Could this be one of those unconscious blunders that even the brilliant criminal makes? But where did it lead?

It led to Canada. That was a very large place, the second-largest nation in the world, geographically speaking. Not many people, however. It wasn't hopeless. He did have another, nebulous, lead to Canada.

What the heck, he thought. He called Peterborough and got through to the school system. Ivy White had graduated from school there. Her records had been sent on to McGill. The university in Montreal, in turn, said that Ivy White had graduated in 1958, in a premed program. Her records had been forwarded to the University of Michigan, in Ann Arbor. She had graduated from there with a medical degree in four years. She had interned at Henry Ford Hospital, in Detroit.

She had spent the early 1960s as a staff surgeon at Henry Ford. Having just looked at DiEbola's medical records, Mulheisen did not recall any instance of him ever being hospitalized, though it may have simply escaped his notice. But it was quite possible that someone DiEbola knew had been a patient there, very likely, in fact. He could have bumped into Ivy White there while visiting someone. Mulheisen was encouraged.

The physician's placement service gave him a link to Ontario, to an indigenous peoples community in the far north, up beyond Sioux Lookout. He groaned. This was getting pretty far afield. As long as Ivy White was in Detroit, he had nourished hopes for this line of investigation. But, what the heck, it had taken him only an hour or two to find out this much: there was a telephone up there, wasn't there?

There was. And for the first time he talked to someone who had actually known Ivy White. Dr. Ivy White, the beloved doctor who had delivered a couple of generations of babies, taken out appendixes, and "cured more ills than a whole tribe of stinkin' med'cine men," according to a garrulous gentleman named Ronnie Heavy Man, who'd answered the phone. This amiable fellow who said scathing things in a laughing voice was willing to inform any and all that "Indi'n med'cines no damn good. 'N' this new quack, Weatherby, or whatever he calls hisself, why he don't know pus from snot. If you could only send Doc White back, why . . ."

Mulheisen finally got from him the immensely gratifying news that Doc White had relocated, "down below." She had returned to southern Ontario to care for her aged mother, who was dying of cancer. It was hoped that once the old lady kicked off, Doc White would come back to Little Loon River Camp, and "The sooner the better—not to wish the old bag an early death, but."

The place Ivy White had gone to was an island in Lake Huron, off the Bruce Peninsula. Mulheisen looked it up on his map. He estimated it was a good day's drive from Detroit. Up to Port Huron, over toward Owen Sound and hang a left. Drive clear out to Tobermory and get a boat out to Shitepoke Island.

He looked in his agency manual. There was an office of the Royal Canadian Mounted Police on the peninsula. A Sergeant McPherson answered. He was happy to hear from Sergeant Mulheisen of the Detroit Police. Yes, indeed, he knew Dr. White. A very nice lady, eh? She lived on "Shypoke" Island. Her mother had died several weeks back. Well, by golly, it was Boxing Day, or thereabouts, now he thought of it. More like half a year, eh? Time flies.

Mulheisen mentally supplied the "Eh?"

What could Sergeant McPherson say about Dr. White? She was about fifty years old, but if Sergeant Mulheisen thought it was more like sixty, he supposed it was possible. Damned fine-looking woman for sixty, he'd say. She had spent many years among the people, up in the blackfly country. Helluva woman. He heard she was going back. He hoped not. She did some work locally and it was a damned good thing for the islanders to have a doctor.

There were probably a couple hundred people out there. Most of 'em old-timers. You know how it is, eh? Kids go off to "Taronna, Monreyall." But now there was an influx of yuppie-types, from "Taronna," even New York. They come in the summer, first, eh? Then they find they can manage their stocks and whatnot on-line, so why live in the city? But it creates problems, eh? The yuppies have money, fancy goods, and they want special things like good coffee, good bread, better groceries, eh? It creates a theft situation, some resentment, tax problems. Gotta build a better dock, better roads for their Jeep Cherokees, more ferry service, whatnot. And they want environmental regulations tightened, more enforcement. No off-season shooting of ducks and geese and whatnot. Eh?

Mulheisen considered calling Ivy White, but then, maybe that wasn't such a good idea. A personal interview would be much better. He went home to pack. Becky was not in a good mood. Nothing serious, just a little grouchy. She asked where he was off to, but he didn't have time to fill her in. He was eager to get going. When would he be back? He didn't know. She seemed annoyed by his incommunicativeness.

He left feeling a little uneasy about her, about the arrangement. But he couldn't think about it. It was still raining. And when he crossed the Peace Bridge, at Port Huron, into Ontario, the rain seemed to get harder. He got as far as Kincardine, on the Lake Huron shore. It was wonderful country, what he could see of it—a dark, wet, north country. He'd always liked that.

It was still raining in the morning. He'd slept in a decent motor inn at the harbor. He enjoyed the sense of being in a foreign country that was, after all, not very foreign. Just different enough to make him aware that he wasn't in Michigan. The country was much like the Michigan lake country, but more sparsely populated, it seemed. Small houses, different signs for things, but still some familiar American-style signs for food and gas. The people seemed vaguely British, what he saw of them while buying gas or eating in the restaurant. It was not quite as *modern*, somehow, as America, not so corporate-captive. He liked that.

The peninsula became more wooded the farther north he drove. It was a tourist destination, but it was early in the season and there was little traffic. Also, the rain had obviously depressed the trade. He saw a few disconsolate families, cars filled with outdoor gear and children staring mournfully out of streaky windows. Others seemed underdressed, in shorts, with wet jackets, waiting under storefront canopies. But the locals didn't seem upset by what now appeared to Mulheisen like quite a lot of incessant rain. They were in sweaters and rain gear, rubber Wellington boots, talking in normal, more or less cheerful voices.

He had arranged to meet Sergeant McPherson in a roadside cafe, along Highway 6. It was steamy inside. McPherson was chatting to the locals. He was a pleasant man with sandy hair and a mustache. He wore rain gear like the rest of them.

"Dr. White's still up there, all right," he told Mulheisen. "I didn't contact her, as you requested. No word of anyone unusual on the island. You'll want to stay at the inn, it's an old hotel. They have vacancies, though, I checked. They're used to a certain amount of tourist traffic, mostly bird-watchers and the like, eh? There's a ferry service from Tobermory, goes twice a day, six and six, on the hour. It's about ten miles offshore, so it takes, oh, a half hour or more, depending on the weather and the sea. They'll carry your car, but the island's only three miles long, so you wouldn't need it. Dr. White's place is only a short walk from the harbor. You got any boots, or a hat?"

Mulheisen's hat was a soft, cotton one. It was soaked just running from the car to the cafe, five steps. McPherson said he could get some gear at a store in Tobermory. He advised him to buy rain pants as well.

"There's a ferry to Manitoulin Island," McPherson said, "don't take that one. Take the little ferry."

"Bird-watchers, eh?" Mulheisen said. "My mother has probably been here. What do they have?"

"Shitepokes, I guess," McPherson said. "That's a kind of heron, a green one. Or is it a cormorant? And gulls, of course. Oh, and orchids. There are supposed to be a lot of orchids. About forty different kinds, eh?"

Mulheisen found the ferry. He had plenty of time to buy a waterproof rain hat, a very nice green jacket that shed water like a mallard, the much-recommended rain pants, and some green rubber boots. It was pretty pricey, considering that he'd probably never wear this gear again. Fancy, breathable, high-tech fabric. He decided not to take the car. The boat ride was brisk, the lake being more than a little choppy, despite what the laughing, fresh-faced ferry girls claimed. He found it necessary to hang on to something when he ventured from his seat in the little cabin where they served coffee.

The boat could carry several vehicles, Mulheisen saw. He talked to the captain, a big fellow with a once-handsome face, now ruined by hard living. He was no doubt competent and friendly enough, but conversation had that tentative feel. He was looking forward to the tavern at "Shypoke," but determined to be the sober captain until he was safely at the dock. Mulheisen didn't want to reveal his purpose, but he wanted to know if anyone who looked like DiEbola had come across in the past couple of weeks. No one of that description. They talked boats a bit, engines, especially Gray-Marines, which led to Detroit, where they were made. A little chat about the recent Stanley Cup playoffs and the Red Wings' shocking failure.

No, Captain Grosvenor hadn't seen a fellow of about sixty, dark hair. He would have seen him, all right, if he'd gone out to "Shypoke," because this was the only way to get there. He'd seen one car with Michigan plates last week, but it was a pickup truck, a carpenter who was doing some work for one of the new people. He'd finished putting in some cabinets and had left already.

It was only a hundred yards or so up the sand-gritted concrete road from the dock to the Shypoke Inn. It was pouring rain, still, and fairly dark. Mulheisen lugged his bag, appreciating the waterproof gear. The inn was a white clapboard affair, vaguely summery looking, despite the rain. Lots of flowering pots dangled from the ceiling of the covered porch that ran the length of the front. It appeared to have, perhaps, a dozen rooms. Only half were occupied.

The proprietress was an affable middle-aged woman who wore a sweater against the chill and jeans tucked into rubber boots, like everyone else. She said her name was Jean. She had the fresh, hearty face of nearly everyone he'd seen. McPherson had warned him that islanders were a little odd—"They refer to the rest of the world as off-islanders, eh?"—but Jean seemed like any innkeeper. Busy, but friendly. She wasn't interested in his business at all. Probably she thought he had no business, had just come out here to soak up the, well, the fresh rain. Evidently, the whole off-island world coveted the delights of "Shypoke" Island.

"Dinner will be up in about twenty minutes," she told him, "but we serve till nine. It's very good. My sister, Janice, is the cook.

Tonight we have her planked whitefish. You'll like it." This was said with genial authority.

Four of the other guests were huddled in the parlor, around the fireplace, nursing hot drinks that surely contained alcohol. Mulheisen's room was upstairs, overlooking the harbor. A large white gull was sitting on the porch roof, just outside his window. It didn't mind the rain. The room had a full-sized bed that sat up high on a brass frame. It seemed a little soft, but comfortable enough. It featured a patchwork quilt and plenty of extra blankets. There was that familiar musty odor of the seashore. A shelf with a good stock of mystery novels. A good reading lamp. A small bath with a tub on legs and a curtain that could be pulled so that the shower, which rose up in a neat plumbing arrangement from the faucet, didn't spray all over everything.

Mulheisen had time for a cigar, if he could manage it in the rain. He took his .38 Airweight with him, if only because the door had only an unsecure-seeming skeleton-key lock. He'd bought his rain hat with an eye toward its broad brim shielding a cigar from the rain. He was gratified that it worked. He smoked a LaDonna as he trudged up the street. There was sand on all surfaces, a slightly disagreeable sensation underfoot. But shortly he came to the end of the finished surfaces anyway and walked on sandy paths through very wet and dense underbrush that by itself would have soaked him to his hips, even if it wasn't pouring buckets, except that he was completely sheathed in rain gear. He was grateful for the breathable fabric, and the pants were indispensable.

He found Dr. White's house without difficulty, after about ten minutes of hiking. McPherson had said it was easy to walk to, and it was. It stood off the sandy road, on a bluff facing out toward the lake, perhaps fifty feet above the shore. It was just a cottage, like all the others he'd seen. Apparently, from conversation he'd overheard, the new people had built some modern extravagances, but he hadn't seen them. This was white clapboard, with a broad overhanging roof that was shingled with mossy cedar shakes. Windows with little panes. Cottagey. Overgrown, of course, with lilacs, roses, and other shrubs that thrived in great profusion here. Doubtless, the famous orchids hid in the damp understory.

The sign was not a faded wooden one, such as he'd seen on others—declaring ROSE HAVEN and DEW REST. But there was an arrow, pointing to a side entry, that said SURGERY. There were lights shining through the curtains, but he could not see any sign of life. Smoke rose from the chimney and was baffled about by the shore breeze. Fog was moving in. He puffed his cigar and returned to the excellent planked whitefish, served with a buttery wine sauce. The same four people he'd seen earlier cheered up with dinner and tried to converse, saying they were from "Taronna," but he wasn't having any of that. He went to bed and slept. It rained and pounded deliciously outside the window, and he slept like the Old Man.

In the morning, the rain had tapered off to something more like a heavy mist. It was still solidly overcast, but the hotel people seemed to regard it as a nice day. After eating half of a breakfast that, if entirely ingested, would have disabled him for the day, he set off for the beach. It was cool, but perfectly walkable. He smoked a LaDonna as he strolled. There were several old rusting turtleback fish tugs, anchored, and numerous souvenirs of the now vanished fishing life, net floats and marine gear, lying about.

The lake was a metallic gray and tumbling. Large ships could be seen at a distance, tankers and ore boats. Gulls wheeled about, crying. Small groups of ducks were driving along at a distance. He didn't see anything that looked like a shitepoke, but there were small shorebirds that scurried ahead of him, peeping plaintively, flutter-

ing onward when he got too close. He walked along the hard-packed
sand, well past the bluffs on which the doctor's cottage perched.
There was a track of sorts up to the cottage, mostly sand, but here
and there reinforced with cedar steps. He decided to finish his cigar
before attempting it. His walk took him around a long curve where
great black and gray boulders stood offshore in the gravelly, stony
lake bed. When he turned about and headed back he realized he'd
walked farther than he'd thought. In the distance, he could see a
dark, burly figure slowly climbing up the path. By the time he was
halfway closer, the figure had disappeared over the top.

It took his breath climbing up the path, the sand shifting
underfoot, except where there was a step or two. At last he stood at
the top. He had to stand and catch his breath. The cottage was just
a few feet beyond the breast of the bluff, too close for his taste. It
had a glassed-in porch, decorated with marine bric-a-brac, nets,
floats, wooden decoys, pieces of driftwood and weathered glass.

He went around to the surgery door and pulled a bell chain.
He could hear the bell tinkle inside. After a brief wait, the door
opened. A pleasant, weathered-looking lady of fifty-five-plus stood
there. She had short, gray hair, a little mussed. She looked at him
through glasses with large lenses in modern, sporty-looking frames.
She wore wool Royal Stewart plaid slacks and a matching red
sweater set. Over this, a white lab coat, unbuttoned.

"Dr. White?" he said, and when she nodded, he introduced
himself. "Detective Sergeant Mulheisen, Detroit police force."

She looked wary. "What's the problem?"

He said he wanted to talk to her. "You're not ill?" she said.
When he shook his head, she said, "I'm sorry, I'm busy just now.
You'll have to come back later."

"Oh. You have a patient?"

She hesitated, then said, firmly, "Yes, I do. What is it about?"

"It's kind of complicated," he said. He realized now that to someone unacquainted with the details of the case, his story and questions would seem, well, far-fetched. But he had not wanted to risk contacting her in advance. "It's about a man named Humphrey DiEbola. You knew him as Umberto Gagliano, a long time ago, when you were children."

"I see," she said. She stood very stiffly, the door only partly opened. He could not be sure, but he felt that she was not quite open with him. She was a woman of considerable poise, however. He could not determine just how reserved she was, or what might be the cause. She didn't seem afraid, exactly, but she was very intent. "I knew him," she said.

"When was the last time you saw him?"

"I'm not sure. Why do you ask?"

"Did you meet him in Detroit? When you were adults, I mean. At Henry Ford Hospital?"

"I may have," she said. "What of it? That was a long time ago, thirty years."

"Then you know that he is known these days as Humphrey DiEbola," Mulheisen said. "He's a well-known Detroit mobster."

She didn't respond to that. Just looked down at him. It was beginning to rain harder now. Where he was standing there was no shelter, except for his rain gear, of course. The rain was swirling about the house in the wind off the lake.

He leaned to one side to look into the hallway. She was not going to invite him in, he saw. But of more interest, on the little entry table, where one might toss keys or gloves, was a familiar-looking cigar box. He had been given a similar box by Helen Sedlacek.

"It's important that we talk," Mulheisen said.

"What about?" she said, not conceding an inch to his inter-est. She didn't seem very friendly, not like what he'd expected: the beloved doctor of the north woods, ministering to poor indigenous peoples.

"Has DiEbola contacted you? Lately?"

"I'm sorry, I have a patient." She started to close the door.

"Dr. White! DiEbola is a dangerous man," Mulheisen said. "If he has contacted you, it could be very serious. Deadly serious."

"Are you staying at the inn?" she asked. "I'll come and see you this evening. About eight o'clock." She closed the door.

18

Payback

Joe Service knew this conversation was inevitable, but that didn't mean he had to like it. It was particularly ominous that the colonel had insisted on holding the little conclave at the boat they had provided for him. Joe was supposed to have returned the boat, but he was supposed to have done a lot of things that he hadn't done. Dinah Schwind had tried to defend him to the others, but even her patience needed relief.

It was pouring rain, which provided for maximum security—nobody was down at the marina on a night like this. The boat was docked at the Saint Clair Flats Boatyard, not far from the restaurant where Joe and Dinah had met earlier. It was also not far from Mulheisen's mother's house, but none of them were aware of that. It had just seemed a convenient moorage to Joe. The Sea Ray, a pretty sleek powerboat, had a tight Cordura canopy that buttoned up well.

The colonel sniffed as he came aboard. "You living here?"

"It's as good as any place," Joe said.

The colonel had brought along a guy whom he introduced as Pollak. He was also a member of the Lucani, the colonel said. Acker and Collins had other business, he said.

"I thought you were just a tight little outfit," Joe said, "four or five of you. How many Lucani are there?"

"Just six," the colonel said. "Seven, counting you."

"Well, don't leave me out," Joe said.

Pollak was a tall, blond man with a battered face. He looked like some kind of agent, once you were told he was an agent; until then, he looked like a hockey player. With Pollak, Schwind, and the colonel aboard, the Sea Ray was cramped. Joe provided the beer.

The colonel said he was disappointed that Joe hadn't come around after DiEbola had been hit. He had some money coming for that nice little piece of work, and they had more work for him. "We know how insistent you are on collecting," the colonel said.

"Yeah, well, I didn't think I could ask for payment," Joe said, "seeing as I didn't do anything."

The colonel was good at hiding his disappointment that his ploy hadn't worked. He frowned and said, "You didn't hit him, then? We thought you had. The FBI, of course, was convinced it was an internal thing. Well, you read the papers."

"I read the papers," Joe said, "but I don't necessarily believe them. Still, maybe it was like they say. But it wasn't me. So you don't owe me anything. As for more work, what have you got? I'm available."

The colonel and his friends didn't say anything for a long moment. Finally, the colonel said, "We were thinking something out of the country, maybe."

"Great," Joe said. "Whereabouts? Someplace sunny, I hope. South America?"

"Closer, actually," the colonel said. He seemed to have made up his mind. "Canada."

"Really?" Joe said. "What's in Canada?"

"Humphrey DiEbola," said Schwind.

They all watched Joe. He looked puzzled for a moment, then he nodded. "So," he said, "the Fat Man pulled a fast one. That guy's quick on his feet. It's like a polka party, isn't it? They have these dances, around here, you know. It's like a marathon, or something. All these big fat guys and their babushkas, wheeling around on the floor, bumping into each other. It gets pretty dangerous toward the end. The band starts playing faster and faster, 'Roll Out the Barrel,' that kind of stuff. The last guy standing is the big cheese, I guess. Or the big pickle in the barrel. Who knows? I went to one a couple nights ago, in Hamtramck. Pretty funny."

They all agreed it was funny. Not that any of them were laughing. They had found out, somehow, that Mulheisen had gone to Canada. A little judicious checking—it hadn't been difficult— had revealed that he'd gone to an island off the Bruce Peninsula. They couldn't be positive, but it looked like Mulheisen was onto something. Whether it was DiEbola himself or just a lead to him, they weren't sure. But there was a woman on the island who had, evidently, some connection.

Joe shook his head, marveling. "The guy is something," he said. "We're all convinced that Humphrey went down, but Mulheisen doesn't believe it. So, why should I go to Canada? If Mulheisen finds him, he'll bring him back."

"We want you to go and make sure," the colonel said. "Take Pollak with you. Mulheisen could have problems, if not with DiEbola, then with extradition. This one looks like a freebie, to us."

"How's that?" Joe asked. "I'm not into freebies."

"We didn't mean it in that sense," the colonel said. "You'll get your fee."

"Which is?"

"Whatever you can recover from DiEbola. And before you ask, let's say fifty grand, if you can't recover anything."

"A hundred," Joe said.

The colonel shrugged. "All right, a hundred. But believe me, the man clearly didn't leave his little mess in the basement without taking along a nice cushion. As far as we're concerned, it's all yours. It could be quite a bit. We know he managed to send a lot out of the country beforehand, and we think we can recover some of that. But he'll have a bundle with him."

Joe managed to look enthusiastic, but he calculated that they must have some other plans. They wouldn't let him keep everything that DiEbola had taken with him. Maybe that was why Pollak was along. "You said a freebie," he reminded them. "What does that mean?"

"Why, the man is presumed dead. Killed by his old buddies. That's the official line. You can just make sure it's true."

Joe looked at Dinah. She gazed back calmly. "I'm not a hired killer," he said to her. "I told you that. The thing with Echeverria was an accident. I never intended to take out Humphrey. That wasn't the deal, you know."

"No, but we figured you had," the colonel said. "Probably the situation got out of hand and you did the best you could, that's what it looked like. And then, you didn't come around, didn't correct our misunderstanding. A suspicious person might think you were involved, somehow."

"In the escape?" Joe said. "I didn't know anything about it. I was keeping tabs on him, through Helen. She seemed to think something was afoot, but she didn't know what it was. The best I could figure, he had some grand reorganization in the works. It looked like something might break and I'd get my chance. But I wasn't going to pop him. I figured once I could see which way it was going to break, I could set him up for you. If you want, I'll still do it."

"It'd be cleaner and easier if you just ran up there in your boat—this is your boat, Joe. Nice boat. And if DiEbola's up there you could show us, once and for all, that you're a team player. Joe

Seven." The colonel was calm and logical. That was the deal. "If you don't want to be on the team, fine. You're on your own."

Joe knew what that meant. It meant he would be fair game to anyone, and the Lucani would provide the direction to whoever came after him.

"I'll go get him," Joe said, "if he's there. You can do what you want when you've got him."

"Pollak will go with you," the colonel said. He wasn't accepting any refusals.

Joe knew what that meant. Pollak was set to ice Humphrey, if need be. And then, who knows? Maybe he'd ice Joe, too. These guys were in the direct-action business. Well, it looked like the complaint window was closed, Joe thought. He'd just have to play his position as the game unfolded. He peered out through the plastic side curtains. The rain was dancing on the deck.

"Not much of a night for a boat ride," he said. "Maybe we should wait till tomorrow, you could get us up there in a chopper, we could rent a boat."

"No," the colonel said firmly. "No choppers. No flying through international airways. No renting of boats. You can run up there, just a couple of fishermen. The Coast Guard doesn't bother. You find the island, find DiEbola. Our information is, he's at a house right near shore. Pollak's got the poop."

An hour later they were in the channel. It was a hell of a run, Joe thought, but it wasn't as if he didn't know the way. He'd brought Humphrey; now the problem was to pretend not to be familiar with the run. More than two hundred miles, the bulk of it across the open sea of Lake Huron, in pitch-black, pouring rain. But the seas were not heavy, the boat was powerful—he had a 205-horsepower MerCruiser, inboard/out, with a four-barrel carb. It took plenty of fuel, but he had gassed up, including the extra tanks on deck.

The navigation was uncomplicated. Once past Point Edward they would be out in the lake. It was mainly a matter of keeping an eye out for lake shipping. Joe figured they could cruise moderately through the night, through the Saint Clair River channel, and by daylight they would be well out in the lake. If the winds didn't get contrary, they should reach the island well before dark. They wouldn't want to be there any sooner.

According to Pollak, Mulheisen had already reached the island. They reckoned he wouldn't approach the woman before the next day. Presumably, Mulheisen could not be sure that DiEbola was even there. For that matter, neither could they. But Mulheisen would have to be a little cautious; a direct approach might be dangerous.

Joe was extremely interested in knowing how they had gotten their information and what it consisted of. Pollak, a man who didn't like to talk much, obviously was aware of Joe's keen interest and knew how much to reveal. Through a variety of sources they had become aware that Mulheisen had blown open the FBI investigation. As they understood it, he had learned that DiEbola had boldly faked the evidence of his death by breaking into a doctor's office and manipulating files. It appeared that the body identified as DiEbola's was really one Angelo Badgerri, a longtime associate of DiEbola's. Apparently, however, the authorities were still clinging to the idea that DiEbola had been the target of an assassination attempt.

It was amazing, Joe thought, how difficult it was for investigators to abandon a scenario once it had been established and agreed upon. This tendency had produced a modified scenario: DiEbola had planned to bolt but was nearly thwarted in his attempt, by an untimely attack by old enemies—or perhaps the mob knew he was bolting and that was why they had tried to hit him. They believed that Mulheisen had ferreted out a connection with an old girlfriend, one Ivy White, now a semiretired doctor living on Shitepoke Island.

DiEbola was presumed to have staged a fake boat explosion and then continued onward by switching to another boat.

This was the touchy part. If Pollak was not conning him, they assumed that DiEbola had provided himself with that other boat and was now at the island. No one had reported him there, but the doctor was known to be on the island. She had continued to see a few patients in the past two weeks, but that didn't mean that DiEbola wasn't present. She rarely went out, anyway, it seemed, and not at all, lately.

Joe and Pollak dined on sandwiches brought aboard by the colonel. Their coffee was soon gone, but they had beer and soft drinks. They took the wheel by turns, sleeping as best as they could in the small bunks forward. Pollak was in communication with the colonel by radio. The colonel informed them that Mulheisen was on the island, that he might have already visited the doctor.

At one point, trying to make conversation as they pounded along through the dark, Joe asked if Pollak was a Pole. There were dual seats, both of them the high, con type, comfortable enough. They could look out through the windshield over the deck. Joe had turned down the glow of the instrument lights, so they wouldn't interfere with their watch for shipping. It was damned bad visibility, so they had to keep alert.

Pollak said he was American. No Polish ancestry. Joe asked if he were Catholic. He wasn't. No denomination. Joe asked if he was a baseball fan. He wasn't. He didn't follow professional sports. Also, he volunteered, he didn't watch TV, hadn't read any good books, and never went to the movies.

"You eat, don't you?" Joe asked. "What's your favorite food?"

"Spaghetti," Pollak said.

"Great," Joe said. "I love spaghetti. What's your favorite?"

"Chef Boyardee. With meatballs."

That shut Joe up. He had been wondering if there was any good reason, should the occasion arise, to kill this bastard. It appeared there was.

They still had good fuel supplies, but they'd have to get more to make it back the way they had come. Pollak said they could run ashore at a village on the mainland, maybe even Tobermory, to get gas and food. It was still raining, but there were intermittent periods when it stopped, followed by heavier downpours and now some wind. The lake was kicking up. The Sea Ray, however, was taking it very well.

They got fuel in Tobermory, with little difficulty, and bought beer. They were fishermen, as anyone could see from the gear lying on the seats aft. They headed back out.

"What's the plan?" Joe asked.

"It's simple as hell," Pollak said. He was loading a Heckler & Koch MP5A3. "We'll beach below the house, walk up, and reconnoiter. If our man is there and no one's around, we grab him and go."

"What a plan," Joe said, smiling. "And what if?"

"We'll have to see when we get there, Joe. If Mulheisen's around, we'll cool it. If DiEbola's not there . . ." He shrugged. "We don't interfere with the lady. If Mulheisen's got him, we better discuss it with the colonel." He nodded toward the little handheld radio.

"How about if he doesn't want to go with us, puts up a fight, is armed, has help?" Joe asked.

They were motoring rather slowly now, angling in toward the island. Pollak had already pointed out the house, sitting up on the bluff and not very visible, thanks to heavy foliage. Joe knew the house all right, but appeared not to.

"We don't want a firefight," Pollak said. "It depends on what we see when we get up there. You about ready? You armed?"

Joe was armed. He had a .38 automatic, a nice Smith & Wesson he'd always liked. He slipped a couple of extra clips into the pocket of his rain parka.

They would move up as close as they could. Joe knew they could run the boat onto a sandy beach, thanks to the tilt function of the inboard/outboard engine, but he couldn't say as much. At any rate, in his previous run he had simply dropped Humphrey and Roman off. For the kind of operation they were envisioning, it wouldn't do to leave the boat beached. It might be difficult to get off. They agreed it would be better to anchor somewhere near the path up the cliffs.

There was no tide to speak of on these lakes, as oceanic as they might seem, so there was no danger of being stranded. There was also very little surf running, which helped. It would have been nice to dock, but it wasn't in the cards. The nearest dock was at the village, and they weren't going there.

Joe suggested anchoring among some of the larger rocks. That might be possible. They cruised along the shore. The best spot they could find for that was more or less ideal, but it was a good half mile from the spot where they would have to descend with DiEbola. Pollak decided that was all right. If DiEbola was mobile—that is, if they didn't wound him in the extraction—he could surely walk the half mile in the dark. And the boat would be much more secure than if it were left to wash in the weak surf. The alternative was to take a line ashore and anchor that way, and there was always the possibility that the boat would get beached and prove difficult to shove off.

It was getting dark. Rain was falling softly but steadily. There was a wonderful fresh smell of pines in the air. Joe nosed the Sea Ray in among some large rocks. It was quite secure here, in a gentle heave and pull. If the wind and the sea kicked up—which certainly looked likely—the boat might get scratched a little, but it was quite protected among these boulders. He could loop a line around a crag on either side. Best of all, they could hop out onto the rocks and, if they didn't slip and fall and skin their shins, they could leap to shore without getting very wet.

They set off.

They could see Roman standing in the kitchen, just staring at nothing. He was listening to something, conceivably. But he stood with his hands hanging at his sides. He was dressed in his usual dark suit, now rather wrinkled and baggy. A woman came into the room dressed in rain gear, obviously the doctor. She talked to Roman for a moment, gesturing toward the front of the house. Roman nodded. She left.

19

Qui Vive

Mulheisen trudged back to the village through the pouring rain. He went to the little tavern, the Shamrock Pub. It was next to the Mercantile, part of the same white clapboard building. It had living quarters above it. The bartender was Casey Gallagher, also the proprietor of the "Merc," as Mulheisen had already learned to call the store. The two enterprises shared an arched passageway with old-fashioned swinging tavern doors. Gallagher moved from one location to the other to take care of customers.

Mulheisen had a welcome double shot of Jack Daniel's, at a hearty five dollars American. He hadn't been drinking much lately, for some reason. It tasted good. There was nobody else in the bar, which was just a long room with a jukebox and several old framed photos of sailboats and fishing tugs on the walls, a pressed-tin ceiling. When there were no customers in the Merc, Casey stayed to chat. Casey was a wiry fellow of middle age with a mustache. He was happy to talk about hockey. He was a Toronto Maple Leafs fan. He was delighted that the Red Wings had thought they'd bought the Stanley Cup, paying far too much for players like Shanahan and Fedorov, to say nothing of Chelios, only to fall in the second round.

The Leafs had battled to the third round, at least, on a quarter of the payroll.

No, he hadn't seen any Detroiters around, although it was early in the season. They'd show up when the weather got warm. Mostly fishermen, boaters. Sure, he knew Doc White, helluva woman. Her folks had lived out here, off-islanders, from down below. They'd retired here. The old man had been a factory worker, at Massey-Ferguson, in Hamilton. Been gone about five years, and now the old lady had died. He hoped Doc White would stick around, not go back up to the Indians, as was rumored.

"Not much of a practice for her out here," Mulheisen ventured.

"Oh, I don't know. She's about retirement age herself, eh?" Casey observed. "She's got plenty to do. Besides the surgery, she's on-line, you know. She consults with some of these tribes up north. She can do that from here, advise the resident nurse, or paramedical people, you know. Not bad, eh? She can live in a healthy place like 'Shypoke' 'stead of the blackfly country, and do her doctoring on-line."

Mulheisen agreed that was quite a deal. He went back to the inn for a bowl of chowder and read an interesting book that Jean gave him, on the history of the lake country, the *coureurs de bois*, the independent fur traders. He wished he had thought to bring the book on Le Pesant. The story fascinated him, with its bizarre resonance in the DiEbola case. He reflected that, like the Algonquians, DiEbola seemed to live by an entirely different code from the conventional notion of justice. Perhaps that was unfair to the Indians, however. They were not, after all, people without a conscience, without a recognizable moral code. Quite the opposite. Whereas DiEbola, from what Mulheisen knew of him, was a man whose code, if he could be said to have one, was strictly personal, a law unto himself. For him, the concept of crime was apparently irrelevant: he did what he wanted.

He was confident that DiEbola had at least been here, and might still be. He had no idea why and he wasn't too concerned.

He hadn't a warrant for his arrest, but he didn't consider that a problem. No doubt he could call McPherson when and if documents seemed necessary.

In these and other thoughts he spent a pleasant afternoon. He hadn't taken much time to relax lately, he realized. He contemplated his recent living adjustments in Detroit, wondered if he'd made a mistake moving in with Becky. Complications. One minute she chided him for calling to say he wouldn't be home, the next she wanted to be informed about his movements. But it was interesting, he thought. He'd been getting stale, no social life. No sex life, either. This was definitely an improvement on that score. But who knew what lay down that road?

He supposed he'd also made a mistake in coming up here, if this turned out to be only a stopover visit on DiEbola's flight. A waste of time, wild-goose chase. Still, the woman had obviously been in contact with DiEbola. She might give some hint about where he'd gone next. That would be worth something. He imagined that they had established some kind of on-line relationship, if what Helen had told him about DiEbola's interest in the Internet was pertinent. The modern thing. What a world, he thought: a mobster meets his childhood crush again, on-line. He had no idea, really, what such a relationship entailed. He'd read about so-called chat rooms, but what were they? Lonely people sitting at a computer late at night, typing messages to one another, discussing topics of interest. He'd heard there were even Web sites for hockey fans, discussing the latest trades, that sort of thing. It sounded pitiful. Still, if you were on an island in Lake Huron, or up in the bush, the Net must seem like a window on the world.

Dr. Ivy White showed up on time. She wore a dress and her hair was brushed, although it was a little disheveled from the rain hat she'd taken off on entering. She had even put on some makeup. She wore her Wellingtons, however.

They sat in the lounge. Other guests were playing cards. Mulheisen and the doctor were served coffee. The conversation got off on a more comfortable tack than earlier, at the house. She quickly confirmed that she had been in communication with DiEbola on the Net. She called him Bert, which it seemed had been his name of choice in his youth. She claimed to be familiar with his reputation, but she also asserted that it was undeserved.

To Ivy White, Bert was a misunderstood man. He was bright, a talented entrepreneur and businessman who had survived a rocky youth to achieve success. Given his background and the milieu in which he'd grown up, it was not surprising that he'd had some difficulties with the law, early on. But he had risen above that, she felt. She didn't expect Mulheisen to believe her, she said. A policeman was bound to believe that young toughs never really reformed. But in her experience among the indigenous peoples, she'd seen firsthand a paradigm of how the greater society can affect, initially, expectations among the underprivileged and, later, through its misunderstanding of their different attitudes and behavior, the sense of self-worth of those same individuals.

In simpler terms, she said, the tribal people she'd worked with had struggled constantly with this problem. It had been a revelation to her, she said. The dominant society wanted everybody to conform, she saw. When they persisted in pursuing their traditional activities they were treated as outlaws. And even when they chose to play the white man's game, their accomplishments were denigrated. She thought that something like that had been Bert's burden, as well. But he'd risen above it. He'd carved out his own, unique niche and style.

Mulheisen hardly knew where to begin. He'd rarely encountered anyone so naive. It was all well and good, he said, to talk about different cultural values, discrimination, and so on. He went along with a lot of those notions himself, maybe most of them. But few societies, he said, accept blatantly criminal behavior as proper, tolerable, or even justified. A society that did that was a criminal society, he said. Mindful of his recent reading, he said that he understood that the indigenous peoples had a different way of dealing with aberrant behavior than modern Western cultures, but he reckoned they were no more tolerant of crime, especially violent crime. When it came to protecting their society and culture, they did deal with it.

But he didn't want to get into a philosophical or sociological discussion, he said. He just wanted to caution her about accepting Bert's version of his activities uncritically.

"You seem to think that DiEbola is just an ordinary businessman," he said, "maybe a little rough, or tough, but essentially one who contributes to the general economy, providing jobs, capital, and so on. I have evidence of a different kind of activity. Until very recently, this man sat at the very top of a criminal combine in Detroit and the surrounding area. He oversaw activities like drug dealing, prostitution, massive organized theft, loan-sharking, intimidation of ordinary citizens to obtain payments to avoid physical harm. And at the heart of it all is murder. That's what drives it all. They murder people for, among other reasons, the benefit of enforcing all other activities."

"I'm not so naive as you think," Dr. White said. "Those activities exist in all complex societies. There are always those who perform those activities. But I can't believe that Bert is a ruthless murderer, some kind of fiend. He may have transgressed, to some degree. People who hope to survive in those societies have to make accommodations. You can only hope that you don't have to compromise too much."

They went on in this vein for some time, rather spiritedly, until Mulheisen tired of the academic argument and simply showed his cards. "I have evidence that your Bert murdered at least half a dozen other men either personally or with the assistance of accomplices. He was there. He ordered deaths. In a couple of cases, at least, I'm sure he did the murder himself."

"I don't believe it," she said.

"Why is it so difficult to believe? If you came to Detroit, I could show you the evidence. What do I have to do to make you think otherwise?"

"I've seen him," she blurted out. "I've talked to him. He's wounded. The people who did those things want to kill him, because he opposed them. He's fleeing for his life. I have to help him."

20

Radio Silence

Joe explained to Pollak that he knew Roman. He would go in and find out what was going on. In the meantime, maybe Pollak should follow the doctor, see what she was up to.

"There's only one place she can go," Pollak said, "to the village. Must be she's going to see Mulheisen. Let's go in and see if DiEbola's here."

But Joe argued against that. "Why do that? No point in showing yourself to Roman, if DiEbola's not around. Besides, maybe she's got a nurse here, or a housekeeper. You can keep an eye on the path, warn me if the doc comes back."

Pollak thought about that for a moment, then said, "She'll be going to the hotel, or some such place, won't she? I can't exactly walk in and stand around unnoticed. Folks'll want to know where I came from."

"It can't be that small an island," Joe pointed out. "What the hell, you're supposed to be some kind of superagent. Figure it out!"

Pollak stubbornly said, "I'll just see where she goes. I'll be back toot sweet." He took off down the trail.

Joe slipped into the house as quickly as he could. Roman confronted him in the hallway, his massive revolver in hand. But as soon as he recognized Joe his face lit up.

"Joe! You come back! The boss'll be happy."

"How is he?" Joe asked.

"No good, Joe." Roman shook his head grimly. "He ain't gonna make it."

"The wound?"

Roman nodded. "What you doin' here?"

"I've got to see him," Joe said. "The feds are onto him. He's got to get out of here."

Roman shook his head. "Don't t'ink so, Joe. He's in here." He led Joe to the door of the bedroom.

Joe stopped. "Roman, there's a guy with me. He went down to the town, to make sure the doctor was out of the way. He's a fed, Roman. He thinks I'm cooperating. If he comes back, don't make a fuss, but keep an eye on him, okay?"

"Joe, you ain't wit' the feds?"

"No, no, don't worry. It's just a gag. Just keep an eye on him, all right?"

Humphrey was in the guest bedroom, downstairs. He was in bed, a large one with a brass bedstead. The doctor had rigged an I.V. for him. He didn't look good. His eyes were red and his mouth appeared dry, he had a yellowish tinge of jaundice. Joe was shocked. When he'd dropped him off he'd been stiff and sore, needing Roman's help, but he certainly hadn't looked like this.

"Slim," he called to him, "it's me, Joe. What's the prob, guy? You don't look so good."

Humphrey opened his eyes. They were yellow. "Joe," he said, hoarsely, "how you doin', kid? Ain't this the shits? That fuckin' Mongelo, he killed me. Or maybe it was the guard, John. That ricochet. How's Helen? She okay?"

"She's fine, Slim. But you don't look so good. Listen, I got kind of boxed in by the feds. One of them's here. I had to bring him. Sorry."

"It don't matter, kid." Humphrey closed his eyes. He groaned as if to himself. He made an effort and said, "I shouldn't have come. It was a dumb idea. A little unfinished business. I thought Ivy deserved. . . . But she ain't the same broad, Joe. I don't know what I thought." He moved his head slightly, in a negative way. "She's wacko," he said, after a moment. "Plus, she ain't exactly Ivy. She's . . . old." He made a gurgling noise, as if laughing. Then he groaned.

"Slim, take it easy," Joe said. "Listen, I got the boat. I can get you out of here. It'll be a hassle, but we could split, maybe go some warm place, lots of sun. You'll get better. There's doctors."

"What about the fed?" Humphrey said.

"I don't know, I'll take care of him."

"You're a good kid," Humphrey said, "but I don't think I'm goin' nowhere."

Joe heard a noise in the hall. He straightened up. Pollak came into the room, pushing Roman ahead of him. He had Roman's revolver in one hand, the Heckler & Koch in the other.

"Stand over there," Pollak said to Roman. Then he came over to the bed and looked down at DiEbola. "Well, the big boss," he said, matter-of-factly. "Looks like he's in a bad way."

"He can't be moved, not by us, anyway," Joe said. "We'll have to get a chopper or something in here."

Pollak shook his head. "That won't be necessary," he said. He stuffed Roman's pistol into his coat pocket, then checked the safety on the H&K.

Humphrey looked at the agent, then looked at Joe.

Joe lifted a hand, as if to halt Pollak. "Just a minute," he said.

"Sure, Joe," Pollak said reasonably. He rested the muzzle of the submachine gun on his free arm. "We've got a minute. What's on your mind? You got a problem here?"

"This looks a little weird," Joe said. "I mean, what's the doc gonna say when she comes back here and finds him?"

"Well, if she doesn't come back too soon, I don't see a problem," the agent said. He talked as if DiEbola were not listening.

"What about Roman?" Joe said.

Pollak looked at Roman, standing at the foot of the bed, watching the scene impassively. "I tell you what," Pollak said. "Actually, this is good. Here." He hauled Roman's gun out of his pocket and held it out toward Joe. As he did so, the barrel of the H&K came up, covering Joe. "Go ahead, take it," he said. "You can pop the monster with it, then pop him." He gestured at Roman with the H&K. "It'll look like . . . well, who knows what it'll look like? Let the mounties figure it out."

Joe took the bulky revolver from him. "What if the doc comes back before we get out of here?" he said. "She might have Mulheisen with her."

"Well, if we stand around here talking much longer . . ." Pollak said. "But let's hope she doesn't. Three bodies are already too many."

Joe wasn't sure if he'd heard that right. Three bodies? Did he mean to include Dr. White, anyway? Or was it a slip? Was there some other third body? He didn't want to debate this point. He laid the revolver down on the bed.

"I don't think so," Joe said.

Pollak shrugged. "Whatever. I can do it."

Humphrey scrabbled weakly at the pistol on his blanket. Pollak hastily reached to stop him.

It was a dreamlike moment for Joe—a very familiar dream. As if in slow motion Joe found his automatic in his hand. This time he didn't even think but shot the agent in the face. The bullet struck Pollak in the center of his forehead.

The dead man spun backward, knocking into a lamp, a chair. But imperturbably, Roman strode around the bed and caught the corpse, still upright. He snatched a towel from a nearby stand and wrapped it quickly and neatly about the man's head.

Joe blinked and glanced down at Humphrey. They looked at each other, amazed. Then Joe walked casually around the bed and helped Roman hold the body upright. "I got 'im, Joe," Roman said, and began to drag the body toward the door, his arms wrapped about the man's upper torso.

Joe stuffed his gun in one pocket, bent, and retrieved the H&K. When he went to the bed and picked up Roman's heavy revolver he looked at Humphrey. His mouth was ajar. "Jeez," Humphrey croaked. "Ivy'll shit."

Joe laughed. "I'll straighten it up," he said. "Be right back." He and Roman hauled the body outside and over to the cliff.

"I got 'im," Roman said. "It's easier this way." He hoisted the body onto his shoulders and started down the path.

Joe returned to the bedroom and very quickly set things aright. There was no blood that he could see. Roman had moved so quickly. But the room still reeked of gunfire.

"Open a window," Humphrey said.

"You think?"

"It'll be okay. You better git goin'."

Joe opened a window. The curtains billowed in, so he lowered it halfway. He looked to Humphrey. "That all right?"

"It's fine," Humphrey said. "Thanks, kid."

"I'm outta here, Slim," Joe said. "Take care."

Humphrey grasped his hand. "You too. Take care of Helen. And Roman. Get outta here." His hand dropped to the cover.

Joe caught up with Roman halfway down the steep path. Together they lugged the body down to the beach, battered by the wind and rain, cursing every step of the way. On the beach they attempted to carry him more or less upright, gripping an arm around their shoulders, but Joe was enough shorter than Roman that it proved too clumsy. Finally, Roman once again simply hoisted the man onto his shoulders in the fireman's carry and hauled him to the boat. There they managed to manhandle the corpse onto the boat, getting thoroughly wet in the process.

"You know, Roman," Joe said, "there's no point in going back up there. You've done all you could for Humphrey. Better than you did for Big Sid. This makes up for it."

Roman nodded.

"Helen's going to need a guy like you," Joe said. "Cast off."

When they were out on the pounding lake, Roman said, "Whatta you going to do, Joe?"

"When we get out a little farther, this guy goes to sleep with the fishes," Joe said. "I'll explain it to his friends, somehow. Or not." His eye fell on the radio that Pollak had used to contact the colonel. He picked it up, stepped back out of the sheltering bridge canopy, and hurled it into the choppy lake.

21

Requiem

"**W**here is he?"

"He's at my place," Dr. White said. "He's not well."

"Not well? You mean he's ill?"

"He was shot," she explained. "It was a ricochet. He narrowly escaped being murdered." It appeared that she was convinced by the physical evidence that DiEbola's story was true. He had told her that he'd discovered that some individuals in his enterprise were engaged in criminal activities. When he tried to put a stop to it, they had tried to kill him. She knew it was more complex than that, she said, but that was essentially the case. She was convinced.

Mulheisen listened to this with something between amusement and outrage. He insisted on seeing DiEbola. After a brief resistance—"He's much too weak"—she acquiesced.

As they walked through the rain she told Mulheisen that Humphrey had, in fact, asked about him.

"About me?" Mulheisen was surprised. "He knows I'm here?"

"No, I didn't tell him you were here. I didn't want to upset him. But I think he's been expecting you. Or, not exactly. What he said, several times, was 'Is Mulheisen here?' He seems to think that you are after him. That you're pursuing him."

"He's got that right," Mulheisen said. "How bad is he?"

"He's very close. To death, I mean. I wanted to have him airlifted off the island, to a hospital, but he wouldn't hear of it. He feels safe here. I think he fears that if he went to a hospital his enemies would soon discover his whereabouts and kill him. Apparently, these gangsters have some kind of ubiquitous network. Nothing escapes them."

"What exactly is wrong with him?" Mulheisen asked.

Dr. White explained that when DiEbola had arrived he was already weakened from loss of blood and shock. The blood loss wasn't critical, she had determined, and he seemed to perk up once he was made comfortable. But she soon saw that the wound was more serious than it had seemed. He hadn't been struck by a bullet directly, but only a ricochet fragment. However, it had perforated the abdominal membrane, and although she had cleaned it, there seemed to be a low-grade infection of some sort. The bullet may have picked up a contaminant en route—perhaps it had passed through another's flesh; she couldn't tell. She had some experience in these things, having treated many wounds, particularly hunting wounds. They could be benign at first and then, unexpectedly, turn nasty.

As time went on he would first rally to the point of getting out of bed, being quite cheerful, and then, soon after, lapse back. She had the feeling now, she said, that for one reason or another, he had taken a fatalistic view of his injuries and didn't believe he could recover. As a consequence, everything seemed to worsen: his fever rose, he was retaining fluids, his systems seemed to be failing. She did not have any fancy equipment; she hadn't come here to practice medicine, although she saw a few patients. She thought he could be helped—or could have been helped—at any modestly equipped hospital. But he would have none of that.

"For fear of exposing himself?" Mulheisen asked.

She stopped in the path. It was very dark. "It's more than that. I think he's disappointed," she said. "In me."

Mulheisen didn't get it. "How could you disappoint him?"

"Perhaps I've gotten it wrong," she said. "He's disappointed that he can't . . . I don't know . . . make amends. He can't atone."

"Atone for what?"

The doctor shrugged helplessly in the rain. "I really don't know. He seems to feel some responsibility toward my brother, Arthur, who died tragically when we were youngsters. I've tried to argue him out of it," she said, as they pushed on through the rain, which was now being driven hard by wind. "He persists in feeling that he was to blame."

Mulheisen told her he had informed himself about the case. He wondered what role DiEbola could have played in it. She had no idea. It was his imagination, she thought. But they had arrived.

Mulheisen was grateful to be out of the storm. He asked if DiEbola was alone.

"I don't have a nurse, if that's what you mean," she said quickly, hanging up their rain gear. "He's in here." She showed him into the guest room. The doctor went immediately to the open window. "Who—" she started to say.

DiEbola opened his eyes. "Leave it open," he croaked. "I like the air. I like to hear the rain."

The doctor hesitated, then lowered the sash until the window was nearly closed.

DiEbola frowned at the other person in the room, but then he realized who was there. His face took on a look of surprise, then he managed a ghastly grin, his lips curling back on his teeth. He had lost weight, and his features, always quite strong, were more pronounced: the nose more beaky, the forehead looming. Only his lips, normally rather red and sensuous, seemed thinner, almost bloodless.

"Mul!" he rasped. For an instant he seemed frightened. Perhaps a pang? But then he relaxed. "It's you," he said. "I was wondering if you'd make it." His voice was little more than a croak. "In time for the wake," he added.

Mulheisen looked to Dr. White. "We'd better get him out of here," he said.

"No," DiEbola said. He shook his head slightly, as if it hurt to move. "I'll stay right here. It won't be long."

Mulheisen ignored him. He started for the door, but stopped when DiEbola called to him.

"Mul," DiEbola croaked, "come and sit down. I got a lot to tell you." He waved feebly at Dr. White. "Wait outside," he said.

Mulheisen caught her by the arm. "Get on to the hospital," he said quietly. "I'm sure you know the procedure. I need to talk to him." Then he went to the bedside and pulled up a chair.

"Dumbest things happen," DiEbola said. "I never dreamed a place like this." He waved a thin hand weakly. "The jumping-off place. I need a token, it looks like, to cross over. You got a token, Mul? A dime?" He turned his palm up.

Mulheisen fumbled in his pocket for a coin. He placed a nickel in DiEbola's hand. "Sure, Humphrey, but what brings you here? I'd have thought you'd retire in Vegas, or maybe Rio. Not out in the woods, on the Lakes."

"Me too," DiEbola said. "Never saw myself croaking in the woods. I wanted to see Ivy, talk about old times. You get my age, Mul, everybody you knew is gone."

"Especially in your trade," Mulheisen said mildly. "You made a lot of them disappear, yourself. So, what was all that business in the bunker?"

"The bunker?" DiEbola seemed confused. Or maybe exhausted. He was silent for a while, eyes closed. When he replied, finally, it wasn't clear at first what bunker he was talking about. "Shou'n't have gone into the bunker," he said. "Funny," he went on, after a long moment, "Carmie went down there too, but Carmie never let it bug him."

"Carmie?" Mulheisen said. "Carmine? What did Carmine do?"

"He went in the hole," DiEbola said. "Shou'n't have done it."

Dr. White came in and whispered to Mulheisen. "I'll have to go down to the village. The phone's out."

"I'll go," Mulheisen said, getting up.

"No, you stay," she said. "I won't be long."

When she was gone, DiEbola said, "Good. We can talk." His face took on a crafty look. "We went in Porky's fort, Mul."

"Yes?" Mulheisen was beginning to get the drift. "You and Carmine? What happened?"

"Porky caught us. He'd a killed us," DiEbola whispered. "Wasn't my fault, I swear. We left him there. We covered him up. Nobody ever knew."

Mulheisen nodded. They sat silently, listening to the wind howl and buffet the house, the rain pelting against the window. Mulheisen sniffed. It smelled funny in here. He supposed it was the medicine, perhaps the infection. But it smelled like cordite, overladen with a damp mustiness. Maybe it was sulfur, he mused: the Devil come to get his favorite.

"But it bothered you," he prompted DiEbola.

"Not Carmie," DiEbola said. "He never gave it a thought. Never mentioned it again. I almost forgot. I been dreaming about it, though. I kept seeing him."

"The Boogey Man," Mulheisen said, quietly.

"You know about him," DiEbola said. He seemed comforted to know that Mulheisen understood.

"Oh yes," Mulheisen said.

"I thought I forgot," DiEbola said. "But then he showed up. We didn't do anything so bad, did we? He'd a killed *us*. Not my fault."

Mulheisen said, "Nobody ever blamed you for that."

"That's how it works," DiEbola said. "Luck and hard work, nobody can pin nothin' on you. Cover him up. Covered everything, after that. Ever' candy bar, ever' muscled buck." He paused. The effort was too much. When he could speak again, he said: "You know what, Mul? It gets to be too much. You can't hide all them bodies."

"Why did you come here?" Mulheisen asked. "What does this have to do with Ivy?"

"I owed her, Mul."

Mulheisen considered that. Then he said, "What did you owe her? What could you do for her? Remind her of a tragedy she got over fifty years ago? No, Humphrey. You came for yourself."

Humphrey tried to nod, but it was too hard. "Sure," he said. "I thought I could explain it to her. She'd understand."

"Maybe she'd forgive you," Mulheisen suggested.

Humphrey smiled. "She's wacko, Mul. She don't know from shit."

"No. She's a good woman," Mulheisen said.

"Sure." Humphrey didn't want to argue. "S'all my fault. You can't blame nobody but me, Mul. The girl didn't have nothing to do with it. Helen. She ain't done nothing wrong. I kept her out of the bad stuff. She liked playing at La Donna, but it wasn't happening.

"Ivy . . . she don't know nothing about me. I found her on the Internet! Accident! Fooling around one night, just 'surfing,' and I found this site up in the bush. Dr. Ivy White. I started E-mailing her. Her ma got cancer and she said she was coming down here, I figured it was a sign. I'd close up shop and come over. She didn't exactly welcome me, but she didn't say don't come. Thought I could make it up to her. Dumb idea. You got that coin?"

"I gave you the coin."

DiEbola lifted his hand, saw the nickel. "Fuckin' nickel? That enough?"

"It's enough," Mulheisen said. DiEbola's fist closed on it, then he closed his eyes. "Need this for the ferryman," he said.

"We have to get you out of here," Mulheisen said. "Dr. White is getting a Mercy Flight helicopter in. You don't have to just lie here and die."

"I don't? Looks like it to me," Humphrey said. "It's just like in Mac, you know."

"Mac?"

"Machiavelli. The Prince. His Prince, Borgia, didn't know when to quit. Not me. Hurts though."

DiEbola struggled to sit up, but he groaned and fell back. Dr. White returned. Mulheisen went into the hall to talk to her. She said the hospital would try to get the chopper out here, but it didn't look good. The weather was really kicking up. The RCMP would send a boat, for all the good that would do.

While she tended to DiEbola, Mulheisen stepped outside for some fresh air. Up here on the bluff, the wind roared, thrashing the limbs of the pines furiously. The rain pelted, paused, then came at you from another direction. Mulheisen retreated to the house.

The doctor had given DiEbola an injection of something, to ease his pain. He was breathing more calmly than he had been. He lay with his eyes closed, but he wasn't sleeping. Mulheisen beckoned Dr. White out of the room.

"How long can he last?" he asked.

Dr. White said she thought he was pretty close to the end. But one couldn't tell. She'd had patients worse than DiEbola hold out for days. But he didn't seem to want to hold out. She thought he'd be dead before the chopper or anybody else got there. They heard a noise; he was calling.

"Sit down, Mul," DiEbola said. He waved his clenched fist at the chair, pointing with a bony finger. Mulheisen sat down. Dr.

White fussed about the I.V. "Leave it, Ivy," DiEbola said. She sighed and retreated to a chair on the other side of the room.

"Mul, talk to me. What's goin' on in town?"

"Nothing's going on, Humphrey. Town's quiet, now that you're gone."

"Tell me a story," DiEbola demanded.

"I don't know any stories," Mulheisen said. He stared at the dying man impassively.

"Sure you do," DiEbola said. His eyelids lifted. He gazed at Mulheisen. "Never know what you're thinkin'." After a moment, he begged, "A story. Some of those cop stories."

Mulheisen thought for a moment, then hitched closer. "I heard this funny story. First murder in Detroit." He related the whole tale of Le Pesant. Humphrey seemed to enjoy it. He smiled, even tried to laugh.

Suddenly his eyes opened wide. They looked bright. "You know what? That was me. I covered the body, then I raised it up."

Mulheisen stared at him.

"I was Porky," DiEbola said. He shifted his head, wondering. "I wish I knew."

He lay back and that was it. Mulheisen stared down at the body. One minute it was a man, alive, thinking. The next, nothing.

Dr. White came to the bedside. She lifted an eyelid, felt his pulse, then laid his hands on his breast. She looked over at Mulheisen and said, "He was an impressive man, but so strange."

"You don't know how strange," Mulheisen said.

"It's funny," she said, "I can hardly remember Arthur, my brother. I haven't even looked at a picture of him in years. He's always been this kind of brutish figure to me. He wasn't nice. But when I think of him, he's always fifteen, but somehow older than me. He was like that for Bert, too," she said. Then she sighed and smoothed back the hair on the brow of the corpse. "Poor man," she said.

Mulheisen nodded, as if in agreement. Privately, he thought, Not like Le Pesant, after all. Not a real chief, willing to assume a burden for his people. Just a shrunken fat man who didn't survive the storm.